MISSOURI MADAM

Spur froze in place at the edge of the kitchen and waited. When the sounds quieted again he moved to the living room off the kitchen. Spur found a fancy lady sleeping nude on a couch. On the floor below her lay a man equally clothesless. He stirred as Spur stepped on a squeaking floor board.

The man came up in two seconds, wide awake and a big .44 in his fist aimed at the noise. Spur shot him in the shoulders, slamming the gun out of his hand. The man screamed and Spur heard action all over the house . . . .

HELENA HELLION

"Don't move, or you're dead men!" Spur thundered.

"You shoot me, you shoot the lady first," he said and began backing toward the other door. As Spur turned to watch Libby, another man reached for the iron on his hip.

Spur's round slashed through his shoulder and he got off a shot that went wide. Spur's second round created a neat round hole in the man's forehead going in, but splattered blood and brains over the far wall as it came out the top of his head.

The Spur Series by Leisure Books:

SPUR

MISSOURI MADAM

HELENA HELLION
Dirk Fletcher

LEISURE BOOKS NEW YORK CITY

A LEISURE BOOK®

May 1991

Published by

Dorchester Publishing Co., Inc.
276 Fifth Avenue
New York, NY 10001

MISSOURI MADAM

1

S am Bass watched from well down the dusty
   street as his four men wandered one at a time
into the train station at Short Falls. The station was
brand new on this just opened feeder line of the Missouri & Texas Central railroad that angled on into
Springfield, Missouri in the southwest corner of the
state.

Sam heard the whistle of the afternoon express
and grinned as he led his horse down the street
toward the station. usually the M & T never stopped
at Short Falls, but it would today. The red signal
would be out and the steam engine would drag the
cars to a halt. Sam loosened the .44 in his holster
and eyed the sawed off shotgun in his saddle boot.

Everything was ready out here.

Inside the station Wyatt Turner had locked both
doors, ordered the three waiting passengers to lie on
the floor, and watched as Louis slapped around the
station manager until he admitted that he could
stop the express, and pulled a lever that would lift
the red flag.

Wyatt went to the telegraph key and ripped the

sending instrument off the wires and pushed it inside his shirt. They might not have another one.

The two trainmen now lay on the floor in a closet, bound and locked inside. Wyatt and Louis ambled out on the platform which was built up to meet the height of the train car boxes for ease in unloading freight. A short time later Joe came out of the station, moved to his assigned spot and tried to look bored.

Hans, the last man out of the rail building had taken time to order the lone woman passenger to stand. He then thrust his hands inside the top of her dress and rubbed her breasts until she screamed and kicked him in the shins. He grinned and hurried outside.

The slow moving train came to a stop at the station platform at the same time Sam Bass walked up after tying his horse to the rail. Wyatt at the head of the platform jumped in the engine doorway and leveled his six-gun at the engineer and fireman.

"Move the train or die in your shoes!" Louis hissed. "Get us two miles out of town and then stop. Now, asshole!"

The engineer nodded and pushed the levers. Steam whistled out of the cylinders as the big drive wheels began to spin on the steel rails, then caught hold and the eight car train moved forward gradually, then slowly picked up speed.

The other four members of the Sam Bass gang had stepped on board the train without incident. When the train was moving fast enough to discourage anyone from jumping off, Louis went into the first passenger car.

"Nobody move or you're dead!" Louis shouted. "Gents get out your wallets and purses, ladies all your jewelry and 'course any gold watches." Louis grabbed a hat off a man in the first seat and held it out.

"Just fill up the hat and nobody is gonna get hurt." To emphasize his point, Louis blasted a .44 round through the nearby window. The noise of the pistol in the confined space was much louder than usual. One woman screamed.

"Shut up!" Louis yelled. "Now get out the cash and jewelry. Don't want to have to yank no necklaces off or anything like that." The people knew not to object or try to stop him. After all, this was the year 1878, and train robbers were the talk of the nation.

At the far end of the car Hans lifted his six-gun and added his comments.

"Just don't get frisky, anybody, cause I'm right here with my trusty .44 looking right down your nose. Now get out those wallets!"

One gang in Texas robbed trains five times near Dallas in fifty days. Everyone knew train robbers were desperados, as quick to kill a person as they were to make conversation.

Sam Bass and Joe had moved through the second passenger car directly to the express car where the mail and valuables were carried and where the safe was located.

The two men in the express car had no warning that anything was out of the ordinary. They often stopped at red flag stations to take on mail or pouches and were moving again at once.

The express door was locked as usual. Sam Bass put three .44 slugs into the locking mechanism. At once Joe drove his shoulder and all two hundred pounds of his weight into the partition and it sprang open.

Sam Bass shot again into the roof of the car, just

9

to stop any gunplay by the expressmen. One was a small clerk, the other was the one Sam wanted.

"No wasted time, gents, open the safe," Sam bellowed. Neither man moved. Sam picked one of them and lifted his .44. He had one round left in it. "You, open the safe or I'll blow your brains all over the car," Sam thundered.

"Please no! I'm the mail clerk," the man Sam aimed at yelped. "I don't even know where the safe is!" The man dropped to his knees. Sam pushed him to one side and swung his pistol toward the second man. Sweat beaded on his upper lip.

"Glad to open the safe, mister, but I don't know the combination. They changed it just before we left St. Louis and wouldn't tell me. Don't get opened until we hit Dallas."

Sam moved the muzzle and shot the man in the right shoulder. The expressman slammed back against the mail sacks and then caught his balance. He held his left hand over the wound, agony painted his face.

"Killing me won't help. I don't know the damn numbers!"

Sam had learned to recognize when a man was telling the truth. He motioned Joe up and took four sticks of the new fangled dynamite out of a sack, fixed it with sticky tape and wrapped more tape around the handle of the safe.

"Move these civilians out to the vestibule," Sam snapped at Joe who herded the two workers to the far end of the car and out the door to the narrow platform between cars.

Sam lit the fuse and went out the other door.

Thirty seconds later, the safe blew. The explosion blasted the sliding side door on the express car half off its track, blew a hundred pieces of mail around the car, but ruined the locking mechanism on the safe and jolted the heavy door completely off one hinge.

When he heard the blast in the engine ahead, Wyatt ordered the engineer to stop the train. Then he tied up both men, dropped down from the engine and walked back to the express car along the cinder filled right of way.

Sam sat on the floor in front of the safe grinning. There was a wooden box sealed with wax that held five hundred freshly minted gold double eagles; ten thousand dollars!

Sam pawed through the rest of the goods, found some stocks and bonds that he didn't understand and left them. He grabbed a sack of silver coins and a packet of what looked like grant deeds. He took the thirty-five pound box of gold coins to the edge of the side door.

The train had stopped. He couldn't budge the sliding door, so went out the one he had come in. Sam dropped to the right of way on the right hand side of the train facing the engine. He saw his four men ready to leave the train.

Down the tracks a quarter of a mile he could see a small trail of dust. That would be Charlie bringing up the horses. Quickly he called his men and then hurried into the brush at the side of the tracks, and only then did they hear two pistols firing at them from the train.

"Somebody is damn brave now!" Louis said. He held up a hat filled with greenbacks and gold and silver coins. "Must have over five hundred dollars in here, Sam! Then we got two gold watches and some rings and things."

"Good," Sam said. "Every little bit counts." Sam was well aware of the value of a dollar. The average cowboy worked for $25 a month and food. A clerk in a store might make $30 a month. They worked all year for $360!

Sam had thought of breaking open the box of gold coins and spreading around the weight, but he decided to keep the box himself. They got to the dirt road that ran a hundred yards from the train tracks and waited. The train still sat where it had been. Nobody had untied the engineer yet.

Three minutes later Charlie rode up with his string of horses and each man grabbed his own and mounted up.

"Which way?" Wyatt called.

"South," Sam said. "Heading for Texas. This is too damn far north to suit me. Nice little valley over there that runs down into the Ozarks. You boys ever been in the Ozark Mountains?"

The heads shook.

"How'd we do, Sam?" Louis called.

"Did a mite bit good, boys. Safe had a box of brand new double gold eagles . . . ten thousand dollars worth!"

Everyone whooped in total joy. Most of them had never seen that much money in their lives.

"That's two thousand for each of us!" Joe bellowed.

Sam grinned and waved them forward like he was in the army horse soldiers. "Let's ride, boys. We'll split it up later."

They rode for three hours and on the gradual up slope they could watch behind them and see that there was no pursuit. Sam knew exactly why. Planning. Good plans produce good results. He had worked on the best methods of robbing trains until he had it down to an exact science.

He took over the station well in advance of the

train's arrival. He ripped out the telegraph key so it would take time to notify anyone of the robbery. Then he had moved the train two miles out of town so no one in town could oppose the robbery. Finally he had placed his men in precise positions with specific jobs to do. His get away was also orchestrated.

Sam could not remember how many trains he and his changing band had robbed. Dozens by now. His first robbery was not so successful. Sam chuckled to himself remembering it.

That first outing had been on March 25, 1877, when he and two friends decided to rob a stagecoach not far out of Deadwood in Dakota territory. They would steal everything of value from the strong box and the passengers.

Frank Towle and Little Reddy McKimmie were the other two members of his gang. They got to the stage, challenged it and told the driver to stop, but Frank didn't get his job done of stopping the horses. He fired a shot, which spooked the horses and they took off charging down the rough stage road.

McKimmie tried to help and lifted his shotgun and fired. The buckshot killed the driver, Johnny Slaughter, who tumbled off the high perch and the reins went slack.

That was all the horses needed and they went wild "running away" with no one to control them. They charged down the roadway, smart enough to stay on the comparatively level area and raced themselves into a lather. Eventually an adventurous passenger caught the reins and pulled the horses to a stop.

The runaway horses had dragged along with them a strongbox with $15,000 inside, which Sam Bass never saw. He kicked McKimmie out of the gang and brought in more men and tried again.

On his very first train robbery he did better. But this job was planned down to the last eyelash. They took on the Union Pacific train in Nebraska near the town of Ogallala. Joel Collins had taken over as head of the gang, and they decided to hit the #4 Express when it paused at the water tank at 10:48, September 17, 1877.

A half hour before train time they took over the small station, tore out the telegraph key, and forced the agent to put out a red light so the express would stop.

It worked to perfection and was a haul that netted them $60,000 in new double eagle gold coins. They tried to get into the safe, but couldn't passing up another $200,000. It was the biggest money robbery that Sam Bass ever participated in. He always kept trying to equal it.

Sam held up his hand now as they topped a small rise along a chattering stream. They had been working up a series of valleys and were nearing the foothills to the Ozarks and their forested slopes ahead.

It was close to dark, when Sam spotted a small rancher's cabin next to the creek.

He talked to his men for a moment, then they vanished into some brush and he rode up to the door and called out.

"Hello. The house? Anyone there?"

A shotgun poked through the open door.

"Yeah? What you want?" a gruff voice asked.

"Mean you no harm. Stranger in these parts and I guess I got lost. I was heading for Branson. This the right way?"

The door came open another few inches, and Sam could see a whiskered face behind the double barrels of the scatter gun.

14

"Yep, it's the way, but you got a long piece to go yet. Riding alone?"

"My Injun squaw didn't want to come," Sam said grinning.

"Hail, you sound right enough. Want to lite and have a bite of supper? We just about to sit down."

"Appreciate it. My name is Sam."

He went to the door and inside the rough log cabin. The man with the shotgun also had a sidearm. Hovering over the stove was a girl of maybe eighteen, who was dishing up stew from a big copper pot. She was tall, a little plump with large breasts straining against the gingham dress top.

"Name's Hawkins," the man said. "Daughter is Hattie."

"Evening, Hawkins, Miss. I'm Sam. That stew smells mighty good."

"Sit and eat," Hattie said evenly. When her father looked away, she grinned at him, her eyes dancing.

Hawkins put down the shotgun and they ate, then when Hattie was clearing away the dishes, Sam lifted his six-gun and trained it on the man.

"Sorry, folks, but I do have some friends who would also like a bite to eat."

Hawkins growled and started to move his hand toward his pistol, but a round from Sam's revolver dug into the wooden table and slanted off into the wall.

"Easy like, Hawkins. Hand me your iron, butt first." The owner of the cabin did, his face angry.

"Come in boys!" Sam called. The other five men trooped into the room, tied Hawkins hand and foot and rolled him on the bunk. Hattie fed the rest of them, then smiled again at Sam.

"Sam, I'm getting me somewhat sleepy. Don't care where the rest of the men sleep, but I got me a bed back here, if'n you be even so little interested."

Sam was not the biggest man in the group. He stood five feet, eight inches tall and weighed one hundred, forty pounds. He had a well groomed handlebar moustache and a full head of dark hair which he parted just off center on the left side.

Sam caught Hattie's hand and led her into the end of the cabin where a blanket walled off one part of the small cabin. She grabbed his hands at once and pushed them up to her full breasts.

"Sam, it ain't often that I see a good looking young man like you! I just can't wait to get you all over and inside me!"

Sam undressed her slowly, played with her breasts until she soared into two climaxes, then stripped her and took off his clothes. He pushed her down on the bed and straddled her. Before he knew it she had grabbed his stiff rod and pulled it up so she could take it in her mouth.

A few minutes later Hattie moved him back down on her hot and ready body and admitted it had been almost a year since she'd had a man in he bed. She made up for it with Sam. By morning he figured he had slept only about a half hour, and he was so exhausted that he couldn't get it up any more.

Hattie pulled his soft pud into her mouth but it was no use, Sam was played out. Hattie took his hand and pushed it between her legs and stuffed three fingers inside her.

"Once more with your fingers, darling Sam, then I'll get breakfast." She kissed him. "Sweet fucker Sam, you send your boys on ahead and you stay on a few days. I'll take care of my old man. I get better the more fucking I do. In about three days I'll really show you a wild time!"

Sam dressed, had breakfast, and told Hattie not

to untie her paw until they were out of sight. He really did have to leave. Hattie swore at Sam, ran for the shot gun and they barely got it away from her before she blasted it at Sam.

Her dress top came open and her big breasts swung out in the struggle, but Wyatt got the shotgun. Wyatt was mad at Sam for a week because Sam made them ride out right then, without giving Wyatt his turn to crawl over the eager farmer's daughter.

Sam Bass had learned that robbing trains and making love to strange women did not mix. One or the other, but almost never both on the same outing. He had made an exception for Hattie, and didn't recover for two days until they were in Branson. By then it was time to take a rest, watch the back trail, and give the men free rein on the two fancy ladies in the small town's only saloon. Sam decided to rest up a few more days.

2

S pur McCoy settled down in the soft seat of the railraod passenger car and looked out the window at the Missouri landscape slashing by at thirty miles an hour. Amazing how quickly these Iron Horses could cover the ground. Coast to coast in seven days if you made the right train connections!

Why, he remembered when . . . Spur tilted his hat down over his eyes and grinned. He was sounding like an old timer, not a young buck ready to take on the world. Spur was not about to challenge the whole place, he had his hands full right now tracking down Sam Bass, train bandit.

Sam Bass had robbed his first stage coach last year, and now in the spring of 1878 he had more than a dozen train heists on his criminal record. He had come to the attention of the United States Secret Service when he robbed five trains near Dallas, Texas within a six week period.

Spur's boss, General Wilton D. Halleck in Washington, D.C. had telegraphed Spur in Denver to get on Sam Bass's trail and to ride him into jail or a grave, either one was fine with Gen. Halleck. The service had been getting pressure from all over Washington evidently.

Spur McCoy was a U.S. Secret Service Agent, and while few in number they were starting to make a name for themselves in the law enforcement field. Just after the Civil War, the Secret Service was literally the only law agency that could cross state lines. The service had been started by Congress with the specific job of protecting the U.S. currency against counterfeiters. Their assignments quickly broadened to almost any interstate or interterritorial crime of dispute.

Spur had joined the Service as soon as it was founded. He had served for two years in the war as an infantry officer winding up as a captain. Then he was called to Washington, D.C. to serve as aide to Senator Arthur B. Walton, a long time family friend and the senior senator from the state of New York.

Spur took the assignment, then went with the Secret Service. After serving six months in Washington D.C., Spur found himself shipped to St. Louis, Missouri where he would head up the Service's activities in the states west of there.

He was assigned the position because he was the best horseman in the Service and had recently won the pistol competition. General Halleck assumed he would need both skills covering the West. The general had been right.

Spur was better educated than most western lawmen. He grew up in New York City where his father was a wealthy store owner and importer. Spur went to Harvard and graduated with a specialty in history. Then he worked for his father for two years.

The train jolted and Spur's hat fell to the floor. Before he could retrieve it a sparkling young woman bent and grabbed it and handed it to him. She had come and sat opposite him while he had been day-dreaming under his hat. He smiled at her, thanked her and she smiled then looked away.

"Thank you again, Miss. That was most courteous of you," Spur said.

She glanced at him, aloof and poised. Then she grinned and dimples punctured her cheeks. "Welcome," she said softly and Spur wanted to get to know her better, but she stood as the train stopped and walked to the end of the car and got off at some small Missouri town.

A tall farmer met her outside the train and kissed her possessively. Spur lifted his brows and went back to his thoughts.

Sam Bass. The man liked to travel. From Deadwood up in the Dakota Territories, to Ogallala in Nebraska, then down to Dallas. Spur had been on his way to St. Louis to head south when he got the new telegram.

SPUR MCCOY. DENVER. SAM BASS ROBBED TRAIN OUTSIDE OF SPRINGFIELD, MISSOURI TODAY. ON THE MISSOURI & TEXAS CENTRAL LINE. PROCEED WITH ALL SPEED TO AREA, AND TRACK DOWN CULPRIT. THIS MISSION TAKES PRIORITY OVER ANY OTHER. SIGNED, HALLECK, SALES MANAGER.

The day before, the train mail had brought him a dozen pages of facts and pictures of Sam Bass. Sam was well known in the press, even posing for pictures with his gang. He was only twenty six years old, but was a master at robbing trains. Spur hoped this would be Sam's last train job.

Spur dug the papers out and went over them again. Sam had been born July 21, 1851 on a farm outside of Mitchell, Indiana. He was one of ten children. Both his mother and father were dead by the time he was thirteen and he was on his own. When he was nineteen he went to Texas to become a cowboy. He got a job on a farm and a year later moved to Denton, Texas where he worked as a stablehand.

He developed a taste for whiskey, and gambling, especially at the small race track in Denton where horses ran every Sunday. Near the end of 1875 Sam was run out of Denton by a posse after he was mixed up in a beating after an argument.

He drifted to San Antonio and in the summer of 1876 with two partners drove seven hundred head of beef to Kansas and the railroad. From there they worked up to Deadwood where they tried to pull a stage coach robbery that went sour.

Then Sam was in on the Big Springs, Nebraska robbery of the train that netted more than $60,000. After that he started his own gang.

Spur pushed aside the papers and stared out the window again. They would be in Springfield in two hours. That meant he was over two days behind the robbers. A mighty cold trail. But at least he had some kind of a trail. Which direction would they move out of the Springfield area?

Spur checked a map spread out over his knees. He guessed they would head south, back to his homeland. That direction led into one of the least populated sections of Missouri and into the Ozark Mountains. Spur had heard some wild tales about the Ozarks, how there was almost no law in some of the counties. That would be an attraction for Sam Bass.

When Spur got to the station he would see what the railroad people knew. Some of them could be most helpful. One of the trainmen must have seen which direction they took when they left the train. It was a hope.

Spur pushed the hat down over his eyes and leaned back on the soft cushion. He was going to be on the trail again soon enough, and sleeping on the ground, waking up stiff and sore. Maybe he should get a nice cushy job as a town marshall somewhere and settle down. Naw!

The jolting of the trail as the cars banged together when the train braked to a stop at Short Falls, eighteen miles east of Springfield, stirred Spur again. This was the site of the robbery.

Spur McCoy grabbed his carpetbag and slid down the steps to the ground and walked across to the small depot. There was no one there to meet him. A quick inquiry showed that none of the train people were on hand who had been on the robbed train two days before. Spur pushed back his low-crowned brown Stetson and scowled at the telegraph operator.

"I'm a federal lawman come here to try and find Sam Bass. Is there anyone who can tell me which direction the gang rode off after the robbery?"

"Fer cats' sakes, course there is, young feller," the key man said staring at Spur from watery blue eyes.

"Good, who is it?"

"Me. I talked to all of them when they backed the train into the station."

"So, kind sir. Which way did Sam Bass ride?"

"South, straight into the Ozarks." He wiped his eyes with a red trainman's handkerchief half as big as he was. "Just damn glad I don't got to go into them Ozarks. Hear tell lots of folks ride in there . . . then they just ain't never heard of again."

"And you'll swear that's the way Sam and his gang rode? How long did these eyewitnesses of yours see them heading that way?"

"Long as they could spot them from top of the train. That string of cars was 'bout two miles out, more or less. Old Clint, he's the engineer on that run, he figured he better back her in and tell us what happened. The brakeman, Arch, he stood on top a box car and watched Sam and his bunch till they went behind a line of trees. Heading south all the way, they was."

Spur handed him a telegram message and a greenback dollar bill. "Send this out right away, if it's no trouble. I'd appreciate it."

The telegrapher became all business again, lowered his green eyeshade over the watery blue eyes and read it out loud.

"Just so I get it right, you know. Says: To General Halleck, Washington D.C. Arrived on robbery site. In pursuit. Signed McCoy. Yep, I can send that."

"Much obliged," Spur said. "Oh, is there a livery stable in town?"

"Nope. But we got a blacksmith who's got an extra horse or two. Down half a block, two houses from the tracks."

Spur thanked him and went to find a horse. He hoped the old nag he probably would find would make it into the Ozarks.

McCoy had ridden a full day now toward the forested ridges ahead of him. He covered about twenty five miles the first day along the thin track of a stagecoach road that was used once a week to haul goods, mail and passengers into Branson.

From what he could find out from the locals, Branson would be the best spot for Sam Bass and his gang to stop and rest a day or so and perhaps kick up their heels a bit before they rode on south—

if that was the direction they headed.

With no other choice, Spur angled along the coach road. An hour before sunset he saw a smoke to the left and rode up a small rise off the trail to investigate. A little ranch showed below, two pole corrals, a small barn, and a log house made from local material. Maybe two hundred head of steers and cows and calves in open range below the house. Maybe he could get a meal and an inside place to sleep for the night.

He rode up and saw pansys and hollyhocks blooming outside the front door. There was a woman here, that was for certain.

"Hello!" Spur called loudly.

A shotgun angled through the front door.

"Yeah, what do you want?" a woman's voice asked.

"Passing through, wondered if I could rent a room or buy some supper? I'm short on supplies."

"You alone? My husband wants to know. You alone?"

"Fact is, I am, ma'am. Heading for Branson. This the way?"

"This is the way." The door swung open and she lowered the shotgun. "Lite and tie your horse. I can find some supper for you if'n you not too picky."

As Spur swung down, he saw she was blonde, hair around her shoulders, younger than the voice indicated, maybe twenty-five or six. She brushed hair out of her gray eyes as he tied his horse. One hand rested on her hip and the other hung at her side.

"Come far?"

"Railroad at Short Falls."

"Anything happening there?" she asked. He saw that her eyes really were pale gray, and her skin was soft and only slightly tanned. She did not spend a lot of time outdoors.

"Sam Bass robbed the train," Spur said.

"Sam Bass, that Texas badman? What's he doing way up here?"

"Looking for more trains, I reckon."

She laughed and he saw the bodice of her dress strain as her breasts thrust forward.

"Come in, come in. We don't get company often up here." She went ahead of him into the one room cabin. It was as neat as a widow's Park Avenue apartment and just as fussy. She had not left her culture or her sense of neatness behind when she moved to this edge of the wilderness.

"My name is Ruth. What's yours?"

"Spur McCoy."

She held out her hand and shook his. "Pleased to meet you, Mr. McCoy."

"I'm pleased to meet you, and to find your ranch just when I needed it. This is a very nice room," Spur said. "Are you from New York?"

She looked up quickly, surprise on her face. She smiled, nodded and went to the wood burning kitchen range.

"I best be heating up some food for you. I don't eat much." She watched him from the stove. "Sit and rest yourself. Wash up out at the pump, you have a mind to." She turned now and he saw that she was slender, yet shapely. "How did you know I was from New York?"

"Just a guess, and the way you have this cabin furnished and how you keep it so neat. Reminds me of an aunt of mine in New York City, Brooklyn really."

"Good Lord, I'm from Brooklyn!" Her face was alive, remembering. Then she turned. "Better get the fire going."

"Let me," Spur said. She stepped back. He put in kindling, then larger wood, and pushed in a pitch stick under the kindling. He lit the turpentine-like pitch which ignited the rest of the wood.

"You've done that before," she said.

Spur saw no signs that a man lived in the cabin, no pipe, no boots, no horsewhip or square of chewing tobacco.

"Husband be gone long?"

She turned and watched him a minute. "For eternity. One of our bulls killed him six months ago. Been trying to make do with all the work around here with my two black hands. So far, so good."

She fixed a meal then. First she fried a thick beefsteak, then warmed up boiled potatoes, beets, carrots and peas that must have come from her garden, and then set out two big slabs of apple pie. He ate it all and drank three cups of coffee.

"Best apple pie I ever had," Spur said.

"Cinnamon. I use just the right amount of cinnamon and it perks up the flavor. Crust always was easy for me."

"The lonesome part must not be."

"True. Will you stay the night?"

"I can sleep on the floor."

"No reason. Bed's big enough for two, used to be, reckon it still is."

She soon finished the dishes and moved to the small couch where Spur sat smoking a thin black cheroot.

"Haven't smelled tobacco in this house for six months. Never liked it much before. Now, seems kind of nice."

She sat beside Spur, trimmed the coal oil lamp's wick a bit to lower the light, then turned to Spur.

"I won't beat around the bush, Spur. I am lonesome. No man's had his hands on me for six months, and I'm more than ready to share my bed with you. You a mind to?"

"Why don't we just see what happens, Ruthie." He bent forward and she moved toward him. He kissed her lips gently, then again. She moved closer and her arms went around him. Her mouth opened and Spur let her tongue dart into his mouth.

Ruthie groaned softly and held the kiss. She made animal sounds in her throat and gently leaned backward, pulling him down on top of her. The kiss ended and she looked at him.

"Oh, lordy, but it has been a long time! I'd forgotten how it always gets me so warm. Lordy!"

She reached up to be kissed again and he moved so he lay half on her and half off. He kissed her, then lifted his hand to one of her breasts.

"Yes, yes!" she said through the kiss. His hand wormed between them through the buttons on the print dress top and closed around her breast.

"Yes, sweetheart! Yes! play with them. They are all yours. Do anything you want to, sweetheart!" Her eyes were closed and Spur guessed she was pretending her husband was feeling her again.

She let him lift the dress up and over her hips, then take it off over her head. Under it she had on only a thin chemise and no drawers or underwear.

"No need," she said in explanation. "No one to impress, no one to entice." She slipped off the chemise and her breasts were hand sized, delicately nippled with small brown areolas.

"Yes, I'm not a virgin. We lost our baby after six months, sweet little girl child. She had been sickly from the start." Ruth shook her head. "I don't want to think about the ones who are gone. I want to feel of the one who is here."

27

Carefully, slowly she undressed him. "I haven't done this in so long!" she said again and again. "I love to undress a man. It gets me all worked up."

Spur lay on the bed and pull on top of him. She lowered one breast into his waiting mouth and laughed.

"Yes! A woman does love that! Makes us glad we're different, and we have tits men love to chew and suck on. No milk now, but there was a time." She blinked back tears, then changed putting her other breast down for him to lick.

Then her hips began grinding against him.

"I can't wait!" she yowled. "Do me right now, quick before the fire goes out. Right not!"

She rolled over and spread her legs, and pulled Spur with her. He lowered and thrust and she swallowed him in one stroke her inner muscles closing around him like a lasso in a crazy way, gripping and releasing.

"Do me now!" she said again and thrust her hips up to meet him. "Faster!"

"You do like it, don't you, Ruth?"

"Yes! Yes! Who says a woman can't like sex as much as a man? This woman does love to get fucked."

The word made her climax and she screamed and wailed, her hips pounding him higher and higher until the spasms shook her, dropping her back to the bed, rattling her like a morning express with empty boxcars.

She scratched Spur's back with her fingernails, shouted again and then bit him on the shoulder. Gradually the spasms faded and she lay limp for a minute staring up at him from the pale gray eyes.

"Glorious! There is nothing half so good! Marvelous! No wonder women let men walk all over them . . . it's all so we can get fucked!

"Heavens! I forgot about you. You didn't make it while I did I don't guess. But then I'd never feel you." She ground her hips a moment under him. "Lordy, but he's still stiff as a telegraph pole." She humped her hips and worked her inner muscles and at once Spur felt a jolt as the freight began to move down the long tube to freedom.

He pumped and groaned and pounded the bed beside her and when he at last climaxed he drove her halfway to the floor through the feather bed and the straw mattress over the springs. She was laughing and crying when he at last shot his final load and collapsed on her.

"Lordy, I never thought you would ever get done. You are some long staying man. I like it that way. No, don't move." She put her arms around his back, pinning them together.

"I like to lay this way for a while, do you mind?"

"No."

"Go to sleep if you want to, I don't mind."

"Not feeling sleepy yet. I say once is never enough."

"Oh good! When I saw you I figured at least four times, maybe five. What do you think?"

Spur laughed softly. "You do love it, don't you? When I get past four I do start to think about sleeping."

"Well, cowboy, we'll have to test you out and try for a new record, your own personal best. I'd say you're around six."

Spur laughed again and kissed her. "I see this is going to be a long night, with not a whole lot of sleep involved."

"Damn right," Ruth said quickly. "I get a big stallion like you in my corral, I'm not gonna let you go with just one or two shots. I got to come out even on all the apple pie you ate somehow." They both laughed.

About midnight they got out of bed and renewed their energy with fresh boiled coffee and more apple pie. Spur had two more pieces and a slab of home-made cheddar cheese. It was a pale yellow and aged only six months, but tangy and good.

He watched her walking around the small cabin as naked as the day she was birthed and not a bit self conscious about it.

"What are your plans, Ruth? You figure to stay here and prove up on your homestead?"

"Plan to. Take me another year and a half. If my two hands will stay on for grub and tobacco and a couple of dollars a month, I might make it. They was slaves in Mississippi before the war. Now they say there are just happy to have a place to live and to be treated halfway like free men." She watched him.

"Man, you are naked, you know that?"

Spur sipped the scalding coffee. "Wondered why I was getting chilly. You think of anything we could do to get warmed up again?"

"I'll ponder on it." She stared at him. "Spur, never did tell me what you do. You know something about ranches, I'd wager. Want to stay on here? We get on great in bed, and you can help run the place. Half of it's yours. No preacher, nothing. Just living together and working the place. Taking it as it comes. Kids is okay with me. Whatever. I like you, Spur."

"And you're not going back to Brooklyn?"

"All that coal dust and grime and all those people? Not a chance in a million. I like the wide open country. Besides, my pa kicked me out of the house. I got more here than I would have back there. How about it, partners in the ranch and in ownership and use of the double bed?"

"Let's talk about that in the morning. We're only half way to six. I used to know a little black girl down in New Orleans who had the wildest way to make love. Want to try it?"

"How wild, Spur?"

"Not anything hurtful, you game?"

Ruth was.

The next morning, she fried him eggs, used the last of a slab of bacon from the cool house in the well, and cooked up more hash brown potatoes than he could eat.

"You thinking of my proposition?" Ruth asked.

"Some."

"So?"

"Got me a job to do, first. Sam Bass. Badass Sam Bass, got to go find him. Afraid I wouldn't be much good as a rancher or a farmer. Like to keep moving."

"Back to some of that New Orleans black cunt, right?" Ruth said. She shrugged. "Never hoped in a year and a half that I could make you stay. A woman has some ways to persuade a man, but you done seen all of mine by now. One for the road?"

"A kiss is 'bout all the strength I have left, you sexy lady. Seven, wasn't it?"

Ruth grinned. "At least I'll have that as a new record." She turned and wiped her eyes, then looked back. "Now get your pretty ass out of here before I start blubbering!"

Spur waved and rode out south back to the road that wound higher into the foothills toward Branson.

3

McCoy never looked back at the woman as he rode away. Yes, it would be something of a relief to swing down, kiss her and help her run her ranch, their ranch, she had said. But Spur McCoy just wasn't quite ready to do that yet. He told her he had to keep moving, to see what was over the next hill.

To find out where Sam Bass was and how he could help bring him to justice and remove a threat to the rail transport of the nation. He moved the nag out at the pace he thought she could hold up under for four hours. Then he would give her a rest, lay in the sun for a half hour and be moving again.

A full, hard day of riding brought Spur McCoy to the edge of the quiet little Ozark mountain village of Branson, population 312, elevation 1,237 feet. Spur didn't like the feel of the place as he sat his horse a quarter of a mile away. There was something about it he didn't understand. He made a small camp in a patch of woodsy brush a half mile from town.

The secret agent left his horse and rifle at his hidden camp and with his .45 Colt on his thigh, walked into town for a beer and to see what he could learn. The town wasn't much. One dirt street with a block's worth of stores and four or five avenues winding off that were filled with small houses built of clapboard and cedar shingles.

He saw a one room school and a small church. Spur counted four saloons, two small general stores and a half a dozen other shops and businesses along the lightly built "commercial" block. Branson was the county seat of Taney county, but he couldn't locate any kind of courthouse.

By then it was nearly dark. The second bar seemed to be the most popular, Cat's Claw, the sign said so he pushed through the bat wing doors. It was mid rustic, even for the mountains. The bar was of varnished quarter cut shortleaf pine and white oak alternated. The bar rail near the floor was an oak two by four well worn down by boots. Along the far wall stood a row of poker tables and a few more small tables for serious drinkers. Six kerosene lamps lit the room in a kind of murky light so the card players had to squint to be sure of their hands.

Spur bought a beer for a nickel and stood at the bar making rings on the polished surface with the cold glass. Plenty of ice in the underground ice house must be available in Branson. They probably had a winter freeze ice pond. Within a half hour he heard that there was a group of six strangers in town. They had moved into the old Parsons house and appeared to be staying for a time.

"Don't know who'n hell they are," the barkeep told a friend. He polished a beer mug and waggled his head. "But they got money, new looking gold double eagles. Brand new ones. The ridges on the edges ain't ever been worn off. Now where would a bunch of shiftless looking hombres like them get just minted double eagles?''

"Does make a feller wonder, don't it?" the man at the bar said, laughed softly and tilted his mug of beer.

At the next saloon, which was less crowded and where a beer cost a dime, Spur asked a stranger where the Parsons place was.

"You got to be new in town to ask that question," the man said. He held out his hand. "I'm Jones, run the general store. You need anything, I probably got it."

Spur shook his hand. "McCoy, just passing through. Trying to locate a friend."

"Parsons place is three houses beyond the school. It's the one with the faded white picket fence around it. Old man Parsons died about a year ago. Nobody knows who owns the place now. Evidently he had kin in Boston, but we don't know much about them. Nobody been keeping the place up much, but somebody rents it out now and then. Banker most likely."

Spur bought Jones a beer and they talked some more.

"I'm looking for some really good range breeding stock. Any around here?"

Jones just shook his head.

"For good breeding stock, you better stick to Texas, or Kansas. Most of the cattle in these parts are hodgepodge bastards, so mixed up they aren't any one breed at all. Mostly sold to locals for beef. Now and then there's a drive down grade to Springfield. Not much of good as cattle country around Branson. Now you move on down toward Springfield, you can find some better stock."

Spur left a while later, walked by the Parsons place and saw lights on in every window but one. He heard somebody singing a drunken, bawdy song and then the wild laugh of a female. It sounded like Sam and his boys were whooping it up. With ten thousand dollars worth of double gold eagles they could buy anything they wanted in town. And maybe anybody.

Spur hoped the whiskey was flowing well for the Sam Bass robber gang. That would make his work much easier. He would get some sleep and surprise the bunch about four A.M. when they were still drunk and too hungover to shoot straight.

McCoy walked back to his camp, slept, and woke up precisely at four A.M. He took his Henry with a full load of twelve rounds, his trusty Colt .45 in his holster and a second six-gun, a smaller, .32 caliber, for back up.

He walked into town and then circled around the house. Everything was quiet. The lights were all out. Spur tried the back door and found it unlocked. Quietly he eased inside and at once found a man sleeping in his own vomit on the kitchen floor, a whiskey bottle was still clutched in his right fist but it had all drained out on his pants.

Spur eased a hogsleg out of leather on the man's thigh, then tied his hands in front of him. The drunken robber stirred, said something in his sleep and laughed softly, then quieted. Spur used another length of heavy cord and tied the man's ankles together.

Spur heard someone roll out of bed overhead and hit the floor. There was drunken swearing, then the squeak of bedsprings, and a woman's giggle. Spur froze in place at the edge of the kitchen and waited. When the sounds quieted again he moved to the living room off the kitchen. Spur found a fancy lady sleeping nude on a couch. On the floor below her lay a man equally clothesless. He stirred as Spur stepped on a squeaking floor board.

The man came up in two seconds, wide awake and a big .44 in his fist aimed at the noise. Spur shot him in the shoulder, slamming the gun out of his hand. He screamed and Spur heard action all over the house.

The man lay bleeding against the sofa, where the fancy lady had sat up and grinned at Spur. "You like my big tits," she asked in a kind of automatic response to a frightening situation. She trembled, then fell on the couch.

Four shots blasted through the living room from a hallway. Spur heard windows open, another one break. He was flat on his belly behind a big bookcase and writing desk. Evidently Mr. Parsons had left the place completely furnished.

Another pair of slugs came through the door, then footsteps sounded down the hall and a door slammed.

Spur ran to the front window. He saw four half dressed men running down the street, looking back, swearing and waving their guns. Quickly Spur got the wounded man on his feet and pushed him into the kitchen.

The outlaw had just come out of his daze and tried to sit up. Spur cut loose his feet and helped him up.

"Either one of you jaspers want to say alive, you do damn quick what I tell you, savvy?"

Both men nodded.

"We're going out the back door and down the alley, turn the other way and find the sheriff's office. Understand?"

"Fer all the good it'll do you," the wounded man said. "First I need a doctor."

"No doctor. Slug went all the way through your

36

shoulder and your arm isn't broken. Only way you'll need a doctor is if you're half dead. Now move it."

They used up a half hour walking cautiously along the dark streets, down an alley and then around the front of the small building that had a poorly lettered sign that said "Sheriff's Office." The outside door was locked.

One of the men Spur had pushed ahead now laughed. Spur shot him an angry look and pounded on the wooden panel again.

"Yeah! yeah! Coming," a voice bellowed from inside at last. Another two or three minutes later the lock clicked, a bar was removed and the door swung open.

Sheriff Lund Parcheck peered out the door over a Remington .44 New Model Army revolver with its heavy octagon barrel.

"What the hell's going on?"

"Sheriff, I have two men to lodge in your jail. They're part of the Sam Bass gang of robbers who hit the Missouri & Texas Central express car three days ago down by Springfield."

"So?"

"So I want to leave them here for safekeeping while I chase the other four members of the gang."

"Don't think so."

"What was that?' Spur asked not believing his ears.

"Said, don't think so. No chance I'm gonna have them cluttering up my jail. Springfield, that's Greene county. Out of my jurisdiction. These boys do anything illegal in my county I'll be more than happy to arrest them. If they didn't, I can't help you."

"You're an elected peace officer, Sheriff. It's your responsibility to assist other law enforcement officers to catch and hold wanted felons regardless of the jurisdiction. Now open the door and get out your jail cell keys.''

"Who the hell are you, mister?" Sheriff Parcheck asked.

"My name is Spur McCoy, and I have jurisdiction here. Let's put these men away and I'll show you my authorization.''

"Nope. That's not what I got elected to do. Take them two back to Springfield yourself, if you got the grit. Me, I'm gonna get me about three more hours of sleep.''

The door banged closed in Spur's face, the lock clicked in place and before Spur could pound on the wood, a bar slid into holders inside.

"Told you," one of the prisoners said. "Told you old Lund wouldn't hold no truck with you. Now what you gonna do, smartass lawman?''

"Shoot you I guess," Spur said thumbing back the hammer on his .45. "You two was shot and killed dead while trying to escape.''

"Hold on now!" the drunk said, suddenly sober as a frosty mountain morning.

"He's joshing us," the wounded man said. "He ain't about to shoot us down in cold blood. His kind never do.''

"You going to bet your life on that idea?" Spur asked softly. "I won't do it here. Wait until we get out of town a mile. Nobody will see, nobody will hear, nobody gonna know. Now move it, dogbreath! Let's walk out of town and north a ways. I want this wrapped up before the sun shows.''

The former drunk stayed sober. He watched over his shoulder as Spur prodded him forward down the street and out of town.

"If I had my piece you wouldn't be doing this,''

the ex-drunk said.

"If I was you, robber man, I'd be worrying about the hereafter, whether there is one or not," Spur snorted. "You try to figure out just how your bullet riddled skull is going to fit into that after life picture."

"Man's got a soul," the wounded man said. "Everybody knows that. It ain't no part of the body, goes right on living."

"You don't say?" Spur said. "You be sure to come back from the dead and explain it all to me. Over there, down through that little swale and up into them shortleaf pine and that mess of white oak. Looks like a damn good place for an an attempted escape to me. A man would just naturally have to shoot to kill a prisoner trying to run for it."

Spur had made his camp in the thicket, and heard his horse whinny as they came up to it. The drunk was getting wild-eyed and Spur was worried he might try something stupid.

"Next to the tree," Spur told the shorter ex-drunk. "Sit down and put your hands behind you."

Spur cut his hand free where they were in front, and tied them in back of him, then tied him to the tree with two tight wraps on a shorter rope. Any more turns around the tree would give too much room to stretch the rope.

He tied the second man the same way to another tree ten feet away. "Stay comfortable, jail birds. I'll have you on your way to Springfield and a real sheriff just as soon as it gets dark. Want to be sure Sam and the rest of his boys didn't follow us."

As Spur turned toward town a piercing, agonizing inhuman scream slammed through the pine trees. It was a sound he had heard too often before, the cry of a horse in deadly peril. He dropped to the ground and rolled behind a tree just as half a dozen pistol shots thundered through the brush and trees from the direction where he had left his horse.

The two prisoners were laughing.

"Come on, Sam!" one of the tied men shouted.

"Sam, you got him belly-crawling to get away!" the wounded man yelled.

Well placed shots gave Spur no choice, he had to move backwark, away from the camp, away from his two captives. He only had his .45 with him. He fired and moved, fired and moved until he got to a big shortleaf pine that he could stand behind. He saw a man dart in toward the captives. By the time Spur shot at him it was too late.

Gunfire boomed beyond the bound men and slugs slammed into Spur's protective tree.

Spur moved again, to the left to another tree for a better field of fire, but when he looked back at his camp, both the men from the robber band had been cut free and were gone.

A closing flurry of shots came toward his position, and then only silence. Spur did a cautious circle route moving back to check on his horse. Far away on the downslope toward town he saw four horses galloping away. Two of them were double loaded. So that's how Sam Bass had trailed him and beat him to the camp.

Spur crashed through the brush to his horse. The animal lay on her side. The grass had been pawed bare where her feet had thrashed in a death agony. Bright red blood painted the whole brushy area around her where blood had sprayed out after her neck had been sliced open.

Spur walked to his camp, picked up everything he had come with including his saddle, and selected a new campsite where he could see the approaches to

Branson and still stay under cover.

Almost all of the Ozark Mountains here were forested with the pines or one of five or six varieties of oak trees. Small valleys and stream gullies were clear and showed some grass, but the man had been right, this was not prime cattle country.

He sat there watching the town. There was no sign that the men he had just seen would ride out of Branson, but Spur knew that a man like Sam Bass would not risk a second confrontation. He had a reputation for clearing out fast, laying low, hiding out and staying inconspicuous between his raids. Maybe that was why he was so successful.

He would be gone as soon as he could get his gang together, get provisions and move out. Which meant Spur had to follow them. He picked up his saddle, Henry repeating rifle, and threw his saddle-bags over his shoulder. He'd come back here for the rest. First he needed another horse, one without a slit throat.

McCoy was a big man at six feet two. He usually weighed in at two hundred pounds in his best fighting trim. It was all muscle, kept lean and hard by long days in the saddle and nights sleeping in a blanket on the hard ground.

He was tanned to a turn, had reddish brown hair and always wore a medium-crowned Stetson, this time a dark brown one and always with a string of silver Mexican pesos strung around the headband. His blue shirt was open at the collar and a stained and well lived-in brown leather vest showed one bullet hole and two grazes.

His hair was longer than that of most men, fighting with his collar and deep on each side with modified mutton chop sideburns. He wore a neatly trimmed half inch wide moustache to keep his upper lip warm. Dark green eyes stared out at Branson with a critical eye.

What kind of a town would elect a sheriff who would not help out another lawman? Spur intended to find out, and to give the man a large piece of his thinking on the subject before he took off trailing Sam Bass. There had to be more to it than simply a lazy sheriff who didn't know the job he was supposed to be doing.

Seeing Sheriff Parcheck was the first item on Spur's list as he trudged into town and dropped his saddle at the livery stable.

"Be back in a few minutes to pick out a horse to buy," Spur told a middle aged wrangler. "You find two of your best for me to take a look at."

"Yes sir," the man said. "What happened to your other horse?"

"She had a bit of a circulation problem. All of her blood ran out a wide slice across her throat. Any more questions?"

The wrangler's eyes opened wide and he shook his head.

4

S pur McCoy marched out of the livery stable and straight to the county sheriff's small office where he banged through the door and stared at Sheriff Parcheck who worked on a plateful of fried eggs, hashbrowns, bacon and a big cup of coffee.

"Yeah?" the sheriff said looking up. "Oh, it's you again, the big federal lawman. You must be federal to claim you have jurisdiction in my county. So you catch the rest of them?"

"You know damn well I didn't. You probably also know I lost the first two, and I'm holding you responsible. I'll be sending a telegram to the Missouri State Attorney General as soon as I can. I'll have you removed from office."

"Don't say. Give my regards to Butch Dolan, he's the attorney general, good buddy of mine. Anything else on your mind? You're holding up my breakfast."

"Do the important things first, Sheriff. Right now you are violating your state oath of office, aiding and abetting a known felon and half a dozen more charges I'll have ready. The Sam Bass gang is pro-

43

bably out of town by now. They were staying in the old Parsons place and you knew it."

"Might have. Might not. Hard to prove what a man knows. You any real business with me? If not I see a young feller who has a real problem."

Spur turned and saw a tall, slender man in a black suit and string tie standing in the doorway.

"If I lose Sam Bass's trail, I'll be back, Sheriff. And you aren't going to be pleased with what happens when I get here." Spur pointed his finger at the sheriff, stabbed it twice at him in emphasis, then spun and walked toward the door.

As he came to the young man he saw a determined, angry look, and knew it must be a mirror of his own. The man walked past and stood in front of the sheriff's desk, his fists balled and placed angrily on hips.

"I see you've managed to kill Frank Davis and not make a ripple in the whole town. Well, I for one, won't stand for it."

"Russell," the Sheriff said in a growning, pained voice. "We've been over this a dozen times. I've told you, bring me some real evidence of foul play and we'll have a look see at the whole situation. It was a house fire, for Christ's sakes. People die all the time when their stoves overheat."

"True, but this one got some help. I found two five gallon coal oil cans just outside the burned out frame of Frank's place. That was before some of your men took them away and destroyed them."

"Those are real bad charges you're making, son. Don't care if you are a damn lawyer. Hell, I could sue you for slander or something. Now you get your ass out of here, and I don't want to hear another word about Frank Davis. You do, and I won't be able to protect you."

"Same way you couldn't protect Frank, right, Sheriff? I don't see how you people keep on doing it, year after year."

"Just upholding the law., Maybe you didn't read for the law long enough, boy. You got a damn lot to learn about practical application of the law. Now get, before I jail you right now!"

Spur had stood at the door in plain sight of both men as the argument went on, now he stepped outside and waited for the young lawyer.

When the man came out, Spur held out his hand.

"I'm Spur McCoy, new to town. Heard your session with the sheriff in there."

"Phillip Russell, attorney-at-law, for all the good it does in this town. My suggestion, sir, is don't stay, ride straight through and then shake any dust off your boots from this county so it doesn't contaminate anyone else."

"Sheriff is a bit high handed?"

"No, inactive. He doesn't do a thing except draw his pay and eat three meals a day. He has no deputies. He never arrests anyone, he looks the other way when a man is gunned down in the streets, hanged outside his house or burned up in his bed. I think he's in with them somehow, but I can't figure how."

"In with them? What do you mean?"

The young man shook his head. "You don't want to get mixed up in this. Here in Branson we have the craziest law set-up I've ever seen. There's no district attorney for the county. They had one but he was run out of town about five years ago, the way I hear. They simply haven't got around to electing a new one.

"There is no kind of local judge. Old Judge Filmore died two years ago, and nobody wanted to run for office. Once in a while a circuit judge comes through, but he usually goes hunting with some of the boys, or catches up on his fishing down at the lake.

"The sheriff is an absolute loon. He knows nothing about law or law enforcement and is proud of the fact. He simply does nothing. But he is good friends with the people at the state capitol up at Jefferson City. Goes up there two or three times a year and comes back sassy as the dickens.

"I've only been here about three months, and everything here is strange. I shouldn't be bothering you about it."

"No, I'm interested. Maybe we should talk some more."

"I have some people to talk to this morning," Russell said. "A will to set up actually. I'll be free right after noon. Come to my office, that's at my small house just two doors down from the little church. I've got a shingle out."

Spur rubbed his chin. "Tell you what. I have to make a run at finding Sam Bass. If I lose him, I'll be back this way."

The two men shook hands and Spur watched him for a moment, then hurried over to the general store and began stocking up on some provisions for a long ride. He had no idea what direction Sam Bass would take. If he headed on South into Arkansas it would be a rough, lonesome ride.

Sam might point for Fayetteville or Little Rock. He would steer around Fort Smith and Judge Parker, the hanging judge.

"Let's see," the store man said. "We got coffee, salt, dry beans, six cans of peaches, slab of bacon, cornmeal, dried apples and apricots and five pounds of raisins. You must be planning on doing a mite of hunting along the way."

"Peers as how," Spur said. He paid the bill of four dollars and thirty-seven cents, and carried it all out of the store in an empty five pound floor sack the man sold for a nickel.

At the livery he checked over two horses. He liked a bay mare the best. She was broad across the chest and like a typical quarter horse, higher in the rear quarters than the front. She looked like she could hit a stride and hold it all day. He saddled her and took her around the block. When he came back he was satisfied. She was smooth, responsive and as calm as a small frog floating on a large lily pad.

"Thirty dollars," the stable owner said. He was a big man, with a fat belly and wore bib overalls so he didn't have to use a belt. He waddled rather than walked and had a birthmark on his right cheek of bright purple.

"Give you twenty, which is five more than she's worth," Spur said. They dickered a dollar at a time and settled on twenty-five, what she was worth and what both were thinking about as the right price all the time. But both were now happy and had the fun of horse trading a little.

Spur tied on his sack of provisions, pushed the Henry into the cross boot and tied it in place with a quick pull loop that made the weapon available to one hand in about three seconds.

He rode to the Parsons place and checked inside. The house was a mess, broken bottles, leftovers of food, and the look of a quick exit by all concerned. The fancy women were gone. He found a hat and a shirt, some female undergarments and one half empty bottle of whiskey.

In the back yard he located dozens of hoof prints. Two of the horses were shod, the others weren't.

Unusual. He moved out to the street and checked and found the same shod/unshod group of prints leading to the south and out of town.

The tracks were easy to follow the first quarter mile on the dirt street, then a country road. There the last signs of civilization ended and the open country took over. Spur rode ahead fifty yards and made a sweeping arc around the end of the trail. He picked up the hoof prints at the far side of the ride. The trail led southwest and Spur followed.

He used the quick trail method he used for long range tracking. Spur figured they were heading out for a far run, so he rode a hundred yards ahead on the general pointing of the trail, then crisscrossed the area until he found the trail again. If the direction left only one good route, he could ride a half mile ahead before he made his arc to find the prints again.

Spur worked for two hours this way, moving up slopes on the Ozark mountains, through sparse growths of oak, and then heavier stands of shortleaf pine. Here the tracking was easier because of the leaf mulch on the ground that left good hoof tracks.

He came over a brow of a ridge and angled down only to find himself on a rocky reverse slope of shale. There was no chance to find tracks here. He rode down the shale to the small stream below, then turned southwest on the far side of the six inch deep water and searched for tracks.

After a half mile of moving downstream he found nothing. He turned and rode upstream, retracing his tracks, then working a mile up the small creek. Nowhere did he find tracks showing that the six men had crossed the stream.

He went back up the shale to the top and found where the riders had hit the rocky area. Now he searched laterally. The shale slope ran for two miles one direction. There were small rock slides and fresh marks on some of the rocky formations, but he had no way of knowing if they were made by Sam Bass's gang.

Spur checked back the other way. The shale slope vanished into vegetation after half a mile ahead but there were no signs that any horsemen had come off the shale onto the oak tree spotted landscape.

The Secret Agent sat on his bay with a feeling of frustration. In the years of working the West he had developed into an excellent tracker. It infuriated him that Sam Bass and his men had outsmarted him. Now he rode back the opposite way to the end of the slate, and now found another rocky formation extending all the way into the water. They could have moved down the stream.

Again Spur followed the brook downstream. He worked one side for a mile, then cut back and worked the other side. At no place was the water too deep for the horses to wade through.

Twice he worked additional mile stretches, and on the third he found a spot the horses had left the water. They had moved at a gallop then, he could tell by the marks in the soft under footing.

Spur followed them to a rise and looked down. There was a wagon road leading from a small sawmill that was turning the larger white oak into saw lumber. Most of it would probably end as flooring.

The problem was the road headed south, out of the mill and he was sure into Arkansas toward the nearest large town. As he watched he saw two wagons each pulled by a team of six move along the road.

The hoof prints and the wagon wheels of just one

such rig would wipe out any chance Spur might have had of following the Sam Bass gang. He had lost them this time for sure.

It was nearly four in the afternoon when Spur turned back north. He still wanted to talk to the young lawyer. There had to be more than met the eye in this small Ozark mountain town. The coal oil fire where a man was burned to death? That type of murder seemed remarkably similar to one other Spur could recall.

It would take him two hours to ride back to town. Spur turned the bay's head to the north and began to ride.

Back in Branson Phillip Russell stood in his small "office" which was in reality his living room converted with a desk and some files and a table. Three men stood across the room from him. All three wore white hoods with small slits for eyes and mouth. His wife huddled beside him. Right then Phillip was glad they had no children.

"I don't understand this at all," Phillip said. "I am a lawyer and representing the dead man's family. We are going to sue the county for a hundred thousand dollars for allowing law and order to become so lax that a band of vigilantes killed this man and set his house on fire to cover up the crime."

"Not a chance!" the middle sized man thundered. "Shoulda stayed where you was 'fore you come here."

"Shut up," a shorter man growled. He had a big belly and a silver buckle in the shape of a big "C." "Too damn much talk. Russell, you been found guilty by the Branson People's Justice Committee and been sentenced to hang."

"No, no, no!" Priscilla screamed from behind Russell. She was a slender woman with soft reddish hair, light skin and dimples in her cheeks. Now her eyes blazed. "You are killers, murderers! You can't walk in here and drag my husband off. There are laws!"

The third man jumped beside Priscilla Russell, grabbed her by the shoulders and pushed her across the room. Phillip started to protest, but the short, heavy set man pushed a six-gun muzzle under his chin and shoved it upward.

The soft tissue drove higher and Phillip lifted his head to lessen the intense pain.

"Leave her alone!" Phillip shouted. "Let her be! This is my doing, not hers!"

The chubby man nodded his hood and the third man with a sawed off shutgun, pushed the woman into a chair and held out his hand to warn her to stay there.

The fat man chuckled. "Yes, now I'd say we have better order in the court here. The lawyer has appealed his sentence. Appeals judge, do you have your ruling on his case yet?"

The third man laughed and Priscilla noticed that when he turned one of his legs was weak and he limped. She knew who did that in town if only she could remember, a limp. Who limped?

"Fact is, Mr. Executioner, this court has come to a decision. The appeal is denied, and the original sentence for Mr. Russell is hereby reinstated, and be carried out immediately."

"Well now, peers we done all we could for the condemned man. Gone through the legalities, and all." The fat man eased the six-gun away from Phillip's chin and pressed the muzzle against the lawyer's heart.

"Inside or outside?" the shorter, rotund man asked.

Priscilla knew she had to keep her wits. They were going to kill Phillip. There wasn't anything she could do about it. She hated them! But she would get even. The man with the limp, she could find him.

The short, fat one, his belt buckle said "C." Where had she seen it? Then she remembered, outside the saloon. The man owned one of the saloons, the Cat's Claw, she thought they called it. But the other one, the tall, thin man. She had no idea about him. He hadn't said a word.

Priscille began unbuttoning the flowered print blouse she wore over the long skirt.

"I have another appeal," she said loudly. By the time the three men looked at her the blouse was hanging loose in front of her open to the bottom. "I have an offer," she went on. Calmly she shrugged out of the blouse. The white cotton chemise hung over her shoulders by thin straps and covered her breasts.

"No!" Phillip thundered. "Damnit, Priscilla, no!"

The shorter man slashed his .44 six-gun across Phillip's head, slamming him back a step, leaving a trail of blood across his forehead.

"Shut up, you! I want to see what the little lady is offering," the short vigilante said.

"I offer myself, for the life of my husband. Now, and anytime in the future." She lifted the chemise with both hands and pulled it off over her head. Her full breasts rolled and bounced for a moment from the motion. They were large, with heavy pink nipples and darker shade pink areolas four inches across.

"Damn, look at them tits!" the tall man who hadn't spoken, said. He had a slight lisp and

Priscilla knew at once who he was, Barney Figuroa, a clerk in one of the stores in town. She had bought groceries from him often.

"Beautiful," the short man said. He moved to her and cupped one breast with his hand.

"All three of you, twice each, right now in the bedroom. Tie up Phillip. When you're all through, you leave, and Phillip and I ride out of town within an hour. Agreed?"

Priscilla could hear the short man's breath come in quick gasps. He rubbed her breast and she hated it, but she would gladly bed them to save her husband's life. The short man reached for his crotch and unbuttoned the fasteners.

"Right here, right now!" he said.

"Shit no!" the man with the limp bellowed. "Damnit, we can get all the pussy we want, anytime. Stop it! We got a job to do here, not worry about our puds!"

The short man jumped back as if he had been slapped. He shook his head inside the hood, and then let out a long sigh.

"Yeah, damnit, you're right. But look at them beauties! I always did go for real redheads. Bet she's got red pussy hair, too!"

"Let's do it," the man with the slight lisp said. He pulled cord from his pocket and started to tie Phillip's hands. Phillip kicked out trying for his crotch, but missed and the man knocked down Phillip with one punch. Two of them tied Phillip's hands and lifted him to his feet.

The short man fondled Priscilla's breasts again, then sighed. "Mrs. Russell, you put your clothes back on. I got to tie you up for a bit here."

Two minutes later she was tied to the chair and they had a hangman's knot noose tightened around

Phillip's neck. They led him out the back door.

Two of them boosted Phillip into a bareback horse, then they all mounted horses they had left and rode to the front of the house where a big black oak forty foot high grew. Now they worked quickly, efficiently.

One man threw the half inch hemp rope over a slanting limb, caught the end and tied it around the trunk. The second man had walked Phillip's horse so he was directly under where the rope went over the limb.

The rope was pulled tight around the trunk and all slack taken up.

As this took place, the short fat man rode a block up the street and walked his mount back, firing his six-gun and shot at a time until it was empty. Then he shouted.

"Execution! Execution! Execution! Everyone come and see the execution of a law breaker and a man who is a threat to this stable and prosperous community!"

By the time he walked his horse back to the Russell house, forty people had left stores and saloons and followed him. A dozen children raced around pointing to the man on the horse with the noose around his neck.

"Bad man! Bad man! Bad man!" they chanted in unison.

When the people were gathered around, the leader nodded and the tall man with the lisp pushed the point of his knife a half inch into the horse's rump. The animal cried out in pain, dug in her back haunches and shot forward in a mighty stride to get away from the pain.

Phillip Russell jolted off the bare back of the horse. He dropped to the end of the slack in the rope and witnesses heard a crack as his neck broke. The horse rushed down the street heading out of town.

Phillip Russell hung by his neck and a hush came over the crowd. His feet twitched with muscle spasms. His eyes came open and his vacant, dead stare seemed to fasten on each witness. His hands twitched and then the three hooded figures looked at one another.

They all fired rounds into the air, then raced their horses down the street and around to the other side of town.

Priscilla Russell heard the first shots, the harangue. She tore at the rope trying to get untied. She could hear the rustle of skirts and the chatter of the people. Then she had the ropes undone and rushed to the window.

"Noooooooooooo!" she screamed. She saw Phillip sitting on the horse. Priscilla rushed to the front door and down the steps, not remembering that she had not buttoned her blouse. She saw the horse surge away from Phillip and saw him slide off the rump of the animal and then fall.

Priscilla screamed and a woman looked at her and rushed up just as she fell. Priscilla was unconscious when her husband's neck broke and he died. The woman lowered Priscilla to the spring grass and fanned her.

Down the street, Spur McCoy rode into town after his futile search for Sam Bass. He saw the man hanging by his neck and pulled his pistol and charged down the two blocks to where a dozen people still stood looking up at the gently swaying corpse.

Spur saw no men left around the hanging. Only a few children and three women who were sitting on the grass with what seemed to be an unconscious woman. He saw that the house stood two down from the church and scowled as he waited for the body to turn around on the rope.

Then he saw what he had feared. The dead man was Phillip Russell, the young lawyer who had argued with the sheriff, the man Spur wanted to talk to. Spur swung down from the horse. From up the street he saw the sheriff approaching on foot.

5

Spur went to the women sitting on the ground and looked at the grandmother who held the unconscious lady.

"Is this Mrs. Russell?" Spur asked.

"Yes, and my friend, and I don't want you to hurt her no more!" The older lady pushed out her chin in defiance.

The sheriff walked past them without a glance in their direction and looked at the body turning slowly on the half inch hemp rope.

Spur stood and walked over where he could face the lawman by looking past the body.

"Nice work, Sheriff. You certainly prevented this vigilante murder, didn't you? Your really have a talent for law enforcement. I'm back, told you I might come back. Just what in hell is going on in your county?"

"Fact is, you're right. This is my county. You hit the nail right on the head with the old hammer. Now, you want to help me cut down this poor soul, or you want to stand there yammering while the widow is over there crying her eyes out?"

Spur flipped out a knife, reached over the dead man's head, sliced the half inch hemp in two, then caught Phillip Russell's body and lowered it to the ground. He put the knife away and kept staring at the sheriff.

"Can't say as if you've heard the last of this, Sheriff. Can't say that at all." Spur turned and walked away down the street and around the corner. He watched the death scene through a bush near the house. The sheriff called to two men passing by and had them carry the body to a wagon which hauled it away. Mrs. Russell revived and went into her house with one of the women.

Spur went down the block, around it and up the alley in back of the Russell house. He needed to talk to the widow, findout what she knew about this place.

He needed some answers from Mrs. Russell about her husband. Spur knocked on the back door, and one of the women he had seen comforting Mrs. Russell opened the screen.

"Yes?"

"I wondered if I could speak with Mrs. Russell? I was a friend of her husband."

"Not now. Land sakes," the older woman said, anger in her voice. "Priscilla just became a widow! You should have a little respect."

"Are you her friend?"

"Why, yes, I guess I am."

"I want to find out who killed her husband and why. I want to know more about this town, this county, and especially about the sheriff. I figure she can tell me."

"Jesus, Joseph and Mary, I hope so!" The gray haired woman pushed open the screen and motioned. "Come in, come in. I ain't seen a man in this town with that glint in his eye and that set to his jaw for a year. My own husband was killed about a year ago. Same bunch. They've taken over the whole county. Won't put up with no outsiders. Phillip and Priscilla are outsiders and they didn't like it one bit."

"Somebody is holding everyone in this whole county as prisoners?"

"More or less, you might say. I'm Wilma. I put Priscilla down in her bed for a minute, but I'm sure she'll want to talk with you. Let me go see her. First off I thought you was from the funeral parlor. You just wait."

Spur sat on the small couch in the living room. It was a spartan house with little furniture, but with family pictures on the wall and a "God Bless This House" needlepoint framed near the front door. It was a poor house, but with warmth and honesty about it.

A few minutes later, Wilma came out of the far door, and a young, red haired woman followed her. Her eyes were red and her cheeks flushed. One hand went to her hair selfconsciously. She was slight, not more than five feet three inches tall and wouldn't weigh as much as a sack of potatoes.

Wilma motioned at Spur. "This is the gentleman, Priscilla. I think he wants to help. Nobody else in town is going to lift a finger, you know that. You've seen it happen before. Now I got to get on over to the hotel and get the food started for the evening meal. I'd say you can trust this young man."

She smiled at them, then hurried out the front door and down the two steps to the sidewalk.

Spur stood with his mid-crowned hat in his hands. Priscilla was a pretty girl, maybe twenty-five, and the soft red hair he noticed before had been combed

carefully. Now her fingers were tightened into fists
hanging at her sides. She looked angry and scared
and furious all at once.

"Wilma didn't know your name," Priscilla said,
her voice soft, lower than he would have guessed.
"I'm Priscilla Russell. The Widow Russell, now I
reckon."

"Ma'am. My name is Spur McCoy."

"Mr. McCoy, please sit down. Wilma said you had
talked with Phillip?"

"This morning. I was supposed to come back and
see him just after lunch. I was interested in the
sheriff. Now I'm even more interested and worried.
Couldn't the sheriff have stopped the lynching?"

"Of course, but he knows his place. The people
who run the county tell him what to do."

"Even to stand by during a lynching?"

"Yes, and worse. But you have one thing wrong,
Mr. McCoy. My huband was not lynched, he was
murdered. Those three men came in here with guns
and tied me to a chair and bound Phillip's hands
behind his back, then pushed him out the back door.
They murdered him."

"Mrs. Russell, that sounds almost impossible
here in this day and age. It's the late eighteen
seventies. This isn't eighteen fifty anymore. Still I
got here just after it happened. This morning, early,
I tried to get the sheriff to hold two train robbers for
me and he wouldn't do it. I think you better tell me
exactly what is going on in this county, and who is
behind it. Can you do that?"

Priscilla Russell nodded. "First, let me make you
some coffee, we're both going to need some. This
story is going to take some time."

They sat across a tiny kitchen table and held
steaming mugs of coffee. Spur worked on a fresh

baked cinnamon roll. Priscilla took a deep breath.

"I want you to know that life is cheap in this county. I'm probably signing my own death warrant by telling you this, but somebody has to. Since Phillip is . . . gone . . . there isn't a lot left I want to live for anyway.

"We came up here from Springfield about four months ago. Phil knew there wasn't a lawyer here, and he figured there would be plenty of civil law for him to keep busy. He didn't figure on the Bald Knobbers.''

Spur frowned. "I'm sorry, Mrs. Russell. I don't understand. You said the Bald Knobbers?''

"Yes. A group not well known except in Tane county here and the next county to the west, Stone. We learned about them in a rush the first couple of weeks we were here. A man was dragged out of a saloon downtown and shot dead by four hooded men. They chased the poor soul, used him as target practice.

"Phillip never carried a gun. He ran out and yelled at the men, but they only laughed and shot into the dirt at Phil's feet so he had to dance. One of the bullets took the heel off his boot. Phil began asking around and learned about the Bald Knobbers that same day. He told me. I figured that Phillip could live with it. Turned out he couldn't.

"The whole thing began during the Civil War when the border raiders from both the North and the South swept through this state and up into Kansas. They called themselves patriots, stealing and looting and gathering gold and supplies for one army or the other.

"But most of the men in both those groups were simply outlaws, criminals, misfits who couldn't stand it to be in the regular army. The Border

Raiders like Quantrel and his men made life unbearable in two or three states for two or three years.

"When the war ended the raiders disbanded, most of them. Some of them became outlaws and went right on doing what they had been doing. Others settled down. A lot of them came to roost here in Taney county.

"There wasn't a lot of law here in the best of times. We're cut off way down here. The state government kind of forgot us. The locals run things to suit themselves.

"It began as a fine, upstanding form of self rule. If the judge didn't come through, some of the townsfolk would elect a judge, and the best men in the community would sit on the jury and they would take care of the disputes and what few criminals who blundered in here. Seemed to work.

"Gradually the self governing became the only kind of law we had around here, and it became ingrown but just and a fine practical system. Then over the years the high principled men who began the whole thing died off or faded from the scene.

"Finally the men who ran things did away with the trials. The men gathered and decided who was good for the community and who wasn't, and the bad ones were run out of the county.

"If the people involved didn't want to go, they were encouraged. The men in power began wearing hoods to keep their identity secret and make it a pure vigilante function so no one could be blamed."

Priscilla sipped at her hot coffee.

"Power corrupts. Absolute power corrupts absolutely."

She looked up at Spur. "You've done some reading. I've heard that. It certainly was true here. Ten years after the war was over the power in these two counties was firmly in the hands of the hooded men who enforced it.

"They became known as the Bald Knobbers. I don't know where the name came from or what it means. But all too soon the men in the hoods were hanging and burning, and running people out of the county who they didn't like. Many times this was on a whim or a personal opinion of one man. It was often done to help one of the Knobbers financially.

"The merchants and property owners all joined the Bald Knobbers so they could protect themselves and their property. Now, thirteen years after the war is over, the Knobbers are riding as strong as ever.

"I know that Phillip thought he could do something to slow them down here. That was all he talked about. He knew the Knobbers were close friends with the state officials. He thought the Knobbers were making payoffs to the state people so they would not investigate the stories they got once in a while from down here.

"That's about it, Mr. McCoy. The Knobbers do whatever they want to. Kill . . . whoever gets in their way. Burn out the businessman who won't pay the 'dues' they insist on. I don't know what can stop them now. Phillip surely couldn't."

"And Sheriff Parcheck?" Spur asked. "How does he fit in?"

"However the Knobbers want him to. He has his orders. He is a figurehead. Goes to the state capitol at Jefferson City twice a year I'm told with a satchel filled with money. He's spineless, that's why the Knobbers ran him for sheriff. There was no one running against him."

"Both counties are in their grasp," Spur said. "So Springfield is the closest real law."

"Yes, but don't count on Sheriff Lacy there to help any. He's almost as afraid of the Knobbers as the folks around here are. He'd just say it's out of his jurisdiction and aim you at Jefferson City and the State Militia."

Priscilla stood. "I better get some supper. I always do. Would you stay and have supper with me? I'd appreciate it. I don't know if those men will come back or not."

"Mrs. Russell, I think I can be here for a while. Is there someone you could stay with for a few days, especially over tonight?"

"No. Just Wilma, the woman who was here when you came. She works till late, then usually takes a room at the hotel. Don't worry about it, Mr. McCoy. I'll get by."

She went to the counter and began peeling potatoes. "I was planning on steaks for supper. Put them in the ice box last night and they're still good. Would that be all right?"

"Yes, of course. I'll be getting a room at the hotel. I'm going to be staying a few days."

She looked up quickly. "Hotel might not be the best idea."

"Why's that?"

"Your argument with the sheriff. Man who owns the hotel is a Knobber. The sheriff probably has told everyone how you stood up to him and that you're an outsider and causing trouble." She blinked back tears.

"Lordy, I don't want you getting hurt because you helped me."

"Don't plan on getting hurt, Mrs. Russell."

She turned, tears streaming down her face. "I almost saved Phillip, did I tell you that? I knew they were going to kill him. I offered myself to them. I took off my blouse and my . . . my chemise so I was bare on top and told them I'd make love to them if right afterwards Phillip and I could leave.''

"That was brave."

"No, desperate! I wanted to save my husband. One of them would have but then the other two shamed him out of it. It was so close! I knew the three men. I'm going to get even with them, even if it kills me. I'm going to shoot them down, Mr. McCoy. Does that surprise you?''

"No. Grief has a way of changing people. But let me handle this. I have some law enforcement connections. I should be able to take care of the whole thing and not endanger you.''

She worked over the wooden cook stove for a few more minutes and Spur smelled the delicious aroma of cooking steak. Soon she had the meal on the table, with warmed up cinnamon rolls, steak, potatoes, fresh peas, applesauce, and lots of hot coffee.

Twenty minutes later, Spur pushed back from the table and grinned.

"Best home cooked meal I've had in months, Mrs. Russell. Now I really do have to go look for a hotel room. If I don't I'll be sleeping on the hard ground for another night.''

She touched his shoulder. "Mr. McCoy. I want to tell you who the three men are who murdered my husband. One of them is Abe Conners, he's a short little man about forty, who is chunky fat and owns a saloon called the Cat's Claw. I think he's also the head man in the Knobbers, but I'm not sure.

"The tall man was Barney Figuroa. He has a slight lisp and works as a clerk at the Branson General Store. The third one was Vern Smith, our friendly town banker. Only one here. Two other bankers had 'accidents' caused by the Knobbers.

Vern Smith also has a slight limp."

Spur listened, his concern for the woman growing. "Mrs. Russell, I hope that you won't do anything for a few days. Let me see what I can find out, what I can do. Will you promise me that?"

"I just want them to pay!"

"They'll pay for their crimes. I'm the one to see to that. Oh, do you have a gun in the house? You might need it for protection."

She went to a drawer in the writing desk in the living room and brought out an old .44. Spur checked it and saw that it had five rounds in it. He took them out and examined them. They were new and the weapon worked.

"Can you shoot a gun?"

"No, show me how."

"All you have to do is hold it with both hands, aim down the barrel and pull the trigger. Never point it at anyone unless you are ready to kill them. Maybe sometime later we can practice shooting it."

"Yes, I want to practice. I have a reason now."

Spur watched her, decided the reason was for her own protection, and let it pass. "Tell me about your husband. Did he think he might be in danger?"

"Yes, from the first time he raised his voice against the unlawfulness. We talked about leaving and moving back to Springfield. I just wish to god that we had done it!"

Tears brimmed her eyes.

"They are going to pay for killing Phillip, Mr. McCoy, I promise you that."

"The law will handle it, Mrs. Russell. If we try to take the law into our own hands, how are we any better than they are?"

She wiped the tears away. Her soft cheeks pale, strands of the red hair hanging limply over one eye.

She pushed the hair back and her face took on a harder, stronger look.

"Mr. McCoy, I might not look it, but I can be as tough as I need to be. The people in this town don't know the real me, but they will before they hear the last of me. I promise them that!"

Spur frowned. "About tonight. You want me to come up the alley and slip in the back door? Nobody else would know I was here. I'll sleep on the couch and you can lock your bedroom door. I owe you for the good dinner."

She shook her head. "No, Spur McCoy, you take care of your hide tonight. That sheriff is going to be telling the Knobbers stories about you."

The big Secret Agent watched the pretty woman a moment, then agreed with her. "They can tell stories, but I can do the same thing. Now, I better get down the street and find a hotel room for the night. I can help you pack if you want to get ready to move back to Springfield. Better you get out of town as soon as you can."

"Not me, McCoy. I have some special business to attend to first."

Spur watched her for a minute, the glint in her eyes was plain to see, and Spur knew she was going to cause trouble in Branson.

6

S pur walked the two blocks from the Russell house to the middle of the row of stores on his way to the small hotel. Spur had not thought much about it until he saw a black family coming down the street. Now he realized the little town was about one third black.

He was in the south, a south still smarting over the Civil War and the freedom of the Negroes. He watched as the five in the black family stepped off the boardwalk and let an older white man and woman walk past. Spur was simply not used to this kind of action. No one told the Negroes to get off the sidewalk, they just did it from long practice, and perhaps local custom.

He continued up the street and saw a black woman ahead of him. She was standing on the boardwalk staring at a white woman who held a parasol and a sneer on her face.

As Spur walked up he could hear catcalls coming and various voices raised in jeers. The black woman was in her mid twenties, the white woman in her forties. They stood and stared at each other.

At last the white woman sniffed. "I am certainly not going to move to let some black no account like you walk past," she said.

The black woman snorted. "Well I sure ain't gonna get my bones off the boards just so some white no account old battle axe like you can step all over my pride."

"Girl, you should be horsewhipped!" the woman snapped. She motioned at the storefront nearby. "Will, you get out here and teach this chippy a leason or two? Just too uppity, she is for her own good."

Two white men came from the store, one had an apron around his waist, the other one carried a short whip that had leather thongs knotted on the ends and a two foot handle.

"Some trouble here?" the apron man asked.

"This . . . this . . . creature refused to let me walk along the sidewalk," the white woman spat.

The black woman looked at the white man. "This is none of your business, mister."

"Making it my business," he said and stepped forward. With his crossed arms, he pushed the black woman off the boardwalk into the dusty street. He waved the white woman past and then stared down at the black.

"Black whore, you got a problem."

"I am not a whore," she snapped back. "But you look like a pimp!"

The man's face flushed. He turned and saw half a dozen other white man and a few blacks watching him. Somebody snickered. A woman giggled behind them.

"Hold on, black trash! You don't talk to Hirum Streib that way. You from the north?"

The black woman looked at Streib, then at the

others watching and began to back up slowly. She turned at last and ran for the other side of the street —and blundered directly into the waiting arms of two white men who had been watching. One man's hand caught her breast and he left his hand there.

"Lookie here what I got!" he shouted. A dozen men roared with laughter as they moved in behind Streib. The men across the street pushed the black girl ahead of them as they ushered her back to Hirum Streib.

When she came near the boardwalk a foot below Streib, the men stopped her, and Streib laughed.

"Black whore, you have a name?"

She ignored him.

"I said, black whore, you got a name?"

She spit in his face and Streib slapped her with his open palm. She would have fallen if one of the men behind her had not caught her.

"Too drunk to stand up!" somebody shouted.

"Little gal is top heavy. Look at them big tits!" one of the men catchers yelled. Everyone roared again. The black woman began to edge away, but Streib dropped off the foot-high boardwalk into the street beside her. His hand caught her blouse front and he jerked down suddenly.

The force of the motion pulled her shoulders down, but as she resisted, the seams of the material broke and the blouse ripped free at both shoulders and the whole front tore down below each arm. She had been wearing nothing under the blouse and was now bare to the waist. Her breasts showed large and uptilted nipples.

"Now, we got ourselves a real black whore!" Streib yelled. "How much am I offered for a quick roll in the hay with this black bitch?"

The woman did not try to hide her breasts. She

swung her hands instead, her fingernails raking down across Streib's cheek, digging four grooves which quickly filled with blood.

Streib roared in fury and swing his right fist at her jaw. She ducked under it and darted away. The two catchers grabbed her again, and Streib ran up to her in screaming fury.

A gunshot stopped the whole affair. Everyone turned and looked for the source and found Spur McCoy standing in the middle of the street.

"Let the lady alone and move back, or eat lead for supper!" Spur bellowed in his best army field command voice.

The catchers let go of the black woman.

Streib stared in amazement.

A dozen men on the boardwalk snorted in surprise.

"Move back!" Spur roared again, firing a round under the boardwalk. Whites and blacks scattered on both sides. Spur motioned to the woman with his left hand and she ran toward him. He and the woman edged back to the boardwalk on the far side of the street. Out of the corner of his eye Spur saw a man draw a weapon on his left.

Spur spun and fired, the round taking the gunman in the thigh and slamming him against the chairs in front of the General Store.

"Anyone else want a lead sandwich?" Spur shouted.

Nobody moved.

Spur backed toward the alley, then into the shadows there and caught the woman's hand and they ran hard down the alley and across the street and behind a row of houses.

Only then did the woman stop shaking.

Spur turned and looked at her. She still did not try

to hide her breasts. Spur slid out of a light jacket he had worn that morning and she put it on. Dusk was fast approaching.

"My name is Spur McCoy, and I have a feeling that you really are from the north. Right?"

The woman buttoned the jacket and looked up at Spur. "My name is Edith Washington. Yes, I'm from the north. I'm in town to try to find my brother. We last heard from him about six months ago when he stopped here."

"Edith, you are now in the south, where the people wish slavery was still legal. Did you get that feeling just now back there?"

"Yes." Tears began to seep from her eyes, then she was sobbing and Spur put his arms around her and held her a minute. She stopped a moment later and wiped her eyes.

'Sorry. I'm usually stronger than that. I seldom break up and cry. My mother was an extremely strong person. I have never been treated like that before. I'm from Philadelphia. My people have not been slaves for over a hundred years."

She moved away from him.

"Mr. McCoy, you must be a northerner, too. I know they'll try to run you out of town, or hire somebody to kill you. I'm almost certain that my brother, John, is dead. Somebody probably pushed him off the sidewalk, too, and he pushed back. John would do that."

She sighed. "Now I guess I'll have to go back home. They won't let me alone here now." She frowned and watched him. "That means we'll never know about John."

"I'll try to find out. Somebody must know. What about the black leaders in the town?"

"There aren't any. The few men here still act like they are slaves."

Edith shivered under his jacket. "What are you going to do now?"

"I was heading for the hotel to get a room for the night."

Edith laughed. "That room would become your grave. The man who runs the hotel is one of the Bald Knobbers."

"That's two people who have told me that, so it must be true. I guess I can camp out another night."

"Then you head back north. No sense dying down here."

"Might. But I'm also interested in who killed that young lawyer today."

"Mr. Russell. I talked with him about finding John. He was asking some questions for me."

"Edith, I can't go back and leave things this way. I'm going to do something about it. I'm not sure what."

"Then you'll need some help and a place to stay. I know a place out of town a ways, you'll be safe there. Get your horse and meet me behind the church in about half an hour."

"Why are you doing this, Edith?"

"Mr. McCoy, it . . ."

He held up his hands. "Hey, call me Spur. Enough of that mister stuff."

She smiled in the fading light. It would be full dark now in another ten minutes.

"Yes, all right. Spur, you probably saved my life back there. They start like that, the fights, the disturbances, then they get meaner and meaner and somebody suggests target practice . . . I saw it happen once about a month ago. They teased this cowboy who was just riding through. Teased him and made him mad, then they took his gun away . . . and killed him.''

She shook her head as if to clear it. "Now, enough of this. You go get your gear, and your horse, and I'll meet you in half an hour. I'll be careful. I'll be safe enough on the black side of town.''

She turned and walked into the darkness.

Spur lifted his brows. It might be good to have a local guide. At least he knew he could trust her. Spur moved down the street and went over a block to where he had left his horse near the Russell house.

He watched for ten minutes before he walked out to claim his mount, rifle and provisions. He could spot no one watching the horse, no one lurking in doorways. Spur mounted quickly and rode into the darkness, glad now for the protection. He wondered if Edith would come. There was nothing he could do now for the widow Russell. He'd check on her tomorrow.

Spur sat on his bay in the shadows behind the church, avoiding the moonlight. The only person he saw moving was a small boy running to the outhouse behind his home, banging the door, then a moment later racing through the dreaded darkness back to the safety of the shaft of yellow light from the back door.

Five minutes later Edith rode up beside him. She was dressed in men's pants, a blouse, a heavy jacket and a hat that hid her shoulder length black hair.

"Ready, Spur?"

"Am now.''

Without another word, she turned her horse and rode. They moved north of town, higher on the slopes, out of the heavy oak timber into taller shortleaf pines.

They rode for half an hour. Spur guessed they were about two miles from the small town. They went into a valley no more than fifty yards wide. A hundred yards upstream on a tiny trickle of water they came to a log cabin.

The place was old, abandoned. The structure was twenty feet square, and the sturdy pine logs were notched carefully and fitted. They even had been well plastered where they met.

"Home sweet home," she said. "It isn't used much. Most folks don't know it's here. Some of us Negroes come up here to hide from the whites when they go on a rampage."

Inside, Spur found that the place had no windows. He snapped a match and was surprised to find a lamp full of kerosene and with a trimmed wick. He lit it.

The place had been cleaned recently. It had two bunks built against the wall with wire strung across them to serve as springs, the blue ticking mattress he guessed were filled with leaves or straw.

A table and a small fireplace stood at the far side.

Edith vanished outside, and Spur followed. He brought in his sack of provisions and she carried a sack from the back of her horse. In it were some cooking pots and some staples.

She looked in his sack and laughed.

"At least we won't starve for a day or two. Were you planning a long ride?"

"Planned, didn't work out."

"Fire?" Spur asked.

"Nobody will be hunting us tonight, so why not have a fire and we can cook up something."

An hour later they had eaten bacon and cheese sandwiches and had coffee and then a can of peaches.

"Will you be going back north to Philadelphia?"

She sighed and stared at him frankly. "Yes. I'm convinced now that John is dead, but we'll never know for sure how or why. My mama would say come home before she loses another child. But I won't sneak out of town. I'll get the rest of my gear and ride down the main street and on to Springfield. No bunch of bastards like this is going to run me out!"

Spur chuckled. "Lots of grit, I like that." He sobered. "But dead grit doesn't help a body much. Remember that."

She leaned back and watched him in the soft lamp light.

"You are interesting. You treat me just like I was white. I mean you aren't put off, or embarrassed or upset. Strange."

"Not so strange. You're a person, a lady, a pretty lady, and I have always liked pretty ladies."

"But I'm black, a Negro."

He caught her hand and rubbed it with his. "None of the white rubs off on the black, and none of the black rubs off on the white."

Edith laughed. "You are a smart man, and wise, and . . . kind." She looked up at him. "This doesn't embarrass you, being here with me, spending the night here?"

"No. Does it embarrass you, bother you? I can take my bedroll out under the pines. I've slept out as much as in lately."

"For goodness sakes, no!" She smiled softly. "Now why would I let the best looking man I've seen in months sleep outside?"

"Just a thought."

"I haven't thanked you for saving my skin back there. Seems to me like this would be a good time."

She had been sitting by the small fire. Now she stood and walked over where he sat in the cabin's one straight chair. Edith bent and kissed his lips. She watched him.

"Does that bother you?"

"Yes. But I'm not sure why. Try it again."

She smiled and kissed him. Spur pulled her onto his lap, and kissed her back. He eased away from her.

"Bother me? Excites me is a better word. Let's try that again." The kiss continued, and slowly she opened her lips so his tongue could bore in.

His hand found one of her breasts through the blouse and she murmured softly. His lips came away and he kissed her eyes.

"Edith, you don't have to do this."

She smiled. "You don't have to either, but I don't want to stop anything we have started, do you?"

He kissed her again, then opened the buttons on her blouse. His hand crept inside and cupped one of her generous breasts.

"Absolutely beautiful!" he said.

"That feels so good!" Edith purred. She unbuttoned his leather vest, then his shirt and played with the black hair on his chest. "You feel so good!"

His hand caressed the mound, teased the standing tall nipple and he felt it grow hotter by the moment.

"Will you be cold?" he asked.

"I'm getting warmer by the second!"

He pushed the blouse off her shoulders and let it fall. Her twin mounds swayed a moment, then thrust out, still pointed and firm.

"Please," she said.

Spur caught both of her breasts, massaging them, fondling them until Edith moaned in pleasure.

"They like to be kissed," she whispered to him.

Spur carried her to the first bunk where she had spread out her bedroom. He sat her on the edge and went to his knees, his mouth closing around the softly dark breast.

He kissed them and licked one nipple and suddenly she climaxed.

"Oh, Lord!" she shouted. "I'm coming! Oh, Lord but it's a good one! Oh, Lord!" She fell back on the bunk, her legs spread and her slender hips pounded upward a dozen times as the sudden vibrations shook her in a series of spasms.

Edith wailed long and loud as the tremors blasted through her. She pulled his head down on her breasts again and went into a second series of long moans and yelps as she thundered through a second climax.

When she finished at last, she lay there a moment gasping for breath. Then she looked at him.

"Spur, tear these pants off me right now!"

He found the buttons down the fly and pulled the man's pants off her shapely legs. Before he could help she had pushed down soft cotton underpants and lay on the bed in the half light bare and delightful.

She sat up and began undressing him. His vest and shirt went first, and all the time she was telling him about the first time she ever made love. She was fourteen and had managed to stay a virgin that long.

Edith pulled down Spur's pants and saw the big bulge in his cotton, short underwear.

"Oh, Lordy!" she yelped. Edith ripped off his pants, then snuggled down to the top of his underwear and began to kiss them downward.

"Wonderful!" she raptured as she came to the forest of dark pubic hair. Then when she jerked the cloth down and his long, hard weapon raised she screeched in delight.

She caught his penis and kissed it a dozen times, then slid it in her mouth and pumped back and forth a dozen times. Spur was about to stop her when she pulled away.

"Quick, Spur! Right now! I've never had a white cock in me and I want you so bad!" She rolled on the bunk and spread her legs wide and lifted her knees.

Spur kicked off his shorts and went over her.

"Positive?" he asked.

"Yes, damnit! Hurry up or I'll get a butcher knife and go after you!"

Spur grinned and lowered. She gasped and helped and then her juices flowed and she moved and at once he rammed into her until their pelvic bones crashed.

"Oh, damn! Oh damn! Oh damn!" Edith screeched. "Marvelous! Wonderful. So beautiful!" She pushed upward so she could whisper.

"Handsome, sexy, Spur McCoy. Please fuck me hard. Fast and hard and then next time we'll do it the way you like. Hard and fast and don't stop!"

Spur kissed her and followed directions. He had never made love to such a thrashing, moving, jolting, responsive woman in his life. She was moving against him, then with him, and squirming on the hard bunk until he had trouble following her. Then she stopped moving and screamed so loud he was sure they would hear her in Branson.

He climaxed and her scream caught in her throat and she launched a series of spasms that made her solo action pale into a beginner's effort. They thrashed and pounded and wailed together as both finished their climaxes at almost the same time.

Spur fell heavily on top of her, then lifted up on his

elbows and knees, but she pulled him down and wrapped her arms around his back.

They lay there for fifteen minutes getting their strength back. Slowly she began to kiss his face. He roused and pushed up. They sat side by side on the bunk.

She looked at him and lifted her brows. "Lordy, I just never would have *dreamed* that we would make love. So *wonderful!* Now, I need to go outside for a minute, then I want something to eat. It always makes me hungry. I may eat up all of your food before the night is over." She kissed him.

'Hey, three, maybe four more times?"

Spur caught both her breasts and fondled them. "Edith, just as long as my strength holds out," he said.

When she came back, they ate cheese and some crackers she had brought.

"I should have some cold beer for you," she said. "Water will have to do, or coffee."

She told him about growing up in Philadelphia.

"Before the war I was just little. I didn't understand much of what happened. I was fourteen when the war ended. I knew we were different from the other folks. But I went to school with the other kids, almost all white. They tried to make friends with me because I was black, and that was the thing to do during the war."

"Then I started to get urges I didn't understand." She laughed softly and played a moment with his flaccid genitals. "This good looking white boy I knew told me he was having the same feelings and offered a try and figure them out."

Edith laughed again. "Boy was I dumb. He helped me figure them out all right. We went behind this big billboard on the way home from school one afternoon. He kissed me and I almost fell over. Then he got his hands on my breasts and I did fall over and he knew exactly what to do make me understand all of those strange physical urgings I had. Three times he showed me all about it that afternoon."

Spur finishd his coffee and picked her up. "I think it's time that you explain some of those urges to me. If you have time."

Edith smiled and kissed him. "Seems to me that we have the rest of the night. I'll try to explain those urges just the best way that I can."

7

The next morning, Spur rode into town the long way, coming around from the north. Edith had assured him that she would be fine in the daylight, and not to worry. She would go to town get her things together and say goodbye to her new found friends then ride out of Branson for good.

They had cooked breakfast and put the food things in a box. She had assured him that everything would be safe there. Nobody would bother it even if someone stopped by to use the cabin.

Spur watched both sides of Main Street as he rode along. There were few people around at seven that morning. He stopped by at the Branson General Store to get some cleaning oil for his pistol and some store bought patches. The tall, thin man who waited on him had a lisp, and Spur wondered if he was one of those who had hung Phillip Russell.

Out on the street, Spur left his horse in front of the store and ambled toward the county sheriff's office. He wanted to have a good talk with the man. There might be some way he could put the fear of the U.S. Government into him. There was little to lose here now.

If Edith were right, the Bald Knobbers would be after his hide sooner or later anyway.

Spur had gone half a block when he felt a change come over the place. It was nothing he could touch or identify. Two men lounged against the outside of a saloon a dozen yards ahead of him. A horseman rode slowly up the street. A farm wagon pulled in at the doctor's office behind him.

Then he knew what it was.

The silence.

Nobody was talking. There were no kids on the street, no women. He slowed and looked around as casually as he could with the hairs on the nape of his neck standing up.

A shotgun roared a dozen feet from him. His head snapped around in that direction and he saw the weapon aimed at the sky, but two more scatterguns pointed directly at his chest.

Sheriff Parcheck grinned from behind the just fired Greener.

"Just so there's no mistake, son, you're under arrest for the murder of Phillip Russell. Lift your hands or get two dozen double ought buck through your belly."

"Sheriff, you know that charge is a lie, why are you doing their dirty work?"

"Doing whose work, deadman?"

"You know who, the Bald Knobbers, the vigilantes who are bleeding this county dry and filling their own pockets."

The rifle butt swung from behind him and he had only a flash of it from the side of his eye before the steel plate thundered into his kidney and he went

83

down in a sprawling, gagging, retching mass.

Somebody pulled the six-gun from Spur's holster and the derringer from inside his shirt.

Sheriff Parcheck stood over him looking down. A bucket of water from the horse trough splashed over his head and torso. Spur gasped in surprise and shook, and them vomited again in the street, not able to lift his face from the remains of his breakfast mixed with green bileish pleghm.

"Now, stranger," Parcheck growled. "You was saying something about our fair county here?"

Somebody grabbed his hair and dragged him to a sitting position.

"You got some complaint about how we run things here, McCoy?" Parcheck asked.

Before Spur could answer another bucket of water hit him in the face and chest almost toppling him over. He sat there, gasping for breath as the pain of the kidney blow slowly faded.

"Get him on his feet and bring him down to the jail," Parcheck said.

Spur let them drag him to his feet, then swung out with both fists, flooring one of the men and jolting the second one back a yard and a half.

A shotgun blasted from six feet behind him, aimed at the sky again. Then the gun butt slammed into the back of his head and Spur McCoy fell forward into the dirt and horse droppings on the street. This time he passed out before he hit the ground.

He came back to consciousness in jail, draped over a plank bunk fastened to the side of the steel cell with iron bars. He blinked, trying to remember. When he did he closed his eyes. No sense letting them know he was awake. He listened for five minutes, but could hear nothing. He was alone, and no one was in the other cells.

Slowly he lifted his arms, then pushed himself up until he sat against the wall. His head pounded like a thousand Apaches on the warpath. Gradually the din faded and only a growing throbbing pain slammed through his head. He could live with one pain.

The jail was the usual; steel bars and thick metal straps to form a steel cell. The door was six feet high and had a heavy lock on the outside and a chain and padlock for double precaution.

Somebody unlocked a metal door down the hall, came in and stared at him a moment, then retreated and a few minutes later, Sheriff Parcheck walked in and laughed.

"Well, our big hero doesn't look so goddamned good right now. Soaked, vomit all over him, muddy, hair all mussed, no gun and no hat. Damn what a shame."

Spur looked the other way, ignoring the lawman.

"I'm talking to you, badass!" Parcheck thundered.

Spur stood up, went to the bars that connected his cell to the one next to it and urinated through the openings.

"Stop that!" Parcheck roared.

Spur went back to the bench and lay down, never looking at the sheriff. The lawman began to rattle the lock, then stopped.

"Oh, you would love to have me come inside, wouldn't you, bit shot? Well, I ain't gonna. Not at all. Fact is we got a trial set for you in just about three hours. You was passed out for some time. Near ten in the A.M. right now. Come one in the afternoon, we hold trial for you.

"The Honorable Judge Abe Conners, presiding."

Parcheck watched him for a minute. "What's that? You say you want a lawyer. Well now, that is a pity. You done hung the only lawyer in town, outside of Nells. Old Nells went into Springfield about three days ago to buy himself a new suit. Won't be back for a few more days. He always spends a week at this little whore house on Ozark street."

Spur concentrated on taking long, even breaths. He was powering his body back into full strength if he ever had a chance to use it. The sheriff kept talking.

"So . . . we'll have the trial. The judge has decided because of the delicate nature of the charges, you will be tried without a jury. The public will be limited in the courtroom for the protection of the accused. The dead man was well liked around town." Sheriff Parcheck laughed long and loud. Then he turned.

"Well, looks like the accused won't have much to say in his own defense. Fine with me. Makes for a quicker trial that way. You'all have a nice sleep now, 'fore the trial. You got most of a day left. We never have hangings in the afternoon. Always sunup round these parts."

The sheriff chuckled as he walked down the hall, the sawed-off shotgun in his hands eased the triggers back down from full cock.

Spur watched his back as Parcheck went down the hall. Time! He didn't have a lot of it left. They would do exactly as the puppet sheriff said they would. Trial, sentencing and hanging in less than twenty four hours. He eased to his feet and found he could walk. Spur did some running in place.

His body was rested and recovered from the two

86

murderous blows. Now, how in hell could he get out of here?

He tried the four sides of the cell. All were sound and secure. The door lock was old, but adequate. He did not even have any wire to fashion a devise to pick it. The chain and padlock ended that hope. The ceiling was ten feet above. It was open beams made of solid oak. The raw sheeting over the beams looked an inch thick. No chance there.

Spur sat down on the bunk. He would have to make a move when they came to take him to the trial. A belly full of shotgun pellets was better than stretching a vigilante rope. At least it would be quick.

For the first time since he had been in the Secret Service, Spur feared for his life. He could very well be dead within eighteen hours. There had to be some way to slow down those bastards, but how?

An hour later he was still trying to figure it out. If there was a way, he couldn't find it. Parcheck and his band of killers had used this method before. They had worked out all the problems and perfected it. This gave them more satisfaction than simply shooting him down in the street. They gave the town the show of a trial and a real law and order hanging.

The door squeaked and keys jangled down the hallway. The voices came softly at first, then stronger. One was a woman's.

"Yes, I know he's the man you say killed Phillip, but he was kind to me. At least we owe him a last meal before the trial. I fixed it myself. Roast chicken, mashed potatoes and gravy, muffins, peas and lima beans and a cherry pie from my own tree. Now you can't deny a condemned man a last meal."

Spur listened closer. The voice had to be Priscilla Russell!

"Hell, all right," the sheriff's voice said. "But Archie, you go along and watch her every minute. Anything happens and it's your balls in the fire. You hear, Archie?"

"Yep. I hear, Sheriff."

Spur was standing at the back of the cell when he saw Priscilla and a guard come down the narrow way between the cells. She looked concerned, but smiled when she saw him.

"Mr. McCoy! Oh, thank God you're not wounded. I heard about you being arrested and I wanted you to have a good meal. Even a killer has a right to that." She was in front of the guard and now winked at Spur.

"Yes, ma'am," Spur said softly.

"Feed him, don't jaw at him," the guard growled.

She passed the covered plate through the narrow hole in the bars for that purpose. Then turned and showed the guard the dull silver knife and a fork.

"The weapons, Archie. Be hard for him to hurt himself with these, right?"

Archie looked at them, nodded and she turned and handed them to Spur. As she did she adjusted the shawl she wore over her dress. She let it come open at her throat and then reached down and unbuttoned two of the fasteners on her dress top so both sides of her breasts showed.

She smiled at Spur then turned back to the guard. She was in front of him so he could not see the prisoner. As she faced Archie she bent forward slightly so her breasts bulged out even more. She put one hand on her stomach.

"Oh, dear. Archie, I forgot the coffee. Shall I go out and get it?"

As she said it her left hand darted behind her back. She lifted the back of her skirt to her waist showing her legs and white drawers. Spur stared in amazement. Then on the back of one leg he saw that she had tied a four inch hunting knife.

Spur edged forward, slipped the knife from the string and touched her back, then he slid the knife inside his shirt. At once he sat on the bench and began eating.

The food was good, he ate all of it as Archie talked to Priscilla. She had straightened up, but let Archie take a good look at the pure white mounds of the sides of her breasts.

She had moved to the side, so Archie could watch both of them. She had decided she didn't need to get the coffee, and talked of the weather and horses with Archie while Spur ate.

"Hurry it up in there," the sheriff bellowed from down the hall.

Spur stood, held out the plate with the knife and fork on it in plain sight.

Archie stepped forward, scowled at Spur, saw that the tools were both there and took the plate from him at the pass through slot.

Priscilla turned to Spur. "Mr. McCoy, I don't think you hurt my husband, and I wanted you to have a good meal. No, no, your thanks are not needed. May God have mercy on your soul."

Spur knew she was putting on an act for the guard, but it gave him a jolt as he realized without the knife she brought he could well be hearing those words as the last of his life just before the trap dropped and he plunged to the end of a half inch of hemp.

Twenty minutes later Spur began to scream. He yelled as loud as he could and a moment later,

Archie rushed down the hallway.

Spur saw him coming and writhed on the bunk.

"Poison! She poisoned me! The bitch gave me poisoned food!" Spur screamed the words as loud as he could.

Archie came to the cell door and scowled. He was confused. He looked at the cell door, then down the hallway.

"Get me the doctor!" Spur croaked as if his voice were going. "Now! I can't live another hour without some medicine!"

Archie ran back to the office. Spur kept screeching. Archie came back a minute later.

"Sheriff is gone. I can't let you out. I'll go get the doc."

"No time!" Spur whispered. "Not much time for me." He slumped against the cell wall.

"Shit!" Archie said. He fumbled at his belt for a key and opened the padlock on the chain. Then he worked on the big heavy door lock and a moment later it creaked and the door swung open.

Archie had his six-gun out as he came into the cell.

"Now, don't move. I'll help you stand up. Can you get up a little?"

Spur had taken the knife from his shirt and gripped it in his right hand which he had slid behind him so the guard would come up his left side.

"No funny stuff, McCoy, or I'll shoot you dead. You savvy?"

"God yes! Get me to the doc. Fast!" It came out as a wheeze that even Spur had a hard time understanding.

Archie wiped sweat off his forehead. He looked out the door, then moved closer to Spur. He tried to lift him with his left hand and arm, but Spur let his

90

weight sag. Archie spat out a string of obscenities and holstered his six-gun. He put both arms around Spur's chest and lifted him to a standing position.

As Spur came erect, he swung his right arm around and drove the four inch blade of the heavy hunting knife into Archie's back, and ripped it out.

Spur kneed Archie in the crotch and when he doubled over Spur brought his knee up again under his chin and snapped his head back, breaking his neck and killing him instantly. Spur grabbed the dead man's keys and six-gun and edged out of the cell. There was a back door, but it was locked. He sorted through the keys, found the right one and unlocked the door.

A quick look outside showed that the alley was deserted. Spur eased out, pushed the six-gun in his belt and put the knife inside his shirt. He walked away from the center of town, toward the small church.

No one seemed to pay any attention to a dirty, bedraggled man walking down the alley. He crossed the street, jogged slowly along the next block and came up six houses from the church. Two houses past it he found the alley and ran down it to the back door of the second house. This was where Priscilla Russell lived.

Spur didn't have to go inside. She had waited for him behind the house with two saddled horses and a sack of food.

She was wearing sensible riding clothes, a heavy split skirt and a hat. She tossed him a blue cotton flannel shirt to put on and an old hat.

"Mount up, they'll be coming any time. The shirt and hat might throw them off our scent."

Spur stepped up on the horse and they rode due

east, away from the middle of town, through a pasture, around a fence, and then into a thick forest of white oak.

When they were hidden, they stopped a moment.

"I don't see how you did it!" Spur said. "That was the bravest, most ingenious plan I've ever heard of. I bet Archie never saw a thing after you bent toward him in there."

Priscilla smiled, but did not blush. "I told you I was tougher than I look. To let Archie have a peek at my titties is a small price for me to pay for saving your life. Now, we better ride like crazy again. I know where there's a cave that Phil and I found one day. It had a hidden entrance. Come on!"

The lady knew how to ride. Spur followed her as she lashed her mount through the timber and brush, down a creek bed, over a low ridge, up another canyon, over another ridge and at last reined in next to a thick woodsy growth not far from a small stream.

She got off her mount and walked forward toward the wall of brush. Slowly she parted the branches and then she and the horse were gone, passing directly through the screen. Spur followed her, found the spot and worked through the brush. There was an opening there that had been enlarged by hand.

A minute later he was inside a tall, airy cave. It had a stripe of sunshine coming in over the tops of the trees, but still camouflaged enough so it could not be seen from outside.

The cave was deep, fifty or sixty feet that he could see. They led the horses in the back and ground tied them. There was a small fire ring, two beds made of fresh pine boughs, and a sack of staples and cooking gear.

"I brought things up here the moment I heard you were jailed," Priscilla said. "I couldn't let them hang the only man in town who could help me."

Spur caught her hands. "Thank you, Priscilla. You have saved my life. There was no chance I could break out of there without help. I had decided to make a try at escaping when they took me to trial. That was about eight chances out of ten that I would be killed when I tried. I thank you again."

She reached up and threw her arms around him and hugged Spur tightly. She stepped back quickly, a little embarrassed.

"Pardon me, at home we always hugged a lot. We were taught that it wasn't bad to let your emotions show." She smiled. "I'm just so happy it worked. I usually don't lift up my skirts that way and I prayed that you would see the knife."

She began building a small fire in the fire ring. "Next we eat and keep up our strength. I have some homemade soup, lots of fresh baked bread and two jars of jam. The rest of that chicken is going to spoil if we don't eat it soon. Then we go outside and you teach me how to shoot the eye out of a buzzard at fifty yards."

Spur grinned. He was still trying to realize that he was free, and not under the heel of a deadly regime that had almost killed him. He laughed and helped with the fire.

"I pretended that you had poisoned me with the food. Archie believed me all the way. The food was good, but I can always use some more of that chicken."

She looked up at him slowly. "What . . . what happened to Archie?"

"Was he a friend of yours?"

"Not really. He usually works in the hardware

store. We bought some things from him. That's all."

"Archie has sold his last pound of nails."

"He's dead?" She asked.

"Yes."

"Good!" she said with sudden determination. "That makes one less of them to gloat over how cleverly they killed my husband."

When the fire had burned down to glowing coals, she put a pot on and warmed the soup and the roast chicken. They spread a cloth over the pine boughs for a table and ate their fill of the slabs of fresh bread, grape jam, chicken and soup.

They cleaned up the leftovers and went to the small creek to wash the pots and bring back drinking water. When those chores were done, she smiled at him and held out her hand. "Now, Spur McCoy, you are going to teach me to shoot."

"Why?"

"Why? You have to ask? I'm going to learn to shoot so I can kill the three men who lynched my husband. Why do you suppose I risked my life to get you out of that jail?"

Spur grinned. "I had wondered about that. You're going to have to do some convincing."

She glared a moment. "Spur, you saw him hanging there. You cut him down! You know he was guilty of nothing more than trying to do what was right. He was a wonderful, naive, crusading child in a forest of bastards. There was no way he could win.

"I'm different. I'm not an innocent. I know how to fight fire with fire, and a thundering .45 with another blasting .45. And I can do it. You owe me, Spur McCoy. You owe me your life! Is there any more convincing you need."

Spur McCoy shook his head. "I just wish we had a rifle. A rifle would be easier for you." She went to the trees the horses were tied at the back of the cave and brought out a Winchester repeating rifle. "Will this do, McCoy? I tried to think of everything. I'm a planner."

This time Spur laughed. "You win. Let's get started."

8

Spur started teaching Priscilla Russell how to shoot the rifle, the Winchester repeater.

"Have you ever fired a weapon before?" Spur asked.

"No. I used to be afraid of guns. Now I'm not."

"Good. You'll have nothing to unlearn. The first rule for you is to get a good solid base to lean the rifle on. Don't try to hold it without any support. Rest it on a fence, a tree limb, a buggy, anything even a big rock. Lying down is a good way to fire a rifle."

He found a gnarled white oak that had fallen over and rested the rifle on a chest high branch.

"Hold it, put the butt against your shoulder and your cheek against the stock. You've seen it done. There, that's the way. Now look through the rear sight. See the front sight? Center the front sight in the rear one. Now move the whole weapon to the target.

He went on giving her basic rifle instruction for an hour. It was over thirty minutes before he let her fire the first round. On her first shot she hit the leaf that he had pinned to a tree thirty yards away with his knife.

She missed the target the next four times.

"Squeeze the trigger, don't consciously pull it. When you do that you jerk it and the front of the rifle moves, spoiling your aim. Try squeezing your whole hand and the finger with it."

She did and hit the target the next five times in a row.

They moved to the six-gun.

"Heavy, isn't it?" she said.

Spur showed her how to hold it in both hands. She caught on quickly.

"How far away can I hit something," she asked.

Spur knew what she was asking.

"No more than five or six feet. With this weapon you get close and make sure." He scowled. "Of course then you have to watch the bullet slam into the man's chest, see his eyes go wild, hear the scream and then the gurgle as he starts to drown in his own blood, and then watch his face as he crumples and dies at your feet."

Priscilla's soft face turned hard, determined. "Good! I want to see one of them suffer the way my Phillip did. Now, where is my target?"

The first time she fired the pistol at a tree six feet away she missed the tree and the weapon flew out of her hand. Grimly she picked it up, asked if it was damaged and planted both feet wide, held tightly, cocked the hammer and then shot the tree dead center, and she did not drop the weapon.

After a dozen shots she said her wrists hurt and they went back in the cave.

She heated up the boiled coffee left over from lunch and they sipped the steaming mugs.

"You shouldn't do this, Priscilla. I shouldn't let you."

"Spur McCoy, you can't stop me, not unless you keep me tied up when you sleep. You said you were some kind of a lawman. Just figure that you're doing the county a favor by letting me get rid of three of the worst bastards we have."

"It's not right, Priscilla."

"Lots of things aren't right in this world, Spur. Was it right when they hung Phillip? Was it right when they chased that black girl down the street after they tore her blouse off? Was it right that they killed that man and burned down his house last month?

"Damn right none of it was right. I'm not a lawman, I don't have to worry about that. I can wipe out the three men who killed my husband and then go back to Springfield and try to pick up where I left off my life. Is that too much to ask?"

"Yes, Priscilla. I'm a United States Government Secret Service Agent. Nobody else in town knows that, don't tell anybody. That's why I can't let you do this."

Priscilla put down her tin coffee cup and walked over to the blanket covered mattress of pine boughs where Spur sat. She knelt in front of him.

"Spur, I guess it's up to me to convince you that I have a *right to enact judgment* on these three men." She reached in slowly and kissed him. Her lips moved on his and before he knew it his lips parted and her hot tongue darted inside.

Spur pulled away from her.

"That's cheating. That is not logical."

Priscilla shook her head. She smiled and the dimples came into her cheeks. She was so cute and perky and sexy right then that Spur could eat her without a spoon.

"Spur, that wasn't cheating at all. This is cheating." She unfastened the buttons on her blouse and in one quick motion took it off, then pulled off a tight fitting undergarment and knelt topless before him.

She had a small smile on her face. "Titties, that is cheating, and I don't mind at all. I've got good ones and now is the time to use them to help me. Go ahead, touch them, play with them. That's part of what I'm offering to convince you."

Spur couldn't help but grin. Her breasts were pure, soft white, redhead creamy white, with faint red areolas centered by pink nipples that were as large around as his finger and now standing tall and he was sure pulsing with hot blood.

"It can't change the facts, Priscilla. This is still something you shouldn't do. Besides, it could be dangerous for you."

"Kiss my titties, Spur. You know you want to. Go ahead. Don't make me do it all."

Spur sighed, reached for her breasts and fondled them. He would always be a breast man. Big, little, medium, swaying, sagging, he loved a good set of tits.

Priscilla bent forward and kissed him again, then kept moving and pushed Spur over on his back on the blankets. He laughed through the kiss a moment, then felt her hips pressing and grinding against his, and he worked her legs apart.

She moved her mouth and nibbled at his ear.

"Now, isn't that better? We can relax and enjoy each other, and you will have no choice but to let me go do what I have to do. Agreed?"

"You're seducing me, lady, not the other way."

She pouted a minute.

"True, but I'll take my chances." She took off his shirt, then the second shirt and smiled at his broad shoulders and muscled arms and torso.

"I like a man with some muscles on him. Is everything else as big on you?"

"Take a look," he said.

At once she unbuckled his belt, pulled down his pants and short underwear and his rock hard penis jolted upward.

"Oh my!" Her eyes were wide. "I've never seen . . . I mean I'm not used to one so big . . . Oh, my!"

They undressed completely and lay on the blanket. At once she rolled on top of him.

"Right now!" she said. "I want to ride you. Help me." She went over him and he assisted and soon she found the right spot and eased forward, impaling herself on his lance.

"Oh, glorious!" she yelped. "Marvelous! It's such a wonderful feeling, so . . . so . . ." Then she was busy, sliding forward and raring back and coming forward until she had worked out a rhythm that looked like she was riding a horse. Spur lay on his back enjoying the attention, then he felt his own steam rising.

Before he could move, she exploded over him. Her eyes shut tightly and she screamed, then she began to cry, but her hips slammed against him as she sought more and more of his staff. She banged against him and cried, then sobbed and pulled his hands up to her breasts.

She shook and vibrated with a long series of spasms, then came away from him and went on her hands and knees on the blanket. She looked over her shoulder.

"Please," she said. "Finish it this way."

Spur went on his knees behind her and she helped with one hand, then he drove forward and she groaned and yelped in delight.

"Now big Spur! Spur me all you can!"

Only a few moments later Spur lost his own control and he jolted his load deep inside her and they fell forward on the makeshift mattress.

Ten minutes later they had dressed and sat watching the fire.

"I'm going to go do it," Priscilla said, her red hair still damp from her perspiration.

"I guess that's your right, Priscilla. But be careful. These men are not the kind who will take kindly to being shot by the widow of one of their victims. Word will get around quickly."

She smiled and reached over and hugged him. "I knew you would come around to my way of thinking. I know where they live. Tonight would be a good time to start."

Priscilla stood and rummaged in a bag she had brought, took out a pair of pants. Without embarrassment she took off her skirt and pulled on the britches.

"I don't want to look like a woman when I'm out there. You realize I can't go back to my house. They will be watching it. The sheriff knows I brought the dinner, he'll figure that out fast that I helped you escape."

"Be careful."

"I will."

He caught her by the hand and turned her around and hugged her tightly. "No, you don't understand. These men are killers. They will fight back with deadly force. If you do manage to kill one of them, the other two will be on their guard. You have to plan each one carefully, then follow through as you have decided will be the safest."

She kissed his cheek. "Thank you for being concerned."

"I'd like to go along and back you up."

"But you can't. You took some kind of an oath. Don't worry, I'll kill them and fade away, probably St. Louis after this, or maybe Chicago."

Spur sipped the last of the coffee. It was nearly four in the afternoon.

"I'm going. I'll wait until darkness to go into town. It should work out fine."

"I might come into town, just stay in the background, an alley somewhere." He watched her.

Slowly she shook her head. "No, I wouldn't like that. You're in enough danger as it is. I have to do this by myself. Do you understand?"

Spur sighed and nodded. "I should tie you up right now and not let you go."

She laughed softly, kissed his lips and backed away. She had hid her rich red hair under a man's hat, wore pants and a shirt that concealed her breasts. She looked like a twelve or thirteen year old boy from a distance. She got her horse, pushed the rifle into the boot and led the mare out of the cave without looking back.

9

J osh Newcomb shook his head slowly as he stared at his wife. "I don't like it, Mary. They are going too damn far!" Josh stood five feet ten, had lots of curly black hair, a tough, strong body from manhandling fencing and posts and hardware most of his twenty eight years. His father had run this store before him.

He stood behind the counter and concentrated on each word.

"Abe is the one going too far. He's got the whole county tied up, and now he wants to squeeze every-one again. I don't know what he thinks he can do with the money, him with the gout so often and that bad heart."

Mary watched her husband. They had two kids home with a neighbor and Mary worked all day with him minding the Newcomb Hardware store. It was a living. Even with the dues they had to pay to the Bald Knobbers.

Josh ran his hands through his hair and scowled. "This killing is what is going to do us in. That young lawyer. That one scares me. No, I wasn't in on it,

103

but Abe said it was bound to happen. Kid was asking too many questions. Should have run him out of town, tarred and feathered, the way we used to do."

"He would have come back," Mary said. "His kind of honest men always do."

"Damn! You're right. But now Abe had this newcomer Spur something arrested. Threw him in jail and all set to have a joke of a trial. But Spur escaped first and killed the deputy. Gonna be hell to pay at the meeting tonight. Abe is going to want him dead too."

"You could always turn in your hood," Mary said quietly. "You know I've never thought much of this way of running a city or a county."

"That kind of talk could get your husband killed, young lady. Stop it. We can think that way all we want, but we have to be careful saying it out loud." He looked around the store but it was empty. Josh wiped a line of sweat off his forehead.

"Even five years ago it wasn't so bad. Then Abe came into town and he really changed the whole scope of the group. We used to have church folks running things. Now it's Abe, saloon owner, gambling hall man and whoremonger."

"Maybe you can elect a new leader," Mary said.

Josh laughed. "We don't elect anybody. Nobody is called president or mayor or anything. The strongest men in the group call the shots and if somebody doesn't like it, he can speak up. Lately the ones who spoke up loudest are now out in the cemetery."

Mary came over and put her arms around him. Her brown eyes were narrow, worried.

"You be careful. I know we agreed you had to be one of them, but just be cautious. Another two years and we'll have enough saved to leave here and sell the store. I've dreamed so of living in St. Louis where my sister is."

Josh kissed his wife on the forehead. "Little Mary, don't you worry. Things will settle down again. First the lawyer, then that strange scene yesterday with the Negro woman, and now this Spur character breaking out of jail. Abe has never lost a man he set his mind on killing. Not before, at least."

Josh looked around the store, saw a man come in and sold him a new spade, then came back to where Mary stood unpacking some hand tools.

"I remember my daddy telling me about the 'group' as he used to call it. Most of it began right after the war, when there was almost no state government and none at all in some of the counties like ours. He said somebody had to hold things together and they did.

"But he said for a long time a man had to be a member of the church and a resident of the town to be on the group. That kept it fairly well in bounds. They were all high minded men, concerned with keeping out the riff-raff after the war, and building a fine community where they could raise their kids."

"I reckon even now Abe Conners would join the church if he had to," Mary said.

"Sure, but that wouldn't change him. He's a criminal himself. That's about the only thing to call him. An outlaw with the power of a whole county behind him."

Mary unwrapped a ten ounce hammer and marked the price on it.

"I saw them with the Negro woman yesterday. Ripped her blouse off and chased her across the street. They were offering her for sale, right there on the street. She looked half dead with fear. But she stood up to them. She sassed that Hirum Streib back right to his face," Mary looked away.

"Josh, I think those men would have ripped her skirt off and thrown her down and done it to her right there in the street if that man hadn't come out and helped her."

"And now both of them are targeted for the undertaker," Josh said. "I can't understand how it came to this. Sure, once in a while the boys used to get out of hand. Like that man from Springfield who came in and started that Oak sawmill. He turned out the best quarter sawed oak lumber I've ever seen.

"Lots better than the quarter sawed old Harry was turning out at his mill. So Harry talked the boys into burning down his mill and hooraying him and his family half way down to Springfield. That wasn't right, but we told them and said no more of that, and everyone obeyed."

"Josh, don't you go getting worked up. You just go to that meeting tonight and be there and don't say much and then you come home before they get into any trouble."

"Wish it was that simple, sweetheart. It ain't." Josh kicked the back of the counter where his money box was. He loved this store and this town. It was the Knobbers who were ruining it. They were taking everything for themselves—some of them.

"I thought the dues thing would break up the whole thing," Josh said.

"But it started off small, you said, like a dollar a month to buy some beer and have the meetings. Early on you said they bought some ingrates stage tickets out of town."

"That's the way it started. Now it's a mite higher. We paid twenty dollars last month, and Abe says the dues have to go up."

"Twenty dollars! That's half of what we make most months, Joshua! You never told me."

"Yep, I knew you would be upset. All the members say the dues are too high, but Abe just grins and says tough, he pays them too. You know they told that young lawyer his dues was fifty dollars a month."

"That's outlandish!"

"Some of us were trying to talk him into leaving town before Abe got his dander up. We didn't make it."

"Lawyer like him wouldn't take in more than ten, twelve, maybe fifteen dollars a month in a town like Branson," Mary said. She sat on the edge of a small chair behind the counter and her face was grim.

"Joshua Newcomb, I don't want you to talk this way at the meeting tonight. You just hold your tongue. Don't do nothing to get Abe and the other leaders angry at you." She went and put her arms around him and pushed close against him.

Josh looked down at her in surprise. "Hey, right here in public?"

She reached up and kissed his lips. "We're married, it's all right. Anyway, I'd kiss you even so. You're the only husband I've got."

He kissed her nose and laughed softly. "Hey, everything is going to be just fine. Don't worry. I know these guys, I know how they operate. I'll be careful."

Josh took a deep breath and checked the cash box. He took out ten dollars and put it in his pocket.

"They'll be asking for money again. Abe ends up with most of it I'm damn sure. He says most of it goes to Sheriff Parcheck for his twice a year trips to the state capitol where he spreads around money like it's water. Abe says that's what keeps the attorney general and the militia out of our county."

"Sheriff Parcheck is the kind of no good who could do that kind of dirty work," Mary said. She went back to unpacking the tools, chisels, files, screw drivers and two boxes of stove bolts.

An hour later, Josh pushed through the bat wing doors of the Cat's Claw saloon, bought a nickel beer from the apron and went through the door marked "Private" into the back room. A dozen men were already there. He waved at some, sat beside Hoss Wilton who ran the livery stable. He had been one of the early members who had been a good friend of Josh's father.

"Evening, Josh."

"Hi, Hoss. Keeping them nags of yours running?"

"Tolerable. What's going on here with the Russell hanging?" He said it softly so only Josh could hear.

"Careful, Hoss. There aren't enough of us left."

"Yeah. I know. Trying to figure out today how to turn this around. Need to export about six people."

"Including one saloon owner?"

"The first one."

Their voices were low, no one else heard or paid any attention. Most of them were talking about Archie, and how he died, and what the hell they were going to do about it!

"Find the bastard and skin him one inch of skin at a time with a good sharp butchering blade," a big man with red cheeks and red hair bellowed.

"Naw, too good for him. Let's make him cut his own balls off, and then slice his pecker off a half inch at a time while he watches!"

That plan got some vocal approval.

"Before that let's find him and that black bitch and strip them both on Main Street and make them give us a dog style fucking demonstration. Then we can cut them both up at the same time!"

Abe Conners walked in and everyone quieted. Abe rolled up to the front of the room where a small table stood beside a chair. He sat down and stared out at the men from small eyes, set close together.

"Men, we have two problems we need to take care of."

"Yeah, Abe, we been chawing on that," Hirum Streib said.

"Good. I've got some ideas too. This McCoy isn't in town. He was seen riding hard to the west. He might be long gone by now. Just in case I want two men to ride out and check that log cabin about three miles out where the niggers hide out sometime."

Two men lifted their hands. Abe nodded. "If you find McCoy and the Widow Russell out there, bring them both back, alive."

"Might sample that Widow Russell a mite, first," one of the men said.

"Don't matter you do, just so you bring them back alive," Abe snapped and waved them off. "Next problem is that nigger cunt who needs discipline. Anybody heard where she might be?"

"Blacktown," somebody said.

"You want to go down there at night and look for her?" another voice asked.

Abe looked around. "So we find her in the morning. We should be planning a deer shoot in the morning. Everyone with rifles and sidearms downtown by eight A.M."

He stared over the group that had grown to eighteen men. He knew each one of them. Most of them he could trust with his life. One or two were marginal, but they were watched and listened to.

"We still got two hours of daylight left," Abe

said. "I want two more men to ride north toward Springfield and then circle back west through the hills, and see if they can spot anyone, or smell out any smoke. I figure McCoy and the Russell cunt are on the way to Springfield, but the woman will slow him down, and they'll camp come dark."

Three men lifted hands. Abe waved at them all. "Remember, we want them alive, back here. Anything else is up to you."

The men left laughing and saying what they would do to Priscilla Russell when they found her.

"We have to hit this hard," Abe said. "This is a direct challenge to our control. We let this go unpunished, and it will be the first step to the end of our rule. Do we want that?"

"No!" the men shouted in chorus.

"Then we have to stick together and keep things running the way they are. We sent Parcheck up to Jefferson City last month with five thousand dollars to pass around. He did a good job. We have a firm commitment from the attorney general, and the Major General of the Militia swears he can't find his way past Springfield, if he ever gets called out by the governor."

The men whooped it up, laughing and chattering.

Two dance hall girls came in with trays filled with mugs of beer. Both girls had stripped down until they were bare to the waist, their breasts rouged and painted.

"Hot damn, tits!" one man shouted.

"Look, but don't touch," Abe called. "At least not until the beer is gone off the trays!"

The mugs were picked up and eager hands reached in for a squeeze and a pat on the breasts. The girls laughed and giggled and at last flipped up their skirts to show off their fancy lace panties. Then they hurried out the door.

"You men know where the girls work, you get the urge," Abe said. "Members get into them pussies at half price!"

Again the man hooted and shouted and started calling out numbers about who would be first.

"Dues," Abe called to quiet the men. "This kind of operation takes money. We don't have a regular county assessor or county taxes, so we get our operating capital by collecting dues. Couple of the boys and me decided that everyone in town is going to pay taxes. Like in any county. I'll pick a man to list all the people and what they own and then set up taxes, fifteen, twenty dollars a family."

"Yeah, great idea," somebody called.

"Then our own dues won't be so much, right Abe? We do all the dirty work. Let the public pay for it."

"Great idea Hirum. Soon as we get our system working, the members here won't have to pay dues. Until then we need another ten dollars from everybody. I'll pass a hat around. Sure hope the total comes out even when I count. I trust you men."

"What about the Negro bitch?" a voice called. "What we going to do with her?"

Abe grinned. "You ever had any black meat, Willy? Hell, lots of things we can do with her. Soon as we catch her. Could have our own private bawdy house, just her and free servicing to members, no more than a dozen a night."

The men laughed and whooped in anticipation.

"Course she might object."

Laughter.

"We find her first."

"How did McCoy get out of jail?" Josh asked.

Abe looked sour. "Hell, I guess everybody'll know soon. We had him locked up tight, took him this morning with no problem. Trial set for this afternoon. Then that asshole Parcheck let the Russell woman in with a dish of food. He said he checked it, no way she hid anything in it.

"Course he didn't search her. He had Archie go along and watch her. Somehow she got a knife to McCoy without Archie seeing it. Don't know for sure, but she could have flashed some leg or maybe let one tit slip out of her dress. Old Archie would have been all eyeballs for her and not worried a shit about his prisoner. Course we'll never know for sure.

"Archie got back the plate and table knife and fork, and half hour later McCoy got Archie back to his cell somehow and knifed him and broke his neck and got away out the back door.

"Widow Russell is gone and so are both her horses, so we figure the two of them lit out somewhere."

As he talked, Abe Conners counted the money in the hat. Then he counted the men in the room including himself. He took a ten dollar greenback from his pocket and put it in the hat. "Yes, exactly right, men. We'll collect from the five who are gone soon as they get back. Anybody not have anything to do tonight, might mosey around town and the safe parts of blacktown and look for that nigger slut."

He looked around. "Anybody have any questions, or anything to say about our operation?"

Nobody said a word.

"Everybody gets another free beer at the bar, after that you're drinking on your own. Stay ready for some action. We got two projects in the works."

10

Priscilla Russell asked Spur again how she looked.

"Is my shirt loose enough so my breasts don't show?" she said not at all embarrassed.

"Yes, but it's a bad idea, you going to town. "These men are organized, they protect each other."

"Spur you men are always talking about 'things that a man has to do.' Well, this is one of those things that I have to do. I couldn't go on living in peace if I don't try to get them. All the rest of my life I would be scolding myself and telling myself what a lump I was.

"I have to settle this once and for all. Then I'll be able to sleep, I'll be able to get on with my life. Right now everything is on stop, until I have a short meeting with those three men. Can you understand that? Do you have any idea how empty I feel inside?"

"Yes. But as a lawman I should stop you. You're doing exactly what they are. Lowering yourself to their level. Is that what you want?"

"No, I want them dead. I hope you understand. I

know you won't try to stop me, and I thank you for that. When this is all over I'll come back and we can ride together on our way into Springfield."

She smiled, a bit of shyness glowing through. "I know my husband has been dead only a day, and I won't even be able to go to his burial, but when we were making love . . ." She closed her eyes. "Well, I hope you understand. I wouldn't mind another few days of being with you."

Priscilla turned, felt a flush on her cheeks as she mounted her horse and made sure the Winchester was in the boot and the big six-gun safe in her saddle bag.

Then she rode.

She knew the way and came to town just as dusk crept over the peaceful looking settlement. She tied her horse at the edge of town and carried the rifle over her shoulder the way she had seen boys do as they came back from hunting.

Lots of them did not bring back any game, so she did not feel out of place.

But she did feel strange. *She was going to kill a man, two or three if she could!* The full weight of it could not slash through her determination. She would cry for the men's widows later. Now was action time.

She knew where Barney Figuroa lived, about a block down from her own house. She wished she could go back there and get some more clothes and some of the food she had canned. But that was not possible. Sheriff Parcheck would have two men watching the place.

She found the spot she wanted after ten minutes of searching. The Figuroa house was near the end of the block. Directly across from it was a vacant home, with a doghouse that had been built alongside the residence. It was exactly the right height.

She could stand behind the doghouse, rest the rifle on the roof of the shelter and be ready for a shot. She hoped that Barney had not come home yet. If he had he might be leaving to go to a saloon or to a meeting of the Knobbers. She knew they met in Abe Conners' saloon. If she didn't find him coming home, she would march up to the house and knock on the front door and use the pistol.

Priscilla watied for what she guessed had been a half hour. Twice she moved and stretched and tried to relax. No one could see her. She had the rifle all ready to fire, the safety off. She heard voices and looked again.

Two shadowy shapes came down the street. One man was tall, the other medium height. They were talking, laughing, saying something about the bar wenches in the Cat's Claw. Then the words came clear as the men stopped in front of the Figuroa house.

"Barney, you are half drunk, you know that?" one man said. The taller of the two shook his head.

"No chance way, that I am drunk about by half as much," he said. Then he giggled. Both men roared in laughter.

"Soused to the top of your old eyeballs," the shorter man said.

Figuroa shook his head again and staggered a step away as he nearly lost his balance.

"Barney, think you can find your way from here to the front door?" the shorter one said.

Barney nodded. "After you leave," Barney said. "Shoo, scat, get the out of here. Hell!"

They both laughed again, then the shorter man waved and walked quickly down the street. Barney looked at the door and took two steps toward it, then he staggered off the sidewalk into the dry lawn. He snorted, got back on the walk and moved two more steps toward the door.

Priscilla sighted through the rifle at the shadow, waited until he got to the steps where he would pause. When he stopped and stared at the steps, she slowly squeezed her whole hand with the sights in the middle of Barney's back.

The rifle thundered and she worked the lever the way Spur had taught her to bring another round into the chamber. When she looked for Barney he was sprawled face down on the small porch. She aimed at the fallen figure and fired twice more, watching each slug slam into the fallen body. Then she put the rifle over her shoulder and walked past the vacant house, to the alley behind it, and down to the far end of the block.

She knew exactly where she was. It was four blocks to her horse, and there were only a scattering of houses between her and the animal. It was dark, she walked slowly, careful not to show any sign of nervousness.

A screen door banged behind her. A woman screamed. Lights flared in some of the houses on the same block the Figuroas lived on. Then she heard hoofbeats on the same street and she walked faster.

There would be no problem getting to her horse. Spur had told her the first man she shot would be easiest. After that the other two men would be on their guard.

Spur McCoy had let the woman ride out of sight, then he saddled his horse, and wished that he had kept the .44 he had taken from the jail guard.

Priscilla had both weapons, and he had none. He would have to take care of that problem when he got to town. His gear had been impounded by the sheriff when he was arrested. He was sure it had all been used and given away by now.

Spur rode hard until he could see Priscilla. He trailed her, staying out of sight, following far enough back so he could close the gap if she were attacked. He wasn't sure what he would do to help her since he had no weapons.

When he saw Priscilla tie her horse and move away on foot, Spur rode on to the alley behind Main Street and left his horse. He prowled that alley for two blocks, but found no drunk who would not mind giving up his six-gun.

He checked the stores and soon found the hardware store. The back door lock was not complicated and he had the lock open in two minutes. Inside Spur found a display of weapons and borrowed a handgun and a new Winchester rifle and shells for both. He also found where the dynamite was stored and took twenty sticks taped into four stick bundles with blasting caps fixed with three foot fuses pushed into each bomb.

Spur left a message on the counter noting his "purchases" and guaranteeing that he would pay for everything as soon as he recovered his funds. He signed Spur McCoy, and went back out the rear door locking it tightly.

Now with some weapons and his own homemade bombs, Spur felt much more like his old self. His job now was to watch and wait. He found a convenient spot in the alley in back of Main Street and settled in behind some packing crates to wile away the time until the town came alive.

It was a little after eight o'clock by his pocket Waterbury, when he heard three rifle shots not more than two or three blocks away. Spur did not run that direction. He was sure there would be plenty of Bald Knobbers there to confuse the problem.

He wanted to see what they would do next. Spur had concealed his identity as well as he could. He hadn't shaved for two days, he rubbed dirt on his face to darken it even more, and the old slouch hat came low over his eyes. The blue cotton shirt looked more like it would be worn by a logger than a cowboy.

He moved slowly up the alley to the street and watched from the shadows. Spur cached the rifle in the alley where he could find it and sauntered onto the boardwalk, then leaned against the General Store front.

Somebody came running past.

"What's going on?" Spur asked using his best southern drawl.

"Christ, somebody's been shot. Old Barney Figuroa somebody said. I'm going for Doc Gibson." The man hurried down the street toward the medical office.

She did it. Spur had wondered if she could pull the trigger when her sights were on a human being. Evidently she had. Now the Knobbers would really start to roar.

He saw six men walk out of the Cat's Claw and march down the street. They all had rifles and side-arms. Abe Conners led the army and he walked as a man possessed.

Abe Conners screamed. "When did it happen? Why didn't you tell me? How could Barney get gunned down that way? That shitty lawman McCoy wouldn't do it. Who? Who, damnit give me an idea just who did this?"

Abe stopped. "Yeah, yeah. From ambush, right, a woman's way of killing. That damned lawyer's wife, the little redhead with the good tits. Had to be her, what's her name . . . yeah, Priscilla. Let's go up to that house of hers and see if she sneaked back and what we can find."

A few minutes later, Abe led ten men into the Russell house. They lit lamps and looked through every part of the residence. Two men found a small strong box which they shot open. Less than a hundred dollars inside in gold. Abe took it.

"She's been here since we saw her last, damn sure about that," Abe snorted. "You men want anything here, help yourself. In about three minutes this place is going up in smoke. Scorch it right down to the dirt, that little barn out back, too. Burn the damn thing down! Then let's see her use anything else from here to hurt us!"

Men ran out of the house with furniture, clothes, and some canned goods. Then Abe nodded and lighted lamps were smashed against walls and curtains on both floors. The coal oil gushed with flames and in five minutes, the whole place was on fire.

The Bald Knobbers stood around and watched. One neighbor tried to get a bucket brigade going, but Abe told him it was too far gone already, just be a waste of time.

Abe waited until the fire was raging, then turned and stomped away with his Knobbers down Main Street to the ground floor office the lawyer had used. They shot the door open and stormed inside.

Here they found nothing they could use. They trashed the files and desk and pictures on the wall.

Abe was still furious.

"Burn it!" Abe bellowed.

"No!" Streib screeched. "It's my building for Christ's sakes. He just rented it."

Abe laughed. "Then drag everything into the street and burn the shit out there! But burn it!"

Abe marched up and down the street as he watched the desk, chairs, file cabinets, book racks and a dozen boxes of papers and books create a large bonfire in the middle of Main Street.

"Got to find her!" Abe kept screaming to anyone he came near. "yeah, house to house. Right now. Streib, Smith, I want you to deputize fifty men right now. Bring the damn sheriff. We're going to do a house to house search until we find that bastard of a woman!"

Smith rubbed his chin. "Think that might be going a little bit too far, Abe?"

"Damnit no!" Abe roared. He took out his six-gun and blasted five shots into the sky.

"All you men, gather round. I've got an announcement to make. Every man in this community is hereby pressed into service of the Taney County Sheriff's Office. You're all deputized. Now round up every man from the saloons and whore houses. Let's move, and keep that bonfire going to give us some light. I need at least seventy five men out here in ten minutes. So move it, NOW!"

Men scattered into the saloons, rousted drinkers and gamblers out. One man leaned out a second story window with his woman, then vanished and came running into the street still buttoning his fly.

In fifteen minutes, Abe Conners had every man awake in Branson standing in the middle of Main Street. He got to seventy, then stopped counting. The time was a little after eight P.M. and the weather was clear.

When everyone was there, Abe stood on a chair on the boardwalk in front of the freight office.

"Men, we've got a tough job to do. A woman

gunned down our friend and neighbor, Barney Figuroa tonight. Cold blood shot him three times from ambush."

There were outraged shouts and yells.

"We're looking for that woman. Her name is Priscilla Russell, a redheaded female about twenty-eight years old. We don't know where she is, but she's probably staying in one of the houses or barns or businesses.

"First we want you store owners to open up so we can look through them, then we'll get to the houses. We're gonna search every building in town and then head for blacktown as soon as it gets light if we need to.

"I figure we'll find her here. So let's get moving. We don't aim to hurt no one, but explain to the good folks of Branson it's for their own good. We got to find ourselves this vicious killer before she gets around to you and me!"

With a whoop the men scattered. There was no direction, no order. It was simply a small army of men working down Main Street poking through every store and business, then swinging half of the men to each side of Main and working down the strings of houses on First and Second streets.

The merchants all cooperated. One man was out of town so Abe was called and they shot his door open, searched the small store and padlocked it so no one else could get in.

A widow on First Street behind Main objected to three men coming into her house. Abe ran to the house, explained patiently to the woman and at last she said the men could search, as long as Abe stood there and waited for them. He did.

The search progressed for an hour. Most of the houses had been checked out, some of them twice.

Down on the far corner of Second Street Vern Smith came up with a prize.

He walked up Main to the fire where Abe had been most of the night and showed off his find.

"Abe, look what we found down there on Second, one little black nigger girl just mad as hell."

Abe turned and saw Edith Washington, the Negro who had given Streib such a bad time the day before.

"Well, well, well. Looks like we caught one fish in our net. Not the big one we wanted, but a little one who needs a few lessons in how to be a nigger in Branson."

Abe walked up to Edith and grabbed the top of the dress she wore and ripped it down the front to the waist. Quicker than he thought possible her hand lashed out at him, slapping him hard across the face.

Abe's reflexes took over and he punched her in the stomach, then his right fist hit the point of her pretty chin and she doubled over and fell into the dirt.

"Get her up, and strip her naked!" Abe roared.

Eager hands tore the dress and chemise off her, then ripped and cut off her white drawers that covered her down to her knees. Abe watched them and laughed.

"Now, high and mighty, northern nigger. We gonna show you where you belong." He pointed to two men. Stand her up and hold her arms and don't let go." The men sprang forward, grabbed her arms and held them out straight so she couldn't bite or kick them.

"You two, get her legs and spread them. You let her move and I'll kick your butts!"

Edith fumed and ranted at them, but she would

not cry. "You touch me anywhere else, and you'll all die!" Edith shouted. "Is this how Branson treats women?" She screeched it, and the men laughed.

"Me first," Abe said unbuttoning his pants. "Then as many of you as she can take. Understand any black cunt is good for at least fifty a night. If she gets too tired, lay her down on the boardwalk."

Abe walked up to face her.

Edith spit in his face and tried to bite him.

"Hold her fucking head and her mouth shut!" Abe thundered. "I don't want my nose bitten off."

One man held her from behind and pushed her body forward as Abe lifted his stiff penis toward her black crotch thatch and probed for the opening.

"Drive it in her, Abe!" somebody called.

"Men, I'll show you how we used to treat these nigger slave girls. Had me ten in one day once. Only two of 'em got knocked up!"

The men roared.

"Abe, we still looking for Priscilla?" Streib yelled.

"I can only fuck one at a time, Streib. Give me about ten minutes."

The crowd shouted and laughed and roared again.

Then Abe drove forward, lifted her buttocks to change her position and blasted into her vagina.

Edith screamed at the sudden pain, but the sound came out muffled behind the hand across her mouth. Abe grabbed her around the waist then and pounded into her. Soon his hands moved to her breasts at the last and he grunted and yelled in anticipation, then pumped hard eight times and stepped back suddenly pulling out of her.

"Damn, Abe. I thought you was hung better than that!" somebody yelled from the crowd. Everyone laughed again.

Abe got back on the chair he had used before.

"All right, now, this is a money raising event, new books for the school. Every man gets a shot at her, but it's two dollars a throw. Streib will collect, so just get in line all you big fuckers. We'll see how good you do in public!"

A laughing group of men quickly formed a line and began digging into their pockets. This was a shameful night all of them would never forget.

11

Spur McCoy had been dodging from building to building to stay out of the way during the search by the angry vigilantes. Once he joined a group of men going through a store then faded away when they left.

Now he came around a corner near the small hotel and saw the commotion down from the saloon. In the firelight he could make out the form of a naked woman. He ran forward and saw Abe Conners pull away from the nude black woman several men were holding upright. Abe made some remark and buttoned up his pants. Spur knew exactly what was happening.

He darted back to the alley, found the best possible spot and planted one of the bombs in a trash barrel and lit the fuse. It would burn for three minutes.

Spur raced two blocks toward the end of town, located the old barn he had seen and checked it quickly. There were no animals inside, just a stack of hay. Quickly he set the hay on fire, made sure it had a good start, then ran back the two blocks to the center of town. On the way he planted another bomb and lit the fuse.

He slid through the alley in back of the yahooing and yelling on Main Street, just as the first bomb went off with a roaring blast. The noise in the street stopped for a minute.

"Let's go see what that was!" a commanding voice bellowed.

Spur kept running away from them. A block the other side of the mass of men, he planted his last three bombs in spots where they would do no damage, but cause a lot of noise. Then he hurried back toward where he had tied his horse. He mounted and rode toward Main Street.

He could see the fire now in the night sky over some buildings. Spur hurried to where he had spotted the black girl being raped. She was Edith, he had seen enough of her twisted face to know that. There were only twenty men around her when he rode into the street.

Just then two more blasts went off on their three minute fuses, and all but three men dashed away from him toward the area the blasts had belched out fire and fury.

Spur brought up the Winchester and aimed carefully, fired and levered in another round and fired again. His first two bullets cut the legs out from two of the men who held Edith. She looked at him, scratched the other man holding her, pulled away from him and ran forward.

The third man grabbed at his six-gun and Spur put a round through his chest, knocking him down.

Spur rode up, reached down and grabbed Edith's arm and hoisted her onto the horse's back behind him. He drew his six-gun and sent two rounds at the wounded men, who screeched in anger and pain on the ground.

A man ran into the street directly in front of the horse. Spur shied the mount to the right. The man had out a six-gun and lifted it to fire. Spur had turned to the right and now the horse's head blocked his right handed aim for a shot. He struggled to get the weapon up in time to shoot around the mount.

The gunman stared at Spur and the naked woman. "My God!" he screeched. Josh Newcomb had a killing shot at either one of them. He lifted his weapon then aimed deliberately over Spur's head and fired two shots.

McCoy fired to the right of the man and spurred the mount and in a moment he was past the man who turned and fired high again. Spur frowned, wondering who the townsman was. Evidently he was not one of the Bald Knobbers or either he or Edith would be dead by now.

Spur charged out of town down a side street, away from where he had planted the bombs. The last one went off and he nodded grimly.

"Sorry I was late finding you, Edith," he said over his shoulder.

She had her arms around him and hugged him so she wouldn't fall off. All he heard were quiet sobs against his shoulders. They rode well out of town toward the cave. A mile away from the light of the barn fire, Spur stopped.

"Figure you're getting chilly," he said. He unbuttoned his outside shirt and took it off. Behind him Edith slipped it on, still without a word. "We have some extra clothes where we're going. Shouldn't take more than about twenty minutes to get there." Still she didn't reply and her quiet cry continued.

He turned to look at her, but Edith had her face averted.

"Edith, I'm sorry. I should have made you get out of town yesterday. Promise me you'll never go back into that place."

She bobbed her head and he angled the horse on toward the cave, furious at the men who had done this, knowing that he couldn't just ride away from Branson. Not after the killings, not after something as flagrant and obscene and terrible as this. Somehow a small measure of justice had to be done here, with or without the correct use of his badge.

Behind Spur, the Bald Knobbers gathered back at the remains of the fire. Some wood was thrown on and it blazed up.

"What the hell happened?" Josh asked the two wounded men.

"Six armed men jumped us!" One of them said. "Shot us up and killed Johnny and grabbed the girl and tore off. We was lucky to stay alive!"

"Six men?" Abe questioned. He looked at the second man.

"Damned if I know, Abe. All happened so fast, the explosion, then the fire, then somebody shooting at us. I went down and then she was gone and Johnny took a round right in the chest."

"Get Doc Gibson over here," Abe growled.

Abe looked around the group. "Anybody else see it?"

"I did," Josh said coming forward. "Wasn't six men, just one and he looked like that Spur McCoy guy you been talking about. My guess is he broke into my store, stole the dynamite and fuses and he set the barn on fire to get us moving around."

"One man! Damnit! You assholes!" Abe bellowed at the shot men on the ground. "Can't you do anything right? What the hell we got left to do now?" He stared around at the twenty men who were still there. "Lot of fucking help you bastards are!"

Abe walked around the fire, his hands clasped behind his back. He stopped and stared into the blazing oak two by fours.

"One damn thing certain, we track him first thing in the morning."

"Abe?" a small voice said.

At the second call, Abe looked up at Curt, one of the two town drunks.

"Yeah, Curt, you have a good time tonight?"

"Right, sure did. Also saw when Mr. Newcomb come running in from the alley and almost shot down the man who grabbed the girl."

Abe looked up, eyes alert, wary. "What did you see, Curt?" Abe asked softly.

"Well, heard the shooting, rifle it was, and I came out of the alley. Bottle was empty anyway. Then I see the girl being held by one man. He dropped her arm and grabbed at his hogsleg, then he got a round right in the chest and fell down."

"What happened then?"

"This big guy on a bay comes tearing in, grabs the girl, boosts her behind him and rides like crazy out east. Then Mr. Newcomb ran out of the street almost into him. Mr. Newcomb shot at the pair, missed. The guy shot back and then he was gone. Mr. Newcomb shot a couple more times, but by then they was out of range."

Abe grinned. "Thanks, Curt." He turned to Josh. "Seems you left something out, Newcomb."

"Nothing important. I should have shot him out of the saddle, I missed. That's it. By the time I got a second shot off, he was gone. I'm not a deadeye shot, not a practiced gunfighter like some of you boys are."

"Shoulda had him," the drunk said, shaking his head.

"Curt, if you saw it all so well, why in hell didn't you put a couple of rounds into him?" Josh said feeling ruffled.

"I ain't no good with a six-gun," Curt said.

"Neither am I, Curt."

Abe Conners stared at Newcomb for a minute, then looked back at the two men with gunshots. "Six men took you, did they, boys? You both got one hell of a lot of explaining to do." He kicked a stick back into the fire where the end had burned off.

"Hell, we ain't doing no good out here. Let's get some sleep and be back here at six A.M. so we can start tracking that pair. Every man bring two horses so we can gallop the whole damn way into Springfield, if we have to."

The men scattered, each going to his home. Abe kicked in the rest of the burned off sticks, swore a minute at the dead man, and decided to let him lay there until morning.

Ten minutes later, Abe was in his home, reaching onto a high shelf in his den for a special cigar box. Inside were neatly wrapped stacks of greenbacks. He added the hundred dollars from the strong box that had been in the Russell house and sat down and put his feet up thinking.

After she shot Barney Figuroa, Priscilla Russell had ridden into the countryside a half mile and waited. She could hear the shouts and occasional pistol shot in the town. When the explosions went off and the fire more than an hour later, she knew

Spur McCoy must be back in town.

There was nothing she could do to help him this time. She just wanted the commotion to die down so she could go back into Branson. There was no chance she could walk into Abe Conners' saloon and shoot him, so she had to get him at home. She figured he would be leading whatever hunt was on for her.

When the chase died down, she would be back in town and ready for him.

It was nearing eleven o'clock when she rode down the side streets of Branson. Everyone in town a week knew where Abe Conners lived. His was the biggest and best house in town, situated on a corner and set at an angle to both streets. The sidewalk came in right from the corner of the intersection.

Priscilla had stuffed her red hair back under the slouch hat, and pulled the shirt loose over her breasts. A boy. She still looked enough like a boy to pass, at least in the dark.

She rode straight to Abe's house and left her horse at a tie rail outside the decorative fence. There were still lights on in the house. She knocked hard on the door with the butt of her pistol hoping Abe would figure it was a man.

She reversed the gun, pulled back the hammer into full cock and held the weapon with both hands. When the door opened with the light on behind him, Priscilla could tell the man was Abe. She was in the shadows. She lowered the weapon and without a word fired a round through Abe Conner's belly.

Abe screamed and jolted back in the entrance way of the big house.

Priscilla stepped inside, saw the hatred and anger and pain on the man's face. But she never faltered.

"Abe Conners, you killed my husband, and a

dozen or so other men in this town. Now it's your turn to be dead." She raised the heavy weapon again.

"No!" he said. Blood dribbled down his chin from his mouth. "For God's sakes, don't shoot me again!"

"Just the same way you showed mercy to all those you have killed? The way you showed mercy before you hung my husband?"

A woman edged around a doorway staring at her. The woman's face was white with fear almost matching the color of her hair drawn into a bun at the back of her neck.

"Die, Abe Conners, the way you have killed so often." She fired three more shots as fast as she could aim and cock the pistol. All the rounds jolted into Abe's chest and he gurgled and died in seconds.

Priscilla turned, walked to the tie rack, got on her horse and rode away to the south. Mrs. Conners fell on her knees, screaming and wailing. It was five minutes before anyone came to investigate the shots at Abe Conners' house. His neighbors figured Abe was just disciplining one of his men.

His next door neighbor found Abe. By then everyone was drained, dead tired and most of the Bald Knobbers were sleeping. Three of his neighbors decided they would wait until morning before they tried to find the killers.

Mrs. Conners was hysterical. Neither the men nor their wives whom they soon called, could make sense out of her rantings.

Spur made one wrong turn in the darkness, backtracked until he came to the right small valley and rode up it to the cave. They went inside and Spur lit a lamp Priscilla had brought. He looked at the woman's things and found a bag filled with clothes.

"Edith, borrow something from here to wear. I'm sure Priscilla won't mind. All three of us are going to have to share a lot in the next few days."

Spur built up a small, warming fire as Edith picked some clothes from the bag and put them on. She came to him and gave him back his shirt.

He touched her shoulder.

"Edith, I'm sorry that I didn't get to that street a little bit sooner. I should have."

She shook her head slowly, then spoke for the first time since he had rescued her.

"No, Spur, you did remarkably well. I'd be dead before morning if you hadn't come. I've heard about men like these, but I never thought they could be real."

"So now you will go back to Philadelphia?"

"Oh, yes! Just as soon as we can ride out. What about food? I can go for two or three days without eating."

"No reason, we have plenty of trail food. This all began when I was tracking a gang of bank robbers."

"I heard, Sam Bass and his cutthroats."

"I lost them."

"But you saved me, twice now. I'm not giving Abe Conners a third chance."

They had sat down beside the fire when Spur had spread one of the blankets. She wore a blouse, a skirt and a jacket, and now hugged her knees up to her chest as she watched the fire.

"Edith, do you need to see a doctor? Did they . . . they hurt you?"

"Just my pride, that's wounded mightily. By body is not damaged." She flashed him a frown. "It wasn't like I was a virgin, was it?"

"You're probably the prettiest woman any of

those men ever touched."

"I want to forget about that. I want to go back home and tell Mama what I found out about my brother, and then get back to work."

"Work?" Spur asked.

"I'm a teacher. I teach fourth and fifth grade at a Negro school in South Philadelphia. Not even in the north do they let the races mix in the schools."

"That will take some time, I'm afraid," Spur said. He was quiet then, staring at the fire. He was trying to figure out what he could do that would be within the law, within his oath of office. There wasn't much.

He could go to the state capitol at Jefferson City and raise hell with the governor. But even that might not do any good. The Bald Knobbers undoubtedly had paid off some politicians somewhere to keep the state people and the militia out of the county.

What did that leave? A federal task force? The Army? Declare martial law? Hadn't been done since the war. You can't jail half the men in town. He scowled and pushed another small log on the fire.

"You're worried. Is it about the white lady, Priscilla?"

Spur shook his head. "No, I think she's quite good at taking care of herself."

"You must be a lawman, probably from the federal government. You must be frustrated because there is so little you can do here. Now you are a wanted man yourself."

"Exactly. If I go into town, I'll be shot dead or arrested by the Bald Knobbers. If I don't go in, they will continue to run roughshod over the whole county. I'm wrong either way."

Edith traced small circles in the sand beyond the

blanket. "I don't know if I can help you, but there's a story I always tell my students. It's about bad things happening. I say that sometimes it's like a rattlesnake. Most of my kids have never seen one, so I show them pictures.

"I explain carefully how poisonous the snakes are, and about the rattles and how the snakes strike. Then I draw a picture on the slate board and I suddenly erase the snake's head. I tell them that every time that the head of the rattlesnake is cut off, it ceases to be a danger to anyone."

Spur looked up and their eyes met. He thanked her a moment without saying a word or touching her. Then his face went grim again.

"Yes, you're right. If half the men in town had better leadership, they would go in that direction. There are only a few, maybe half a dozen in all who are the root cause of this whole problem."

He put another stick on the fire.

"Edith, how can I justify going into Branson and shooting down the six men who must be eliminated before the town can set itself straight again? I don't see any way that I can come near to convincing myself that such an act would be in the best interest of justice. If I killed them wouldn't that make me a Bald Knobber just like them? It means I'm taking the law into my own hands, the same way they are."

She watched him, then leaned in and kissed his cheek.

"Spur McCoy, you are a brave man, and a wise one. But twice I was caught in a street with a hundred rattlesnakes between me and freedom. And both times a brave man rode in and rescued me. The last time he had to kill one of the snakes to do it.

"Tonight there are three hundred people in that town, and most of them are just waiting to be rescued. A dozen at the most would move out and find some other place to rob, if Branson became a law abiding town. You know that, Spur McCoy.''

"Then you are suggesting that I wade in there and wipe out half the Knobbers?''

"I can't give you that kind of advice, Spur. I only know what happened to me, and that one man died, and now I'm free.''

Before he could answer Spur heard noises outside. He leaped to his feet, grabbed the revolver and slid toward the far side of the cave. His gun covered the form that walked through the forested opening. It was Priscilla Russell.

Spur relaxed, lowered the hogsleg.

"Glad it's you,'' Spur said.

Priscilla eyed his pistol.

"I'm glad it's me too, otherwise whoever I would have been could be dead right now.'' She looked around. "Company?''

"Priscilla, this is Edith Washington. She ran into trouble again tonight in Branson.''

Edith stood and smiled at Priscilla. "I think I'm wearing some of your clothes. Abe Conners wanted mine so he took them, all of them.''

"Edith, I'm sorry. You're welcome to anything you need.'' She looked around. "Where's the coffee?''

There wasn't any. She got the pot and started some boiling on the edge of the fire. Priscilla edged two stones into the coals so the pot would sit on them and not tip over.

Spur watched her. Priscilla's hand was steady as she set down the coffee pot.

"I'm sorry, Edith,'' Priscilla said. She paused. "I hope Spur got there in time.''

"Almost. I'm still alive. I am grateful to you for the clothes."

Priscilla smiled. "We have enough for both of us until we get to Springfield. We can't have Spur getting all worked up all the time looking at naked females, can we?" For a moment her hand trembled, then she began to cry silently. She bowed her head and when it came up her eyes overflowed and she sobbed.

Spur sat down beside her and held her as she cried.

"You did it then?" he asked.

She sobbed and nodded.

"Barney Figuroa, right?"

She looked up. Tears streaming down her face. "Yes, and Abe Conners. I shot him too. Right at the door of his house. He's dead for sure. I had to do it, Spur. I had to!" She sobbed again, clinging to Spur as if he were the last person in the world.

When the coffee boiled, Edith used a cloth and took the pot off the fire and poured out three cups. Priscilla sipped at the brew black and unsweetened. Slowly her sobbing tappered off and then stopped.

After five more minutes she told them about the two shootings. Edith stared at her wide-eyed.

"These bastards have been getting away with murder too long," Priscilla said. "Edith, I recognized the three men who invaded my home and dragged my husband off and hanged him, for no legal reason at all. He had simply asked too many questions." She caught a big gasp of breath and sipped the coffee.

"Tomorrow I'm going back to town for the other one. I don't care now if I never get to St. Louis. But I want the third man who hanged my husband, the banker, Vern Smith."

"Is he one of the leaders?" Edith asked.

"Yes, Abe, then Smith and probably Hirum Streib are the three top ones."

Edith nodded. "One of them is dead already. Their leadership is shaken. If the next two men were to be eliminated, do you think the Knobbers would survive in Branson?"

Priscilla wrinkled her brow. Her dimples vanished. Then she shook her head. "No, I don't think so. Those three are the top leaders."

"Just a thought," Edith said looking at Spur McCoy.

Spur fidgeted where he sat, put two more sticks on the fire and drank his coffee. He glanced at Edith, who only smiled and looked away.

Spur drained his cup and reached for more. It could be a long night for him before he decided what to do the next day. He had made up his mind about one thing. As a lawman he could not simply ride away from an outrageous illegal operation such as this.

The ticklish moral question he kept asking himself over and over again was what could he do about it, and still stay within the law?

12

Word of Abe Conners' killing rocketed through the small town at sunrise. By nine A.M. everyone in Branson knew that Abe had been shot down in his own doorway the night before.

The Knobbers had started gathering at dawn in Main Street, but when they heard about Abe's killing, they all went to the saloon he had owned and sat around in twos and threes talking quietly. There was an ugly desperation generating.

Vern Smith came by at seven-thirty and took over the small table where Abe had sat. No one else had moved toward the chair. It was done. He had inherited the leadership of the Bald Knobbers.

"We're going to get him!" Vern said so softly and with such hatred that some of the men in back did not understand Vern. "We're going to track down this damn Spur McCoy and blow him into little pieces, tear him apart, cut his balls off one at a time!"

The men shouted their approval. He looked around. "You guys we sent out last night on patrol, did you find anything, smell any smoke?"

"Caught some smoke smell about three miles out, but danged if we could find any fire. Wind whipped up and the way that little bit of smoke swirled through the trees, we could have been a mile or two off. Found not a damn thing, really."

"So McCoy did land and stay. Which means he'll be back. He's a hardhead, that one is. Anybody who could get away from Parcheck has to be. Think we can just take it for granted that he killed Abe. Figures. But how would he know where Abe lived? How would he know a lot of things?"

Vern looked around. His slight limp was no handicap now. He was talking, his long suit, and he could sway people.

"What I'm saying, is that I think it's time we cleaned house. I know that we have a traitor in our midst. We have a spy, someone who does not truly believe the way we do. Before we go after this Spur McCoy bastard, we must root out this traitor and put him on trial.

"We do it this morning, right now!"

The men looked around at each other. They were in the back room of the saloon, and only the hard core were there. There had been twenty men, but now they were down to eighteen, minus one who went to Springfield.

"Christ, Vern. You sure?" one man asked.

"Yes, I'm sure and it isn't you. How else could this McCoy know that both Abe and Barney were in on the execution of that young lawyer? How else would a stranger in town know where both the men lived?"

Vern looked around at the men. "Most of you have been active in our work lately. But three or four have not. Makes a man wonder." He stared from man to man. "Does anybody have any charges to make against one of our members about treason?"

There was no response.

"Then I'm going to ask some questions." He glanced at the men and his glance stopped at Josh Newcomb. "Josh, how long have you been in the Band of Twenty?"

"About four years now, Vern. Ever since I took over the store from Pa."

"Yes, that seems about right. Your father was a good man. As I remember, you haven't ridden with us often."

"I'm alone at the store most of the time, Vern, you know that."

"Yes. True. But most of our work is done after store hours. Is there some special reason you don't participate more?"

"I guess I'm not a violent man, Vern. I know we have to keep outlaws and gamblers and gunsharps out of town, and I support that."

"Are you saying, Josh, that some of our actions are not against these kind of troublemakers?"

"I think that is a fair statement, Vern "

"Then you don't agree with our basic principles, do you?"

"It depends on who tells them, I guess."

Vern motioned Josh to come forward. "Josh, come down here and let's talk this out."

Josh stood slowly, there was a faraway look in his eyes. He moved slowly, then stood in front of the small table. Vern did not stand.

"Josh, did you have a good shot at Spur McCoy last night when he rode past you?"

"Yes. But I'm no marksman with a pistol."

"You shot and you missed him from ten feet?"

"That's right."

"There has been some talk that you missed him on

purpose, that you disapproved of our fun time with the woman. Is that true?''

"Vern, is it true that you run our banker out of town because he was a better money manager than you are?'' Josh asked in an even voice.

"Bastard!'' Vern exploded. He jumped to his feet waving his arms. "That man was a cheat! He was foreclosing on property.''

"Folks who knew said he was within the law, he was doing nothing that you haven't done over the years on bad debts. Vern, how can you accuse me of missing a shot with a .44 when you ran old Harvey out of town because he was hurting your business?''

"Enough! I am not on trial here.'' Vern's face was red, his heart pounding. He sat down and straightened his shoulders. "Josh Newcomb, you are hearby charged with being a traitor to the Group of Twenty, that you have not participated in our work, and that you deliberately failed to shoot Spur McCoy when you had no excuse to miss. Your trial will begin at once.''

There was a chattering of voices.

"Vote'' a voice said. "We always used to vote on things like this.''

"No!'' Vern thundered. "There will be no goddamned vote on this matter. The trial has begun. Is there anyone who wants to act as Josh's defense lawyer?'' Nobody said a word.

"I'll act as my own defense,'' Josh said. "Not that it will make much difference. When Vern smells blood, there is little that can stop him. Where did you get such a blood urge, Vern? Was it when you rode with Quantrel? I heard that's how you got enough money to open a bank in the first place.

"Seems you looted this northern bank and turned

over about half of the gold to the Rebel treasury, the rest went into a hole in the ground that you came back for later on."

Vern jumped up and slammed his fist into Josh's belly, then his other into Josh's jaw. Josh jolted back a step.

"You never did have much power without a gun in your hand, Vern."

"Shut up! This court is now in session. I'm the first witness. Last night this man, Josh Newcomb, had a chance to kill Spur McCoy, but he deliberately missed the shot. That makes him a deadly traitor to the cause of the Group of Twenty. If Newcomb had killed the madman, McCoy, as was his duty, then Abe Conners would be alive right now, and we would not be having this meeting."

"Yeah, yeah!" someone shouted.

"Vern is absolutely right," Josh said. "Abe Conners was killed last night, only I didn't do it. I was home with my wife after our search and the fire ended. Abe was killed an hour later, I'm told. Your job is to find out who did the killing."

"Wives are not able to testify for their husbands," Vern said. "They use crotch logic and it never washes. What we need here are some more witnesses about Josh Newcomb. He's the one on trial."

Hirum Streib stood up. "Vern, I got something to say. I knew Josh's dad. The old man was all right, but fussy. He never really joined with us. He didn't oppose us, but he wasn't really one of the Twenty.

"Now as for Josh, I've been watching him. He ain't never dirtied his hands, know what I mean? He even went along a time or two, but no blood on his hands. If I didn't know better, I'd say he was a spy for somebody at Jefferson City. He's writing down names and places. Bet he has a diary of things he don't like around Branson. Far as I'm concerned, Josh is our traitor."

Josh stared at Streib for a minute. "Hirum you are an asshole!"

Somebody laughed. "Can't argue with that!" Somebody else said. Everyone roared.

"Hirum you were always an asshole, and you always will be an asshole," Josh thundered. "You wouldn't know an honest man if he rammed a pitchfork handle six feet up your dingus and it came out your mouth!"

The men roared again. Hirum had never been a favorite of the Group of Twenty.

"Enough of the name calling," Vern said sternly. "This is a court, let's maintain some order. Are there any more who wish to speak for or against the defendant?"

"Always been fair and honest with me," a man at the side said. He stood, and Vern waved at him.

"Hans, we're not concerned if he's fair or honest, is he a traitor to our cause? That's the question."

The man sat down.

Josh looked at Vern. "Face it Vern. You don't have any evidence at all that I did anything against the Group. You just think that I tried not to shoot a man. For that you're going to hang me?"

Vern grinned. "Now there is an idea. We ain't had a good public hanging in weeks. Looks like most of the evidence is in. Since I'm operating as the jury here, guess I should give my verdict."

He stood and marched back and forth twice. "I the jury do hereby find the defendant, one Josh Newcomb, guilty as charged."

There was a chorus of hurrah's. One or two of the men frowned deeply.

"Sentence is that the condemned by hanged by the neck until dead. Place will be the old black oak next to the hotel, high noon today. Any objections?"

There were none. Vern didn't think there would be any.

"Tie up the prisoner so he won't be tempted to run away. He's got another hour and a half to live."

One of the men bound Josh's hands in front of him and tied him to a chair. Nobody went near him. It was as if he had a plague and they would catch it.

Vern sent four men to follow Spur's tracks where he went out of town last night. "He's riding double, we know that, so try to find the deep set of prints and follow them till hell freezes over. Might look for that smoke again. I want one of the same men who was out yesterday to be along."

The team was formed and rode off. The men were cautioned not to tell anyone about the upcoming hanging. It would be a surprise. There was less chance for opposition that way.

Vern waved as the men left. "We want to make sure of this. I want three men with repeating rifles on roofs overlooking the hotel. Get in spots where you have a good field of fire. We don't want nobody spoiling this hanging. Rest of you scatter and keep your mouths shut until high noon."

In the hardware store, Mary waited on a man for some fencing, said he'd have to load it himself since Josh wasn't back yet. The man paid and said he could do that.

Mary looked down Main Street from the store's front door and saw some of the men she knew were Bald Knobbers coming out of the Cat's Claw. She frowned. Where was Josh? She decided that he would be along in a minute. She hummed as she went back to the counter. It had been a good morning.

She had sold two batches of fencing, and several other good sized orders. Maybe the day she could get away was coming closer and closer.

Where was Josh? She walked back to the front door as Hirum Streib sauntered by. He tipped his grimy hat and nodded at her, but he looked away quickly. She frowned. Hirum was not one of her friends, but she knew him, the way she knew almost everyone in town. A few people moved in each year, but they soon found their way into the hardware store.

Small towns were like that. She liked it here. But she was also excited about the thought of moving to St. Louis. The city would give the kids a chance to be somebody, to get a good schooling and learn things.

Another man came along the boardwalk and she knew he was with the Group. She called to him.

"Wilbur, did you see Josh? He should be back by now from the meeting."

Wilbur shook his head. "No ma'am, didn't see which way he went when we left. He . . . he should be along soon." Wilbur nodded and almost ran down the street.

Mary frowned and went back in the store to help a man find the size of stove bolts he needed.

Ten minutes before noon, Mary looked out the window again. Her stomach was drawn up so tight she could hardly breathe. It wasn't like Josh to stay away this long and not tell her what he was doing. Something was wrong.

Another man had come in for some binding twine, and he had hardly looked at her. He paid and left quickly. She wasn't sure but now that she considered it again, she was sure that the man was one of the Bald Knobbers.

She hated the name, she tried never even to think of it. Then she heard the first shots.

Men were at both ends of Main Street, walking toward each other. They fired their pistols in the air and then shouted. At first they were too far away to understand what they were saying. Then she heard.

"Big hanging at high noon! Oak tree at the hotel. Come one, come all! Big hanging at high noon!" The man closest to her took ten or twelve steps and fired his piece and shouted the words again.

Some people passed on the sidewalk and Mary called to them.

"Who is being hung?" she asked.

Two women and a man shrugged and moved on. Mary locked the front door and hurried down the street toward the small hotel and the big black oak that grew beside it. There had been hangings there before. She shivered.

"Who is getting hung?" she asked someone else. The man shook his head.

At the black oak, Mary saw that there was no scaffold. So it wasn't a legal hanging. A black mare stood there, with a bridal but no saddle. Mary cringed. It was to be a vigilante hanging! Well, she just wouldn't watch, but she had to know who it was.

There was not a chance that Josh was to be hung, she couldn't even consider that. Josh found something he needed to do. He would be at the store wondering why she had closed up in the middle of the day.

She saw Vern Smith and hurried up to him. He scowled when he saw her coming, but there was no way he could avoid her.

"Vern. Vern Smith. Just who is it who is being hung?"

"Nobody can say, Mrs. Newcomb. We all just wait and see."

"But isn't this . . . The Group. Surely you know."

He shook his head and turned away.

Mary stood there in the heat of the midday, staring at Vern, not even trying to swat a dozen flies that left horse droppings in the street and attacked her. A man looked at her, shook his head and turned away. She saw him but before she could get to him, he had vanished into the growing crowd.

Soon there were fifty people in front of the hotel. Five minutes later at noon there were over a hundred.

Vern Smith rode into the center of the crowd on a horse and lifted his hand. On the signal two men walked out of the front door of the Cat's Claw saloon, pushing a man ahead of them. He had his hands tied behind his back and his arms bound to his sides with a second rope.

The crowd saw it and hushed. When the trio was close enough somebody recognized him and the name slammed through the crowd.

"Newcomb!"

"It's Josh Newcomb they're hanging!"

"Josh! Josh! Josh!"

Mary heard it almost at once. She rushed past the others, ran as fast as she could toward the three men. She jolted into one of the men beside Josh who carried a rifle. The surprise and force of her charge bowled the man backwards until he lost his balance and fell.

Mary set upon the second guard, clawing at him with her fingers, tearing down the corner of one eye before he brought up the rifle and pushed her away. Josh stood there watching. His legs were tied together by a short rope so he couldn't kick anyone.

"No!" Mary screamed. Tears flowed down her face. "No, no, no! Josh has never done a bad thing in his life! NO!" Two men from the crowd rushed in and caught her from behind and held her, then on a signal from Vern Smith they marched her along behind her husband.

At the tree the same two men held her.

"Murderers!" Mary screamed. "Isn't there just one man in this town strong enough to stand up against the kill crazy Bald Knobbers? They are vicious animals. They're ruining our town. Do you want to live in fear of your life?"

Vern turned to her.

"Mrs. Newcomb, shut up."

"Bastard!" She screamed. "Vern White is a murdering bastard and I hope he rots in hell for it!"

A third man came up behind Mary and pressed his hand across her mouth so she couldn't talk.

Vern nodded. Two men boosted Josh Newcomb onto the horse so he sat facing its rump.

Mary squirmed against the men, then got the hand out of position enough so she could bite a finger.

"Murdering bastards! All you Knobbers are killers. Start on women and kids next why don't you!" The hand clapped back over her mouth, then a dirty kerchief replaced it and was tied tightly behind her head. Tears streamed down her face.

Two men on horses rode up and threw a half inch rope over the big, strong oak limb. The other end of the rope held a hangman's knot noose. One of the riders fitted the loop over Josh's head and cinched it up tight. The knot lay against the left side of his face.

The other man took the rope back to the tree trunk and tied it off as tight as he could.

"For crimes against the people of Taney county, Josh Newcomb has been sentenced to die by hanging." Vern said from his horse. "The execution will be carried out now."

Josh sat on the horse with his shoulders back. He looked at Mary.

"I love you, Mary! I talked back to Vern Smith! That was my only crime. He's crazy. Somebody should shoot him right now. He's the worst . . ."

Vern signalled to the man on the ground near the black horse. The man lifted a wooden handled whip with six long leather strands and lashed it across the black horse's rump.

The animal bellowed and jolted forward. Josh Newcomb slid off the back of the quarter horse and dropped a foot to take up the slack in the rope.

The crowd was deathly quiet for a moment. Josh's neck did not break. His eyes were wild with fear and fury. In the dead stillness the crowd could hear him gasping for breath as the half inch rope pressed aginst his throat, then crushed his windpipe and his legs thrashed and his body jolted and twisted as he slowly strangled to death.

Not a person spoke.

Not a soul moved.

The quietness came rushing at everyone's ears.

They could hear their own hearts beat.

Then the man at the end of the rope stopped moving. A man rode up and looked at Josh, lifted his eyelids, put his ear to Josh's chest.

"He's dead," the rider said.

"The body shall hang there twenty-four hours as a warning to all who try to violate the laws of Branson," Vern Smith said.

The crowd exhaled long held breath and drifted away. There was no shouting or talk. Everyone felt the same terrible, awesome wonder about death. What was it? Was there really a life after death? Or was it one long, dreamless sleep? Nothingness?

Mary Newcomb sagged in the hands of the men holding her. At last they let go of her and she fell into the inch think dust of the street. She sat there staring up at the body of her husband. But she she would not cry. She would not let them see her weep!

Not now. The time for crying was over. She knew what she had to do. Vern Smith would not let her live long if she stayed in town. She had to get her children, rent a wagon and load what she could from the house and the store. Then tonight in the dark she would slip out of town and drive as fast as she could for Springfield.

She had kin there who would protect her. They would hide her if they had to until she could get on a train to St. Louis. She was going there after all. Not the way she had hoped. There was nothing here now for her except death.

How she wished she had insisted a year ago that they leave this hell hole of a town!

Mary Newcomb lifted from the dirt and brushed off her skirts, then walked back to the store. It would be closed the rest of the day. She had certain things to get ready. She had to be prepared if Vern tried to come and bring her back. Quickly she worked getting two double barreled shotguns ready. She loaded both, took along twenty five more rounds. Slowly she worked with the unfamiliar dynamite sticks.

She remembered what Vern had taught her. She made two stick bombs, tied them together with string and pushed the dynamite caps into the powder, then put a six inch fuse on each one.

It was only the beginning of her preparations.

13

D oc Gibson knocked on the front door of the Newcomb Hardware store but there was no response. He went around to the back and knocked again. Slowly the door edged open. A six-gun muzzle poked through.

"Your name and your business!" a woman's voice snapped.

"Doc Gibson is the name, a little sympathy is my business."

The door swung open and Mary Newcomb caught Doc's hand and pulled him inside the back storage room of the store.

She closed and bolted the back door at once. Mary blinked back tears and then reached out for him and fell into his arms crying softly.

"Doc! I didn't think anybody would even look at me again in this town," she choked out through her sobs.

"The Knobbers need me here, Mary. Up to a point I do as I please. You're right, they all are bastards. Some day things will get straightened out here, but not for years." He looked at the boxes and bundles on the floor by the back door.

"Good, you're fixing to leave. Tonight will be the best time. I'll go get a wagon so nobody'll know it's for you. Right after dark I'll drive it past here, then we go to your place."

Mary wiped the tears away and leaned back from her friend of many years.

"I begged Josh not to speak out against them, but he felt he had to, I guess. Wish I was strong enough to take a shotgun and go blow Vern Smith's head off."

"A lot of us wish we were that strong, Mary. No, best you get out of town fast with your kids. What are they, about four and six or seven now?"

"Melissa is five and Josh Junior is almost eight."

"What can I do to help you here?"

"Nothing, Doc, thanks. I'm just near done. Next I go home. Oh, I won't be here for a funeral for Josh. Could you see that it's done proper? A marker and all. I'll send you money when I get situated."

"No trouble. I'll do it. And don't you dare send any money." He looked down at the two shotguns and the boxes of shells. Beside them was a cardboard box with the dynamite bombs ready to use. He picked up one of the bombs and looked at it.

"Yes, wanted to be sure they were set up right. You've got twenty seconds or so after you light the fuse before it blows up."

"Thanks, Doc."

"I'll have the wagon here at seven o'clock. You try to drive straight through to Springfield."

Mary let him out of the back door. First she thanked him with a tight hug and a kiss on the cheek. Doc was a widower and he appreciated a hug now and then. She looked around, then slipped out the back door and locked it.

Five minutes later she had walked down the alley behind her home and hurried in the back door. Her neighbor looked up from where she sat watching the kids and Mary knew she had been crying.

"You better go home, Celia," Mary said. "I don't want you to get in any trouble count of us. Come on now, I know, I know, but you best be thinking about yourself, too." Mary gave her a greenback dollar bill and the woman was still too upset to talk.

The children had heard the neighbors talking. They both came out of the parlor where they had been playing caroms on the big board with the gold rings.

"Is it true, Mama?" Josh Junior asked, his face stiff and ready to cry.

"Yes, Josh. Your daddy is gone, he's . . . he's died. We're moving out of town."

Melissa ran up and hugged her. "Why did Daddy leave?" she asked.

Josh Junior scowled at her.

"He had to go, he couldn't help it. We'll talk more. Now, both of you get boxes and put everything you want to take in them. Your clothes and toys. We're going to leave as soon as it gets dark, but don't tell anyone!"

Mary stood a moment in the kitchen where she had lived for almost ten years. So long! She rushed then, using two old suitcases and cardboard boxes and packed her clothes and all of the personal things she could find.

She sobbed as she passed up Josh's clothes. There wasn't time and there wasn't room. In a fury she threw things into the boxes that had folding tops, and tugged them to the back door closest to the alley.

The last box she packed was food. Josh Junior came and helped then. He was grim faced, brimming with questions, but he didn't ask them. She would have to explain sometime.

They had a good dinner, she wasn't sure when she could feed them again. Then she made sandwiches, enough to last them for two days, and put it all in a box.

The time rushed past. When she finished the sandwiches it was dark. She and Josh Jr. carried the boxes out the back door to the closest place to their house where a wagon could drive in the alley.

When they were done, she told the kids to stay inside the house and not let anyone in, then she hurried down to the store's back door.

Doc Gibson was waiting with a farm wagon with two foot sides on it, and pulled by a pair of plow horses that looked sturdy enough. He nodded and she unlocked the store. She lit a lamp, then took a piece of paper out of her reticule.

"What's this?" Doc asked as she gave it to him.

"Don't ask a bunch of fool questions, just sign it on the bottom line under my name and keep it."

"Why?"

"Because I don't want the Bald Knobbers to get the store and all the goods. I'm selling it all to you for $3,500. But you don't have to give me any money. This is a legal bill of sale, that not even Vern Smith can contest. It'll be safe with you."

Doc nodded. "And I'll get somebody to run the store for me and send every bit of profit to you. You give me your new address and a new name as soon as you get settled. Then the Knobbers won't know it's you."

"Don't have to do all that. But if it does make some profit, it sure would be helpful."

"Yes, now let me load these boxes."

Mary loaded as many as the doctor, and soon everything was on board. They fixed a seat near the front for some boxes, and Mary put the shotguns under a blanket so one pointed to each side of the wagon but were out of sight. She could reach both of them easily.

In back she put a short mattress for the kids to sit on.

Doc jumped up and drove as they went through two more alleys and then came up in back of her place. She went inside to get the kids and Doc Gibson tussled the home boxes into the wagon. He rearranged the mattress and had everything on board by the time the three came out of the house.

"Melissa, we're going on a long trip. You can play in back and sleep on the little bed. Won't that be fun?"

Melissa frowned, shrugged and climbed on the wagon.

Josh Junior was already on the makeshift seat holding the reins. Mary gave Doc Gibson a hug and kissed his cheek. "You take care of yourself now. Don't let the Knobbers hang you, too. I'll worry about you."

"Good. Feels fine to have a pretty woman worried about me. Now get out of here."

Doc said a small prayer for their safety as Mary Newcomb climbed into the wagon wearing sensible trousers and a work shirt. She picked up the reins and quietly headed out of town.

They drove all night down the rutted track of a trail like road to the north and Springfield. By midnight both of the children were sleeping, and the horses were getting tired. She cracked their backs with the reins and they plodded forward at maybe three miles an hour.

She knew that as soon as morning came, Vern would find out she had left town. Doc said he would put up a notice on the front door of the hardware stating that it was now his legal property and anyone interested in working the store as clerk and manager, should see him at once. There would be somebody, Mary was sure.

Now her job was to get as far from Branson as possible. If she got enough miles, perhaps the riders Vern would send after her would give up and go home. Perhaps.

She ate another sandwich. She wasn't hungry, but the action of eating gave her something to do and kept her awake. She was sure if she went to sleep the horses would stop.

Mary watched the Big Dipper. It was true that it did rotate around the North Star. Early on she had seen it low and to the right, maybe where the hands of a clock would be if it were four P.M.

She watched it now and saw that it was almost straight over the top of the North Star. She wasn't sure what time that would make it.

Mary finished the sandwich and drove on. The ruts bounced the whole load and Melissa rolled to the side of the small mattress. It woke up Josh Junior and he pushed her back on the softness without waking her.

"Thank you, Josh. You know you're going to have to be the man of the house now for a while."

He sat up rubbing his eyes. "Uh huh. I know. Want me to drive?"

Mary smiled in the darkness. "No, you can drive tomorrow while I sleep. Now, you get your rest. I'll need you tomorrow for sure."

Twice she went to sleep before daylight. The first time she fell to the side and woke up. Mary was not sure how long she had been sleeping. She looked up at the Big Dipper and found it lower to the left of the North Star. The horses stood stock still in the middle of the trail waiting, perhaps sleeping themselves, she was not sure.

Mary whacked them with the reins and they snorted and moved ahead grudgingly. She did not recognize any of the area they were passing through. That was not unusual, she had only been to Springfield once in the past ten years.

The second time she dropped off to sleep the wagon went off the trail and the horses stopped as they faced three big pine trees. She got them back on the road and saw that there were tinges of dawn in the east.

She had another sandwich for breakfast, wishing she could stop to build a fire and make coffee, but she knew she didn't dare. Every mile farther she moved north, was another mile toward safety, and a free and fair life for her children.

The route ran down hill almost all the way so there was no strain on the animals. When sunup came and the chill of the night began to fade, she stopped the rig and roused the children and gave them each a big drink of water from a canvas water bottle and a sandwich to eat.

"Sandwich for breakfast?" Melissa asked.

"Yes," Josh Junior said. "This is a picnic, a

special trip. You be good and don't make trouble.''

Mary smiled at her son and got the rig moving again. Soon he was sitting beside her.

"Mom, are they going to come after us, the bad guys who . . . who killed Pa?''

"They might, Josh. Yes. I think they will.''

"Then I'm going to be a lookout, a guard. Can I have one of the shotguns?''

"No, Josh, I don't want you being shot. The guns are where I need them.'' She had put Josh's two six-guns in one of the top boxes. She could get to them if she needed them. She concentrated on driving but got sleepier and sleepier.

"Josh, you drive for a while. When the sun is half way up toward noon, you wake me up.''

"Yes, ma'am!'' he said and jumped to the seat and took the reins.

She would lay down for just a minute, maybe ten minutes. But it had been a long day and a long night.

Mary slept for two hours before Josh woke her. Mary had a bite of her sandwich and drank some water and felt almost as good as new. Almost.

She had driven down the road a mile more when riders suddenly came out of the brush along both sides of the road. There were three of them. All were laughing and talking. One came close to the right hand side of the wagon.

"Ma'am. This road is closed. I'm afraid you'll have to turn back.''

She knew the man, a Bald Knobber.

"Now why would I have to turn back, Wes? Some good reason you can give me?''

"Yes, ma'am. Vern Smith says so. He says he's going to put you in a new house he's setting up. He calls it his five dollar house and there'll be special ladies there for fucking."

She was supposed to be shocked. Mary smiled and reached under the blanket beside her. "Well, in that case, we can't keep Vern waiting, can we. I'm sure he'll be my first customer. I'm charging him twenty dollars." Her hand closed around the shotgun and her finger found the trigger. She pulled it once.

The 12-gauge shotgun shell exploded and a full load of shot blasted through the thin blanket, expanded out of the long barrel into a pattern a foot wide before it caught Wes in the chest.

The force of the shot slammed him off the horse, shattering a dozen ribs, ripping his heart and lungs into a mass of bubbly red froth as he died in mid air even before he hit the ground.

Mary jerked the weapon from under the blanket, swung it a foot to the left and pulled the trigger the second time, dropping the firing pin on the second barrel.

The roar of the gun was louder this time and the target twenty feet farther away, but he took ten pellets into his face, five of them crashing through his nose and eyes directly into his brain, splattering nerve endings, brain tissue and a thousand small blood vessels, jolting the man into eternity while he still slumped forward on the horse.

"Christ!" someone yelled from the other side of the wagon. A pistol fired into the air, and the rider came up fast. He was Hirum Streib, and he was five yards from the wagon but out of the sight lines of the second hidden shotgun.

"What the hell you doing, woman?" he screeched. His six-gun covered her and she let the shotgun drop into her lap. She wanted to throw up, but she knew she couldn't. She had to get Hirum forward more so the second shotgun would kill him.

She had never even hurt another human being before. Now in ten seconds she had killed two men. And she would kill the third one if she had the chance!

Hirum moved his horse forward carefully but stayed out of range of the shotgun.

"Mary, you wouldn't have another scattergun under that blanket, now, would you? Just pick up the blanket easy like. You try to gun me down and you're one dead bitch, I can tell you that. I'm a better shot than your late husband was."

She sat still. If she moved the blanket . . .

"Pull the damn blanket away or I'll shoot your little girl. That get some action?"

"You wouldn't! She's just a child."

"The blanket, Mary. Then you and me gonna have a naked party under the trees over there. Next we'll take the bodies back and let you explain to Vern Smith why we shouldn't hang you for murder."

Mary sighed. It had been a good try. At least it would be two dead for two dead, an eye for an eye. She had avenged her husband's murder. Slowly she took the blanket away from the double barreled Sam Holt breech loader scattergun.

"Yeah, just as I figured. Push it off on the ground. Careful! Right now I'd just about as soon shoot you dead as pull down your panties. Do it!"

She pushed the weapon off the edge of the wagon. It hit the ground and she was surprised it didn't go off.

"Yeah, better. Now stand up and take off that jacket and your shirt. I want to look at me some tits!"

She hesitated.

"Come on, whore, you got nothing to lose now. Might as well use what you got left." He began to laugh as Mary unbuttoned the jacket and took it off.

Behind her a six-gun roared.

She snapped her head around and saw Josh Junior holding one of the big .44's with both hands. She looked at Hirum and he clutched his right shoulder, his gun jolted out of his hand. Almost at once the six-gun fired again, and then a third time, and Mary saw the bullets slam into Hirum Streib's chest, blasting him off the horse and into the soft leaf mold beside the trail.

Josh Junior stood and aimed the weapon at the man lying deathly still on the ground.

"Enough, Josh. Hirum can't hurt us anymore." She stepped off the wagon, picked up the shotgun and put it back in place. Then she looked at the three men. All were dead. She took the guns from their holsters. She could sell them in Springfield.

Back at the wagon, she saw that Josh had picked up the first shotgun and reloaded it. He angled that one to the rear and covered it with part of the blanket he had used last night.

Mary held out her arms and he came to her.

"I know it isn't right to kill anybody, Mama. But . . . but . . ." Then he burst into tears.

She hugged him and let him cry it out. A second later Melissa squirmed against them and Mary held them both. Melissa cried because Josh cried.

She talked softly to them as they sobbed. Told them that sometimes a person has to do something that doesn't look right, but this time it was right. These were bad men who would have taken them back to Branson and done terrible things to them.

"So remember, this was not a bad thing. This was

a good thing. Of course we will never have to do anything like this again, because we will be safe and free of the bad people back in Branson.''

She wiped their tears, dug into the food box and came out with apples and gave them each one.

"Now, we have to drive on to Springfield. You kids have never been there. It's really quite a big town. We'll stay there a while and then get on a train and ride all the way to St. Louis.''

She kept talking to them for another ten minutes. At last the agony had gone out of Josh's eyes, and he was more relaxed. He wanted to drive again, so she let him.

She figured they had been riding for ten hours. They should be over half way, more than that, thirty miles from Branson. Only another fifteen miles to go. They should be safe now. By the time Vern Smith sent someone to find out what happened to Hirum Streib and his two men, she and the kids would be in Springfield and the wagon unloaded and it and the horses sold.

Mary Newcomb lifted her head and squared her shoulders. She was a lady who could do what had to be done. She wasn't worried any more about what she would find in St. Louis. She would do just fine, thank you, and so would her two children.

14

Spur McCoy had been up half the night. He kept a small fire going and boiled a second pot of coffee. By morning most of it was gone. He had watched both women sleeping near the fire on the bough beds. They were exhausted.

Edith was content to stay at or in the cave until Spur was ready to ride for Springfield. He and Priscilla had argued for an hour after Edith went to sleep. There was no way he could convince her not to go back into Branson.

After she went to sleep, he nursed his java by the fire and tried to come up with some plan of attack that would put a crimp in the Bald Knobbers' power, yet still let him keep his oath as a peace officer.

It was nearly morning when he had the spark of an idea and he drifted off to sleep leaning against his saddle to let the idea germinate and grow while he slept.

Priscilla was up before he was and had a fresh pot of coffee boiling and bacon and hash browns cooking.

"Sorry we're out of eggs," she said as he wiped the sleep from his eyes.

"Put it on my tab and buy a couple of dozen," he said. He went out to the spring to wash up, and came back hungry and with the new idea worked out well enough to get it moving.

As he entered the cave, he saw Priscilla getting ready to ride out.

"Don't go," Spur said. "You've made your point. You've paid them back two for one. It's too risky to try for Vern Smith. He may even be the head Bald Knobber by now."

"It really doesn't matter," Priscilla said slowly. "We had no children to worry about. I can take the risk. I won the first two times, there's no reason why I shouldn't come away unscratched this time as well."

"There are several good reasons," Spur said. "It's going to be broad daylight. You might not be able to catch Vern Smith alone. By now he almost certainly is armed everywhere he goes. He may even have a Bald Knobber or two as bodyguards."

"He might just have a chance then. But I have all day. I can wait until I find the right moment."

"Wait ten minutes and I'll ride part way into town with you."

Priscilla grinned and her dimples popped in, her eyes danced. "You thought of a way to blast the Knobbers and still stay a lawman?"

"Working on it. What do you know about the preacher?"

Priscilla laughed. "Yes, good idea! He isn't the best preacher in the world. Non-denominational. His name is Dutch Van Aken. As far as I heard he never took sides on the Knobbers. No praise, no damning them. Sounds like a good man to start with for some

166

kind of local resistance to the Knobbers."

Spur and the two women ate the breakfast of bread and jam, hashbrowns and bacon, then Edith waved them off.

"I'll do the cleanup and get everything ready to ride. You two be back before dawn so we can get a head start in the dark." She laughed. "I have an easier time hiding in the dark than you two will."

Spur and Priscilla led their mounts out through the hidden entrance, made sure the brush and branches swung back in position, and then mounted and rode.

They talked little until they could see the town. Then Spur stopped and rubbed his stubbled chin. He was still in his disguise as a down and outer.

"One last shot, Priscilla. Don't go in there. You're too pretty a woman to be risked in this kind of a game. I should tie you up right here and pick you up on my way back."

"You wouldn't dare!" she snapped. Then she grinned. "McCoy, relax. You've got two women, one of us is bound to be around for you to make passionate love to after this is over."

"Don't joke about it, Priscilla. I know you're still furious about their hanging your husband, but now is the time to use your head, too."

"Not a chance, McCoy. I've got one more man to kill. See you back at the cave." She waved, kicked her mount in the flanks and rode away from him angling more to the south so she could come in through the least populated section of town.

Spur sat there for fifteen minutes watching her until she was out of sight. Then he nudged his horse into motion and rode through all the cover he could find to the west side of town, and left his horse in some brush. He carried only the new six-gun he had taken from the hardware store.

His clothes were mud caked and dirty. He had discarded the blue shirt, and wore a brown one that was as filthy as his pants. The same slouch hat perched on his head and another day's black stubble growth made him look like anybody but Spur McCoy.

He waded in the creek for a dozen yards to soak his boots and pants legs to the knees. He came out of the brush beside the creek and slanted to the start of a street. No one seemed to notice him. He shuffled down to the first alley, and walked into it, peering into a trash barrel as if looking for some discarded food.

A merchant chased him away from his trash box. On down the alley he saw the church steeple, and he turned on the next street and went around to the church's back door. The parsonage was next to the white building, and he knocked on the rear door there.

A slender man with spectacles on answered his call. The man wore a high collar and garters around his dress shirt sleeves. He had a thin moustache, and suspenders on blue serge pants.

"My good fellow, our poor box is empty this week. I might find you a bit of breakfast, but that would be about all."

"Reverend Van Aken, I'm not here to beg or for breakfast. I need to talk to you about an urgent matter. May I come in?"

"Yes, yes, of course. I didn't mean to insult you. Your appearance . . ."

"Understood. Can we talk inside?"

The parson hesitated only a second. "Yes, of course." He pushed open the door. "Come in, we can talk privately here in the kitchen. I'm a widower."

"Sorry. Rev. Van Aken. There is a serious

problem in this town that I'm sure you're aware of, the Bald Knobbers. You must know how they have taken over the entire county, run it the way they feel, kill anyone they don't like." Spur stopped. "Sorry, you know the whole story better than I do. I want you to help me do something about it."

The preacher frowned. "Just what could we do? I don't understand."

"We need an opposing force. We need to rally the honest and God-fearing men of town so they will face up to the thieves and killers who run the county. If we could get fifty men to line up on one side of the street with their pistols and rifles, and show that they were willing to go to war to save their county, I'm sure the Bald Knobbers would pull up their stakes and walk off their claim."

The preacher took off his glasses, removed a handkerchief from his pocket and polished the ground glass.

"Well, I guess it's possible. But most of our churchgoers are not the kind of men who would be good fighters."

"We won't have to fight, that's the glory of the plan," Spur said. "We get the men to meet and form a power group and then we put on a show of strength and the Knobbers will have to back down."

"Interesting, yes, interesting. I'm sorry I didn't catch your name."

"True, I didn't give it."

"Why are you so concerned about our town? I don't remember seeing you around here before."

"I've only been here for two days, Reverend Van Aken. But in those two days, two innocent men have been killed by the Bald Knobbers, and I understand two of the Knobbers have been killed by some irate citizen."

"I see. That still doesn't explain your interest in our town. We're a small place. You just riding through?"

Spur took a deep breath. If this were going to work, he had to take some chances. "Rev. Van Aken, I came into town trailing Sam Bass and his bank robbing gang, then I lost them. The sheriff wouldn't cooperate with me when I caught two of them, and then all sorts of wild things began to happen.

"Mr. Van Aken, I'm a United States Secret Service Agent, sworn to uphold all the laws of this land. That's why I'm so interested in seeing some justice returned to Branson."

"Well, I am surprised and delighted. You must be in disguise then. Do you have a name?"

"Yes. I'm Spur McCoy, which I afraid is an unpopular name now in Branson with the authorities."

"Well, well, well! Yes, I have heard that name bandied about. Now, let's see what we can do about gathering a list of men. The church membership rolls would be the place to start."

"Sounds helpful."

"Mr. McCoy, I'll need to get them from the other room. Why don't we move into my study. It's a bit messy I'm afraid. Oh, no, the records are in the church office. I'll only be a minute. Sit down here in my chair and I'll be right back."

Spur sat on a chair in the cluttered study that had a big desk littered with papers, a wall filled with books, and a wall hanging that had been hand worked in cross stitch showing the Twenty Third Psalm. Spur stood and walked around the room.

He passed the window and saw the preacher walking toward the house on the far side of the

170

church. He returned to the church and a minute later came in the back door and then the study with a large black book.

"Here it is, church history and membership book. Dates back to well before the war, near as I can tell about seventeen eighty-five." He moved to the pages half way through.

"Now here is the current membership."

As he spoke two men came into the room's open door. One had out a six-gun and he aimed it at Spur.

"Not a twitch, McCoy, or you'll be dead meat in a pine box."

Spur sprang forward, grabbed the preacher who did not move fast enough to clear the gunman's target. Spur used the minister as a shield, then kicked forward and the gun flew out of the man's hand.

Spur drew his own .44 and the weapon responded to his figner pressure and the second man in the doorway with a gun out toppled into the hallway halfway to heaven before the sound of the weapon faded.

"On the floor, now!" Spur thundered at the first gunman still holding his half-broken wrist. The man went down. "Hands over your head, lace your fingers!"

Spur spun the preacher around. The benign look that had been there before was now replaced with a snarl.

"Damn! I should have gut shot you when I had the chance," the preacher said.

"Van, I done just what you said, I tried hard," the man on the floor whined.

"Shut up, fool!"

Spur slammed his pistol down across the preacher's face. The man groaned. Spur felt up and down his body, found no weapon and pushed him to the floor. He picked up the dropped pistols from both men, then aimed at the minister's face with his hogsleg.

"Who are the top three leaders of the Knobbers, Van Aken? Tell me now and live another five minutes."

"No. I can't. They'd kill me."

Spur kicked him in the side just over his kidney. The preacher doubled up in pain. Spur waited.

"Another minute, Van Aken, then you'll find out for sure if there is life after death."

"No! no. I'll tell you." He gasped for breath and shuddered, then swallowed. "Abe Conners was top man. Then Vern Smith the Banker moved up. I guess Hirum Streib is next in line and then I'm the next."

"You've been a Knobber all the time?"

"Since I came to town, five years ago."

"And you're not a real preacher?"

"Hell, no! Abe and me rode in. We heard about the new preacher coming, so we met him at the stage outside of town, took him off and damned if his clothes didn't fit me tolerable good. That preacher didn't need them six feet under where he was by then. I keep track of the brethren this way."

"You used to keep track of them," Spur said. He looked at the first man on the floor, then back at the preacher. All he saw was a blur of the fake religious man's right hand as it swung up a derringer and fired. Spur's reflexes triggered a shot at the phony minister that caught him in the forehead and killed him instantly.

The derringer's round slashed past Spur's cheek and punctured the wall hanging. Spur aimed at the other man, then he let the hammer down easy.

"Bald Knobber, you're through in this town. You get to a horse and get on it, and ride like hell out of town. I see you around here in an hour and I'm putting five slugs through your left eye. You understand me, scum bag?"

"Yes . . . yes. Yes sir. I can . . . I can be gone in half an hour . . . easy."

"Don't tell anybody what happened here. You savvy?"

The man nodded. He shivered so hard he could barely stand. Spur kicked him in the butt as he ran out the door. Spur faded through the back door and down the alley. Nobody had wondered why there had been three shots in the preacher's house.

Spur took his time, looked in garbage cans, trash barrels, got run off by another merchant, and at last wandered to Main Street and turned down toward the bank.

There was only one left in town, the Branson First Bank. It sat on the corner, looked substantial with its solid brick construction, and two big windows so people could see there was no funny business going on inside with their money.

Spur hunkered down on his heels and leaned against the front of the hardware store.

Within ten minutes he had heard about the store owner's hanging, and how his wife had raced out of town last night just after dark. The note was still tacked to the door. Spur read it, then squatted down again and leaned against the wall.

Evidently the Bald Knobbers were so nervous they hung one of their own men. Doc Gibson was acting for the widow. Maybe he was an honest man. Maybe.

Spur had been watching the bank, but nowhere did he see a redheaded woman who looked like a young boy, who had a grudge to kill the banker. Spur waited another half hour, then he rose, stretched, got outraged looks from two matrons and ambled off down the alley to find the doctor's office.

The place was a block down on Main. Half of the building was where the doctor lived, the other half his office space. There was no nurse, no receptionist, just a bell over the door and a pad of paper for the patient to write down his name and his complaint.

Spur wrote down George Washington, for the name, and sudden death syndrome—hanging, as the complaint. There was no one else in the waiting room.

Spur put the pad of paper back on the small stand and waited. A minute later a man came in dressed in tan pants and a white shirt with the sleeves rolled up. He wore glasses and looked first at the pad.

He saw the name and glanced up, saw Spur and grinned, then looked at the complaint. The doctor frowned, motioned Spur with him and tore off the sheet of paper and wadded it up. They went to a small room and the doctor closed the door.

"Doctor Gibson?" Spur asked.

"Yes, George, bad problem you have."

"Isn't mine, Doctor, it's the town's problem. I want to do something about it, any suggestions?"

The man in front of him rubbed his hand across his face. "You're here because of the note on the hardware store door. That figures. The Knobbers might figure it too, but somebody had to help that lady. I just hope to God she makes it."

"You helped her get out of town?"

"Yes. This morning I heard Vern Smith sent out three men to bring her back."

The doctor stared at Spur again. "Saw you one

day. Your real name must be McCoy, Spur McCoy. That's got to mean you're some kind of federal lawman. Don't matter. Not anything legal you can do here."

The man lifted his head and stared at Spur. "Unless you're the one who cut down Barney Figuroa and Abe Conners."

"That pleasure was not mine."

"Then who?"

"You might not believe me, Doc."

The doctor walked around the room. "The only other person would be the Negro girl, Edith, I think her name was. Or . . . Mrs. Russell, Priscilla Russell."

Spur shrugged. "Doctor, what else can the town do? I figured the preacher would be a good man to approach. Turns out he's the third man in line to run the Bald Knobbers."

"Van Aken? Well, mercy me."

"He isn't even a real preacher. He told me he and Abe Conners waylaid and killed the real preacher and Van Aken took over his Bible, his clothes and his church."

"What won't they do next?"

"Without their leadership would they wither up and die out?"

"Possible."

"I've got a hunch Vern Smith might not live out the day. That leaves Hirum Streib."

"Streib in line too?"

"Third or fourth."

"He's a no account."

"Fight them, Doc. Set up a Committee For Justice, get honest men and run the hooligans out of town. You got a lot fewer now to worry about."

175

"What about the sheriff?"

"He should be run out too. Trouble is he was duly elected."

"Election was fixed, don't mean a spoon full of beans," Doc said. He paced the office again. "If we could do it without more of the innocents getting killed, I'd try." He stared at Spur a minute.

"McCoy, Sheriff Parcheck arrested you, violated your rights, misused his office. You can arrest him on a federal charge and haul him off to Springfield. You get him out of town and we'll figure out how to take care of Streib and the rest of the Knobbers. We can even deal with Vern Smith."

Just then somebody came in the front door and rang the bell.

"Doc! Doc! Come quick. Some crazy woman just shot down Vern Smith. He looks deader than hell!"

"That would be Priscilla Russell," Spur said. The doctor took off running. Spur ambled up the street in the same direction.

15

Priscilla Russell adjusted her shirt again so her bound breasts would not show and swung down off her horse at the edge of town. No use attracting any more attention than needed. She did not wear a gunbelt, it would look out of place on her. Instead she carried a small box that held the .44 Colt pistol.

This time she was a young boy going on an errand. No one would glance twice at her. She had smeared mud on one cheek to detract from her clear-skinned look, and she had not washed on purpose this morning.

She still made a girlish looking boy of about sixteen, but it would have to do.

Priscilla had thought a lot about what Spur had told her. That Vern Smith especially would be watching for someone to try to kill him. He knew he was the third one on the lynching party that had hung Phillip Russell, and Vern was the only one left alive. He would try to keep it that way.

She walked along the street toward Main, dragging a stick in the dust the way she had seen countless boys do. She watched the people but not obviously.

Phillip Russell's widow knew Vern Smith by sight, that was one big advantage. He didn't know who was trying to kill him. Surely he would not suspect her. She sat down on the boardwalk with her feet in the street a foot below, and watched the town. She had never really stopped and studied it.

People were rushing every which way, just like they had something important to do.

Main Street. Horses, wagons, buggies, a few people meandering along on the boardwalks. Each merchant built his own walk in front of his store. Some met flush, some were higher or lower than the one next to it. Most of the boardwalks were eight to twelve inches above the dust and dirt, and often mud, of the raw dirt street.

Down a block she could see the Branson First Bank solidly stationed on the corner. Nobody came or went from it yet. It would not open until ten. Why did bankers keep such short hours, she wondered.

A sudden chill slanted through her. For a moment she remembered the agony, the horrendous fear in Abe Conners' eyes when he knew he was going to die. Now Abe was dead, but so was Phillip! Somebody else was going to die today, and Priscilla prayed that it would be Vern Smith.

She frowned. That was no such thing to be praying for. For a moment she felt remors, then she closed her mind to it. No! Vern Smith had killed wantonly, he deserved to die. And she was the only person who could exact that deadly vengeance. It would be done!

She stood and wandered up the street. For a while she sat outside the saloon trying to listen to what the men were saying.

"Hanging," she heard the word again. Then she looked the other way down the street toward the hotel and saw it. A man had been hanged to the big black oak near the hotel. His body slowly turned in the morning breeze.

The name came then, Josh Newcomb, the hardware man. They had struck again. But she thought that Josh had been with the Bald Knobbers, not against them.

Soon she found out about Mrs. Newcomb taking a wagon and running away in the night with her two children. Silently Priscilla grieved with the new widow, then prayed that she would get safely to Springfield.

Two men went into the bank. She wondered what time it was. A clock in the next store, a big Seth Thomas striking clock that was for sale, showed that it was ten twelve. The bank was open! She was sure that by now Vern had to be inside.

Back door. He would come in a rear entrance. She stared at the bank. How should she do it? Should she wander in looking around, curious. Find Smith, open the box and shoot him? By now she was sure everyone in the bank would be armed. Even the tellers.

She walked past the bank slowly. Tried to hit a tossed up stone with the stick but missed. She stared inside. All boys are curious. She saw one customer, and the usual partition and the tellers' cages. No Vern Smith. He would be behind a desk.

She had been in the bank only once before to sign some papers with her husband. Slowly, she walked on past. Down the side street she could find no back door to the bank. Not even on the alley. One way in, one way out.

For a flash of a second she wondered that maybe

Spur McCoy was right. Maybe two for one was enough.

"No!" she said sharply out loud. She looked around, but there was no one near her. She retraced her steps to Main and went to the far side of the street and sat in the shade. More people came and went from the bank.

Priscilla sat up straight, her whole body quivering. A man had just left the bank. It was Vern Smith. He wore a six-gun on his hip. A man followed him closely with two guns looking at everyone in front of and behind Smith. A bodyguard.

She gripped the box tightly. Smith walked the other way, down three doors and vanished into the saloon called the Bar--B. She frowned. She could not walk into the bar. The apron would toss her out as being too young. She had to wait for Vern to get up his Dutch courage and come back out.

Suddenly she was hungry. A good cup of coffee would be fine right now. Money? Did she bring any money with her? She had taken all the cash from her house when she fled with Spur—about twelve dollars. But she had brought none in her pants pockets with her.

For a minute she had an urge to walk up the block and look at the house she and Phil had bought the first week they were in town. What a mistake that had been! She knew there was no time for her to look at the house. She could miss Vern. She slouched on the boardwalk, then went to a string of empty chairs backed up against the Branson General store and sat in one of them.

It was only fifteen minutes later that Vern Smith came out of the saloon, hurried to the bank and went inside. The bodyguard walked two steps behind him all the way.

Priscilla knew she should have a plan. She knew that she should be near the bank and wait for him to come out. But planning was not her best talent. She stood, brushed off her pants, saw that her shirt did not have breasts bumps in it and walked toward the bank.

A cold sweat touched her forehead but she ignored it. Now was the time. She had no reason to put it off. She might get hurt in there, but there was no other way. She would walk in, find Vern and shoot him. Then she would worry about trying to get out.

Not that it mattered that much.

The important job was to kill Vern Smith!

Each step seemed like a mile now as she walked the half block down the street. For a minute she waited for two wagons to pass, then stepped off the boardwalk into the dust of the street and went around horse droppings to the far side.

The bank was two doors down.

Priscilla took a deep breath, checked the box. Yes, the top flipped off and the weapon was there. She had cocked it so all she had to do was aim and pull the trigger—no squeeze it. She would be so close she couldn't miss.

The door was heavy.

A man reached beside her and pushed the door open, then they both were in the bank. It had a fancy tile floor and varnished teller cages with real metal bars in front of them.

She looked around.

Two tellers stared at her, dismissed her and she walked to the far end, away from the tellers. There was a door there and a desk in front of it. No one sat at the desk. She didn't see the bodyguard with the two guns.

Priscilla paused a minute at the desk, then walked

to the door. It had to be Vern Smith's office. Then she saw the plaque on the door that said: President, Vern Smith.

She moved quickly, grabbed the knob and turned, thrusting it open. Inside she saw Vern look up from his desk. The man with two guns was behind him. They both frowned at her for interrupting them.

"Yes, son?" Vern said. "Do you want to open an account or maybe take out a loan?"

Vern laughed and the bodyguard laughed. She turned with her back to them, opened the box and grabbed the weapon. When she spun around she swung up the gun and fired. The first round killed the bodyguard.

She thumbed the hammer back and before Smith could reach for his gun, she fired again. The bullet went through his heart and he fell dead on his desk.

Priscilla let out a held in breath, dropped the six-gun on the floor and turned for the door.

The teller nearest the president's office had heard the first shot and he grabbed a sawed-off shotgun and raced to the door. He saw the boy fire the second shot and turn. The teller stared at the boy for just a second, then pulled both triggers.

The twin shotgun blasts from only six feet away tore into Priscilla's man's shirt and blasted away half of her abdomen, almost cutting her in half. Her body flew backward against the desk, and then slid to the floor. Blood and bits of flesh and clothing sprayed over the back wall and the desk.

The teller ran to Smith and saw that he was dead. He checked the guard. There was no reason to look at the boy. By the time he turned the door the other two bank workers were there.

"Close the bank," he said calmly. "Send someone for Doc Gibson and the sheriff." Then the teller slumped to the floor and threw up.

The sheriff got there before Doc Gibson did. He had closed the bank and kept everyone out. Doc Gibson checked the three and shook his head.

"All dead, Lund, you should have known that. Nothing I can do for any of them." Doc stared at the bloodied remains of the boy. He reached down and pulled off the old hat. A riot of shoulder length red hair tumbled out. Doc wiped the smudge off the cheek.

"Here's your vicious killer, Sheriff. Her name is Priscilla Russell, the widow of the man Vern Smith and two others hanged a few days ago. Guess it's an eye for an eye, wouldn't you say?"

Sheriff Parcheck stared at the woman.

"Christ! I don't believe it! She had the guts to walk in here and blast Doug and then Vern, in broad daylight?"

"Looks so, Sheriff. I'd wager she's the one who shot both Abe and Barney too. From what I hear those three are the ones who hanged her husband."

Doc stood there a minute. "What you going to do now, Sheriff?"

"Well, guess we should get these bodies over to the undertaker. Or have him come get them. Yeah, his job." The sheriff walked out of the bank like a ship that had lost its sail. He had no one left in the Knobber group to tell him what to do. Doc Gibson snorted and wondered if Spur McCoy had some surprises fixed up for the sheriff. He hoped so.

Spur McCoy munched on a square of four big cinnamon rolls he had bought at the bakery and lounged against the side of the bank. He had heard what happened inside. The bank teller had revived and was telling everyone.

Then the word rocketed through the street that

the killer had been a woman, not a boy. It was Priscilla Russell, the young lawyer's widow.

Spur relaxed in the sun. When Doc Gibson came out, he fell into step beside him.

"Priscilla?" he asked.

"Yep. Blown half in two with a shotgun. Damn messy. Nothing I could do."

"Damn it to hell!" Spur shouted at no one, at every one. "I told her not to try it, but the only way I could have stopped her was to tie her up. I don't tie up pretty ladies." Spur walked for several paces in silence. "The sheriff seems a bit unsure of himself."

Doc Gibson was grim. "He damn well should be. The top three leaders of the Knobbers are dead. He's worried he might be next. And now he doesn't have anyone to tell him exactly what to do every minute. He might not be able to get his pants on tomorrow without someone to tell him how."

"I'll tell him how. By then I'll have arrested him for a variety of charges and have him on his way to Springfield and points east."

Doc stopped. "You truth telling?"

"Damn right. Then the Knobbers will have no leaders, they will not even have the appearance of legality, and you should be able to put together an interim county government that can last until you call a special, honest election."

"Sounds good. Damn't, I know four or five who will help me. We'll tack up a notice that any former members of the Bald Knobbers have twenty-four hours to get out of town or face arrest. Then we appoint a temporary sheriff and get a bunch of county councilmen or supervisors or whatever they're called. Lots of work to do."

"Serves you right for volunteering," Spur said.

Spur dug into his dirty pants and came up with a

gold double eagle. "Would you see to the funeral for Priscilla? She deserves a marker and all."

Doc nodded. "Glad to. That little lady had more nerve and will power than most of the men I know. She had to figure if she got to Vern that she'd never come out of the bank alive. Still she marched in there and took out a fast gun bodyguard and Vern before he could get off a shot."

Spur shook hands with the doctor, turned down a side street where he found a horse trough. He washed off his hands and face, wiped dry with his hands and adjusted the gun on his belt.

Now he had to have a run-in with the sheriff. He hoped the man was still there and had not cleared out of town.

Before Spur got to the sheriff's office a man rode into town leading three horses. Over each horse a dead man had been tied. Men ran to the street and lifted heads to identify the men.

"Wally Perkins," one man said. "Shotgun blasted him into kingdom come."

"Turk Johnson," another voice said. "Another shotgun I'd say."

"Shit, look at this! Old Hirum Streib done caught himself two slugs. One dead through the heart."

"Where you want them?" the stranger said. "I come on them back down the trail, and rushed right along to get here. Nobody else around. Did see some fresh wagon tracks though, heading toward Springfield."

Sheriff Parcheck ran up and looked at the bodies. When he saw Streib's body his shoulders sagged.

"Take them over to the undertaker. He's gonna have more business than he knows what to do with."

Spur knew Hirum Streib was a Bald Knobber, one

of the leaders. These could have been the three men Vern Smith sent to bring back the widow Newcomb and her kids. If so that meant there were three more Knobbers down and dead. That could be eleven of them in graves already. The rest of the hard core must be having serious doubts by now about the whole movement.

Spur caught up with the sheriff just as he went inside his office. Spur looked around and saw no one else in the small room.

"Sheriff Parcheck. I understand that you're looking for me." Spur pulled his gun and covered the lawman. "My name is Spur McCoy and you're under arrest for violation of laws of the United States, and of this state and county."

16

Sheriff Lund Parcheck stared at Spur in disbelief. "You . . . yeah, maybe you are. Clean you up a lot. What the hell's the weapon for?"

"Parcheck, you're under arrest for kidnapping, assault and battery, malfeasance in office, giving a bribe, taking a bribe, violation of citizens rights, grand larceny and for being an absolute asshole."

"You're joking. I'm the law in Taney county."

"You were, right back this way to the jail cells. Remember what happened to the four top leaders in the Bald Knobbers, Parcheck. They are all dead, along with seven more of the Knobbers. You want to make it twelve instead of eleven?"

"Knobbers? I ain't one of them. I'm the duly elected sheriff of Taney county."

"Election was rigged, only one man allowed to file and run. Move it, Parcheck. I want you locked up safe and sound." Spur grabbed a ring of keys off the desk and pushed the man to the hallway and down the row of cells. He shoved Parcheck in the second cell, slammed the door and locked it, made sure there was nobody else in the jail and went back to the front office.

Two men stood there. "Who the hell're you?" one asked.

"New deputy," Spur said.

"Better take a bath and get some clean clothes."

"Just as soon as I get my first pay day."

"Where's the sheriff?"

"Busy at the minute. Said I should talk to anybody."

"We ain't just anybody." One of them shut the front door.

"Yeah, we special friends. We need to know what the hell to do now. Everybody been killed off. Who's in charge? Who sits at the table?"

"Got the answer right back here, boys," Spur said, drawing his iron. "Just ease them shooters out and put them on the floor, nice and slow like." One of the men started to draw, and Spur slammed a bullet into the floor an inch from his boot.

"Easy, next one goes in your balls. Put down the iron!"

Both did. "What the hell is this?" one of them asked.

"Change of command, boys. The Knobbers are all through in Taney county. Some of the good old boys took off, most are dead. You can stay if you want to volunteer to dig your own grave."

"Told you we shoulda rode for Springfield," the shorter one growled.

Spur prodded them into the first cell, locked it and let them yell at the sheriff. Back out front, Spur locked the outside door and went to Doc Gibson's office. He was setting a boy's leg. Spur helped hold the leg straight as Doc wrapped on the bandages, then lathered them with a half inch of plaster of paris cast.

When the cast was done, they sat in a small office.

"Doc, we got something of a problem. No sheriff. I just arrested him. I'm appointing you as chairman of the Temporary Governing Committee. You have until five o'clock to get five members, and then until six to appoint a new interim sheriff. Your mandate is to have elections within three months to fill all of the vacancies in the county government."

"Spur, I'm not a politician."

"Good, that's why this is a temporary appointment. In three months your job is over and the county will have a government."

Doc rubbed his chin. "I did say I'd take a stab at it if you got rid of Sheriff Parcheck." He walked around the office once, then thrust out his hand. "Deal, McCoy. How soon do you need a new sheriff?"

"About twenty minutes ago."

Doc hesitated. "What's going to happen to Parcheck?"

"I figured like you that he couldn't get an honest trial in Missouri, so I'm taking him down into Arkansas to stand trial. Him and two more Knobbers. At least we're going to start that way. I've got an idea how we might smoke out some more of the hooded characters."

"You hold down the jail for half an hour and I'll have a new sheriff for you. He's a good man. Used to be a lawman back east, then came out here. Honest as the long cold of winter. Name is Cully Jacobson, about thirty. Now git."

Spur grinned as he left the doctor's office. It was getting along to afternoon. He bought a fresh apple pie at the same bakery as before and ate it all on his way to the jail. Inside the three prisoners were yelling.

Spur pushed open the door. "Any more screeching back here and nobody gets any supper. Understood?"

When he closed the door all was quiet.

Cully Jacobson came in a short time later. He was a strongly built man, with a moustache and close cut hair. He wore a .44 with a long leather holster that hid a long barrel. Cully grinned.

"Hear I'm the new, temporary sheriff," he said.

"Soon as I swear you in. This is for not more than three months, and you do right by these people, or I'll come back here and kick your ass all over the county."

"Sounds right by me," Cully said. "I done some law work back in Kansas, about five years ago."

Spur swore him in, not sure if he had the power, but knowing it would be a million times better than what Taney county used to have.

"My only orders are that you do no executions. Nobody is hanged in the county until a proper group of elected officials take over."

"Fine."

"Right now you have three prisoners. One is the former sheriff, and right hand man of the Bald Knobbers. The other two are Knobbers. I'm taking all three down to Arkansas tomorrow so they can have a fair and just trial."

"Feed them twice a day and charge it to the county at whichever cafe or eatery will hold the tab."

Spur sat down at the desk and motioned the new sheriff in closer. "Now this is what I have planned for tomorrow. I'll need your help and that of two friends you can trust with your life."

Ten minutes later, Spur walked out on Branson's Main Street and it seemed to feel different. There were more people moving around. He saw that the Newcomb hardware store was open and busy. The stage pulled in and two people got off and three got on. Two of them were men eager to leave town.

Spur walked out to his horse and rode back to the cave, getting there slightly before dark. He told Edith what had happened to Priscilla. Edith cried.

"I was getting to like that lady. She was so strong and proud. I don't think I could ever use a gun the way she did."

Edith had cooked some beans, after soaking them all morning, and mixed in the rest of the bacon before it spoiled. They had a good meal, and Spur told her she could come back to town if she wanted to. She shook her head.

"No, too many bad, bad memories. I'm ready to ride to Springfield and get back home, though. When can we go?"

"Day after tomorrow," Spur said. "If all goes well tomorrow in town, and outside of town."

"Are you really going to take the former sheriff and those two Knobbers all the way to Arkansas for a trail?"

"Might, but I don't think we'll get that far."

"Oh."

They cleaned up the supper things, Spur watered both horses and tied them outside where they could eat some grass. Then they talked for a while sitting around an easy fire.

"I've never known a white man like you before," she said. "Now, I've not known a lot of white men, but most of them were overly polite, or downright rude. You treat me just like any other person."

"Hey! didn't mean to. You are a special lady. The way you stood up to those goons was wonderful. You're strong and you believe in standing up for your rights. You just tried once in the wrong place."

They went to bed early. Spur had settled down when she brought over her blankets and lay beside him. She put her hand on his shoulder.

"Spur McCoy. I'm not trying to seduce you, I . . . I just want to touch you, know you're there. Do you mind?"

Spur laughed softly. "No, just be careful where you touch. Lying here so close to a beautiful, sexy lady could get me all worked up."

"I'll be careful. But maybe tomorrow night I won't be so careful."

Spur leaned over and kissed her lips softly, then turned away.

"Pretty lady, that is a definite appointment."

The next morning, Spur rode to town early, had a big breakfast at a small cafe and got to the sheriff's office at 7:30. The new sheriff was there, having slept overnight on a cot in the hallway.

"McCoy, I got one man to go with you. We'll have the prisoners handcuffed so they can ride and the horses tied together. Shouldn't be much of a problem getting over the old Indian trail through the Ozarks and down to a place called Harrison. About thirty-five miles or so and county seat of Boone County."

Spur walked around the three horses and the one man who was to ride with him. Both he and the other man had a sack of provisions on the back of their horses. It was a two day ride so they wouldn't take much food. The three prisoners sat glumly on the horses, their wrists bound together with shackles.

"Special deputy Roger Zilke is your guard," the new sheriff said. "He's a good man with a rifle."

"Looks like we're ready," Spur said. He changed horses, mounted up on the loaded bay and led the contingent out across the street and south out Main toward the old Indian trail. There was little traffic between the two states at this point since there were only small towns on each side.

Spur talked briefly with Zilke, then the guard moved to the back of the line of three prisoners.

"Long damn way from here to Boone County, McCoy," Parcheck said.

"Yeah. Maybe we should make you walk. You want to walk, Parcheck?"

The former sheriff made no reply, just glared at Spur and they kept riding. As they rode out of sight, Doc Gibson stood beside the new sheriff.

"Damn, I hope it goes the way we want it to go," Cully said.

Doc Gibson scratched his ear. "Way he set it up, should work. All we can do now is wait and see."

Spur led the men along the trail for half an hour. Branson was well behind them. He came to a gully where they had to start a climb toward a low pass ahead, where Spur called a halt.

"Dang horse threw a shoe or something," Spur said, getting down. He lifted the mount's foot and led her to the side and tied her reins to a bush.

"You men get down," Spur ordered. "We'll tie you to a tree. I think this broken down nag needs a slight rest, then we should be able to move again. Zilke, start a small fire and let's have some coffee. No sense wasting a half hour."

The coffee was brewed and Spur stretched out next to a fallen pine tree. Zilke had taken a cup of coffee, laid his repeating rifle over his knees and squatted beside a two foot thick shortleaf pine.

Spur kept working lower and lower until he was perfectly protected from two sides by the big log.

It came a little later than Spur figured it would. Three rifle shots blasted into their small camp. One nicked the log behind where Spur lay, and the second one caught the tip of Zilke's boot but did no damage.

Parcheck and the two prisoners dropped into the dirt as low as they could go.

There was a whoop from above them on the sides of the ravine. Six more shots slammed into the rocks around the five men huddled behind whatever cover they could find.

Parcheck screamed in delight. "Come get them, boys! Only two of them here. One's behind the log. Circle around and nail his ass. Zilke is over by the big tree."

Spur pushed his hat up over the log on the barrel of his Winchester repeater. A rifle round slammed through his low-crowned topper, spinning it around. He pulled it down.

"Damn, that was a new hat!"

A dozen more shots came into the area.

"You all right, Zilke?" Spur called.

"Fine, no problem. Where is the damn cavalry?"

As he said it they heard shots from higher on the slope from both sides.

"What the hell is that?" Parcheck yelled.

"The cavalry, Parcheck. Greetings for your friends up on the side of the hill. How many you have up there, three or four? I hear the rest of the Knobbers rode out of town last night."

The rounds stopped coming at the men below. The battle raged above now, as the Knobbers fought with someone higher on the hills. A scream echoed down the canyon.

A dozen more shots, then the sound of one horse charging away. Before any of them below could move, six more shots jolted into the rocks, with the hot lead bouncing off the boulders every which way.

A scream from one of the prisoners, and then all was quiet.

"McCoy!" a voice called from above.

"All right down here," he yelled back.

"We nailed two of the bastards, one took off, but he's heading south. Good chance we'll never see him again."

"Good work. Take the bodies back into town. We'll be along directly."

Spur stood and looked around. Two of the prisoners were flat on the ground rolled into small balls. Parcheck lay sprawled behind a small boulder that wasn't big enough to protect him.

"Parcheck, you all right?" Spur called. The Secret Agent walked over and nudged the ex-sheriff. When Spur rolled him over he saw where two slugs had cut into Parcheck's chest. He was dead.

One of the prisoners caught a ricochetting round and had a small gash on his upper leg.

Spur took the handcuffs off both men.

"Now take off your shirt and tie up that leg wound," Spur told the man.

"Just get me back to town, Doc Gibson can fix it," the man snarled.

"You aren't going back to town," Spur told the man. He ordered both of them to strip naked, boots, everything. Zilke picked up the clothes, tied them in a bundle and tied the boots together, then lashed them to the saddle of one of the horses.

When the man's thigh wound was wrapped, Spur pointed to the south.

"That way, Bald Knobbers. It's less than forty miles to the first town. When you get there you can worry about what to do about clothes." He tossed them a four inch knife with a folding blade.

"You should be able to live off the land for a few days. Have a nice walk."

"You can't do this!" the unwounded man roared.

"Can't?" Spur said moving toward him. "Maybe you'd like one of your heel tendons cut so you can't walk right. You want that?" The man moved away shaking his head.

Spur motioned with his pistol and made the men walk past Parcheck.

"Consider yourselves lucky. You could have caught a slug like Parcheck did. You suppose those Bald Knobbers up there shot him on purpose?"

Spur yelled at the two prisoners and they hurried up the trail, picking their way carefully on tender feet.

Together Spur and Zilke loaded the ex-sheriff on his horse, belly down, and tied his hands and feet together under the nag's belly. Then they mounted up and sent two rifle shots at the naked Knobbers who worked up the canyon toward the pass at the top. They would be able to see into Arkansas from there.

"That pair will never set foot in Missouri again, I'd wager a year's pay," Zilke said.

"Let's hope so," Spur said and led the string of horses with one dead man back toward town.

The three dead Bald Knobbers were laid out in a row outside the sheriff's office. Kin was invited to claim the bodies. Nobody did. The new sheriff called some of the onlookers together and told them about the attack in the mountains.

"Parcheck got killed, the other two prisoners escaped, and two of the attacking force were killed. That accounts for at least fourteen of the hard core of the Bald Knobbers who controlled this county for so long. From now on, justice and law is going to prevail in this county. Anybody has any problems with that way of life, this is an invite to mount up and ride out."

The sheriff turned his back on the crowd and walked into the office to clapping and shouts of approval.

Spur McCoy bought Doc Gibson a noontime meal at the hotel dining room. They had steak and all the trimmings.

"It's a start toward honest self rule," Spur said.

"Damn well about time," Doc said. "We've got notices up for the election. Dug up the laws on it, and who we need to elect. I'll be going to Springfield next week for some advice from the county people there."

Spur cut off a slab of the medium rare steak and worked on it for a minute. "Good steak," he said. He gave Doc Gibson a scrap of paper with his St. Louis office address. "You have any problems, you write me a letter at this office. Word will get to me wherever I am."

"Don't expect any more trouble," Doc said. "But we'll have to see." He paused for a while. "I got one worry, that's Stone county next door. They have a bunch of Bald Knobbers over there, too. Don't know how much they talked to this batch."

"Stand tough, Doc," Spur said. "Stand tough."

After his dinner, Spur stopped by at the Branson general store for some supplies for the trail, then rode toward the cave. As he had done every other time, he watched his back trail, did a quarter mile backtrack, and made sure nobody followed him. He wanted no surprises between now and tomorrow morning.

17

When Spur rode into the small clearing near the hidden mouth of the cave, he found Edith sitting in the sun on one of her blankets. She had washed her hair and let it dry in the sun and had combed it out into a black halo.

Spur swung down, unsaddled his horse and set it to grazing on a long tether and put the sack of provisions by the tree. Neither of them had spoken.

He sat down beside her. She made room so he could sit on the blanket close to her.

"Tell me what happened," she said.

He told her, quickly, in detail. "As far as I can tell that band of Bald Knobbers is finished. Fourteen of the twenty core members are dead. As far as we know the rest of them have left town quickly for other parts."

"All of this and you never violated your oath as a lawman, I'm proud of you."

"It worked out. Someday there may come a time when it won't."

"What will you do then?"

"Depends. I'll weigh the benefits against the

personal loss, and if the benefits are great enough to enough people, I'll probably do it."

"Honest, you're so damn honest. I've never known anyone like you before."

"Why aren't you married? You're beautiful, smart, educated, have a good job. Why hasn't some smart man married you?"

"One did. He was killed by a white man in a fight three weeks after we were married."

"Oh, God, no!"

"Yes. It's one of the backlashes from the war. I was waiting for my husband to come, and . . . and this man walked up to me and backed me against a wall. Then he began touching my breasts."

"The bastard!"

"Will came up and saw him and I pushed the man away, but Will wouldn't let it be. He yelled at the man, and ran at him and hit him in the face. The man was a Southerner and before Will could move, the white man drove a knife into my Will and he died in my arms."

"The bastard! How long ago?"

"Two years." She took a long breath and brushed her hand across her eyes. "I kept Will's name." She looked up at Spur. "You remind me a lot of him. About the same size. Strong. A square cut face, and you get things done. Will wanted to be a policeman. He was going to school." She stopped and looked away.

Slowly she moved until she leaned against Spur. She caught his hands and put his arms around her.

"Just hold me tight a minute, it helps."

They sat that way a while, then she moved and he let go of her and she edged away.

"We're heading out in the morning?"

"Yes. Early start and we'll be in Springfield the second day sometime."

"Good. I've had about enough camping out." She stood and stretched, caught his hand and pulled him up. "Help me get us some supper. We can heat up some beans. Did you bring anything from town to eat?"

She looked in the sack and yelped in surprise. There was bacon, eggs, canned peaches, a sack of fresh cherries and two big apples.

"We'll have a feast!" She frowned. "I wonder if that woman and her two children ever made it to Springfield?"

Spur told her about the three bodies that were brought into town.

"Mrs. Newcomb could have killed them. She must have been angry and frightened enough. It doesn't take a good shot to use a shotgun effectively."

"I hope she did, and I hope that she is safe."

"We'll ask when we get there."

An hour later they relaxed after a full supper. Spur cleaned up everything, built up the fire and brought in the blankets from outside where she had aired them.

She spread them out near the fire and sat down. Edith patted the spot beside her and Spur sat there. She reached over and held his face and kissed his lips gently.

"Spur, I've never slept with many men. But I do want to make love with you. It seems so right, so natural. It . . . it's not just gratitude for your saving me twice from that mob. I want to be sure you understand that."

"Yes, Edith, I understand." He reached over and kissed her lips. She responded for a moment, then pushed him back.

"I want to say this. I'm serious. I teach children. I know I have to be a little stronger, a little cleaner, a little better dressed and more careful than other people. These students look up to their teachers. We're models for them.

"So, in Philadelphia I am pure and pristine. But right now I feel like I want you a dozen times. Does that makes sense? I want you on me and in me and loving me every way possible. Even though I know when we get to Springfield I won't even get to ride on the same passenger car as you do. I'll be on the one marked 'Colored Only.' But I don't care. Why is this, Spur McCoy?"

"I don't know, Edith. It has something to do with the perpetuation of the species, I'm sure. But it also has a lot to do with how two people feel about each other. There has to be respect and honesty, and love, even if for just the moment, there always has to be love."

She kissed him and pushed him down gently on the blanket.

"Spur, take off my blouse, please."

He did. She wore nothing under it. Her hanging breasts dangled toward him and he caught one in each hand.

"So good! That feels so good!" She nestled on top of him then, crushing her breasts against his chest, her lips reaching for his.

A minute later she sat up.

"I want to undress you. To do it slowly, to tease you. Can I do that?"

He bent and kissed her breasts and smiled. "Of course, Edith. You can do anything you want to, here with me and back in Philadelphia. Remember that."

She undressed him with loving gentleness.

When they were both naked, she lay across him and stared at the contrasting skin in the firelight.

"Look! So dark, so black, and so white, pink, tanned brown, really. Such a difference!"

"Not so much difference. We both have two legs, two arms, two eyes, one heart, one mind. If we are hurt we cry, if we cut our skin, we bleed. We live, we die. Not so much difference."

"The Knobbers thought so. To them I was an animal."

"The Knobbers were criminals, they were Southern criminals."

She kissed him and smiled. "You're right, not so much difference." She pulled him over on top of her.

"Soft, and easy and slow. Can you make it last a long, long time, Spur not-much-difference McCoy?"

"An hour?"

"I'd die!" she said giggling like a school girl.

She parted her legs and lifted her knees. Spur kissed her and probed gently, found the opening and worked in slowly. At last they were locked together.

"Oh, yes!" She kissed his nose. "Don't move for a minute, or two." She sighed. "Heaven. Now I'll know what to expect when I get there." She moved gently under him, then kissed his chest.

"Tell me about Spur McCoy. We have a whole hour." She gripped him with her internal muscles and Spur yelped. "Just want to be sure you don't go to sleep on me."

He told her about his youth, his life, his fighting in the war.

"Did you kill men, in the war?"

"Yes, from far away with a rifle, in one hand to hand battle with a rebel major when we overran their position. I had to use a knife before he could bring up his pistol."

She shuddered.

He moved gently inside her and she smiled, the terror forgotten.

"Do that again," she said, kissing him hard. Then she climaxed gently and opened her eyes watching him. "I don't want to get you over excited. One time for you, six or seven for me." She kissed him again. "This night, this whole trip, is going to be something I'll remember for the rest of my life."

"Tell me about Edith Washington."

"Not much to tell. I was born in Philadelphia, went to school there, went to two years of special Normal School to get my teaching credentials. Now I teach."

"Brothers, sisters?"

"Two of each." She was silent a minute. "Spur, I'm being unfair. I'm using you shamelessly. I didn't even ask."

"What do you mean?"

"After, after what those men did to me in the street . . . I needed another experience, something to take the bitter taste from my mouth. I might have hated all men forever after that. It was so . . . so brutal . . . like I was a dog in heat. So . . . so . . ." He touched her lips.

"I understand. I'm glad to be able to help. I'm ashamed of those men."

She began moving her hips under him. She grinned at him.

"Good. Now, Spur, let's see how fast you can get where you're going. You've held back long enough." She pushed upward with her hips, lifting him a foot off the ground, then dropped down and he laughed and felt her muscles gripping him and releasing, and within a minute he was counting the stars as he sailed past them on his way to the moon.

They lay locked together for a long time. Then they got up and built the fire, found the cinnamon rolls Spur had hidden from her and ate and drank cold water from the stream.

They made love again, and ate again, and then lost track of the time and the night and when they woke the next time, a sliver of sunshine streamed in the top of the cave.

Gently he kissed her good morning, then they got up and had coffee and packed for the trail.

Outside, Edith stood in her borrowed clothes and looked around.

"I really hate to leave," she said. "So much has happened to me here. I'll never, never forget Branson, Missouri." She looked up at Spur. "And even if I have a dozen reincarnations, I'll never in a million years forget last night."

"You might," Spur said.

"How could I? It was romantic, and honest, and I think I learned something about human nature. How could I ever forget that?"

"About ten miles down is a good sized stream. By the time we get there it will be getting hot and we could decide to take a swim and then warm up on the grass and we might even feel like getting romantic again. Have you ever made love in the water?"

Edith looked at him a minute in surprise, then they both burst out laughing, mounted up and rode down the trail toward Springfield.

[AUTHOR'S NOTE: The historic town of Branson, Missouri exists today. Stone County and Taney County are still there. Both counties were literally independent kingdoms following the Civil War. For twenty years after the war clenched fists and six-guns were the only law there.

The Bald Knobbers controlled Taney and Stone Counties as tightly as the Mafia ran Chicago in the 1920's.

Extortion was their main purpose. If you didn't pay the price, you might be visited on late night raids by horsemen. Beatings and hangings were common. The only law was the law of the Bald Knobbers.

These vigilante groups gone bad were not routed out of power until a pitched battle took place with the Missouri militia which was called out in the late 1880's to settle things once and for all.

Dr. Gibson's new honest government lasted in Branson for almost five years, then the Bald Knobbers from neighboring Stone county moved in and took over until the militia arrived.]

HELENA HELLION

1

The man on the road looked barely able to ride. The horse was in little better shape. Both were haggard, underfed, bone weary. The man's hair was shaggy, matted, his beard unkempt and the body odor of a dozen weeks without a bath was now overpowering. His eyes were a shade of light brown and red lines mapped most of the whites.

He lifted his head and stared down a quarter of a mile lane at the small ranch spread ahead of him. It was typical for Western Kansas. A small frame house, a larger barn and two corrals made of poles and inch-thick planks. A sixty foot Kenwood steel tower held a windmill spinning lazily in the afternoon breeze. The wind always blows in Kansas, the wanderer remembered.

He kicked the roan into motion and she walked reluctantly down the lane, then smelled water, perked up her ears, and moved faster toward the small frame house with smoke coming from the chimney.

Someone was home.

There was no blanket roll tied on the rider's saddle, no sack of provisions or clothing. The man wore a castoff homespun shirt that had all but two buttons missing. His hat had been found left in the street after a drunken brawl, and his pants had been stolen from a clothes line in Nebraska. He had put them on wet and let them dry as he wore them.

He slowed the horse. Maybe this wasn't the place.

The rider stopped the thin roan and looked around again.

Same house, same barn he had built with his two hands and strong back. New windmill, not even seven years ago could he afford a fancy four-post, angle steel tower like that. But it was over the same well he had dug a bucket full of dirt at a time. Thirty feet he had to go down.

The thin wanderer stared at the place again, then nudged the tired horse forward.

Home.

Damn! Home after such a long time.

The roan caught the scent of water in the horse trough. Yes, it was in the same place, but now it had a pipe to send the water from the pump on the windmill directly to the hundred gallon galvanized watering tank. He remembered paying almost four dollars for it back in . . . when? Must have been 1863 just before he went off to war.

He blinked to clear the moisture from his eyes.

Home!

He rode to the side door of the house and started to slide off the horse.

"Far enough mister, stay astride!" The voice came from the door and through a sliver of an opening a rifle barrel extended.

"Easy, just want to talk," the rider said.

"Talk. Who the hell are you?"

"Name is Will Walton, and this is . . . this is my ranch!"

There was a moment's silence, then the rifle lifted and the door opened. A rawboned, rail-thin man stepped out, the rifle's muzzle still centered on Will's chest.

"You a mite mixed up, stranger. This is the Bar S ranch. Sure you got the right place?"

"Damn sure. I built this house, that barn, bought the damn horse trough. Lived here until sixty-three . . ."

The man at the door lowered the rifle.

"Possible. I bought the place in sixty-six, nigh onto four years ago now. My name is Hirum Smith."

Will nodded. "Pleased to meet you . . . but this is still my ranch. Homesteaded back in . . . must have been February, sixty-three."

"Fraid not, Walton. I bought it fair and legal off this widow lady. Said she wanted to move on West. She had a hired hand named Hans, a big German guy. He went with her."

"Widow . . . don't understand. She warn't no widow."

"Said she was. Anyways I got the sale all legal, bill of sale, grant deed, whole thing recorded down at the county court house." Smith looked at him closer. "You feeling all right, mister? Look a mite peaked."

Will Walton sagged even more on his saddle. His hands shook for a minute. "You say she claimed she was a widow?"

"Yep."

"That was . . . you say four years ago . . . don't understand. Just don't . . ." Will looked up quickly. "Lying, got to be lying! You holding my woman prisoner inside? That it?"

"Easy, take it easy. I'm a bachelor. Aim to get married first of next year. Nobody's inside. Bought this place fair and square."

Will shook his head, then shivered. It couldn't have been four years! The war is just over, not a month ago. Got mustered out and headed home. Yes, he got held up a time or two. It was all so mixed up.

He scowled, looked back at Smith. "What year did you say it was when you bought my ranch?"

"Back in sixty-six."

"And that was how long ago?" Will asked.

"Christ! Don't you even know what year it is? This is eighteen and seventy. Whole new decade and U.S. Grant is our president. A Republican, by God!"

Will shook his head. "Can't be five years since the war was over. Ain't taken me five years to ride home. What's going on? Am I crazy or something?"

"Easy there. You were a soldier. War did funny things to some men. I was there, too. Got wounded and discharged early on. Say, you want to lite a spell and have something to eat? Look like you could use it. Come in and I'll tell you all I know about the folks who lived here. Woman said she was a war widow, lost her husband at the Wilderness she said. She had a boy, said his father never saw the lad. He was two or three at the time, I guess."

"A boy? She had a boy? This woman who was short and fat and had long yellow hair?" It hit him as nothing had since the war. A new wave of joy and wonder swept over him. He had sired a son!

Will sat there shaking his head. "Five years. You say I been wandering around for five years? Ain't possible. Just can't be!" He slid from his horse, staggered and Smith caught him by one shoulder.

"Yeah, come in and I'll heat up some of the stew I

made. Damn good stew. Sure looking forward to a woman's cooking again, but this ain't half bad. Sit and rest and I'll tell you everything I remember about the woman and her son.

"This Martha was a short woman, little on the plump side, with long wheat straw color hair."

Two hours later former Lt. William Walton of the Ohio 25th Infantry Regiment, thanked the rancher for the meal and information. They had watered his horse and given her a muzzle bag filled with oats.

Then he rode into town. Plainview wasn't much of a settlement. Two hundred people called it home and even that number was going down. Seemed like everything clustered around the railroad, and the new magic tracks were far to the south of Plainview.

Will stood on the boardwalk in front of the general store. He saw two men he knew, but they walked by without a second glance at him. The third man looked again and held out his hand.

"Will! Damn good to see you. Haven't seen you for years. Damn good to talk again. You are looking a mite sickly, Will. Better take care of your health. Sorry I have an appointment at the bank about a loan." The man in the black suit and fancy vest hurried down the street.

"I'm glad to be back," Will said after him, but the man kept walking. In the Cattleman's Saloon he found a familiar face behind the bar.

"Jesus, Mary and Joseph, look who done come back from the dead! Will Walton!" Charley held out a meaty hand. "Damn, they all said you was dead. Wilderness got you I heard. Pretty little wife of yours sold the ranch and moved some damn place."

"I'm finding out," Will said. "Look, I ain't got a penny on me . . ."

"Beer's on the damn bar," Charley said. He was a

grossly fat man, short, naturally stout and when fueled with beer he ballooned. He drew the brew and pushed it before Will.

The ex-army officer had to blink back tears so they wouldn't show. A real man didn't cry, leastwise not in public. He sipped the beer.

"Christ, Will. Guess you're trying to find your woman. Didn't hear where she was heading. West though, as I remember. She took along that foreman she had. Hans somebody. Damn big German who could drink twenty beers and walk a straight line. Never seen a beer drinker like him. Never got filled up. Every twenty minutes by the clock he used the privy out back. That son of a bitch could drink beer all night!"

"Out West? Martha moved out West. Damn big place, Charley."

"Best I can do. Heard they was heading west."

Will spent a half hour with the beer, nursing it, reveling in a luxury he hadn't had in months. It was all he could do to get odd jobs to find enough to eat. He rode the grub line whenever he could, moving from ranch to ranch asking for work.

It was the Code of the West. A hungry man was never turned away from a ranch cook house. Ranch owners and hands knew that someday they could be in the same fix, and so they fed the grub line riders and wished them well.

An hour before dark, Will thanked Charley for his kindness and rode out of town. He stopped in a clump of trees next to a small stream and made a fire to stay warm as night descended. He was just ready to curl up with his head against his saddle as a pillow, when he thought about the war. Had it really been five years since the war was over? Where had the time gone? What had he been doing all those years? Why couldn't he remember? His hand rubbed the scar on the back of his head.

He knew he joined the army in sixty-three. Then he fought and bled and recuperated and fought again. He got out in sixty-five, he was sure of that. The smoke drifted into his eyes, and for a moment he thought of the Wilderness.

Lt. Will Walton lifted his pistol when he heard cannon fire and he went flat on the ground, his eyes staring into the brush, the thickets. There were Rebels out there! He knew there were. What did the generals know?

His commander, Colonel Richardson, said he had scouting reports of masses of troops less than a half mile from the XI Corps' front lines. Not even Brigadier General Nathanial McLean thought there could be any kind of a flanking attack without some of his own scouts reporting Rebel movement.

Lt. Will Walton lay beside his men on the picket line. They could see no more than ten yards ahead in most places because of the thick brush, thorn bushes, vines and saplings.

Will knew the Confederate skirmishers were getting closer. He could *hear the bastards moving!* His men reported shots, quite a few, but the woods so hushed the sounds that it was almost impossible to tell from what direction the sound came. Will was positive that none of the generals or their colonels could hear the shots or they would be moving troops to meet the advance.

Lt. Walton talked quietly to his men.

"Hold steady. The colonel himself told me that no sane man would try a mass attack through that wilderness of brush out there. Those thorn bushes would cut up a division."

A twenty round barrage of fire sounded almost directly in front of them and Lt. Walton saw one of his men go down.

"Keep low and hold your fire!" Lt. Walton bellowed.

"The colonel told us nobody is out there," a Yankee private whispered.

"Hell, the same colonel told us nobody could attack through the brush and brambles either," a sergeant snarled. "But the damn Rebels are coming!"

A wild falsetto Rebel yell shattered the silence, then a sound the men hated crashed in on them, the ominous roll of hundreds of weapons firing as the infantry charged forward.

Lt. Walton scanned the brush. No figures yet. Ten yards! Rifle bullets sang through the air around them. He dug lower into the mulch of the woodsy floor.

"Fire when you see them!" Lt. Walton cried at his men of the Third Company.

Six rifles went off at once. The nervous soldiers hastily reloaded.

Six Rebel grey uniforms jolted through the brush directly ahead of them. Rifles cracked and roared. The six men were replaced by twenty more then those by twenty more and soon a solid wall of Rebels stormed over the brush and the bodies of their own men, trampling everything into the ground, sweeping over the hastily set up Yankee picket line.

"Back!" Lt. Walton shouted. Only four men from his forty staggered to the rear, firing at the surging gray uniforms behind them. A round caught Lt. Walton in the thigh. He plunged on. He saw two of his men explode as an artillery shell hit to his left. Only a spray of red mist was left of the men as he stormed ahead.

Everywhere he saw running Yanks, some trying to fire behind them, some trapped when they had built fortifications facing the wrong way. The enemy had swept both flanks and got behind the main force.

He heard that Von Gilsa's skirmish line of two German regiments was swept away by a screaming, bellowing mass of Rebels who charged forward like wild men, smothering all resistance in front of them.

Word spread among the survivors that Colonel Lee and Colonel Reily's regiments were soon battered and routed. Within minutes General Charles Devens' whole division had collapsed and men were streaming to the rear, making no pretense of fighting.

Will swung around and stared down the long road. It was a floor of blue uniforms. Behind him he saw that the two "knuckle" guns which had been positioned to protect his flank, had been swung around by Rebels and they were firing them down the road with grape and canister and anything they could ram down the barrel. It was a slaughter.

He heard the cannon go off and dove into the ditch just as a six-inch length of railroad tie slammed into a corporal's chest three feet to his left, tearing the torso in half, and dumping him against a tree where he hung as if nailed there.

Will plowed into the brush twenty feet, then ran north following the edge of the roadway, away from the death, away from the blood. His leg burned like fire where the rifle ball had penetrated. He limped and then staggered. He found a branch to use as a crutch.

Behind him the Rebel tide rolled forward. On the road he had heard a captain say that Stonewall

Jackson had hit the soft spot in the Yankee lines with twenty-eight thousand men, and nothing could stop them.

At last Will fell behind a tree. He could run no farther. Struggling over pain and horror he had moved back far enough so he was out of the heavy fighting. Either that or the Rebs had all surged around him. He was near the Chancellorville house somewhere but off the road still hidden in the brush. He wrapped up his bleeding leg the best he could. There was no chance to get medical attention. Whole regiments had been wiped out, companies ground under the surge of the Rebels. Everything was massive confusion since the back areas had become the fighting zones.

Most commands were disorganized, frantic and confused. Rebel troops had overrun and bypassed thousands of Yankees. He still had a pistol on his hip. He drew it now and huddled against the felled tree.

A dozen men passed by five yards from him but in the half light of dusk they could not see him. He didn't know if they were friends or foe. He waited another hour, tried to determine which way to the river, but could not.

Someone staggered toward him, turned and fell almost at his feet. It was totally dark now, the brush cutting out most of the faint moonlight.

Will stared at the man for several minutes. He did not move. Slowly Will crawled up to him. In a splash of light through the heavy brush he made out the gray tunic. The man was a Rebel!

Will pulled his four-inch knife he had brought from Kansas and lifted it to strike, when the Rebel mumbled something.

Will pulled back his hand. The Rebel's eyes

flickered open.

"Water!" the man whispered.

Will found his canteen still on his belt. He tipped it and gave the enemy a drink. Now he could make out his face better. He was maybe twenty-one or two. His uniform was torn, a bloody slash across one arm and his chest was a mass of blood.

Will stared at him. The eyes watched him with fear.

"Yank?"

"Yes."

"Looks like we're both shot up."

"Yes. How can you even talk?"

"Most can't. I'm . . ."

He coughed, spitting up blood.

Will raised his hand. "Don't talk, and I don't want to know who you are, or where you're from."

The Rebel watched him. He had no weapons showing. The man's eyes mirrored pain and he closed them a moment. Then they jolted open, the fear plain.

"You'll aiming to kill me?"

"Seems to be the general idea. Your boys killed all of my company."

"That's what they tell us to do."

A moment later the air buzzed with rifle rounds as two forces began firing at each other. Both men pressed into the ground. Will pulled his pistol, but he saw no soldiers from either side.

The shooting and shouting soon died out.

"Get on with it you gonna kill me. I ain't got . . . but a few hours anyway. Coughing blood . . . always good as dead. Seen two buddies die that way. Use . . . the knife, quieter."

"I'm not going to kill you, soldier."

'Your job. You being an . . . officer and all."

"Forget it. You know where your lines are?"

"Ain't no lines. Advanced so fast, lost contact with both sides. Don't know where . . . the hell we are." He wheezed and spit up blood again. But went on. "Then I got hit bad, some canister . . ."

"Reb, I've got to move. Back north to the river. Your people will find you in the morning."

"Not a chance. Be stiff dead then." Tears seeped down his cheeks. "Don't matter. Hurt most gone . . . that's bad sign. Watched too many wounded die. Hell, don't matter. I never 'mounted to much nohow. You best get. Us Rebs own this hill . . . and woods. Stay off the road. Damn death trap." He coughed again.

"Oh, Jesus!" the man whispered, then spewed blood from his mouth in a thick red torrent. He looked at Will once more, then sighed and his eyes closed in pain, then drifted open but he saw only eternity.

Will slid away from him, and stood. He used the cane and hobbled north, he hoped it was north. Then the bullets began to fly again and he dropped to the ground. It was cold.

The cold of the ground penetrated his hands and chest. Will shook his head. Where was he? Not at the Wilderness, damn sure. He held a saddle, smelled a fire. Damn, he'd done it again! The war was over. He was in Kansas in his camp, just outside of Plainview, and somebody *was shooting* at him.

"Don't reach for that six-gun or you're deader than a headless rattler!" a man growled.

Will looked up slowly. The man in the faint firelight was grubby, hair matted, teeth black and gone, beard as scruffy and ragged as Will's. But he held the gun.

Another man strode in, kicked away Will's Colt and picked it up.

"Nice piece," he said softly and pushed it in his belt. Then he reached down and backhanded Will in the face.

"Stand up and take off your clothes 'till you're mother naked."

Will hesitated. The man kicked him in the side. Will tumbled to the ground from his half kneeling position, then stood quickly.

"Strip, asshole!" the first man said and fired into the ground between Will's boots. Will pulled off his tattered homespun shirt, then wiggled out of the pants and tossed them to one side.

"Time enough?" the younger one asked.

"Hell no, he's too old. Wait for a young one."

The older robber watched Will carefully. "Now your boots and socks. Rush it!" Will pulled off his boots standing up. They were too big and fit him loosely. He shivered in the chill.

"Flat on your belly, arms over your head," the younger one ordered Will. He stretched out. For a moment he could see neither man, then they laughed. One whistled and horses trotted up.

A moment later they had mounted and both guffawed again, then wheeled and rode off, shooting twice into the air.

Will sat up cautiously. They were gone. So were all of his clothes, his meager sack of food, his saddle and his horse. He was alone and naked and didn't own a penny's worth of anything, not even a homespun shirt! But for once he was absolutely sure where he was and what he was going to do.

He had to find his family! Naked or not, he had to find where Martha had gone and where she had taken his son. Because now for the first time he knew he had a son. An heir! Every man wants a son. He had a reason to get a new ranch and build it up, he had a son!

The headache came and without thought he touched the scar deep in his hair where the rifle bullet had slashed through the back of his head. It had been deep enough to cause him severe problems and pain, but not deep enough to kill him. How often he wished that the lead had killed him in the Wilderness.

Will Walton sat on the cold ground and looked at the few yellow lights in Plainview. He had to find his family, he had to find his son! Now he had a great reason. He rubbed his head without thinking and the unseen harpies flew around him bringing a headache that almost made him scream.

Instead he smiled. He had to find his son!

2

Spur McCoy sat in the stagecoach and bounced along over the rutted trail as the Concord coach did its best to absorb as much of the shock as possible. The Concord was the best stage coach made, the standby of the Wells Fargo Overland Stage routes.

Now Spur was luxuriating in the space. On three upholstered benches inside the coach as many as nine passengers were often seated. The center bench was always the hardest to ride, and the last occupied, since there was no back rest to lean on.

But now there were only three passengers on the stage, all headed to Helena, Territory of Montana and the end of the line. There was no easy riding railroad up this high in the United States.

Two lines were starting to work to put in northern rail service, but nothing was past the talking stages yet. Spur rode the trains as often as possible now in his job as a United States Secret Service man. But he marveled at the quality of this land schooner he rode.

In these days when a cowboy made $25 a month

and found, the Concord coaches cost as much as $1,500, and were all built in Concord, New Hampshire at the Abbot-Downing factory.

Their best features were the thoroughbraces, a pair of wide suspension straps an inch thick that served to absorb many of the jolting shocks of the road. This often created a rocking motion that some people objected to, but Spur said it lulled him to sleep like a good rocking chair.

Depending on the territory, four to six horses pulled the rig, commanded by the driver who sat up front on the box. Below him was the leather enclosure known as the front boot where mail, express, and valuables were kept during transit. Luggage was packed on top or in the rear boot, which was larger than the front one.

Spur shifted his weight and looked out the window. He knew it took six horses on this part of the run to pull the Concord up to Helena, which sat at more than four thousand feet above sea level, and not far from the famous Rocky Mountains. He had never been to Helena before, and he might not come back until they had a respectable railroad.

They had left the gamma grass and bunch grass behind on the edge of the Great Plains, and wound through foothills and small mountains as they worked higher into the center of Montana.

There was game enough to satisfy any sportsman. From the rocking coach that day Spur had seen two kinds of deer, a bouncing antelope herd of ten, as well as puma or mountain lion, which quickly moved into cover. There were black bear, moose, grizzly bear and wolves in the higher reaches of the mountains as well.

The forests were magnificent with Douglas fir, ponderosa pine and western larch mixed with lodgepole pine and Engelmann spruce.

But right then Spur was more interested in getting to Helena, settling a small problem and getting back to a real law problem. He snorted as he thought of his assignment:

"PROCEED TO HELENA, MONTANA TERRITORY. MEET WITH LIBBY ADAMS WHO HAS BEEN LIFE-THREATENED. PROTECT HER, BRING TO JUSTICE ANY LAWBREAKERS IN THIS MATTER, YOUR LENGTH OF STAY THERE AT HER DISCRETION. BY ORDER OF WILLIAM WOOD, DIRECTOR OF THE SECRET SERVICE. CONFIRM."

A second wire from General Halleck, the number two man in the agency and Spur's usual boss, explained matters a little more fully.

The woman in question, a rich widow, was stirring up a fuss about women's rights, and demanding the vote. She had the right to complain, but there was no chance she would succeed. She also was a personal friend of William Wood, and Spur WOULD WITHOUT FAIL allow her to campaign for women's suffrage, protecting her at all times until they both felt the danger to her life was over.

Spur sighed and looked out at the trail ahead. They were working downward, which meant they were coming off the mountains into Prickly Pear valley, where Helena was located. He looked out the window and ahead could see smoke drifting into the sky and the outline of buildings three miles away. They should arrive in time for him to take a bath before supper. It had been a long trip from the train at Rawlings, Wyoming.

When the stage pulled into Helena it was a festive occasion. The big red and gold coaches came only twice a week and brought mail, a little freight and mail order goods from the big catalogs.

A dozen dusty boys ran alongside the coach the last block to the Wells Fargo station. The driver heaved back on the reins and the sweating horses came to a stop as the shotgun guard above clamped down on the big rear wheel brakes.

Spur let the woman get out first, then the drummer who had his showcase of fine knives and cutlery with him in the coach. He would not trust it on top.

When Spur stepped into the inch-deep dust on Helena's Main Street, he avoided the horse droppings. The shotgun guard on top tossed him down his carpetbag. Spur caught it and headed for the boardwalk that fronted the row of shops and stores.

Helena was a big town for Montana, with more than 3,500 souls—half of them still looking for gold, the other half in lumbering or cattle or farming, and the rest trying to satisfy the retail needs of everyone.

A strange sound assailed Spur's ears. He looked down the street and saw an interesting sight. Wagons and horses cleared the wide dusty avenue to make way for a parade of sorts. Six or eight women all wearing pure white blouses with long sleeves and dark skirts marched up Main Street waving banners.

In front and beside them marched a ten piece German band with tubas and trumpets.

Spur got to the boardwalk and watched the marchers. The first sign he could read said: "The Vote For Women Now!" The next one read: "We Pay Taxes, Too!" then "Taxation Without Representation!" There were two of each kind of the neatly painted signs being carried by the women.

Men hooted at them from the boardwalks.

"Get home and get my supper ready!" one man shouted. Men laughed and clapped. Women on the sidewalk stared, laughed embarrassed, or turned away. A few shouted in favor and went and joined the parade.

"You get my pants sewed up yet, Katy?" a man called. One of the marchers turned, her face red.

"No Barney, I didn't. And you'll be sleeping in the stables for the next week!"

Then everyone hooted at Barney, who wasn't sure the whole thing was so much fun anymore.

Spur looked at the woman leading the pack. Tall, midnight black hair, a proud carriage and a slender, enticing body. She had to be Libby Adams.

Spur watched the lady, the way she walked, the way she bounced her sign up and down and stared hard at the men along the boardwalk. As she passed by him their eyes locked for a moment and then she moved on.

A drunk staggered off the board walk, tripped, rolled forward and then stumbled and crashed into Libby Adams. Spur jumped of the wooden walk and darted into the street. He picked up Libby Adams, nodded, then grabbed the drunk and dragged him twenty feet to the horse trough.

Spur upended the man, held him by the ankles and dunked him head first into the wooden horse drinking tank. The man sputtered pushed up with his hands, roaring in protest. Spur dunked him in again, then dropped him lengthwise in the water to the roar of approval of the marchers and audience alike.

The march, which had stopped when Libby went down, began again, the band playing, the women waving their banners. Libby looked at Spur and smiled, nodded, then marched forward waving her placard.

Spur stepped up on the boardwalk as a man came through the crowd and stared at Spur. The big man tensed, then saw the watcher smile. He came forward and held out his hand.

"You got to be Spur McCoy, right?"

Spur took the hand in a sold shake. "True, just got off the stage. I didn't get your name."

"Sheriff Josiah Palmer of Lewis and Clark County. We should have a talk. I got a letter that said you might be coming."

"Word travels fast. That lady in front of the line is Libby Adams?"

"Yep, just wish she'd stay in that big house of hers or in her bank. Getting tired of these parades."

"Legal though, right?"

"True, unless they get disruptive or violent, then I can refuse a parade permit. Oh, yes, we have laws here too, McCoy." He nodded to the left and both men turned that way.

A shot slammed through the sound of the oompha band and Spur spun looking back at the street. Libby cried out in pain and fell backwards into the other women who caught her. Blood smeared her left arm.

Spur and the sheriff ran into the street. Spur looked to the left where he thought the shot came from. An alley opened there and before anyone else could move, Spur charged through the crowd and down the alley. New brick buildings showed on both sides at Main Street. Then there was a void before he came to houses on the next block.

He saw no one. He stopped but there were no frantic hoof beats of an escaping bushwhacker. He saw something ahead, a nearly new red handkerchief tied into a neck band. Nothing else. He ran back through the alley, checking trash barrels and boxes, but no one hid in any of them.

The shooter either went into one of the side doors of the stores, into the houses or through the empty area between them. No chance to catch him now.

When Spur got back to the street, the sheriff led Libby along the boardwalk to a doctor's office.

Spur followed and took off his hat when he came to the door. McCoy was a big man at six-two and an even two hundred pounds. He was tanned and fit from spending more time outdoors than under a roof. His reddish brown hair was longish, fighting with his shirt collar, hiding part of his ears. On the sides he wore half mutton chops with the sideburns below his ears.

His upper lip sported a neatly trimmed half-inch wide moustache. Right now his hands were hard and rough from doing some rope work on a cattle spread. He was an excellent horseman, journeyman cowboy, crack shot with rifle and pistol and he practiced twenty rounds a day when he could get the time.

He pushed open the medic's door and stepped inside. There was no office as such, just a plain room with benches around three walls. Through an open door he saw Libby sitting in a chair. Spur moved to the door and looked in.

"Doctor Harriman, I'm not about to die," Libby Adams said. "Just bandage it up so I can get back with my ladies and finish the march."

"Afraid not, Mrs. Adams," Sheriff Palmer said. "I cancelled the rest of the march . . . violence. Part of the conditions you must remember."

"But . . ."

Spur moved so he could see the whole room. Libby

sat on a chair and Doctor Harriman looked at the wound on her bare upper left arm.

"Ouch! Oh, that hurts, Doc."

"Going to hurt a lot more if you don't hold still," Doc Harriman growled. "Got to be sure that the slug went right through."

"With two holes in her arm, it's a good possibility," Spur said. They all turned to look at him.

Sheriff Harriman spoke up quickly like the good politician he was.

"Libby Adams, like you to meet Spur McCoy. Your dang fooled notions is why he's here. This old sawbones is Doc Harriman."

Spur nodded at the woman. "Saw your parade."

"Should I know you?" she asked, her voice smooth, pleasant somehow amused.

"McCoy is the gent sent out by Washington to keep an eye on you, just like your little friend, Governor Benjamin F. Potts said they would," Sheriff Palmer said in a neutral voice.

"Thank you Josiah, I absolutely will not fight with you today. I got shot so I should be a heroine. I'd much rather talk to this nice Mr. McCoy who rescued me not once, but twice. Are you really from Washington D.C.?" she asked.

Spur grinned. "No Ma'am. I'm from St. Louis."

"Oh?" She was disappointed.

"But I work for William Wood, who I would guess is a good friend of Governor Potts. My official title is United States Secret Service Agent, and I'm at your service."

"Well, isn't that nice?" Libby smiled. Her soft brown eyes sparkled and her smile showed even, white teeth. She was a pretty woman, striking, self assured, and, he remembered, rich. She swirled her long hair around her shoulders and turned so she could stare at Spur as the doctor worked on her arm. Apparently she had forgotten about it.

Spur knew how painful an arm wound like that could be. He saw her wince only once as the doctor completed his probing of the wound, then began to treat and bandage the violations.

"You're much younger than the expert I expected, Mr. McCoy."

Spur laughed, watching her eyes. "Thank you. And you are much prettier than what I expected."

It was her turn to laugh. "Pretty is as pretty does," she said. She looked down at her arm. "Thanks, Doc. Sorry I was such a crybaby."

He reached up and kissed her cheek. "Libby, you took that better than nine out of ten cowpokes I patch up." He looked at the sheriff and Spur. "I'm over sixty, so I get to give all my pretty patients a kiss on the cheek. Part of my day, actually." Before he could move, Libby reached over and kissed his weathered cheek, then stood.

When she lifted her left arm, a small yelp of wonder seeped from her lips.

"Yep, gonna hurt a mite before it heals. Just no heavy lifting or pitching hay or digging graves. Outside that, Libby, you should be fine."

She smiled at him and stood in front of Spur.

"Mr. McCoy, I wouldn't mind at all if you wanted to treat me to some ice cream over at the Helena General Store. They just put in a new machine that makes it, but they can't keep it frozen very long in the ice box. I heard they made some this morning, game?"

"I haven't had any ice cream since I was last in Denver," Spur said holding out his arm to her good right hand. "I just hope they made strawberry."

She caught his elbow and they walked the two blocks along the boardwalk to the general store. There were half a dozen people around a small table at the back of the store where a clerk with a white apron was dishing out ice cream.

The people parted when Libby came up. The clerk looked at her and smiled.

"Not quite as firm as it was when you were here this morning Mrs. Adams. But I like it better softer."

"Two of your large sized dishes, Lester," she said. Spur fished in his pocket for change and came up with four quarters.

"Nickel a dish," Lester said setting the soup dishes filled with creamy vanilla on the counter. Spur gave him the quarter and carried both dishes to a free spot around the table.

"Seconds on ice cream today, Mrs. Adams?"

"My one vice," she said looking at him. She smiled mischievously. Her voice lowered. "No, that's just one of my vices."

As they ate the ice cream, Spur was surprised and pleased. She was not at all what he had expected.

"You're serious about getting the vote for women?"

"Of course. Women had the vote in New Jersey from 1790 to 1807. Then the men 're-interpreted' the state constitution. I bet you didn't know that the first national convention on women's suffrage was held in 1850 in Worcester, Massachusetts."

"Afraid I was too busy to attend that one," Spur said.

"Don't patronize me, Spur McCoy. I'm deadly serious."

"That's my job, keep you serious but not dead."

She licked off her spoon and stared at him. "I'm

not sure yet how to know what you mean when you talk that way. But I'll figure it out. I'm a fast learner. I bet you didn't know that right now, today, there is one territory where women have the vote. Do you know that?"

"Which one?"

"Wyoming, of course. They got the right to vote from the beginning. The very first legislature voted on December tenth last year to extend the right of the ballot to all women over twenty-one years of age in the state!"

"A person can learn something new every few days," Spur said.

"Now I understand. You *are laughing* at me." She stood. "I don't like people who laugh at me. I hope you don't continue this when you come to supper at my house tonight. We will serve promptly at eight. Come at seven. We will have a chance to do some planning about security, and what you think you can do to protect me. I'll see myself out and home, thank you."

Spur watched her leave, then finished his ice cream. It was delicious.

An hour later Spur had made all the needed arrangements and had a metal bathtub brought to his room along with the five pails of hot water. It was scald yourself first and freeze toward the end of the bath.

He had been on the road for a week getting to Helena. A week of sweating and grime and the second class accommodations at the few stage stopovers they had. Now he wanted a bath and some clean clothes before he crossed swords with Libby Adams again. He smiled as he stepped into his bath. That Libby Adams was one hell of a woman, and she knew it.

Spur could sit in the long, narrow tub and extend his legs, but not lie down. It was enough. He soaked, then scrubbed and soaked again. After three scrubbings he decided at least half of the grime was gone.

McCoy dressed in clean blue pants and matching dark jacket, then he pushed the tub and buckets into the hall and searched out a barber shop. He had a fresh shave and a haircut to bring his wild hair into more control and a moustache trim. Then he moved on to the best saloon in town and asked questions about Libby Adams.

The barkeep grinned.

"One hell of a woman, that one!" he said. "You see her this afternoon marching, shouting, and then when she got shot she never cried or wailed or even said it hurt! Make a damn good soldier that woman." The apron shrugged. "Course it don't hurt that she's the richest lady in town. Richer than any of the men as well. She owns the bank and about half the retail businesses.

"Hell, when the town burned down last year, she started putting up new stores before the damned ashes was cool!"

Spur took a pull on the lukewarm beer. "How did she get all of her money, property?"

"Married it. Some folks put her down for that, don't bother me. Hell, she did right by old Phil for as long as he lived." The bartender motioned Spur closer. "See, she was twenty-one or twenty-two, and old Phil was sixty-one when she married him. Didn't make no difference to either of them.

"She kept his books, and tended his house and helped him with business for five years. Then one night old Phil climbed on top of her and got too damned excited. Doc says the old boy went out with a hardon that wouldn't stop. He just plain fucked himself to death!''

"That the story?" Spur asked.

"Hell, no story, God's truth. Undertaker said the old boy was buried with a hardon. First time he'd ever seen it."

They both chuckled and Spur looked at the time. It was a quarter to seven. He asked the barkeep where her house was, gave him a fifty cent tip and walked up the street and down a block to the biggest, fanciest, most ostentatious mansion in Helena.

At eight o'clock in Helena that time of summer, it's still daylight. When Spur was still two blocks from the big house, he sensed someone behind him, and stepped quickly into an alley. A moment later two men ran down the street toward him. Both held pistols. Spur dropped back deeper into the alley and waited. The first came in fast and flattened against a brick wall behind a large trash barrel.

The second came forward as if to draw Spur's fire, then darted backward. He slid around the corner out of danger. A half a minute later the man at the mouth of the alley ran in and rolled toward the same protection where the first man had vanished.

Spur leaned out and blasted three rounds at the tumbling man. He was not sure if he hit him, but then he had another problem. Before he could move back to the protection of the large cardboard boxes, he saw an object hurled toward him. He had seen small hand bombs during the war.

This looked like a homemade variety. He guessed that two sticks of dynamite had been tied together. The fuse sputtered in the air and Spur figured it would fall near where he lay. He dove under a pair of two by twelve timbers that had been nailed together and leaned against the wooden wall of the store.

A second later the bomb went off with a cracking roar and hundreds of pieces of metal slammed into the boxes and the boards. Spur crawled out and waited, his six-gun ready. He heard cautious steps. One man looked around the cardboard box which Spur saw had been riddled as if by shrapnel. When the head peered over the protection, Spur shot him in the forehead, then jumped up.

The second man ran toward the alley. Spur leveled in and held the weapon with both hands and fired twice. Both slugs caught the man in the shoulders and slammed him to the ground.

Spur looked at the riddled boxes again, shook his head and ran forward to the downed man. He had lost his weapon. Spur rolled him over with one boot. He had never seen the man before.

"Who sent you to kill me?" Spur asked.

The man snorted.

Spur put his boot on the shot up shoulder and pressed down. A scream of pain slanted through the alley.

"Who?" Spur asked again.

"Just a man. Never knew who he was."

Spur kicked the shot shoulder, and the man screamed again.

"I can hold out much longer than you can," Spur spat. "I'd say you'll bleed to death in about fifteen minutes."

The man remained silent. Spur knelt before him and backhanded him across the mouth, then jolted the shoulder. For a moment the gunman almost passed out.

He looked at Spur with hatred. "True, never saw the man before. Said he was from out of town. Told me I could earn an easy fifty dollars. I got help.

Didn't know you was a one man army. How did you get away from that dynamite with roofing nails taped around it?''

"Easy," Spur snarled. "Now what was the man's name?"

"Might have been a fake name. Said he was from Virginia City if I was in that area. Said his name was Laidlaw."

Spur hoisted the man to his feet and marched him over to Doc Harriman's office. He told the doctor to patch him up and hold him for the sheriff. Charge: attempted murder.

"I'd wait for the sheriff, but I'm late for a dinner engagement with a beautiful black haired lady."

Doc Harriman chuckled. "Guess I can manage. Just wish I was going to dinner up there in your place."

Spur was twenty minutes late getting to dinner at Libby Adam's big mansion.

3

Spur McCoy started to lift the fancy knocker on the front door of the Adams mansion when the massive panel unlatched and swung inward. Before him stood Libby Adams.

There was only one word Spur thought of, so he said it softly, with surprise an awe.

"Dazzling!" She was. Libby had prepared, too. Her hair was swept up and piled on top of her head making her appear nearly six feet tall. The richly decorated dress she wore touched the floor but left uncovered both shoulders and plunged deeply between her breasts showing the sides of both firm mounds. The dress pinched in at the waist and curved out over good hips before falling to cover her shoes.

Her face was radiant, with only a little rouge and a touch of red on her lips. She smiled.

"Mr. McCoy, I presume?" She smiled. "Won't you come in? My, you look so much more handsome than you did this afternoon. A haircut and shave do help, don't they?"

Spur found his voice at last and stepped inside to a thick rug, and a beautifully decorated entranceway. Doors led off in three directions.

"Are you sure this is the same woman's rights marcher I saw shot and then dumped into the dust this afternoon in Main Street?"

She laughed and caught his hand. "The same. I enjoy dressing up when there's someone to dress up for. You are extremely naughty, you know, you're quite late."

"Sorry, I was held up."

She led him down a short hallway with a carpet runner on the floor and original oil paintings on the walls. At the second door she went into a large square room that held a six foot walnut table set up for a banquet for two.

"Before we talk business, we have supper; dinner, some people in New York call it. I hope that out here in the rough frontier we can be elegant enough for you."

"This will do nicely. I haven't seen anything this elaborate since a dinner reception for the Duke of York in the White House in Washington D.C. during the war."

"She smiled. "Thank you, I'm delighted that you're impressed." They sat down and then the food began to come. It was a seven course meal with appetizers, soup, salad, then an entree of fresh fish followed by steak and four kinds of vegetables, followed by three courses of deserts.

At last Spur pushed away from the table.

"I don't think I can even stand I ate so much," he said. "I had forgotten how much I had missed good food on the stage coming up here. Do you know it took me eight days to get here from the railroad?"

"Yes, I remember. Eight days of little sleep and

less food. I came in that way myself, about a
thousand years ago. Let's move into the drawing
room for some business."

When they were seated in strikingly upholstered
chairs looking through a window into a carefully
tended garden, Libby stared at him.

"Spur McCoy, I was shot today. Does that mean
someone is really trying to kill me, or only to scare
me?"

Spur stood and walked to the window, then came
back. "Either way, it's my job to stop them. I want
you to clear with me before you make any talks in
public or go on any more marches. That slug
through your arm could just have easily been
through your pretty little head. You take no more
chances until I find out who fired that shot."

"Yes, sir."

"That easy?"

"Who wants to get shot? I never argue with
experts. I make it a rule always to find the best
people in the field and follow their suggestions."

"That doesn't sound very liberated. What about
all of the woman suffrage work? What about
Elizabeth Cady Stanton and Susan B. Anthony?"

"Who are they?"

"Suffragettes in the east. Oh, I have another
name for you. On my way here two gentlemen
insisted that I do one thing, but I didn't want to."

"What was it they wanted you to do?"

"Die." He told her about the brief encounter with
death in the alley.

"So far one man has died in this little drama. I
don't want you to be the second corpse. The man
who lived agreed to my logic and told me who had
hired him. I wondered if you might know him. He's
from Virginia City, evidently."

"I do know some people there. What was his name?"

Spur watched her closely. "The man who was mentioned was someone with the last name of Laidlaw."

Her reaction was instant.

"Oh, damn! I never thought he would go this far." She stopped. "But the men who shot at you, may not have been the same ones who shot at me."

"True, I'll ask the gentleman about that first thing tomorrow. Now, what about Mr. Laidlaw? There must be more to this than a simple little campaign to get the vote for women in the Territory of Montana. Now is the time to tell me what this whole caper is really about."

"The vote for women," she said.

"Mrs. Adams . . ." he stopped when she held up her hand.

"Please, call me Libby. Everyone does. May I call you Spur?"

He nodded. "Now, Libby, start relying on your expert. Men in the street were hooting and laughing at your parade, at your try to get the vote. This is not an issue to call for assassination. Not even the governor would send a plea to Washington for that alone. What else is involved?"

"I'm not sure. The man in Virginia City is Rufus Laidlaw. He's the Secretary of State, a powerful office. Virginia City is our capital."

"I've never heard of Virginia City in Montana."

"That's part of the problem, no one has. The state capital should be here in Helena."

"So that's part of this mess. He wants to keep it there and you're working to bring the capital to Helena?"

"A lot of people are working toward that goal, but

they're not getting shot."

"With a move here, land values would skyrocket, right?" Spur demanded. "And businesses already here would grow tremendously. But land values in Virginia City would slump, and the town would end up as a ghost town."

"Yes. But that's not the point of the move. Helena is where the most people in the state live. It's a natural center for trade, transportation, business. The capital should be here."

"What's Laidlaw's stake in Virginia City?"

"He owns a lot of property there. I guess he's afraid he would lose most of his money." She looked up quickly. "But a move of the capital is more important to the state than any one man."

"Or woman, voting or not," Spur said.

"But the vote is still one of my main interests. I have a bill introduced into the legislature in Virginia City to give women over twenty-one the vote. It would change the state constitution to read any legal resident over the age of twenty-one shall have the vote regardless of race, creed or religion. It's been introduced and is now in committee. We hope to have it brought to a vote before the end of the session."

"But it probably doesn't have a chance to pass, right?"

"Probably. But many good ideas have had to be tried a dozen times before they become law. It's the way things work in politics."

"Still this is not a reason to kill you. I understand two railroads are starting to send survey teams out to pick a right of way across the northern states. Would that have anything to do with Helena?"

"We hope so, Spur. If we could get the Northern Pacific to bring their tracks through Helena, it would give our economy a boost just like trains have to other western cities."

Spur rubbed one big hand over his weathered face. "Yes, yes, the old railroad route fight. Now we're getting somewhere. I've seen a dozen small local wars fought over where the tracks should go. And sometimes the survey teams are prone to allow local causes and even bribes to alter their judgement."

"I've heard that, but Helena is the logical route for them, the best grade level. They probably will come west along the Yellowstone River to get the easy grade, then cut northwest through Montana heading for Seattle."

"Then it's the railroad route that this is all about?"

"Partly. If we can get the state capital here, the railroad would be a lot more willing to come this way. We would have everything to offer them. It would be good for the state, good for the railroad and good for Helena."

"And bad for Virginia City."

"True," Libby said. She divided her long hair over her shoulder in three strands and began braiding them, then unbraided them and combed them out.

"What else aren't you telling me, Libby?"

"In a day or two there will be a meeting here in town of the Montana State Legislature Capital Relocation Committee. They'll be looking over the area, checking out where the city says the new capital can be built, talking with residents, generally gathering information about whether or not to move the capital here."

"Which doesn't make Mr. Laidlaw happy. Will you be testifying before the committee?"

"Yes. It's probably one of the most important contributions I can make to Helena. If I live that long."

"You will." Spur watched her. She was beautiful, she was nervous, she was so lovely and vulnerable right then that he wanted to take her in his arms and hold her, tell her that he would let nobody hurt her. But she still held back. There was something she wasn't telling him.

"Libby, what's the other problem? Something else is coming along that you're not telling me about. Right?"

She looked up and her hand came up to her mouth in surprise. Her lovely brown eyes went wide in surprise, and then her face set grimly.

"Yes. I just got word this afternoon. A railway survey crew is working its way toward Helena. They should arrive in a day or two depending on their progress. We think it is significant that they are moving through here with one of their three or four proposed routes."

"Tomorrow or the next day. Them here as well as the relocation committee. Sounds like Mr. Laidlaw will be in town as well, in fact I'd bet he's already here."

"I could check with my hotels."

"You own all four?"

She nodded.

"No, I'll find out. One other problem. You're an important person in this town. You own a lot of property, businesses, control the lives of a lot of employees. Do you know of any of those people who might want to try to shoot you?"

She stared at Spur for a moment. Then slowly shook her head. "No, I don't know of any. I don't think there are any. You see, Spur I came from a poor family. I've lived all my life here in Helena. My father ran a small hardware store for Alexander Adams.

"A kinder, more generous, more gracious man never lived than my late husband. His first wife died in childbirth along with his son. He was a widower for years, then one day he took a fancy to me when I was eighteen. He courted me for a year, then married me, and we had seven beautiful years together.

"He taught me everything about business. I can never have children, Spur. We found that out after two years of trying." She laughed. "Lordy, did we try! Then he concentrated on teaching me how to run his business firms so I could carry on when he died. He was forty-one years older than I was, but it didn't matter to us, except this one way. He knew he would never have an heir.

"I've tried to run things the way he would have, or perhaps a little softer, a little easier. The bank has never foreclosed on a loan since I took over. Neither have we ever lost money on a loan.

"In six years I have never fired an employee. We have a way of taking care of our own. One man was a drunk. We talked to him and his family, and spelled out what they all had to do. We helped him, and now he's the manager of my bank. I try to be as fair as I can with all of my fellow workers."

"I've heard that," Spur said. "So we're making progress, ruling out suspects. What about the gold mines? You have two or three I understand."

"Gold isn't as important to this town as it was. We began in a gold rush, true. Four old prospectors were about on their last legs. They decided to make one more try, then give up and go back to honest work. They dug into this ravine with a trickle of

water down it. Those four men called it the Last
Chance Gulch. The gulch runs down what is now
Main Street here in Helena. They hit it big, worked
out the panning, found the mother lode and made
them all rich. Now we've taken out more than ten
million dollars worth of gold around here. The
experts say we have at least that much left, but the
real mining riches will be in other areas, copper,
silver, other minerals."

She stood and he enjoyed watching the way she
moved. "No, Spur, the gold mines are not a factor in
my wounding."

"Which brings us back to Laidlaw, the relocation
committee and the railway right of way."

"Yes. Spur, I want you to stay here in my house,
that will be added protection. We have plenty of
rooms, for goodness sakes. I'll send someone to get
your things out of your room. We'll leave it
registered in your name as a decoy. Might be a good
idea to register at the other three hotels as well."

Spur grinned. "Yes, be glad to stay here. I'm sure
your cook is better than they are at the hotel. You
sure you haven't done detective and law enforcement work before?"

"Just my business training."

Spur stood. "I'd like to make a tour of the saloons.
Find out what I can about what folks are saying, the
gossip, the speculation about who shot you. Bound
to be some talk. Some of it might be helpful. Also, I
want to try to find Mr. Laidlaw."

"Be careful of the man. He's a snake."

An hour later, Spur had sipped beers in four
saloons, and everywhere he found the same feeling
toward Libby Adams. No one had a bad word to say
about her. In two taverns they drank a toast to her
recovery. Spur had never found this sort of feeling

toward the town's rich person anywhere in the west.

A man at the bar next to him began talking about Libby. Spur had not brought up her name.

"Woman is a gem, she's about perfect. Know what she did for the Johnsons? The man of the family got himself killed in a mine shaft. Wasn't even her mine. She paid off the loan on the little house they built. Put the wife to work in one of her stores, and rounded up another widow lady to move in with the Johnsons and take care of the two young uns.

"Know this for damn sure, 'cause the Johnsons is my in-laws. She tries to help out. More than you can say for most rich folks. Don't remember anybody in town going hungry. Libby always sends somebody over with a sack of groceries, a hundred pounds of flour and a sack of spuds."

Spur bought the man a nickel beer and moved on. Libby Adams seemed to be the best liked person in town. He checked at the three other hotels, registered, and said he'd move in later that night. None of them had a Rufus Laidlaw registered.

When he got back to the Adams house, Spur let the solid brass knocker drop and almost at once the maid answered the door. She was about eighteen, barely five feet tall, and fair.

"Evening Mr. McCoy. Your things come and I put them upstairs in the big guest room. Mrs. Adams gone to bed and she said I should show you up to your room."

Spur followed her up the curving staircase to the second floor. The whole house was a showcase. He wondered how much Alexander Adams had spent on it.

The room was nearly twenty feet square, with a huge four poster bed with a canopy, two windows that looked out over the town, a sofa and chair, and a small table, as well as a dresser and writing desk. Over a hundred books showed their bindings in a wall-built bookcase.

"Mrs. Adams said I should lay out your things," the maid said. "My name is Charity."

"Thanks, Charity, but you don't need to bother."

She opened the carpetbag and looked up smiling. "It's really no trouble, and if Mrs. Adams said do it, I must." She put his clothes in the dresser and the carpetbag beside it.

He sat on the sofa chair and watched her. She was small, barely five feet tall, he guessed, but had a fully rounded figure. Her hair was blonde, cut short and he remembered her eyes were blue. She finished with the carpetbag and came and stood in front of him.

"Mr. McCoy, is there anything else I can do for you?"

"Thanks, Charity, you've done plenty."

"I could perhaps help in other ways." She knelt on the floor in front of him and slowly began to unbutton her blouse. Spur noticed that she wore little under it. He could see her nipples straining through the cloth.

"Charity . . . you don't need. . . ."

"I know." She looked up, and smiled. "I thought you might want some relaxation. I give good back-rubs!" Her blouse was open now and it was plain that she wore nothing under it. The sides swung back showing the edges of her breasts.

When Spur sat down his legs had spead and now she moved on her knees between his legs and looked up at him, smiling broadly.

"Mr. McCoy, you're the handsomest man I think I ever seen. I'd be proud to relax you a little . . . just however you need to be relaxed." Her hand came out and rubbed his crotch, where Spur could not stop his hardon from growing. She found it and cried out softly in delight.

She shook off the blouse and her breasts bounced from the movement. They were fuller than Spur guessed, still childless pink areolas with soft brown nipples that had filled with hot blood and enlarged and risen.

She leaned forward and unfastened his belt, then opened the buttons down his pants and spread the fabric. She worked through his short underwear and claimed the prize.

"I found him!" she yelped in delight. "Oh, such a big boy! Him and me gonna get along just fine!" She popped his penis out of his pants and bent at once and kissed the turgid rod. The purple head throbbed and twitched and she giggled.

"Oh, lordy, yes, but him and me gonna do good things for each other!" She bent, kissed his staff again, then opened her mouth and sucked him inside.

Spur's hands reached down for her breasts and toyed with them as she bobbed up and down on him. He caught her head and pulled her up and off him.

"Maybe we should talk about this on the bed. Does the door have a lock?"

Charity darted to the door and locked it, and was back at the bed when he got there. Her eyes sparkled. She reached up and helped him take off his vest, and then his shirt.

"Always wanted to do that," she said. Spur caught her skirt, found the buttons and undid them. She kicked the skirt away and was naked.

"I hoped that you would let me stay," she said. She stepped off the bed and finished undressing him. Then she jumped up on him and wound her legs around his torso.

"Standing up?" Spur said.

"Never have that way," she said. "Is it possible?"

Spur lifted her with one hand around her soft bottom and moved her to one side slightly, then lowered her. His shift slid into her waiting, hot sheath and she yelped in surprise and delight.

"Oh, yes!" She bounced back and forth on his hard pole and made small sounds deep in her throat. Spur watched sweat bead on her forehead as she rode him like a pony. Soon her breath came in short gasps and she began pounding harder and faster.

She erupted into a jolting climax as her whole body shivered in joy and release, then vibrated and shook as spasm after spasm tore through her. She closed her eyes tightly and her face grimaced as she made the joy last as long as it possibly would.

Charity pushed her sweating face against his chest and hugged him tightly, then wiggled in his arms.

"Move down on the bed without letting go of me," she said. "I want you on top of me hard and heavy!"

He made the maneuver and she relaxed. Spur came out of her until only the head of his shaft was in her delicate neither lips, then he drove in hard.

"Oh, damn!" she yelped.

He repeated the movement a dozen times and with each thrust she panted and said "Oh, damn!" He could tell she was building again. Now he concentrated on his own desires and pounded short and hard, driving her soft fanny a foot into the down featherbed as the powering unstoppable surge came and he exploded deep inside her, splashing her with his stored up seed and draining him into the mini-death as he sagged on top of her.

She put her arms around his back, pinning him in place, as she finished her own climax and kissed him hard on the mouth before turning her head to suck in lungsful of new air to replenish her spent body.

Five minutes later she reached up and kissed him.

"Again, lover. Do it again, right now!"

Spur stirred and found he was still erect and began to make love to her again. She looked at him.

"I want to be on top, please?"

He rolled away from her and she sat on his chest a moment, then lowered her breasts one at a time into his eager mouth.

"It feels so good when you do that! Like all the wonderful things in the world all at once! It's like I just want you to be in me and around me and chewing on me and fucking me all the time!"

"How about all night instead?" Spur asked.

"Oh, yes! Anyway you want to. In any place you want!" She pulled her breast from his mouth and moved down. Slowly she came over his turgid, pulsating shaft and guided it into her heartland.

"Just wonderful!" she screeched. "So beautiful! I want to stay just like this all night!" She laughed. "But then the next position I'll want to stay that way all night too!"

She hung over him, rocking back and forth. Spur found her breasts with his hands and held them, massaging them tenderly. Quickly she climaxed, her whole body shaking and bouncing. She growled and whined as the passion blasted through her. Then she was back in her position using him like a rocking horse, moving them both toward the next explosion.

It was nearly midnight when Spur leaned up on an elbow and stroked her cheeks, and throat, then her smooth sleek breasts.

"We should have brought something to eat from

the kitchen," Spur said. She rolled over top of him, bounced off the bed and went to a box that he had not seen in the corner.

"We did! I figured you would be hungry or thirsty." She spread out the food and drinks between them on the bed.

"We have three kinds of hard sausages, two kinds of cheese, lots of crackers, and dill pickles and two bottles of wine and just for emergencies a bottle of whiskey. Anything else that you might want?"

He used the knife she had brought and sliced the hard sausage into slices and put them between crackers along with slices of the dill pickle and then uncorked a bottle of red wine.

They drank and ate the crackers. Charity ate a little, then played with him, teased him and soon she had him back in bed. She pressed his face into her stomach and moved it downward. Spur found where she wanted him to go and his tongue rimmed her nether lips then plunged in and she climaxed at once and screeched in such rapture that Spur had to clamp his hand over her mouth to quiet her.

They came together three more times and Spur shook his head.

"I'm finished, Charity. You outlasted me."

"Seven times is wonderful!" she said, kissing his chest. "Now get some sleep and we can start again in the morning." Spur kissed her breasts, they cleared the bed of the food and drink and softly lay down in each other's arms. Before he dropped off Spur resolved to wake up at five-thirty. He had developed that ability and now used it whenever he needed to.

Charity went to sleep at once. Spur nuzzled her gently, then lay back and let sleep overtake him.

4

Will Walton knew where he was headed. He tried to keep that one fact clear and straight in his thinking. Usually he could, except when the headaches came. Then he went out of his mind. He knew he did. He could remember some of it.

Now he gritted his teeth and rode on. After that bad day in Kansas when he discovered he was officially dead and his "widow" had sold his ranch, things had been a little better.

He knew he had a son!

Will had been naked and without a penny to his name after that day, but he had survived. He had learned well in his wanderings how to survive. By instinct he lived one day at a time. He had taken clothes off a line at night. Walked around the town until he found a horse in front of a saloon after the place had closed.

He stole the animal and rode out of town quickly, used his saddle "O" ring and a pair of pliers to alter the brand on the horse, then traded saddles with another saloon patron and soon no one could identify the horse and saddle.

He had worked north from Kansas.

In North Platte, Nebraska he ran into trouble again. He had worked for a month at a ranch outside of town, had nearly twenty dollars in his pocket when he moved on north and stopped in the general store in North Platte to buy enough supplies for a two week ride.

He never could remember what happened after he had been in the store for a while picking out supplies. He must have thought he was in the war again. That's what it always was. He came back to reality in the local jail and the sheriff had told him he wounded a man and almost scared the store owner's wife to death.

"You acted crazy," the sheriff said. "Kept yelling about Rebels coming, and something about the Wilderness." The lawman paused, passing in a plate full of dinner through the bars. It was home cooking from his wife.

"You were in the war, Walton?"

"Yes sir. First Lt. Will Walton of the Ohio Twenty-Fifth under Colonel Richardson."

The sheriff rubbed his lean face. "That was one of the outfits slaughtered in the Wilderness for damn sure. I barely got out of there with my life. Still got a minie ball from an old muzzle loader in my hip. Some Reb was using black powder and a ball that day."

Will ate the food. He hadn't had a meal that good for a month, or maybe two months he couldn't remember. The ranch food had been barely palatable.

"I thank you kindly for the victuals, Sheriff. What happens now?"

"Where you heading for?"

"Worked out at the Bar S for a month to get a

grubstake. Moving up to Montana to try to find my family. Wife thought I was killed at the Willderness. Damn near was."

"Know how you feel. You had twenty dollars in cash on you when I brought you in. Month's wages all right. Jenny said you was buying trail food. Everything seems to check."

"Figure I can look at the brand book in Montana and see if my brand is up there, the WW. Ain't one registered in Nebraska. One in Kansas is mine, but I ain't there."

"Like to help," the sheriff said. He lifted his right leg off his left and stood with a limp. "You know you shot up the store?"

"God no!" Will blinked back the start of tears. "Damn! Just went crazy. Happened before. Got this slug across the back of my head."

The sheriff unlocked the cell and looked at the scar. He shivered.

"Lucky you ain't dead and buried," the lawman said.

"That's what the Rebs kept telling me. Prisoner of the Confederates for about a month before it ended."

"Expenses, let's see. We got a store window for ten dollars, and ruined merchandise of about five more." The sheriff said it half to himself. "How much you need for grub?"

"I figured five dollars of dried goods and coffee and possibles would do me for near a month."

"Got myself a little fund I use from time to time," the sheriff said. "I'll have a talk with the people concerned."

Will thanked him and rolled on the hard bunk, but he couldn't sleep.

The next morning the sheriff was back at his cell.

"Time to move, Will," the sheriff said.

"Where?"

"North toward Montana, and a bit west."

"How come?" Thought I owed some money, had some charges against me."

"All cleared up. Talked to the wounded man into not pressing any charges. We put it down as drunk and disorderly and I fined you two dollars, plus expenses. They came to twelve dollars for the window and the goods at the store.

"Then it costs you five dollars for that list of grub you wanted at the store. He threw in some extra I think. I took care of most of it from my fund. Which leaves you fifteen dollars pocket change to get you to your next job."

Tears streamed down Will's face.

"Don't know how to thank you . . . Most folks don't look kindly . . . God bless you, Sheriff!"

Will had no idea what brought on his "spells" as he called them. Sometimes he had no recall of how long they lasted. After he got out of jail he remembered working his way into Scotts Bluff, Nebraska and then on to Casper, Wyoming. But then things faded again.

Now he stared around, not sure where he was. He had no understanding at all about what month it was, let alone the year. The last period of time he could remember had been in Nebraska. He sat up on the edge of a small stream. He still had a horse, and some provisions. For that he was thankful.

Casper was somewhere behind him, but where was this? He had little idea which direction to move. For a half hour he sat on the small stream bank and studied the land around him. He was into some mountains, but could see no signs of life. There was no road or trail, no smoke, no railroad, no wagon road, not even a cow grazing on the grass in the valley.

For a moment he thought he heard a shot, then he was sure, two more shots. Pistol, he knew at once and wondered how he was certain.

From the west! He hurried to his horse and rode in that direction up a small slope to the top of the ridge. When he stared down on the other side he saw a cabin with smoke rising from the chimney. Two men with masks over their faces were riding around the cabin, shooting through the windows.

Automatically Will reached for the rifle in the boot and to his surprise found one. He dove to the ground behind cover, levered a round into the chamber and killed one of the attackers with his first shot. The second rider turned, surprised, then began to ride off when Will's second round took him in the shoulder and knocked him from the horse. Will's next rifle slug powered through the robber's chest, killing him instantly.

Will remained where he was, out of sight.

Ten minutes later he heard a screen door hinge squeak and saw the cabin's back door opening. A face peered out.

"Hello out there. I belong here. Don't shoot no more. They was just the two of them."

It was a woman's voice Will figured.

"You all right?" Will asked still concealed.

"Rightly so, now I am. Come on down. Don't want to dig in these two trash all by myself. I ain't got no man no more."

Will lifted from his concealment, took the reins to his horse and walked down the hill.

The woman came out of the cabin. She was older than her voice indicated. Pushing thirty-five, he decided. She wore a gingham dress that covered her neck to wrist to ankles. Brown hair had been done up in a bun at the back of her neck.

He stopped a dozen feet from her.

She looked at him and he could see the disappointment there.

"Thanks. Thanks for saving my life, and Sally's. We're obliged." He hesitated.

"I got to be riding on," Will said quickly. "Just don't like to see nobody get shot at who ain't shooting back."

"Ran out of rounds. Damn polecats knew about it. They was both rawhiders. Knew they was around here someplace."

"Just where is this, ma'am?"

"You don't know?"

"Got myself lost."

"Easy enough. We about twenty miles from the Montana line up in the Bighorn Mountains. Not too far from little place called Sheridan, Wyoming."

"Appreciate it, ma'am. Well, I better be moving on."

"Most evening. You could stay for supper. I would appreciate a hand with the burying, too, if'n you don't mind."

"Oh, yes. I did kill them." He dropped the reins to his horse confident that it wouldn't move more than a few feet to graze. "You have a shovel?"

He kept the revolvers and two rifles the pair had, then gave one of the horses and saddles to the woman, and said he'd take the other and sell it somewhere.

It took him two hours to dig through the rocky soil to put the two rawhiders underground. At that they only had a foot and a half of dirt and rocks over them. But it would be enough to keep the wolves away from them.

When he was finished the woman brought out a cup of hot coffee, and when he tasted it, he smiled.

"Best coffee I had in years," he said.

She smiled. "I got a boiler filled with hot water. You a mind for a good bath and a shave, I won't complain none."

"Bath . . ."

"You could use one. You see I don't go between the blankets with no man without a bath."

"Between . . ."

"Figure I owe you. Them rawhiders was telling me what they would do to me and Sally, and she not fourteen yet. So you get inside and Sally will scrub your back if you have a mind to. I'll be along soon as I feed the chickens. We'll have a late supper and then you stay the night. Lite out first thing with sunrise if you want. Figure I owe you."

"Well now . . ."

"You don't want me, just say. Reckon you could have Sally, even though she ain't been spoiled yet."

"Not, not that at all. Just been so long. I mean a real lady and all."

"No different last time I heard. A woman is a woman." She smiled. "Fact is, I'd enjoy you staying over. Been three years since my husband died . . ."

Will went inside, found Sally, a miniature of her mother and well developed fourteen, a grown woman already. She helped him fill the round white cedar bath tub then he shooed her out and stripped off his clothes. He was grimy. He washed for a half hour then heard the door open.

"My name is Shirley, it matters any."

She walked in front of him where he sat cross legged in the tub. He made no move to hide himself.

"Wish there was room in there for me." She smiled. "I sent Sally to the long well. We got time."

As he scrubbed once more, she slowly undressed until she stood naked before her. She watched with satisfaction as his penis progressed from limpness to a stiff erection jutting out of the water.

She bent over the tub. "Wash my tities so they'll taste better."

He did, then she stood as he did and she dried him with a towel and led him through a curtain to her bedroom.

"No man's slept in here for three years," she said. "Hope to hell you are good in bed."

"Everybody is good in bed," Will said and they rolled onto the blankets spread over a straw mattress.

"Oh, damn!" she said and laughed.

"What?"

"Your shave. You'll get that right after the third go round in bed here. I got a powerful need to be filled."

The next morning, Will sat on the bed. He had dressed and started out into the rest of the cabin when he heard the girl. She was asking her mother what it felt like to be poked with a man's long "thing."

Shirley just laughed and said Sally would find out some day.

When he came out they both laughed and he grinned and hadn't felt so good in months.

Over breakfast she suggested it. "No sense you moving on. Got yourself a ready made family. Preacher comes around once a month. He could do the marrying. Sally needs a Pa. The ranch here ain't much, but a man could make it pay. I got three hundred head of cattle somewhere in the hills."

Will told them about his quest.

"So I'm still married and I have to find my family.

They could be in Montana.''

Shirley scowled. "Most likely they ain't. Wasn't in Wyoming or Nebraska or Kansas. You got Texas and Arkansa and Nevada and about twenty more states and territories. You aim to try them all?''

"If I have to,'' Will said softly.

Sally laughed. "I don't think he liked the way you did him, Ma,'' the girl said. "Let me try.''

Mother slapped daughter and spun her around. "You mind your tongue, girl!''

She shook her head. "I know how you men are. You get something in your craw and you got to go find it. Gold or silver, or a new ranch or an old wife. I know.

"My man didn't die, he ran off for gold somewhere. I figure he got himself killed because of his quick temper. He ain't coming back. I got to fend for myself. You want one more try on the bed, just to be sure you don't like it here?''

"Shirley, you were remarkable, delightful. But it's a matter of conscience. I must find my son. I must know what happened to them.''

She did lure him to the bed again, and this time neither of them bothered to tell Sally to go away so she stood by the bed watching it all with youthful delight as her hand under her dress rubbed at her crotch.

He left an hour later, clean shaven, with three sets of pants and clean shirts in his kit bag. They were a little large for him, but Shirley said her husband would never need them. She packed him enough cooked food to last two days and cried when he left.

He rode north and east for Sheridan the way she told him. Before noon the headache came again. Just before he found Sheridan, he was back in the Wilderness firing at the Rebels as they stormed through the brush. He left his horse and charged away to the rear with the rest of the blue coats, and ran until he fell from exhaustion.

When he came back to reality all he had was an empty six-gun in his hand and the clothes on his back. He had no idea how to find his horses, his food or his clean clothes.

With a futile sigh, Will tried to blink away the headache as he walked toward a smoke to the north. It should be some town. He couldn't remember the name of it, and he wasn't sure even what state this was.

One thing he remembered. His name was Will Walton and he was heading for Montana. Exactly why, he wasn't sure.

5

The next morning, Spur's mental alarm clock misfired and he slept in. Libby was up and off to her office in the bank by 7:30. It was her normal work time and she went over various reports and made some business decisions just the way Alexander had trained her to do years before.

She sat back in her big chair and looked out the second story window of the bank and down the tree shaded main street. This was a great little town, and she was going to put it on the map and make it the capital of Montana! It was logical, reasonable, and Alexander would have wanted it that way. She had been in the fight from the first three years ago for the move to Helena.

She looked at a scale map of the town's business district which she had specially prepared. Each of the blocks was represented with the individual stores and houses showing. Those she owned were shaded in light blue for residences and light pink for businesses. She had twenty-one retail firms along the three blocks of Main Street and twenty rental houses she had brought over the years.

Not bad. She had picked up six new commercial operations since Alexander died. They were logical acquisitions to get rid of competition or to open a new venture. Things were progressing well. But she was disturbed about one thing.

She was only thirty-two years old, and already she was thinking about what had bothered Alexander for many years. She had no heir. Who would carry on after she was gone? It was a fact that she should think about. She could not marry some young man and have an heir, the way Alexander hoped he could. She would give a hundred thousand dollars if she could bear a child!

She could always adopt. Usually a single woman could not adopt, but with her resources and contacts she could probably make it work for her. She put the problem out of her mind. Her secretary knocked on the door and came in.

Mrs. Unruh was almost forty, wrote the most beautiful hand of anyone Libby had ever seen, and was a highly organized and efficient person.

"Hal Barnes is here, Mrs. Adams. He's with the hardware store, lost his wife few months back."

Libby's frown faded. "Yes, bring us some coffee and send him in."

The man who came in her office was slight, his shoulders stooped and he had a look of intense concern on his pale face.

"Sit down, Hal. I thought it was time we had a little talk." He looked up with a worried expression. She hurried on. "Hal, the hardware store has been doing well these past few months. New construction is up in town and that always helps, but the hardware business is a problem solving service. People tell me you're the best problem solver in town."

Hal looked up, a smile creased his face, then vanished.

"Thank you, Mrs. Adams."

"Hal, your total sales are up and so is the profit on the store. You're doing just remarkably well. I'm arranging a bonus for you at the end of the month over your usual profit percentage."

"Oh, really? Well, thank you, Mrs. Adams. I appreciate it." The smile stayed this time, his shoulders came back a little and he sat up straighter.

"Hal, we were all shocked and saddened by your loss. Emmy was a wonderful woman and we all miss her. I have been concerned about you these last two months. I know it's been hard. I've been through the tragedy of having a spouse die, Hal, I understand."

Hal looked at the floor, his shoulders slumping again.

"Hal, I also know that there is a time for grieving, and a time to stop. I think you're at the stopping point, Hal, it's time to do something else other than throw yourself into your work. I appreciate your diligence, but I have another problem I want you to help me with."

Hal looked up, a small frown building on his face.

"You remember Ken Farley. He passed away about six months ago. He worked in one of the mines, a foreman and a good man. His widow has been having a difficult time since then trying to support herself and the two youngsters. Usually I'm not much of a matchmaker, Hal, but I've seen her watching you in church lately on almost every Sunday morning.

"Hal, I think Marie Farley would be pleased if you would call on her now and then. She's a fine woman, but she has her needs, just the way you do."

"But, but she's so pretty . . ."

"Hal, pretty doesn't do a woman a bit of good when she has to go to bed alone every night. You understand what lonely is, I know for sure. I'd be more than pleased if you'd consider calling on Marie. If nothing happens, what have you lost?"

"She wouldn't laugh at me?" Hal asked.

"Hal, you're a fine looking man. You have a good position and are earning more money than half the men in town. From what I've seen of her watching you in church, I think she'd be delighted to have you come calling. After that, see what happens. You might be surprised."

Hal stood taller. His shoulders came back and a smile lit his face like she hadn't seen since his wife died.

"Much obliged for the suggestion, Mrs. Adams. And thank you for the kind words about the store. Gonna make that the best dang hardware store in the state!" He started for the door but turned. "Thanks for the hint about Marie. She comes in the store once in a while." He grinned. "Think I might go up to her place right now and see if there's any handyman jobs I can do for her around that big house of hers. Must be something, no man being there for six months now." He nodded and smiled.

"Thank you, Hal," Libby said a broad grin on her face.

Mrs. Unruh came to the door when Hal had left. "Your only other business this morning is Orville. He's from the livery stable."

Libby frowned. "Yes, ask him to come in."

Libby stood with her back to the window on a foot high platform so she would not have to look up at the man. He would have to squint to see her against the light. In this case everything she could do to help her commanding management position would be a plus.

Orville walked in wearing his stable clothes, dirty jeans, boots, a shirt with sleeves torn off at the elbows, and a grimy hat he twisted in his hands. He was about thirty, unwashed and irreverent. He had a half sneer on his face as he stopped in front of her desk.

"Yes, ma'am?"

"Orville, Greg says you've been stealing money from the cash box at the livery stable. Is that true?"

"Hell no! Pardon me, Ma'am. I ain't stole nothing."

"Very well, Orville. I guess I'll have to turn it over to Sheriff Palmer. He'll arrest you for grand theft and put you in jail until the trial. You'll need a lawyer, of course. Can you hire one? They ask for half their fee in advance. Most charge only twenty dollars a day."

Orville stared at her. "Twenty . . . Hell I only borrowed thirty dollars. . . ."

"Orville, you're changing your story?"

He sighed, his hat turned faster. "Yeah. I guess so. Don't want to go to jail. Greg really signed a paper against me?"

"He did. I told him to. He says you've been stealing a dollar a day, and he told you to stop five or six times."

"Like to gamble a little after work. Nothing else to do. But even on the nickel table it takes money."

"So you admit you stole from the livery?"

"Yes, ma'am."

"Orville, do you know in six years I've never fired anyone who works for any of my businesses?"

"Heard that, yes ma'am."

"I could break my record with you. Is that what

you want?''

"No ma'am."

She sighed and looked out the window. How did she get to be a judge and jury here? She turned back. "Orville, exactly how much did you take from the cash box?''

"Thirty-four dollars. I kept track. I was gonna win big and pay it all back. I . . .''

She held up her hand. "Orville, you can keep working at the livery but you're going to have to do a few things. First, you'll be docked two dollars a week from your pay until the thirty-four dollars are repaid. Is that perfectly understood?''

"Jeeeze . . only make four dollars a week. That cuts me to two dollars . . .''

"Think hard before you steal again. It's only for seventeen weeks. Second, Orville you must promise never to steal from the livery again. If you do, I'll have you arrested and tried. Is that understood?''

"Yes, ma'am.''

"Third, you are not to gamble ever again. No more cards or dice or faro. Nothing.''

"But . . . no cards?''

"Play for matches, it's just as much fun.''

"Damn! . . . all right.''

"Can you read, Orville?''

"No ma'am, just never had the chance.''

"You will now. You are to wash up good, put on clean clothes and report to Mrs. Unruh in the outer office every week day morning at seven-thirty for an hour of reading lessons. When Mrs. Unruh is satisfied that you are literate, you can stop coming.''

"No . . . Not a chance. I . . . I'd feel silly.''

"Orville, how old are you?''

"Twenty-two.''

"Lots of time yet for you. After you learn to read and get a haircut and shave regularly, I might be able to find a better job for you, something that would pay in relation to your new knowledge and ability."

Orville frowned. "Pay more? Maybe in two or three weeks?"

"No. First you repay the $34. And you finish learning to read. Maybe three months."

"Maybe ten dollars a week?"

She smiled. It was a fortune to him. "That's possible, Orville. Now get cleaned up before you go back to the stable. Shave every day, and come tomorrow morning for your reading lesson."

"Yes, ma'am." He paused. "Appreciate this, Mrs. Adams, only don't tell nobody about the readin'." He turned and hurried out of the room.

Spur McCoy came into her office before the door closed. She looked up and smiled. A stab went through her. She sat down behind the desk and felt her knees give way. Almost at once there was a burning between her legs and she was wet down there. She took a slow, nervous breath and tried to control her voice.

"My most difficult caller all morning," she said. "Sleep well?" She tried to sound normal, but already her breath was coming faster. Damn it!

He evidently saw no hidden meaning in her words. Spur sat down in a chair next to the big desk.

"Matter of fact I slept extremely well. That bed is better than the ones in your hotels."

"That's true. Seen the sheriff yet?"

"On my way. Just got outside of that big breakfast that Charity brought me."

"Glad you liked it." He had liked Charity well last night too, she knew. God, could she keep up this front?

"I have a couple of questions."

She watched him, waiting.

"Is Laidlaw the main person who would suffer if the state capital moved here?"

"No. Most of the merchants in Virginia City would eventually have to close up and move. There isn't enough basic work or any industry there for the people."

"Is the Yellowstone River the most logical route for the rail line through Montana?"

"Absolutely. They can use the river bed for a gradual grade and through natural passes for over four hundred miles. There hasn't been an easy grade like that anywhere else in the West for any of the railroads. It's a hundred times out a hundred that the engineers and grade surveyors will pick that route."

"Just wanted to make sure. Looks like Laidlaw is fighting against a stacked deck."

"But he's still going to fight. I know the man. He is not a good person."

"A good man is hard to find these days."

"I know," Libby said with a big grin. For one wild second she almost jumped up and pulled open her bodice. Instead she laughed to cover up her emotion. "I've been hunting one. They all want my money. How about you?"

"I'm not interested in money. I've been in that situation and walked away from it."

Her brows lifted. "You'll have to tell me about it sometime."

"Glad to. A reminder for you and your safe-keeping. No public speaking engagements, and no damn parades."

She laughed and nodded.

"Now, I have to go see the sheriff about a man in jail."

Libby watched him go and a strange feeling seeped through her. She had not felt anything like that in a long, long time. She knew at once what it was, raw, animal desire, sexual wanting and so strong that she knew she was damp and a burning came between her legs again.

The feeling was so intense that she cried out, and Mrs. Unruh hurried into her office.

"Yes, Mrs. Adams?"

"Oh, no, Mrs. Unruh, I changed my mind, not right now, please. Do I have any more appointments this morning?"

"No ma'am."

"Thank you, please don't disturb me for a while. Thank you."

The door closed and she was alone. Libby had forced herself not to think about the night her husband died. Now that was all she could think about. It had been wonderful.

Alexander Adams was a talented, tender lover. He had responded to her sleek young, firm, energetic body like a teenager. They made love every other night and couldn't wait to get to it.

On the night he . . . died, he had been more anxious than usual. They had a lovely dinner, then bathed each other in the big specially built bathtub, and luxuriated on the feather bed. The second time they made love he said he felt a pain in his chest, but he decided it was only stomach gas.

An hour later in the middle of the third love-making he had screamed and died of a massive heart attack just before he could climax.

She had been frantic. Somehow she knew he was dead even as she dressed and had one of the servants run for the doctor.

Since then she had not known any man.

Sex!

She had put it entirely out of her mind. She had concentrated on what Alexander had trained her to do. She ran his companies with such efficiency and drive that they became even more prosperous. She had no time for sex. There was no overpowering need. Once or twice her "happy fingers" had snuggled between her legs and rubbed herself to ecstasy, but that had ended after the first month or two.

During the past six years many men had wooed her. Some had been subtle, some blatant, one almost raped her before she hit him with a lamp. But she had not *needed sex*. That was before yesterday. Before Spur McCoy had lifted her from the dust of the street. He had *touched her!* She had thought of little else since then. Last night she had planned on seducing him, but after dinner she had made excuses to get away from him.

She had been as shy and frightened as a virgin!

So she had sent Charity to him, with instructions to take care of his sexual needs and to be sure to stay all night. That morning Charity had told her in the minutest detail everything they had done in bed the night before.

It had taken all of her willpower to come to the bank this morning. One part of her wanted to dash into his room and waken him and tear all of her clothes off for him. But six years of celibacy had conditioned her. She had come to work.

When he stopped by, she had been moist and flushed in an instant. What was happening to her? She was acting like a fourteen year old who suddenly discovered that sex must be glorious if only some man would show her.

Libby looked down and one hand had curled inside her dress and was rubbing her breast through a tight wrapper.

What in the world?

She pulled her hand away. She had to keep busy. Libby knew that Spur McCoy had work to do, he had to keep her alive. Maybe tonight she could . . . talk to him again. Perhaps he would be interested enough to . . . kiss her.

Her mind surged ahead from the kiss to his fondling and then the foreplay and the undressing and . . .

"Mrs. Adams."

The voice came again, and slowly Libby turned her chair from where she had been staring unseeing out the big window to find Mrs. Unruh standing at her desk.

"Yes, Mrs. Unruh?"

"There's a man here to see you about that parcel of land you wanted to talk about on the north side of town. He says he's interested in selling, but says it has to be today because of a death in his family back East. He will be taking the stage out day after tomorrow, early."

"Yes, Mrs. Unruh. Please ask him to come in. Then send someone over to bring in Mr. Leslie. We may need the lawyer." She would do it, she would throw herself into her work again . . . today. Tonight was going to be a different matter!

6

Spur left Libby's second floor bank building office and walked straight to the jail in the small courthouse. Sheriff Josiah Palmer was finishing his breakfast, and pushed away the tray.

"Figure you want to talk to our prisoner again," Palmer said. Spur said he did and together they went back to the cell.

"Keep him outa here!" the prisoner bellowed. "He's the guy who shot me and tortured me."

"You're breaking my heart," Sheriff Palmer said.

"What else does Rufus Laidlaw have planned for Helena and for Libby Adams," Spur asked.

The man with the two bullet holes in his shoulder now wrapped in bandages shook his head.

"Don't know what the hell what you're talking about. Just told me to discourage McCoy there from staying in town long. Nobody tried to kill McCoy. Scare him, that's all we was trying to do."

"Who taught you to make a grapeshot grenade that way?" Spur demanded.

"Hell, we made them almost like that in the war.

Get a newspaper and roll it into an inch wide tube. Fold over the bottom, fill her with black gunpowder and wrap the nails around the outside. One about a foot long used to make just one hell of a hole in a company of Rebs.''

"Never heard of doing that in my outfit," Spur said.

"Maybe you was never short on cartridges and long on powder," the prisoner said. "Hell, Sheriff, we was just trying to scare him. Nobody hurt him. What's the charges for?"

"Attempted murder, assault with a deadly weapon, and using blasting powder in the city limits," Sheriff Palmer said. "Maybe I can think of a couple more. Circuit judge should be through here in about a month."

"I got to stay here for a month?"

"About the size of it. Judge Poindexter just went through on the stage last week. We didn't have no business for him to do."

Outside in the sheriff's private office, the lawman shook his head. "Not much chance this Laidlaw is going to show up and bail him out. I've heard of Laidlaw. He's a man who rides just inside the law, when somebody is watching him."

"He's tied in, that's for damn sure."

Shots sounded down the street.

"What the hell?" the sheriff asked. "Too early in the day for drunk miners. Better see what's going on."

Spur followed him out the door. Half a block down the street a dozen miners and farmers were in the street outside the Golden Nugget saloon. People stood gawking at a fight of some kind.

The two lawmen ran up to the crowd and pushed their way through.

Bud Stoner saw the sheriff and waved. "All over, Sheriff. Damn Yahoo over there shot up my brand new mirror behind the bar, the six-footer I ordered from Chicago. Crazier than a hoot owl, that one is. Claimed the Rebs was charging at him through the thorn bushes and the saplings."

Spur looked where Stoner pointed. A man in tattered clothes crouched behind a horse trough. He had lost his hat and his hair was dirty strings around his shoulders. He had a shaggy beard and farmer shoes. Slowly he edged out from behind the trough, held his hand like a six-gun and "shot" by bending his thumb.

"Bang, bang, bang! Got you, you dirty Reb! Back this way, men, to the rear, fall back. Not a damn chance in hell we can hold off that many Rebels!"

"Crazy is right," Sheriff Palmer said.

Spur put his hand on the lawman's shoulder. "Let me talk to him. Sounds like he had more of the war than he could handle. Yes, I know it's been over for five years, but some men cave in long after the shooting stops. I'll talk to him."

Spur saw the people move back from the man where he cowered behind the trough. He looked like he could be about thirty years old. Spur crouched at the other end of the trough.

"Sergeant, how many men did you lose?" Spur said in a sharp tone. The man behind the planks ignored him, "shooting" his imaginary gun at the crowd of people.

Spur changed the rank. "Lieutenant! I need a casualty report, right now!" Spur snapped. The man behind the trough looked at him.

"Yes, sir! We've had twenty of forty killed, at least ten more wounded who can't move. We had to leave them. Got overrun, the poor bastards. I've got one sergeant and five men left ready to fight."

"Good. What's your name, Lieutenant?"

"Walton, Sir, C company of Colonel Richardson's 25th Ohio. Afraid we're not much of a force to help you fight, Captain."

"Have your men fall in behind you and follow me. We'll get out of this area, too damn many Reb snipers slipping in. Let's move, Lieutenant!"

"Yes sir," Walton said. He stood, slung an imaginary rifle. "Fall in by twos, on me, moving out. Look sharp for Reb snipers!"

Spur turned and walked through the crowd to the closest alley and went down half way along an old brick building. He had no doubt that Walton would follow. The clumping shoes across the boardwalk proved it. When they were out of sight of the crowd, Spur stopped and turned. There was something vaguely familiar about the man's face.

"Your first name, soldier?" Spur demanded.

The bearded man snapped to attention, saluted. "First Lieutenant William Walton, sir."

"You say that's all that's left of Charlie company of the Ohio 25th Regiment?"

"Yes sir. They come through the Wilderness at us, sir. Colonel said nobody could get through there. Right through them bramble bushes that could tear the uniform right off a man. But they come, thousands of them. Blew our picket line right back into the road and across it.

"Heard Stonewall Jackson used twenty-five thousand men in that advance. Smashed us, sir. Cut us into ribbons. Lost all but five of my company."

"Then Spur knew. He had been with the Ohio 25th under Colonel Richardson before they got hit at the Wilderness, just outside of Chancellorsville. He had seen Lt. Walton at Regimental meetings.

"Walton, I'm Captain McCoy, with Baker company. I remember you. I was transferred out a short time before Chancellorsville. But that's all over now. The Reb's are a long ways off now."

Somebody came down the alley, and when Spur turned the man threw a bucket of water at Walton. It hit him in the chest and splashed into his face with a shocking suddenness.

Spur drew and sent a .44 slug winging over the man's head who ran like he was mule kicked out the alley.

When he turned, Will Walton was himself again. He looked at his soaked clothes, then at Spur.

"Must have done it again, right? Acted like I was back in the war. Hope I didn't hurt nobody." He reached for his weapon but found his holster empty. "What happened?"

Spur watched him a moment. "Remember me, Walton? Captain McCoy of Baker company, Ohio 25th."

Walton screwed up his face, squinted, then wiped the water out of his eyes and looked again.

"By damn, it is you, McCoy. Little heavier, more face hair, but the same man." He looked at his ripped cotton flannel plaid shirt and pants too big for him over farmer shoes. "Things been bad for me since the war. Got wounded."

"Let's talk about it, Walton. I'll get a couple of bottles of beer and we'll find some shade and talk."

Ten minutes later they sat under some trees at the edge of town by a little stream.

"Somebody told me this is 1870 already," Walton said. "That's right?"

"True, Will. War's been over for five years."

"By damn! Seems like yesterday. Picked up a head wound there at the end of the Wilderness, then later on I got myself captured by the Rebs. But the war was over soon after. Didn't feel none too good after that Rebel ball sliced through my noodle."

"Been a long time since the war," Spur said.

Walton tipped the beer, then stared at Spur. "Yeah, I remember you now. B company Ohio 25th. Part of Major General Oliver Otis Howard's XI Army Corps. We all got the hell beat out of us down at the Wilderness."

"Didn't you go back to that ranch in Kansas you were always talking about?"

Walton's eyes glazed a minute, then he shook his head. "Oh, yeah, I went back. Nigh on to five years after the war. About two three months ago. Met some Jasper I never seen before. Said he owned my spread. My WW brand was his. Had a bill of sale, and the grant deed signed over by my wife. He said my widow. She thought I got war-killed and sold out and moved."

"Where did she move to, Will?"

"Hell, he didn't know. Nobody knew. I been trying to find my wife. Guy told me I got a son, five or six year old. I got to find my family, McCoy!"

"Did they take the brand with them? The guy in Kansas, was he running your brand on his stock?"

"Nope, guess they must have taken it. Brands. Yeah." He stopped and held his head with both hands. For a minute a high whining sound came from Walton, then he shook his head and looked back at Spur.

"Yeah, the Stockman's brand book. Checked it in Kansas, but no WW. Checked Nebraska and Texas. Missed Wyoming but got a look at the Montana one. There's a WW listed, here near Helena somewhere."

"And you plan to ride out to the ranch and see

who owns it?" Spur asked.

"Figured to."

Spur looked up and saw the sheriff standing in the edge of the shade.

"First, Will, I better talk to the sheriff. Be right back. He went up to the lawman.

"How much does the barman want for the mirror?"

"Twenty-five dollars. Had it shipped in from Chicago."

Spur gave the sheriff the money. "Any other charges?"

"Not if you take care of him. Don't figure he's dangerous. You say this is all some kind of a throwback to the war?"

"Yes. Some men saw too much killing, did too much blood letting. I've seen it happen in the middle of a battle. One man stood up and began singing a lullaby to his baby daughter. Before we could get him down he was hit with ten bullets."

"Take care of him," the sheriff said and walked away.

Spur intended to. An hour later he had Walton in one of his hotel rooms. He arranged for a bath and went and bought some new clothes for Will. Then they stopped by at a barber shop where Will had his beard shaved off and a proper haircut.

He stood outside the general store looking at himself in the window.

"Sakes! I peer to be about twenty years younger! Don't know why I never shaved it off before. Too dang much trouble, I reckon. You find out where this WW ranch is?"

"Nope, figured you'd want to do that yourself. First, it's time to get some good food into that shrunken belly of yours."

They went to the Bakery Cafe and Spur enjoyed watching Will eat. He began with six hotcakes the size of a dinner plate, four eggs and six slices of bacon. By then it was almost noon so he had a steak and a bowl of chili.

"You ended the war as a prisoner of the Rebels?" Spur asked.

"Yep. Only about two months, but longest damn two months of my life. Rebs didn't have no way to treat the crease on my head. I was out of my mind for about half the time. Lucky they didn't shoot me or let me starve."

"But you came through the Wilderness," Spur said. "We had a lot of generals who didn't know what was happening that day."

"That's not lying at all," Will said. He stared at a man who just came in the cafe door and suddenly he crouched beside his chair.

"They're acoming again, men! Make your shots count!" Lt. Walton checked his line again. Forty men were dug in facing the Wilderness. Nothing but thorn bushes and saplings out ahead them. Everyone said no man in his right mind would attack through there.

But he knew they were coming. He could *smell them!* They were out there.

"Look smart now, lads. Fire and load, fire and load. Keep up the order."

Twenty rifle shots roared fifty feet below them, then directly ahead he saw the gray uniforms. He was calm. It hadn't been this way before.

"Fire when you have a target men!" he shouted, aiming his pistol.

The first rounds from the enemy slammed through the thicket. One caught Private Golloway in the jaw and tore half of his face away. He flopped at Lt. Walton's feet, his one good eye pleading with his commander to help him.

All Will Walton could do was push him aside, flop on the ground behind a log and fire around the end at the blur of gray uniforms working through the brambles. Then the bullets sang around him like hornets.

He saw another man go down, dead without a sound. On the other side of him Corporal Schmidt lifted over the log to fire, but before he could, two Rebel rounds slammed into him. One powered through his forehead, blowing the back of his skull off, showering Lt. Walton with fragments of bone and splatters of brain tissue and rich warm blood.

Lt. Walton screamed and emptied his pistol, then picked up a rifle and saw that it had not been fired and aimed at a running soldier and triggered it. He saw the round jolt into the man, tear through his ear and come out his left eye, throwing the lifeless corpse against a pair of saplings which held it a moment, then it slid to the ground.

Will shook his head and looked at his line. Ten of them were dead. Half the rest wounded. The gray tide of men ran forward, less than five yards from his picket line. There were two hundred infantrymen in front of his forty!

"Pull back, men!" Lt. Walton bellowed over the sound of gunfire. Then the grenadiers ran up and threw their bombs and he saw another of his men die, this one blown in half by the explosion.

"Pull back, damnit!" he roared, but by then there were only a handful of his men could move. They crawled away from the picket line and darted to the rear. Lt. Walton found another rifle and he fired it at the howling horde, then dropped the useless weapon and ran as fast as he could.

He lost track of his men in the brush. The saplings slowed him, the thorn brush clawed at his uniform.

Lt. Walton paused beside a tree to get his breath. A Rebel corporal came around the tree and the men stared at each other for a second in total surprise. The Rebel dug for his pistol. Lt. Walton jerked a knife from his belt and slashed at the enemy's throat. He only nicked his shoulder.

Before the Confederate could upholster his pistol, Lt. Walton had lunged forward, slashed again, cutting across the man's neck deeply. Will jerked the knife back and thrust forward with all his weight behind it at the Rebel's chest. The knife pierced cloth and skin, broke a rib and drove deeply into the dying man's heart.

They both fell to the ground where the Rebel flopped like a straw doll. Will rolled over and reached for the knife sticking from the corpse's chest. He stared at the blood, then heard a rasping wheeze as the final gush of air came from the dead man's lungs.

Will grabbed the knife and ran. For a moment he had no idea which way to move. Then he heard firing in front of him and he turned and ran the other way. He came to a road and found hundreds of tattered, wounded Yanks streaming north. He joined them, then heard the cannon fire behind him and darted into the edge of the thick woods for protection.

Lt. Walton still held the bloody, four-inch knife in his hand. Only then did he notice that his hand and arm were spattered with blood. The left sleeve to his shirt was gone, ripped off somewhere on a thorn bush.

He stopped. The surge of blue shirts kept moving north up the post road. He couldn't take another step. His leg ached and burned. He looked down and saw blood. He had been shot in the leg and never even knew it.

Will slumped beside a tree, his eyes closed.

Later he shook his head. Had he slept? It seemed so quiet. He could see the road but it was empty now. Darkness was coming fast.

Behind him! Someone was coming. He crouched in back of the log, waiting. Someone working through the brush, quietly, a scout? He peered over the fallen log. A gray blur of a Rebel surged toward him. In a reflex action, Will thrust up the bloody blade and saw it drive into the man's chest.

The gray uniform rolled over him and fell to the ground. Will's blade came free. He lifted it ready to strike. The body rolled and he saw the face.

It was a boy, no more than fourteen! He had no weapon. The knife had wounded him high in the shoulder. He bled.

The boy was blond and frightened. He stared at Will for a minute.

"You gonna kill me?" the youth asked.

"Don't know. Where you going?"

"Scouting for General Jackson. Used to live nearby. Know the woods. He sent me."

'How far back is he?"

"Maybe a mile. Front line is about three hundred yards trying to get organized. Advanced too fast."

"You're my prisoner. Stand up, I'll take you to the rear and you'll be questioned, then we'll patch up that shoulder."

Will was on his feet at once. All memory of his wound gone, just the prisoner and his knife. He needed a better weapon. The road, he would be able to find one on the road.

He prodded the boy out of the brush to the dirt trail, found an abandoned rifle that was still loaded and marched his prisoner down the line.

They came around a small bend and before Will could call out, he saw three blue coated troops aim in the dusk and fire at the Rebel uniform. All three bullets crashed into the boy and flung him backward.

Will darted into the brush and the safety of the cover. Damn them! Why had they shot so fast? The Reb had just been a boy! Tears splashed down his cheeks as he ran north. He had to get back beyond the front lines, wherever they were, he had to.

His leg ached now. He limped and used the rifle as a crutch. Why did the boy have to die? He could have been a useful prisoner.

Will stumbled on, then his leg hurt so much he couldn't stand to put any pressure on it at all. He slumped down behind a log and rested. He'd go on in a minute. Just a short rest.

He felt strong hands on his shoulders, then a voice.

"Will. Will Walton, it's all right. They are gone. The war is over, Will. It's all right. You can stand up now, Will. The war is over, you're safe. The killing is over, Will."

Will Walton blinked, stared at the cafe, and at people around watching him. Strong hands urged him to sit down at a table and he did.

Slowly he remembered. He looked at the man who sat across from him.

"God, McCoy, did I do it again? Was I out of my head again? When is it going to stop?"

Spur shook his head. "We don't know, Will. The war did strange things to people. I've seen men run screaming from their first taste of combat. I've seen men who swore they would be cowards turn into the best fighting men I had. The human mind is a strange duck we dont know much about yet. Maybe in a hundred years the doctors will figure us out."

"I was there again, McCoy. It was the Wilderness all over again, the same damn thing. We're on the picket line and the damn Rebs overrun us and we retreat and I come away with only one or two men out of forty. It's horrible."

"Relax, Will. The war is over. You just had a square meal and this afternoon you're going to find out if the WW brand has anything to do with the WW brand you registered down in Kansas. I'll get your six-gun back from the barkeep at that saloon. You'll need some protection riding around here. Just no more shooting up bar mirrors. My expenses can't cover another one."

7

Rufus Laidlaw sat at the back of the Golden Nugget saloon in Helena brooding over a bottle of whiskey. He had downed three shot glasses full already and another sat in front of him waiting.

He knew he shouldn't be here. It was a risk, a gamble. But where the hell would he be today if it hadn't been for some of the risks he had taken?

He picked up the shot glass, then put it down. He knew some people in Helena, but most of them were back in Virginia City. Nobody would recognize him. He tugged the low crowned hat lower over his eyes.

Damn! How could everything go wrong all at once? He had seen the dimwit shoot Libby Adams in the arm. The arm for Christ's sake! How could the asshole have done that? Then he sent the same man and a partner after the Jasper who picked her out of the dust, and one of those men was killed and the other one wound up in jail probably screaming his head off. Laidlaw knew the big man was a whole lot of trouble.

Now he found out that the big stranger who just

got off the stage when Libby was shot was a United States lawman of some kind. What was he doing here?

Laidlaw lifted the shot glass and poured the drink down his throat. It burned. Good. He was feeling too bad to feel good. The State Capital Relocation Committee would be here tomorrow or the next day, and he was sure now that the Helena mayor, a committee he appointed as well as Libby Adams would all testify about the glories of bringing the state capital to Helena. Damn them! What else could he do?

Just before Montana became a Territory, he had bought up all the land he could around Virginia City. If the seat of the territorial government moved, he would again be living off only his territorial salary.

His hand was steady as Laidlaw poured the shot glass full again.

He came to this saloon because it was one of the few in town that Libby didn't own. He was sleeping in her hotel under an assumed name. He ate at the best restaurant in town even though she did own it.

"Damn her eyes!" he muttered and stared at the whiskey bottle. He'd meet the committee members whenever they got to town and provide them liquid and female refreshment for them. Couldn't hurt.

If they decided to move the capital to Helena, that would just about make it certain that the railroad would come here too. Shit! Then Virginia City would be a way station on a stage line that sent a coach through there once a month!

Laidlaw was a big man, six feet tall and half that wide. He weighed well over two hundred-eighty pounds. The only place he could weigh himself was at the feed store on the big scales that went up to five hundred pounds. Once or twice a year he went down after the store closed and paid the clerk to let him in and give him the bad news.

His face was fat and pinkish. He shaved meticulously every morning and kept his hair short and sideburns cut short and close above his ears.

Still his eyes seemed lost in the flesh, but burned brightly with a soft green tint. His nose had been mistreated when he was young, usually over arguments about his weight which resulted in fist fights which he almost always lost.

Laidlaw pushed back from the table and headed for the outhouse in the alley. Once out the back door he found the small structure, but realized the door was too small for him to enter. He utilized the side of the outhouse for a splash panel and completed his business there.

Laidlaw wandered out the alley to the street and went down to the Montana Hotel where he entered by the side door. His room was two in on the ground floor. He hated steps.

The big man ordered his noon meal from the room clerk, and gave him a quarter to see that the tray was delivered to his room promptly. As with many fat people, he avoided eating in public. When he was alone or in the privacy of his house or room, he gorged.

Now he had three steaks, and three orders of two vegetables, two bowls of stew, six rolls, three bottles of beer, and half a cherry pie. When he finished eating he lay down on the bed for a rest.

A moment later he looked at his gold vest pocket watch. Only a little after two P.M. He had to try again. He went out the side door and to the smallest saloon in town where the beer cost only a nickel and where the down and outers openly panhandled for drinks.

He found the man he was looking for and waved him over. The man had done jobs for Laidlaw in Helena before. He was small, weasel faced, and whiskey thin. Usually he couldn't remember when he'd had his last meal. He subsisted on beer and crackers, but usually he forgot to eat the free crackers.

He was known as Skunk Johnson and took baths only when he fell dead drunk into a river. He sat down at the back table across from the ponderous bulk of Laidlaw and eyed the mug of draft beer waiting there.

"Help yourself, Skunk," Laidlaw wheezed.

The small man leaned forward in the chair, scooped up the mug and downed half of the amber fluid without taking a breath. Then he set the mug down and stared at Laidlaw.

"You want something," Skunk said. When he opened his mouth black stumps of teeth showed past thin lips. "Always want something when the beer is here first."

"Most people want something, Skunk. You want something, you want to stay drunk for a month. I can fix it for you. I can leave thirty dollars with the barkeep for you as a tab. Then you can buy a dollar's worth of beer a day for thirty days. That should keep your nose red for a month."

"Yeah, probably. But I can't do it."

"I haven't even asked."

"Know what it is just the same. You buy me another beer?"

Laidlaw waved at the barkeep who brought two more beers and set them in front of Skunk.

"I hear things," Skunk said. He finished the first beer and turned it upside down on the table. Not a drip ran out of it. "Talk gets around. There's a federal lawman in town. Your boys missed him and one got his head blown off, the other asshole's in jail."

Skunk swilled down half the second beer, and peered at Laidlaw through barely open eyes.

"You still want the lawman planted out in the graveyard, right?"

"If he had an accident I wouldn't cry over it."

They looked at each other for a minute. Skunk drained the second beer and belched. Laidlaw wiped sweat off his face with a linen handkerchief and moved back on his chair.

"You know anybody who might like to arrange an accident?"

"Can't say, off hand."

They watched each other again. Skunk snorted, shook his head.

"Shit on a platter, Mr. Laidlaw. I wouldn't touch an accident job like that for under five hundred dollars."

Laidlaw laughed. "That's two years pay for a working man, Skunk. Outrageous."

"So is losing everything you own on land down in Virginia City. Might find some help for you for five hundred." He downed the third beer without taking a breath, belched again and stood. "You get your price up where it's worth a man's life to take on the job, and I might be able to find you three good men."

"Three?"

"That's Spur McCoy, you're talking about, Laidlaw. He's known all over the West from San Francisco to St. Louis by men who claim to make a living with their guns. He's a hard man to go up against. Don't plan to fight fair if you want him to eat lead. Come to my office anytime." Skunk turned, and walked toward the bar where he slouched at his usual end spot waiting for an unwary stranger from whom he could cadge a drink.

Laidlaw finished his beer and rolled off the chair. He went out the back door. His form was easy to spot, and he had no wish to be identified yet in town. He went through the alley that led to his hotel and in the side door and to his room.

He rested on the bed for a while, then a commotion out on Main Street brought him to his window. He pushed aside the curtains and looked out. Someone was screeching down the block in front of the bank.

Even from a half a block away he knew the woman talking was Libby Adams. Why must the woman haunt him so? She was off on another tirade. This was her town. How in hell did he shut her up long enough to win his battle with the relocation committee?

Damn! With a good rifle he could almost do the job himself from here. No, the federal man would still be there. It would do no good to win the battle for the capital only to wind up at the end of a stretched hemp rope with a noose around his neck.

He had to get the lawman out of the way first. Laidlaw called the room clerk and had him send a messenger to bring Skunk to his room. He went back to the window and watched down the block. He could almost hear what the woman was saying.

In front of the bank on a quickly put together platform, Libby Adams stabbed her finger through the air at the twenty some persons listening to her. She was just getting warmed up.

"I remind all of you ladies, that we must be equal partners in the home. We are not some chattel that can be bought and sold. We are not the property of our husbands. We are individuals in our own right! We are human beings. Without us there would be no family unit. We should have an equal say in everything that goes on in the home. We can own property. We can be accused and tried under the law.

"And since we are subject to laws, we should be able to voice for or against those laws and to elect the lawmakers. Women are just as smart and intelligent, and compassionate as men are. Men have not given us a chance to show what we can do. But my husband did. Alexander Adams had no male heir, no heir at all, so he trained me to take over his businesses.

"I've done a good job managing them and making them grow. Ask anyone in town.

"Another thing. Women pay taxes. I pay taxes. Do you know how much tax my companies paid to Lewis & Clark county last year? You would be surprised. It amounts to almost one third of the total budget of the county!

"Yes, over thirty percent. Yet I have no say whatsoever in how that money is to be spent. I don't even have a vote to elect the members of the board of county commissioners! That is simply taxation without representation. If you remember correctly, we fought a war with England over that one. Maybe I'm about ready to fight a war with the county over taxation."

She paused and looked around. There were more men than women. She saw two members of the county board listening intently to her. Good!

"What do you think would happen if I refused to pay my county taxes? What if the county suddenly had one third less money than they had last year?

Mr. Commissioner, what would you do then? What if I deny you the right to vote in the state and county elections? What would you do? Walk in my moccasins for a mile and see how it feels!"

The women in the group cheered and she let a soft smile touch her stern face.

"Gentlemen, ladies, all I'm asking for is what the women of Wyoming have. They have the vote. They had it from the very first plans to form the Wyoming Territory. All women over twenty-one in that territory vote on state and local officials and every concern on the ballot.

"You must give us the vote. We deserve it. You must start treating us like equals, not inferiors. If you don't, the day is going to come when the women will rule, and men will be treated as second class citizens!

"Look at it another way. The law says women are too dumb to vote. Fine. Then I am too dumb to vote, and I'm also not smart enough to run my businesses here in town. I made a count. I employ over four hundred people here in town. Of those four hundred, three hundred and forty-seven are heads of households.

"If I'm too dumb to run my businesses, I better just close them down. That means three hundred and forty-seven families in town will be out of work. Will the men of the county support them? Will the county poor farm take them in? Will the Board of Commissioners find food and clothing for them all?

"Makes you stop and think, doesn't it? The only conclusion has to be that women are just as smart as men. If we educate our girls as well as our boys, they will be doctors and lawyers and engineers and just as smart as their male counterparts. It's long overdue for the United States, and the Territory of

Montana to wake up, and give women the vote!''

Spur came running up. He had spent too much time with Will Walton. Damn, she was at it again. He saw a man in the crowd touch his six-gun. Spur was on him in a whisper. Grabbed the hand on the gun and powered the man six feet to the rear of the small crowd.

"What the hell?"

"Take your hand off that iron, mister!"

"Damn, what's the matter with you?"

"Looked like you were about ready to use that hogsleg."

The man shook his head. "Hell no. Happens I agree with the lady. I'm telling our representative in Virginia City to vote yes on her bill when it comes to the floor. Like the idea."

"Oh, fine. Excuse me. Just trying to protect the lady."

Man nodded. "I hear there's some cause to do just that."

Spur left the man, went to the edge of the platform and stared hard at Libby. She saw him, grinned, then waved at the crowd and stepped off the platform.

"I thought we agreed that you wouldn't make any more speeches?"

"I agreed that you said it, I never told you I would follow your suggestion."

"Let's get inside the bank," Spur said holding her elbow. She went with him.

"Spur McCoy, you should know that I'm a direct descendent of John Quincy Adams, the sixth President of the United States. No one is going to keep me quiet until they bury me."

"That's exactly how I'm afraid someone is going to shut you up. Now let's figure out how we can come to some agreement on what you will and won't do the next two days."

"I'm a descendent of the President on my mother's side, not my husband. Her name used to be Adams, too."

Spur bobbed his head at her and they went up the steps to her office.

"I didn't plan on speaking today, the mood just hit me and I went out and did it."

"Keep better control of your impulses next time until we can talk over your plans," Spur said. "You're being unfair to me, you know."

"Unfair? How?"

"If somebody kills you, I'll probably lose my job."

She looked up at him quickly, saw his crooked grin and punched him in the shoulder.

"We certainly can't let you lose your job, now, can we?" She sighed. "All right. I'll be more careful. I'll talk over with you any more speeches I want to make." She watched Spur closely. "Did you enjoy the present I sent to you last night?"

"Enjoy? What present?"

"You know what I mean, Charity."

"She was delightful. But usually my tastes run to someone a little older, more mature, experienced."

"Are you just putting in an order?"

"Just making an observation. Oh, I also prefer brunettes." He watched her and saw her look up at him quickly, a small smile faded as she turned away. He wondered what she was thinking.

"Nice try at changing the subject, but you still must be more careful. Do you think Laidlaw is in town?"

"Probably. He's more than likely planning a party for the relocation committee as soon as they hit town. It's always been his style."

"Wine, women and song?"

"At least wine, women and whiskey, plus lots of food. I've seen him operate before."

"Describe him for me. What does he look like?"

"You'll have no trouble spotting him. Rufus Laidlaw is obese, probably around three hundred pounds and about six feet tall. He is a hard man to miss. He has a fat face, tiny eyes and he's a made to order politician. He's usually within the law, but has no moral handicaps when he wants something done."

"I'll watch for him. Are you through here, ready to go home?"

"No. I have more work to do."

"When you're ready to go, I want to take you home, just in case. I think Laidlaw will try to kill you again today."

"What about yourself? Aren't you a target, too?"

"Secondary, you're the prize."

"Oh, I did hear that the surveying crew on the right of way is moving closer. They should be in town sometime tomorrow."

"Know anything about them?"

"Not much. Most of them are trained engineers who specialize in grades and routes and finding the best passes through the mountains. I've heard that some of them can be bribed to route the line a few miles this way or that. But I've also heard that some of them are so strict and professional that they would never even listen to the offer of a bribe. They are honor bound to put the road where it should go, period."

"Sounds like a good crew."

"Spur, we simply have to get the railroad to come through here. It's the best route, nobody can dispute that. I'm just afraid of the politicos, men like Laidlaw. Somehow they might come up with enough money to sway the decisions. They'll say the route should swing south with the Yellowstone River at Livingston for about twenty miles, and then cut west through the Madison Mountain range to Virginia City."

"Railroaders hate the mountains. They'll pick the easiest way through, no matter the politics."

"I hope so. If we get the railroad and the state capital relocated here, this town will be set up for a hundred years!"

Spur left then and toured the saloons. He saw no man who looked big enough to be Rufus Laidlaw. He asked in two of the saloons if the barkeep had seen him, but the two men said they were not sure who he was.

When Spur described Laidlaw they said nobody that big had been in their places all day.

The Secret Agent cruised the three blocks long Main Street and when he saw no sign of the fat man, he leaned back in a chair next to the Helena General Store and soaked up some sun.

An old timer next to him looked over with disapproval.

"New in town?" the old man asked.

"Yep."

"No wonder. These chairs is reserved for residents and customers. You either one, young feller?"

"Nope."

"Figures. And you're too big for me to pitch out of that chair so Wally can sit there, right? Probably the next thing you'll want to do is sit there and talk all afternoon."

He looked at Spur who had his eyes closed letting the sun warm him.

"Yeah, like I figured you'll probably talk my arm

off if'n I give you half a damn chance. One thing I can't stand is a body who wants to run off at the mouth all the time. Just can't bide that no way. I had me a wife for a time, and she was of that ilk. Just talk, talk, talk, all day long so a man couldn't get a word in lengthwise. You hear that blamed woman up there at the bank today?

"Now, there was a talker. Course none of us agree with her. What she needs is a man to get her pregnant and keep her barefooted and without no clothes on and in her kitchen cooking." He grinned and then snorted. "Yeah, like to see that. Libby bare assed in her kitchen." He looked at Spur again.

"Damn, you still jabbering? Be glad when Wally gets here. Least I won't have to listen to him chattering all the time. You know what I figure about this Libby woman? I got it all thought through. Now stay with me on this. I figure that . . ."

Spur tuned the old man out and let the warm Montana sun soak into his bones. There wasn't a thing he could do right now until Laidlaw or one of his men made a move. He had Libby covered, and so far they had been lucky. He hoped that their luck was not going to change. But then with luck you can never tell.

He knew he should rock the chair down on all four legs, and get up and tour the town again. Maybe he would do that in another ten minutes. Spur McCoy relaxed, and smiled. He couldn't even hear the old man beside him in the tilted back chair talking up a storm.

8

Will Walton left the eatery on Main Street, with a full belly and a lot more positive outlook than he knew he had felt for years. He flipped a twenty-dollar gold piece in the air, caught it and headed for the livery. Spur McCoy had given it to him as a loan because of old times together. Fine man that McCoy.

Will had left his fine black at the livery that morning early when he got into town, not quite sure how he would pay for the stable rent and the feed. Now he could.

He had his pistol and a box of shells, and his saddle and small sack of possibles he had left at the livery. He was set! Now what he wanted to do was ride out and find the WW ranch. He had asked at a saloon and when two people told him the same directions he believed them.

About six miles out toward the mountains, along a stringy crick and up a small valley. He paid the livery man, saddled up and rode out with confidence brimming over. This was going to be the end of a long search for him. He as sure of it. He would find his family, his son, today!

He had tried three states before where there had been WW brands registered. At two of the ranches they were obviously not the right family and they had no idea what he was talking about. The people were not his people and he faded away quickly. The third one had been burned out by Indians and the owners had left a year before.

Now he had another chance. It *just felt different* this time. Somehow, he knew this had to be the right place. He was going to find his family . . . his SON!

Will blinked back the sudden moisture in his eyes and galloped out of town to the west, then reined down and walked the mount, not wanting to burn her out before they got to the valley. The closer he came to the right spot, the more certain he became.

All those years of wandering, not sure who he was for months at a time, chasing the ghosts of men killed five years before in the war, trying hard to remember where he should be going, all of that was going to end . . . and soon.

He had ridden away with confidence from the Rebel prison camp that first day after they got the word the war was over. He had been lucky and drew a half worn out horse from one of the Northern companies that opened up the camp.

He had turned west and galloped for Kansas. But somehow he never reached it. Where had he been for those five years? What did he do to stay alive? Will shook his head. He would not even think about that anymore. He was going home! The words made emotion surge up in his throat and he could hardly breathe for a moment. His eyes misted and he wiped at them with his hand.

Home!

He came to the rise where he could see the valley and the crooked little stream that came out of it. The valley was a mile long, half that wide, plenty of graze for three hundred head in this green!

At the far end he saw a house, log construction, with a barn to one side and what looked like two corrals. He rode then, anxious to be sure, to tie it down once and for all that he was home, that his wandering and hunting were over.

The horse stopped at the stream to drink, and he stared ahead. The log cabin was closer now, must be twenty-four feet square, maybe bigger! Lots of work involved there.

He walked the horse then, memorizing every tree, the patches of bright green along the stream. He saw where it had overflowed with spring rains, turning the low meadow into a marsh for a while but now thick with belly-deep grass. Ahead, fir and western larch stood as sentries around the cabin and peppered the far end of the valley where the hills rose.

It was perfect! A great looking little spread. He saw the cattle long before that, but hadn't wanted to concentrate on them until he was closer. Now he did and saw that they were a mixed breed, but he could recognize none of the stock he had used.

Seven years! None of the animals would be the same even if they drove some breeding stock up here, which would be doubtful.

He came out from behind a copse of brush and hardwood trees along the creek and headed down a narrow lane the last quarter mile to the house.

It even had hollyhocks growing by the corner. His wife, Martha, had always been partial to hollyhocks.

He was two hundred yards away when a young boy of six or seven came away from the well house with a hoop and stick, when the hoop fell over, the boy saw him. He stood still for a moment, then when he was sure the man rode toward the house, he ran quickly to the side door and vanished.

A woman soon stepped from the side door a shotgun in her hands. She was short, chunky with stringy yellow hair. His heart skipped a beat. So long! It had been such a long damn time! Was it her, was this woman really his wife?

He rode forward, kept his hands where they had been on the reins. He didn't want to come all this way, all five years, and then be shot down as a robber.

His horse kept walking forward. He stared at the woman's face. Too far yet. At fifty yards he wasn't sure. Then at twenty he was. A surging joy filled him. Will walked the black horse up to within ten feet of the woman.

"Hello Martha, it's been a long time." He had practiced a hundred thousand times what he would say when he found her. Now only this had come out.

She looked at him. "How come you know my name?"

"Don't you recognize me, Martha. Mite older now, been seven years. Don't you remember back in sixty-three when I left the WW ranch in Kansas and went to war . . ."

Small muscles tightened around her mouth. She looked toward the barn, then on west.

"You best get moving on. My husband don't allow no grub stake riders around when he's not here." She made no move to lift the shotgun which now pointed at the ground.

"Martha, I hear you had a baby, a boy. I never did see him. Didn't you get my letters?"

"Why would I get letters from a stranger? You

best move out of here before my husband comes."

The shotgun muzzles came up now, both pointing dead square on his chest.

"Martha, I'm going to take off my hat, slow and easy. Don't do nothing rash with that scattergun. Slow and easy take off my hat. You'll recognize me then." He slid off the battered black hat and held it over his chest. "Remember, Martha? I met you on Tuesday and the next Saturday I came courting and we got married a week later. Remember, Martha? Emmy Lou James stood up with you, and my best man was Hic Warren. Remember?"

"Best just move on, stranger."

"Martha, I've been hunting you for five years. I got wounded in the war, made me forget things, sometimes for months at a time . . ."

"My husband got killed in the war, at the Wilderness. Nobody seen him after that. Don't know what kind of stories you been hearing."

"My name is William Walton. That WW brand is still mine, legal and registered in Kansas City. You're my wife Martha, and that boy must be my son. What's so hard to believe about that, Martha?"

"My husband got war-killed. Told you. Can't stand here all day."

She put her finger on the trigger. "You aiming to move on, or do I have to dig a grave?"

"Why did you sell our place in Kansas, Martha? It was a good little spread."

"Sold the place when I was a legal widow. Judge said any soldier not coming home twelve months after the war was legal and declared him dead. Made me a widow. Got the paper somewhere. My husband was war-killed. Admit you look something like he used to. But you old now."

"So are you, Martha, but I know you."

She called the boy who came and stood beside her.

"You bring those extra shells, Will, like I told you?" she asked the lad.

He held up four more 10-gauge shotgun shells. She lifted the muzzle and blasted a load of shot six feet over Will's head.

"Martha, I got my discharge paper. I can prove I'm Will Walton."

"Don't matter none. I got my paper too. All legal and honest. I'm married again. Good man. Big German man who would break you in half. You best move on down the trail."

Quickly she broke the shotgun open pulled out the spent shell, pushed another one in and had it trained on Will before he could move.

"You always was good with weapons, Martha. You dead set on this?"

"My man got war-killed. Got a paper."

Will took one more good look at the seven year old boy. He had Will's brown hair, his lean chin and long nose.

"Reckon I better move on, then, your mind made up. You owe me for the ranch. Gonna ask a lawyer back in town about it. Legal dead ain't real dead."

She motioned with the weapon.

He turned the horse.

"Still time to change your mind, Martha. Court might figure you moved a little quick after that twelve months."

She shook her head.

"What's my son's name. You can tell me that. Looks just like me. What's your name, son?"

"Will, William Walton, Jr. Are you . . ." He looked at his mother who was grim faced staring at the man on the horse. "Are you my real Pa?"

"Shore am, Will. Mighty proud to meet you after

all this time. I got hurt in the war, forgot who I was for a long time. Not too sure where I was even. But now I'm well, I know who I am and I know who you are. I'm your real Pa. You tell your Ma that when I ride off."

He turned and kicked the horse in the flanks. The black exploded away from the spot and three seconds later the shotgun roared, speading instant death where he had been sitting only moments before. He looked back and saw her swing the gun, but he was out of range of the pellets by then.

Tears streamed down his face. He stopped the black and turned to look at the spread again. The woman went in the cabin at once, came out and took the boy with her to the barn. A minute later he saw them both mounted, and riding to the east. He moved down trail.

She would be going to talk to her husband. Now there was nothing else for him to do. He had to go back to town and talk to Captain McCoy, then see a good lawyer. Some lawyers would not even talk to you unless you showed them money first. He would see, he would see.

Behind him Martha Walton rode toward the east range.

"Is he my real Pa? Is he Ma?"

"You just ride and forget what he said. We do have ourselves a problem. Hans will know what to do. That's why he's around. You don't worry none about your Pa. If he had wanted you or me he would have found us a long time ago. That man was just somebody your Pa talked to during the war. Still happens. Strangers bothering us war widows."

"He did look like the picture you got, Ma."

"Hush up and help me find Hans."

"Looked a lot like me, Ma."

"You tryin' to get a clout 'long side the head, boy?"

"No, Ma."

"Then hush up. We got troubles enough without you starting to yowl like some old hurt tom cat."

"Hans said he was going to find those strays," Will Jr. said.

"Where's that?"

"Out by the far windmill."

They found Hans twenty minutes later. She told him straight out what the man said.

"Is he who he says?" Hans asked, his broad German face stern.

"Don't matter for sure, he thinks he is."

"I want to know. It does matter."

"Reckon he probably is. Been a long time."

"Then we have a problem. You have a problem."

"We both at fault, Hans. You just as much as me. You said to do it, showed me how and all. Law will say you're to blame, too."

Hans frowned and put his hands on his hips. They all were dismounted around the stock tank beside a twenty foot tower windmill. The blades spun around, the drive arm worked up and down and with each cycle, another gush of water ran down the wooden trough and into the tank.

"There's only one way to take care of it," Hans said.

"We could move again."

"No, I told you, this was the last time we move," Hans said. "We're on a good spread. We stay put. He's the one who rides on."

"He won't, not Will. Stubborn man once he thinks he's right."

"So we're back to the one answer," Hans said.

"What's that, Ma? What you aiming to do?"

"Shut up, boy!" Hans roared. "When we want your mouth working, we'll ask you." He looked back at Martha. "You're in this feet first too, you know. You got a better way to settle it?"

"Move on. Or take him in. We could take him in and . . ."

"He's your husband. Think he'd take kindly to your living with me these past five years?"

"No, Will wouldn't understand that. I thought he was war-killed. We both did. A year after the war and he wasn't back yet. Judge agreed with me. Then when you come to the house that night, just seemed natural."

"Now Will suspects, he'll blow my head off. I got to get him before he kills me."

"Must be a better way, Hans."

"If you figure one out, you tell me. We're riding back to the house so I can get a rifle and some more shells. Then I'm heading out to do what has to be done."

None of them spoke on the way back.

At the ranch house, Will Jr. took two of the horses to the corral and unsaddled them. When he came back, Hans was ready to ride.

"You gonna shoot my Pa, Hans?"

"Shut up, kid."

"Hans, we could tell Will flat out it's all legal. I got the judge paper making him legally war-killed. We're legal anyway we want it. We could give him half the ranch somehow. Must be a better way than this."

"And when he finds out about the other?"

"No way he has to find out. I won't tell him. Will here didn't know nothing about it."

"He'd find out. There's more coming the letter

said. They'll want to check his signature for sure this time. Him being on a long cattle drive won't work again."

"I've changed my mind, Hans. I can't do this to Will. He was my husband for three years."

"I been with you for five years, that mean nothing?"

"Course." She turned and let the tears come. When she looked back she wiped the wetness away. "Hans, don't go. Stay here and let's think through all the ways to settle it. Must be a better way than this."

"Sure, for you. Turn me in and say I done it 'cause I signed the paper, and they send me to prison, you get your husband back and all the hard work I've put into this place." He swung up on the gray and shook his head. "Not a chance, woman. I've earned what I have here, and no wandering range bum is going to cheat me out of it!"

He turned and rode away.

"No, Hans, don't!"

Her plea was lost in the clatter of hooves on the hard ground of the trail toward town.

9

Will Walton paused on his black at the far end of the mile-long valley and turned, staring back at the spread where his wife and son were. Once he saw them riding across the valley toward a far finger canyon, then they were out of sight.

He couldn't simply ride away. Not after such a long search, so much pain and hurt and anguish. He had to get off the black and sit on the rich grass. He never had graze like this in Kansas.

Why wouldn't she admit who he was and take him in? He was legally dead she had said. A judge gave her a paper. She had probably married again. Reasonable.

He looked away and shouted. "No!" Why had it happened to him? Didn't he have enough problems? For a moment he recalled one or two of his days of wandering. The times came back in snatches, and none of them were pleasant. At least he could not remember ever being in jail.

He watched the clouds skittering over the mountains far to the west. The Rockies! He had often heard of them.

Why had she turned him away? It had to be more than a new husband. What? He stirred, then lay back in the grass and stared at the sky. Someday he would know. Now he had to do the logical, rational thing—go back to town and talk to McCoy, then talk to the best lawyer Helena had.

Will rode slowly. He had no great desire to bring the law against his former wife. Or was she still his wife? He knew some of the missing during the war had been declared legally dead. But what happened to him? Was he still married or not? He would let a judge decide that.

He would live with it either way. He admitted that he hardly recognized his wife. She had changed. She wasn't just plump now, she was fat, and not that pretty anymore. Ranch life was cruel to any woman, it wore her down, destroyed her youth and beauty and soon she was another work animal. It was twice that hard on a man.

He came to a long arm of timber that slanted diagonally up a ridge, down through a small feeder stream valley and upward into the foothills. He knew enough about the terrain now so he could save a mile by cutting over the ridge and through the timber.

Mostly lodgepole pines here and a few Engelmann spruce, so there was less underbrush. Someday the loggers would move in here. But not until the railroad came through so they could get the lumber out at a fair price. The days of wagon trains hauling goods out of the mountains was almost over.

The trains would revolutionize commerce in the next twenty years. It was an exciting time to be alive. So much happening. The West opening up so quickly, people on the move. New inventions coming out every year.

A half mile ahead he saw what looked like the same horse at the side of the trail. The rider was off giving his steed a blow. He wiped the horse down as Will rode up.

The man looked up and smiled. "Crazy horse tried to run away with me. Just broke her couple of weeks ago. I think she's got it out of her system now. Heading for town?"

The man was big and blond. Will said he was going that way. The man eyed him a minute.

'Wouldn't be looking for work, would you? On my way to town to pick up a good man with steers. Got some roundup and branding work to do, and I could use another hand. Just a small spread. You interested?"

Will pushed his hat back and crooked his left leg around the saddle horn. He took out makings and rolled himself a brown paper smoke.

"Could be. I been around cattle most of my life."

"Look a little thin. Sure you could put in a dawn to dark day on the range?"

"Does a horse have four feet?"

The man laughed. "Well, guess I should know your name."

"Will Walton," he said. Will saw in a haze as the man dug for his six-gun. Will's came up fast and first and a shot sang past the man's right arm so close it stopped the man's draw before he had iron out of leather.

"You know me, but I'm not sure about you. Must be Hans, who's been living with my wife for past five or six years."

"Got me all wrong, friend," Hans said, his hands well away from his weapon. "Me, I'm just a ranch hand. Woman didn't know nothing about cattle and

I did. When you didn't come home after the war, she just natural kept me on."

"Most ranch foremen don't sleep with the owner."

"Hell, after three years it just sort of happened."

"That's the way you die, it just sort of happens, today. You stole my ranch, my cattle, my wife and even my son. Why should I let you live?"

"I'm not even sure you're who you say you are. You got a paper says so? You prove it any way?"

"I can. Martha. When she's naked she's got a silver dollar size birthmark on her left thigh, high up to her crotch. That enough? She's also got two moles on her left breast. Now how could I know that less I had bedded the lady, who is my wife. You got anything else smart to say before I kill you?"

"Yeah, where the hell you been the last five years? Why didn't you come back? She waited for you a year after it was over? You didn't come 'cause you was crazy out of your head, right? I heard about men like you. Got so sick of killing that they went crazy and tried to forget it and forgot everything.

"While you were running around all crazy, I was doing your work on the ranch, branding, cutting out stock to sell, driving them to the railhead. I worked for everything I got, I didn't take it away from you, I built up the herd."

"My herd. It was still my ranch, my wife, my son."

"So go ahead and kill me. But I bet you can't. You killed too much during the war. Now you can point that thing, but you won't gun me down in cold blood. Not a chance."

"Try me and see, asshole!"

"Aim to. You still half out of your head. Crazy man."

"I was, but I saw my son. I'm fine now. No more

blackouts, no more spells when I can't see straight and don't know where I am. That's all over. First I kill you, then take over my spread again and my wife if she wants to stay. But my son stays, that's for damn sure!''

Will wondered if he was slowing down, or maybe he *couldn't shoot a man anymore.* Hans faked to the left, surged back, then went left and kicked out with his boot, spinning the six-gun from Will's hand. Hans turned and ran.

Will dropped to the ground, grabbed his gun again, but by then Hans was into the timber, past two big lodgepole pines. Will rolled to get behind some protection as a round slammed into the ground where he had been.

"I got plenty of time, Will. You're a dead man. You'll never get to town. I know every inch of this woods and the range. We're still four miles from Helena.''

Will sent a round into the brush where he thought the voice came from, but heard only a laugh.

Will saw the man running for his horse which he had whistled for. He had a shot but didn't pull the trigger. For just a flash his mind saw a Reb soldier and his horse. The smoke of the Wilderness came and the saplings and thorn brush, but Will beat the images back, smashed them down, refused to accept them.

Slowly his vision cleared and he was still in Montana. The gunman was on his horse and vanishing into the pine trees.

Will mounted and rode after Hans. He was trailing him, which meant going slower, but making sure he didn't walk into an ambush and be shot from his saddle.

He saw the angle the horseman took led uphill and

away from town. That figured. Spur tracked him for a half hour, then came to a dense woods, that reminded him too much of the Wilderness. A rider could sit in there ten yards without being seen.

A simple trail double back would put a man in perfect position for an ambush. Will rode to the left, around the ambush spot by fifty yards, then doubled back and waited in an ambush of his own.

Hans came out of the dark woods, fast, charging through the lighter brush and trees, aiming for the top of the ridge. Will waited until he was not more than twenty yards away and fired three times with his pistol.

He knew the first round was high, pulled it down but by then, Hans had leaned almost out of the saddle. Will's next round hit the saddle horn and slanted away and his third round would have unseated a rider in the saddle.

Then Hans was away into the brush.

Will followed him. There was nothing else to do now. He figured Hans had decided to make Will stay dead with a pair of .44 slugs. That would solve his and Martha's problem. Will wasn't enthusiastic about the solution. He got off his mount and checked the ground where the trail faded, came up with it across a hard packed earth area where the horse had gone hard through a small creek and up the far side.

The tracking became slower. Will worked deliberately. Now was no time to make a mistake. It could be his last if he did. He checked the route, moved ahead a hundred yards and found the tracks again, then once more leaped ahead only to lose the prints and have to go back to the last sighting.

The trail led up the slope into heavy forest of Douglas fir and ponderosa pine. A sudden shot slammed into the intense silence of the woods. No round came near Spur. The man ahead could have dropped his six-gun, or shot at a snake.

Will galloped ahead quickly toward the sound of the shot. He came around a pair of three-foot thick Douglas fir trees standing almost side by side and saw the problem twenty yards ahead. It was a draw, free of brush, but heavily matted on each side.

Hans sat on his nervous horse facing the biggest Grizzly bear Will had ever seen. It had reared up on its hind legs and stared from small eyes at the man and horse. The bear stood nine feet tall and looked down on the rider.

Hans had his six-gun out but did not fire again. A wounded Grizzly is a horrendous foe, Will had heard. The bear roared and swiped at the horse which jittered backward, head twisting and turning. Hans had trouble enough just to stay seated on the animal.

He fired again into the dirt beside the Grizzly's big feet but the huge beast stood his ground.

There was no time for Hans to pull the heavy Sharps rifle from his boot. He moved the prancing horse backward, looked at both sides, but there was no way out. He had to back uphill.

Will had drawn his pistol and sighted in on Hans, then let his weapon's aim drift over toward the bear.

In a move that caught both men by surprise, the Grizzly jolted forward and with one ponderous swipe of a huge front paw, slammed the side of Hans' horse to the left, breaking its neck, tumbling Hans to the ground. He rolled as he hit, came to his feet running and wedged between a pair of trees on the edge of the ravine and scampered into the thick brush where the monster Grizzly would have trouble following.

Will's horse had heard the death cry of the other animal. It bucked unexpectedly and Will barely held his saddle. He swung the animal around and charged back up the gully. At the first opening he turned right the same direction Hans had moved.

He rode past a big ponderosa pine into a small opening in the brush when a pistol shot slapped at him. The hot lead ripped apart the air an inch from his skull and faded into the distance.

Will threw himself off the horse to the left, hit the ground hard and held onto his pistol. He was infantry, not a horse soldier. Will listened to the horse crashing through the brush for a dozen yards, then she stopped and all was quiet.

A branch broke to his right. Will lifted around a ponderosa and scanned the area. A slight movement of a young pine tree caught his attention. It stopped, then moved again. He watched the spot. A leg swung forward and Will pounded two shots into the space just above the leg. He heard a groan and something crashed to the ground.

As soon as Will fired he rolled to the left to another tree and stared around it on the opposite side as before.

Nothing.

He heard nothing, saw no movement. Slowly he began to circle the spot. He had to know for sure if Hans was hit, dead or only playing dead.

It took him fifteen minutes to worm through the woods silently, using cover wherever possible. At last he came to the spot he wanted, about ten yards from his former target and slightly above it.

There was a body there, all right. Will stared at it, torso, legs, one hand, the other arm thrown over the head. He could not see the man's face.

Dead? Will wondered. He moved closer, but there

was no reaction. He threw a rock at the body, but it did not flinch or move. Was he wasting time on a dead man?

Will lifted and slid behind a big pine. He looked out from ground level. He was six yards from the body now, still there was no way to see the face. It was covered by the one arm and some brush.

Will held the six-gun in both hands and walked forward, ready to fire at a moment's notice.

There was no notice. The hidden hand held a gun and it exploded twice in the blink of an eye. Both rounds hit Will. The first caught him high in the thigh and spun him around. Before he fell a second round slammed into his chest, on the right side, shattering a rib and puncturing his lung.

He jolted backward from the second round and lay stunned. He was in such deep shock that he couldn't move, couldn't speak. His eyes were open but for a few minutes they were frozen in place.

Hans, the "dead" body, lifted from the branches he had used to cover his face but leaving room for him to see out, hurried to Will. He held his six-gun trained on Will.

With one boot he lifted Will's right arm. It dropped like a dead weight. With his knife he drew a thin blood line down Will's cheek. Will didn't react. He couldn't, for the moment he was paralyzed.

Hans stood, aimed at Will's forehead and said, "Bang, bang," laughed softly and then turned.

"Now to find his goddamn horse before it wanders off." He frowned for a moment. "He died too easy. I wanted it to last longer." Hans shrugged and hurried to find Will's black horse.

Will lay there as if dead.

But he was still alive. He had heard everything Hans said. Now he waited for his body to die or give him back some powers. The sensations came slowly. First his eyes rolled and responded. He could move them, look at what he wanted to!

Next his sense of pain returned. His chest exploded with an agonizing pain that made him want to be paralyzed again. The agony seemed to peak, and then recede enough that he could manage it. His leg began to hurt and that's when he realized he had been shot in two places.

Hans had played possum on him, and the trick had worked. It had killed him. Will knew he was going to die. Doctors just didn't know how to patch up the kind of wound he had in his chest. His lungs were both on fire.

Slowly his legs began to work, then his arms. He rolled over and tried to sit up. It took him five minutes. He was a dead man, he knew. Will wasn't sure where he was, but it had to be a mile off the old wagon road he had followed. His only hope was to get there and pray help came past on the road.

Each time he breathed, fresh fires scorched his lungs. He tried to suck in air as gently as possible.

How could he move a mile through the brush and timber?

If only his horse were here he would have a fighting chance. His horse. He called. His voice came out a croak, but the name, "Blackie" somehow made it through. He clutched at his chest after the call. It hurt so much tears sprang to his eyes.

Four times he called the horse. The last time it was almost a shout, and he had some hope. Then he remembered that Hans' horse had been killed by the Grizzly and he had tried to find the black.

Will checked the position of the sun. Getting low. Maybe three in the afternoon. Time had flown on him again. He could sit right there and die. Or he could rip up his new shirt and make a bandage for his leg to stop that blood. No way to stop the blood starting to pool in his lung.

Five minutes later he had his leg wound wrapped and bandaged. The bleeding stopped. Good. Nothing he could do for his lung. He made one more try at calling the horse.

After the call he coughed and spit up blood, and he remembered what the Rebel soldier had said at the Wilderness about wounded men who spit up blood. Half dead already.

He heard something behind him. With a great effort, Will turned his head and saw his black mount push her head through a clump of brush. He called again, softly. The mare nickered and walked forward, stopping six feet in front of him.

Now what? He did not have the strength to get on the horse. There was no convenient stump of fallen log. The horse was not trick trained to lay down so he could roll into the saddle.

He thought it through again, then whistled and the horse came forward again, nearly stepping on his extended leg. She stopped beside him.

The stirrup! If he could reach up and grab it, and he could convince the horse to walk forward, she could drag him to the wagon road.

He reached as high as he could. The bottom of the stirrup was still three inches above his head. Will closed his eyes. He would die right here if he didn't catch that damn iron! He used one arm and pushed up, then surged upward with his right hand and grabbed for the stirrup.

A wave of pain battered through his body such as he had never felt before. He screamed, his whole system seemed to be on fire and bombarding his nervous system with agony signals.

He missed the stirrup.

Again he tried it to the same kind of pain, but this time his fingers closed around the iron and he held on. The horse unused to that kind of pressure on the saddle skittered toward him, then away. He held on.

"Whoa, girl. Whoa down!" She steadied. He tried to pull himself up to a standing position, but there was no strength left in his legs. He had lost too much blood, he decided. A wave of blackness swept toward him, but he dodged it and held onto the stirrup.

He had to get her moving. "Okay, girl, let's move. Giddap!" She took one hesitant step and stopped. "Come on, girl, Giddap!" She took another step, then a third and he felt his heels drag in the dirt as she pulled him along the ground.

How did he direct her? He didn't. He couldn't. He had to hope that she headed downhill toward the wagon road. It was the only thing he had left.

After fifty yards he swung around and let the pains sear through his chest as he reached up with his left hand and now held the stirrup with both.

The pain in his chest came in surging rushes that left him giddy and light headed. When the blast passed, he could open his eyes again. He saw now that the black had picked a downhill course through a gentle valley that had no timber and little brush.

For a moment he felt strong enough to try to stand, but after getting one leg up the other buckled and he nearly lost his grip on the stirrup. As he looked around he remembered none of the landmarks. He had never been in this valley before. The black wanted a drink, so she walked into the foot deep stream and stopped and drank.

The ice cold water on his feet and legs buoyed his spirits for a moment, then he realized his shoes had filled with water and there was nothing he could do about it.

The mare moved again, pulling him out of the water, back to the soft grass. His arms were like lead clubs. He had lost most of the feeling in them. He figured his arms would tear away from his shoulders at any minute.

Then they did.

He fell with his face in the grass as his hands came off the stirrup and it took him a moment to realize it. The relief in his arms was so wonderful he wanted it to go on and on.

"Whoa!" he called. The black stopped six strides away. If he called her back, she would turn around and drag him back the way they had come. He had to go where she was.

A few inches at a time would be the best he could do. He had to move forward. He pushed with his good leg, and pulled with his hands and elbows. Pushed and pulled, inches at a time.

It took him five minutes to cover the ten feet. Then he surged up and missed the stirrup. The pain in his chest almost knocked him out. He lay there gasping.

The second time he tried he caught the metal stirrup and got the black moving again.

Will began to count to take his mind off the pain. He closed his eyes and counted horses in a field, he counted steers as they came down a branding chute, he counted buffalo as they charged across the railroad tracks in Kansas.

"What the hell is this?" a voice boomed out at him from the darkness.

Will opened his eyes, looked up at a man towering over him. He was a farmer in overalls and a straw hat.

"God A'mighty, you're shot up bad!" He bent and pried Will's hands from the stirrup. "Easy now. Easy. Got a wagon here loaded but plenty of room for you on some loose hay for a mattress. You like a shot of whiskey? Shouldn't hurt that wound none. Gonna hurt some as I lift you into the wagon."

It didn't hurt, it spun Will into a frenzied scream that carried him into blessed unconsciousness.

The farmer grunted and lay Will on the straw, then covered him up with a blanket and got his rig moving down the road toward town. He urged the two plow horses along at a faster rate than usual. The farmer scowled as he watched the man. He'd been shot at least twice, but he was still alive. He wondered how far the horse had dragged the man. By rights he should be dead.

The farmer stopped in front of Dr. Harriman's office and ran inside. The medic came outside and shook his head. Between them they carried Will into the office and lay him on a table.

He regained consciousness when Doc Harriman poured whiskey over his leg wound.

"Oh, damn!" Will said.

Doc looked at him. "Bad way. Who are you? What happened?"

"Will Walton. Spur McCoy knows. Tell him ... tell him ... Martha ... I saw my son!" Then Will drifted back into unconsciousness.

Doctor Harriman tried for five minutes more, but there was nothing else he could do. Sheriff Palmer sat in the outer office. Doc came out and shook his head.

"He's gone. Amazing he lasted as long as he did. Lung a mass of blood, probably filled full by now." He told the sheriff what Will had said, word for word.

"This Spur McCoy knows him. He might know what it's all about. Thanks Doc."

10

Rufus Laidlaw watched the farm wagon wheel into town and heard the excitement about the man who had been shot. Tough luck. He was interested in other things. He went back into the saloon he had been drinking at and stared at his glass. He should have a report from the clerks at the hotels soon. He had paid them to tell him when any of the railroad men got to town.

He finished the afternoon with the whiskey and a moment before he left one of the desk clerks came running in.

"Just registered a man who said he was a railroader. He's in the dining room now at the Montana House hotel."

Laidlaw waddled over to the hotel and the clerk pointed out the rail man. Laidlaw sent a bottle of wine to the man's table with a card bearing his name, and waited, then walked up.

"Sir my name is Laidlaw, and I'd like a word with you if that would be possible."

The man was in his late thirties, clean shaven with

a soft look about him. He stood at once.

"Mr. Laidlaw. Thanks for the wine. Please sit down. What can I do for you, sir?"

For the moment Laidlaw was surprised by the man's cow-towing ways. He sat and let the man pour him a glass of wine.

"Understand you're a railroad man?"

"Deed I am, Mr. Laidlaw. Been in the trade for over ten years now."

"Working the area around here?"

"Not hardly. No roads in this part, not yet that is. Hear two lines are coming this direction but could be ten years before the steel and ties get here."

"I heard the same thing," Laidlaw said sensing a winning hand. "Know what route they might be taking?"

"Rumors are that they will follow the Yellowstone most of the way, maybe four hundred miles across the state. Then, God only knows where they head."

"Wondered if you might have some say in that?"

"Me? No, I'm afraid not, Mr. Laidlaw."

"Aren't you on the survey team from the Northern Pacific?"

The man smiled, sipped the wine. "Not at all. I'm a railroad engineer by trade. Right now I'm going to Omaha after a visit to my kin up in Washington Territory. I hear there are some good jobs opening up for qualified engineers so . . ."

Rufus Laidlaw pushed back his chair and stood.

"Sorry I bothered you, sir," he said, turned quickly and walked away. Railroad man my foot! Laidlaw stormed as he hurried out to the desk clerk to demand his money back.

Laidlaw moved on to the smallest hotel, but the one in town he thought had the best food. He went into his room after ordering dinner sent to his room through the room clerk. He was surprised to find a woman on his bed. Then he remembered, he had ordered one from Marie's, the best whorehouse in town.

She sat up and stretched. She wore only a thin chemise and he could see her breasts pressing outward.

"You finally get here. It costs extra to wait, you know."

He snorted and went to the bed. She pulled off the chemise and she was as ordered, big breasts and small waist. She was partly redhead and mostly blonde.

"You ready or do you just want to look and jerk off?"

"Does your mouth ever stop running? Hell, I know how to fill it up with something." He unbuttoned his fly and tugged down his pants then kicked them off.

"Get on the floor between my knees," he said.

"Jesus . . . nobody told me. . . ."

"You want me to lay on top of you, bitch?"

"God no!" she thought about it a minute. "Hell, for five dollars you got a deal."

"Thought so. Money always does it."

She stood in front of him and let him play with her breasts, then knelt and began to work over his less than totally interested third leg.

"About time," he said when she slid his erection into her mouth and began bobbing back and forth. "Don't take all night, I got work to do."

She pushed him over on his back on the bed and moved higher. Then she slid over him, plunged his hardness into her waiting vagina and pretended he was a small pony and she was the rider.

"Damn, you are a real whore, aren't you? Bet you

could make a worn out hound dog get a hardon. Oh damn!" He thrust into her hard once bellowed in satisfaction and pushed her away and reached for his pants.

"That's it?" she asked surprised.

"Hell, I ain't sixteen anymore. I don't cum for a week and a half without stopping on an all night fuck."

"Yeah, but you ain't seventy either. Had me an old codger who was sixty-five and was he a good fucker!"

"Did he pay you five dollars?"

"Nope."

"Then get dressed and get out of here before my dinner arrives. I don't let anything spoil my eating not even a sweet little pussy like you. Now move your ass."

"Yeah, that's plain to see you like to eat." She jumped back when he swung at her, then finished dressing. She grabbed his pants and took out a bulging wallet, extracted a five dollar greenback and two ones, and threw his pants back at him.

"The two dollars is a tip, you got any complaints about the service?"

"No, now get out!"

Five minutes later the room clerk let the dining room steward bring in the dinner cart. Tonight Laidlaw had ordered three complete dinners: a two pound steak, medium rare, a large plate of spaghetti, and another dinner of fresh caught fish. Each came with vegetables, salad and soup. He ate everything in sight even the half dozen rolls in the covered basket.

As he ate, Laidlaw formulated his plans. He could always think better when his stomach was filling. He had to concentrate on Spur. Once the federal officer was taken out, he would have more luck eliminating the woman. Both had to be done tonight.

The first job was to set up a small vacation for the lady. Nothing fancy, just something away from Helena for two days. That shouldn't be hard.

When he finished eating he sent for Skunk Johnson at the saloon. Ten minutes later Skunk was in his room. He told the man exactly what he wanted done, and how much he would pay. Skunk could find his own men.

"No trouble. I've got the men to do it. She'll be home tonight. I'd suggest just after dark. Now, you said two jobs."

"I have five hundred for you for those three good men we talked about before. But there has to be a guarantee. If Spur McCoy is still living my midnight, you get ten dollars a man, period."

Skunk looked at him, tipped the beer Laidlaw had provided, then nodded. "Done. You don't know nothing about it. I'll need the thirty now, to sweeten the pot a little."

Laidlaw gave Skunk three ten dollar greenbacks and the derelict walking like a man slipped out of Laidlaw's room and then out the side door. He had walked the back streets and alleys all of his life.

Spur McCoy had just finished eating dinner with Libby in the mansion, when a messenger brought him an envelope. He tried to see who delivered it, but the person was gone quickly.

Spur opened it and read it, then showed it to Libby.

"McCoy. I know you want to find out who shot Libby Adams. I can tell you who it was, but if anybody knows I told you, I'm a dead cowboy. Meet me in back of the livery stable corral tonight at eight-thirty.''

Spur checked the Seth Thomas on the dining room mantle. It was a little before seven.

"You won't go," Libby said. "It's a trap, a set up to get you alone in the dark.''

"Not many bushwhackers will take on a federal agent. They know three more will show up to find out what happened to the first one. It could be a lead. I'll be careful. Getting there early is part of that. I'm gone.''

He grabbed his gunbelt, put an extra box of rounds in his brown vest pocket, and checked the Remington .44 New Model army revolver and shoved it into the holster. On the way out he picked up the Henry Repeating Rifle he lived with these days. it was a .44 caliber rim fire ammo model, with a 24-inch octagonal barrel with six rifling grooves inside. It weighed over nine pounds. He liked the long tubular magazine that slid in under the barrel and held twelve cartridges.

The Henry worked with a trigger guard lever. This was the weapon the Rebels said the Yanks loaded up on Sunday and fired all week.

"I don't want you to go," Libby said moving up to him. She reached in and kissed his cheek. "I was hoping we might be able to talk tonight and have a cozy fire, get better acquainted.''

"Soon," Spur said. "I had something of the same ideas, maybe with a bottle of wine and some cheese thrown in. Later. I've got to check this out. I'll be careful.''

He ran out the back door and the house and over two blocks before he stopped. There would be at least three of them, he figured, and it would be a kill try. But a lot of men had tried to ambush him before. He went straight out of town three blocks into the countryside, then swung around behind the livery stables. He could see the two lanterns inside where men were cleaning stalls. There was little cover behind either corral. He chose the one with the best cover, a smattering of brush about twenty yards away.

Spur settled in the back of the brush and began his watch. Just before eight o'clock he heard a horse coming. It was cloudy and dark now. Whoever it was had not taped down his saddle rattles. He had never been in battle with a horse.

Spur picked him up out of the gloom. As the horse bored into the brush, Spur moved parallel to it, barely ten feet away. The rider was not looking for any surprises. He rode to the middle of the fifty foot wide patch of brush and dismounted. He tied the horse to a tree and moved to lift a rifle from the boot.

Spur clubbed him with the side of the Remington pistol and he went down without a sound. Before he came back to consciousness Spur had stripped him of two knives, a hideout gun and a pair of revolvers.

He appeared to be about thirty. Should know better. Spur waited for him to come back to consciousness. When he did Spur could see in the moonlight that his eyes were wild.

"What the hell . . .?"

"Sloppy work," Spur said. "If I was going to try to bushwhack somebody, I'd get there an hour early, hide well, and wait. Not come jangling in on a horse ten minutes before time."

"What you talking about?"

Spur hit him in the jaw with his fist knocking him down. He sat up holding his jaw and Spur hit him again.

"Who hired you?" Spur snarled. "You've got a minute to tell me, then your own knife is going to start slicing up your hide."

"Nobody hired me. Just out for a ride."

"That's why you were pulling out a rifle?" Spur hit him again sprawling him from his sitting position into the dirt.

He sat up slower. "No more! Okay, I was waiting. I was just support for the main two up closer to the fence."

Spur had learned the information he needed. He whacked the man with the Remington pistol again, knocking him out. Then he tied his hands behind him. Tied his feet and put a gag in his mouth.

Spur moved like a moon shadow across the open space to the edge of the corral fence. It was still fifteen minutes to the deadline. He found the best hiding spot on the left side. A feedbox had been placed just outside the fence. Ten yards way were a dozen bales of straw. He slid between an alley in the bales and stood the rifle beside him. By crouching just a little he was totally hidden.

Five minutes later he heard someone coming. A man hurried to the feed box and went over the fence hiding behind it just inside the enclosure. The dozen horses moved a little but most had settled down for the night, sleeping where they stood.

At eight thirty, Spur assumed the other man was in place. He lifted up and cupped his hands pointing his voice back toward the stables.

"Hey, McCoy here." he said speaking loud but not shouting. "Who the hell am I meeting?"

The man behind the feed box spoke.

"Over this way. I got to be sure you're alone."

"I'm alone. Where are you?"

Spur saw him lift then behind the box. Spur

tipped a bale of hay off the end of the stack so it bounced near the fence.

The man behind the box powered off three rounds from his pistol. Spur had the Remington up and snapped off two rounds aiming just over the gun flashes.

A scream rattled the boards of the corral as the man behind the box slammed backwards, his weapon firing twice more into the air before he hit the ground.

Spur moved from his firing position to the end of the hay. He stared across the corral but could detect no third man. He had to be there. Then he saw a shadow gliding across the field behind the corral. The first man was the set up for the real professional gunman moving now. Sacrifice a man to get your target positioned. This guy played dirty.

The man stopped and knelt, waited, then moved again, quickly but carefully, like an army scout moving through enemy territory. Spur watched the man come near the far end of the stacks of hay. The Secret Service Agent had his Remington up and ready. When the shadow became a man, Spur thumbed back the hammer on the weapon.

The third ambusher stopped, holding frozen in place.

"One more step and you're dead!" Spur snarled.

The man tried. He jerked up his weapon, firing as it came. The first round went into the ground near his foot, the second in the ground five feet in front of him.

Spur's first round tore through the bushwhacker's chest, ripped apart his heart and drove him backwards so the spasming of his dying fingers on his gun hand sent three more rounds into the dark sky.

Spur moved up and checked him. He was dead.

A lantern came out the back door of the livery. A man held it high.

"What's going on back here?" he yelled.

"Dead men," Spur called. "Send someone for the sheriff."

Ten minutes later the sheriff had identified both men. One was a part time rancher, the other a drifter who had been in town for a month.

"The third one in the brush can talk," Spur said. He might also tell you who hired him."

"Hope so," Sheriff Palmer said. "Both these Jaspers have a new ten dollar bill in their pockets. Not a hell of a lot to get paid to try to kill a man."

"Especially not if it works the other way," Spur said. He left the sheriff to question the witness and hurried back to the mansion. He didn't like leaving Libby alone for this long at night.

Unseen at the edge of the crowd, Rufus Laidlaw scowled as he heard the news and moved away. Damnit! What now? He had taken three good tries at killing this man. Evidently he was going to have to do it himself. But not tonight, perhaps tomorrow. He would see how the rest of his plan worked out.

There might be no need after tomorrow, if the plans all worked to perfection. He continued down a side street to his hotel and slipped in the side door. There was a note in his box behind the desk man.

"Edward Scott arrived late today. He's a surveyor with the Northern Pacific. He's in Room 14."

Laidlaw continued to his room for a bottle of whiskey and two glasses, then knocked on the door to Room 14.

The panel opened and a sun burned face stared out.

"Yeah? So?"

"Mr. Scott?"

"So?"

"I understand you're with the Northern Pacific railroad."

"True."

"Do you have a minute to talk? I and my friend would like to have a small discussion with you."

"Don't see no friend."

Laidlaw held up the bottle of whiskey, and the grim faced man in Room 14 turned into a wide grin and he swung open the door.

"Always have time for an old friend, come in, come in!"

They sat on the edge of the bed and toasted each other with the good whiskey. After the fourth toast, Laidlaw got down to business.

"How is your progress on finding the route for the new railroad?"

"Fair. The Yellowstone is a godsend. Wish she extended all the way to the Snake River."

"Mr. Scott, I know the route of a railroad is usually a closely guarded secret, but these are exploratory routes as I understand, and there are three being run."

"Four, and most everybody knows where they are going."

"But the Yellowstone is the best, cheapest to build and probably will be the one chosen," Laidlsaw said.

"Hail, you said it, I didn't."

"But it is true, isn't it?"

"Probably. If you was a betting man."

"My problem is just where you'll leave the Yellowstone. I'm hoping you'll cut south with the river for about thirty miles and then drive through the mountains to Virginia City, the capital of the Montana Territory."

"Can't say, can't say. I've got a suggested route . . ." He stopped and drained his whiskey.

"You were saying there was a suggested route?"

"Yep. Just a suggestion. Figure to keep on west past Livingston to Bozeman, then swing between mountains northwest more to a camp I call Three Forks. There I'd like to charge due north and a little west to bring us right here to Helena. From there we head west and then northwest."

"I'm still hoping for Virginia City."

"Why, you got property there?"

"Sir, I am not pleased with that remark."

"Though, it's probably true. But I never insult a man when I'm drinking his whiskey so I ask your pardon."

"That's all right. I understand. I've heard that in some cases officials of the line have changed routes to run through favored towns and areas."

"True. But don't blame me for what the bosses do. I'm just a route finder, a pathfinder."

"Say you were to recommend a path through Virginia City. What would you say to a gift finding itself your way?"

"You mean take money to make a different suggestion for the right of way?"

"Couldn't hurt. Nobody would know except you and me."

"What kind of a gift are we talking about?"

"We start with a young lady I'd like you to meet for the night. She is delightful, unspoiled, clean as my sister. Then there's an envelope in my safe with five thousand dollars in it. Both those gifts are yours for that Virginia City route recommendation."

Scott picked up his glass and finished the whiskey. Then he set it down and stood. Laidlaw puffed as he stood and smiled at the raw railroader.

Laidlaw never saw it coming. The smashing right fist caught him in the eye and drove his three hundred pounds of flesh a foot backwards, ruining his precarious balance and dumping him on the hotel room floor beside the bed.

"Mr. Laidlaw, I drank your whiskey and I listened to your ideas. Don't like them. Don't like being offered a bribe to corrupt my morals and my professional integrity. Ain't nice to offer men more money as a bribe than they make in five years. Just ain't proper." He helped Laidlaw to stand.

"Hope there ain't no hard feelings. I'm a working man. Struggle to do a good job. Fact is I'm one of the best grade engineers in the country. A damn insult to offer me five thousand dollars to compromise my professional standards."

Laidlaw felt of his eyes, shook his head. He wanted to bolt for the door but the railroader was between him and that freedom.

"You should learn, Laidlaw, that if you want to bribe a railroad man you should make it worth his while. Now I ain't saying some men won't take five thousand, but not me. My reputation is worth a lot more than that."

Laidlaw felt he had heard some glimmer of hope.

"What would you consider a reasonable amount, Mr. Scott?"

"A million dollars, hard cash. That's what my reputation is worth. No idiot is going to recommend going through the heart of the Rocky Mountains just to get to Virginia City. But for a million it would be worth considering."

"Sorry, I don't have that kind of money."

"Damn shame," Scott said. This time Scott hit him on the jaw and Laidlaw went down again. It took most of the china pitcher of water from the washstand to bring Laidlaw back to consciousness. Then Scott helped him out the door, but kept the rest of the bottle of whiskey.

Rufus Laidlaw staggered back to his room and fell on his bed. His jaw ached. He was wet from the top of his head to his waist. He was supposed to check with one man about the other part of his night's mission, but he couldn't now. He rolled over on his back and bellowed in fury. He prayed that by tomorrow he did not have a large black eye. It would not be easy testifying at the Relocation Committee hearing if he had a shiner. He bathed the eye in cold water for a half hour, hoping it would keep the blood from settling in the flesh. At last he went to bed. He made a new rule for his business ethic: Never try to bribe a railroad grade engineer for less than a million dollars.

11

Sheriff Palmer told Spur about Will Walton just before he left the corral. Spur had been saddened, but not surprised. When a man comes home after seven years, he's got to expect a few changes have been made. At least Will found his family. For some reason the woman must have turned on him. There must have been a man around to help her. From what Will said just before he died, he must have seen his son, and Martha. That was good.

Spur would ride out there first thing in the morning and check with the family, try to find out what happened. He had almost nothing to go on, but in his gut he knew that Martha or some man she knew had shot Walton. That angered Spur. He would tend to it and see that the killer paid. He owed that much to Lt. Walton.

Spur hurried now as he went back along the street to the big house at the end of the block. The Adams mansion, the people called it, and it was. He bounded up the front steps and let himself in.

Charity was usually near the door. He didn't see

her. The house was strangely quiet.

"Damnit no!" Spur thundered as he ran through the house. He found Charity in an upstairs closet. Her blouse had been ripped off and her breasts showed. She was tied and gagged. Spur untied her, found her blouse on the floor and she began to cry.

It took him three or four minutes to get her calmed down. Then the story gushed out.

"They came just after dinner, four or five of them. They just opened the front door and ran inside. One of them grabbed me and two ran into the living room and found Mrs. Adams."

"Five men. Did they wear masks?"

"Yes. They were rough talking. Clothes like they were working men, miners or cowboys. One man took me upstairs and told me to undress, but I clawed his face and he slapped me and pushed me on the bed and then ripped off my blouse.

"Somebody called from below, telling the man to tie me up and push me in a closet. He wanted to do me, but he didn't have time. So he put me in the closet and I heard him leave. Then I tried to get out, but I couldn't."

Spur put his arm around her and let her cry again. Then he took her downstairs, found a bottle of brandy and told her to have a drink, to lock the doors and not to let anyone in until he or the sheriff came.

"You going after them?"

"I'm going to try. First I'm going to talk to the sheriff again."

Five minutes later Spur had told Sheriff Palmer the story. He shook his head.

"No telling where they might be. Could be here in town, but I doubt it. More likely they could be in any one of a dozen abandoned mines and mine shacks around here."

"Does the name Laidlaw, Rufus Laidlaw, mean anything to you, Sheriff?"

"I been around here for a long time. Known a lot of men. Laidlaw. He the same one who's got some Territorial office?"

"Libby says he's some kind of officer for the Territory."

"Could be Rufus Laidlaw is the same one who had the old Laidlaw mine about three miles out of town. That was one of our famous flash in the pan mines. Produced great for about fifty yards, then the vein took a right angle into another claim. Laidlaw wound up losing everything he had in the deal."

"If he's behind this kidnapping, could his men have taken Libby out there?"

"Couple of buildings still standing, but sure as hell don't sound like a smart move to me."

"That could be it. He'd figure it was such an obvious place to look I'd never think about it, or know about it."

"Possible. Can't really track them until morning, anyway."

"Draw me a map how to get out there, and I'll need some kind of flares in case I have to go into the mine."

"Got some you can have. You want me to send a few men along with you?"

"No thanks, but I would appreciate it if you could get a search started here in town, and some of the close in abandoned mine buildings."

Ten minutes later Spur had memorized the map the sheriff drew for him and was riding. He had the Henry repeating rifle and his pistol, plus extra rounds for both. Five to one, the odds sounded about right.

It took him two hours to find the right lane leading off the main stage road. He took the wrong branch and wound up at a working gold mine. After backtracking he came to the old Laidlaw dig and at once knew it was no longer abandoned. Out in the clear air he could smell a smoke for a mile, and now the smoke came clear and strong from one of two buildings ahead.

Spur left his horse by the lane and circled around the lane that led in. He spotted a lookout in a tree a quarter of a mile from the buildings. He slid past the man and left him in place.

Soon he could see a dim light in the smaller of the two structures. Working without a sound, Spur crept up to the building until he was twenty yards away in some brush. Nobody came in or out for ten minutes. He could see smoke coming out of the chimney.

He checked the area again. There were no exterior guards that he could see. He slipped from shadow to shadow, then walked across the last ten yards to the side window. It was so dirty he could barely see through. At last he rubbed some of the outside dirt off and he could see inside.

Before he recognized anyone, a gun muzzle jammed into his back. Spur spun automatically, knocked the gun away from the surprised man, kicked him in the side the way a Japanese had once taught him, and then slammed his fist into the man's unprotected jaw, dropping him to the ground unconscious.

Spur tied up the man, gagged him and rolled him under the downhill side of the cabin. He found the gun and stuffed it in his belt, then looked in the window again.

Libby was the first thing he saw. She sat, cool and

at ease at a small table playing cards with three men. A box of kichen matches sat on the table. Libby had the biggest stack of matches in front of her. She was also talking up a storm, but he couldn't make out what she was saying to the men.

Spur crept around to the front door, tested it, then turned the handle and kicked it open. He charged into the room with a pistol in each hand.

"Don't move, or you're dead men!" Spur thundered. One man dove for his gun. Spur put a slug through his chest and he flopped over dead or dying.

One man grabbed Libby and used her as a shield.

"You shoot me, you shoot the lady first," he said and began backing toward the other door. As Spur turned to watch Libby, another man reached for the iron on his hip.

Spur's round slashed through his shoulder and he got off a shot that went wide. Spur's second round created a neat round hole in the man's forehead going in, but splattered blood and brains over the far wall as it came out the top of his head.

The man with Libby drew his six-gun and Spur dove for the floor and tipped over the table as a shield. Two slugs thudded into it, then the door slammed and the man was gone.

Two men dead, one tied up, one out the back door and one in the tree. Spur jumped up and raced after the man with Libby. The odds were getting better. Spur saw him tugging Libby with him in the moonlight, but he couldn't fire.

The kidnapper pushed Libby in the mine tunnel and Spur ran up to it. From what the sheriff said the tunnel was short and there were no shafts down to other levels. How did the man intend to hide for long in there?

Spur found some torches at the front of the abandoned tunnel and lit one, then held it to the side of his body and began moving into the hole. He stopped frequently to listen, but heard nothing.

The mine tunnel extended thirty yards into the hill. He checked out occasional "drifts", lateral tunnels off the main one. But most were only a few yards long.

The man and Libby were still somewhere ahead.

He worked to the end of the tunnel where he found steel stakes driven into the ground. A hand painted sign said: *No trespassing. From here forward is the Jefferson Mine. Do Not Enter.*

Spur read it again, and remembered what the sheriff said about the vein of gold running directly off the claim. The metal bars had been pushed aside and Spur squeezed through. Ahead was more mine, only this one had been worked extensively. There were large "rooms" were pockets of ore had been dug out giving the tunnel a ceiling sometimes twenty feet high.

Every dozen feet there was another drift Spur had to clear. Twenty yards into the new mine he came to a shaft dug directly in the middle of the tunnel with walking space around the sides. This one still contained a block and tackle and pulleys to lift up buckets of ore from somewhere below.

Spur checked the rope and the bucket and saw that a layer of dust covered it all. The bucket had not been used for months, maybe years. Libby had not been taken down that shaft.

He moved ahead, saw something move on the tunnel almost at his feet and jumped back as a four foot rattlesnake slithered away into the darkness. He was sure the reptile had been blinded by the sudden light of the flaming torch. There could be more. He heard that snakes loved old mines.

Spur checked two more drifts, then another shaft that fell away to darkness below. This one had a wooden ladder fastened to the wall. It looked sturdy. He checked the rungs and found the center of each clean of dust. The ends were dust covered.

Someone had descended the ladder recently, maybe within the hour. He touched a piece of paper to his torch and dropped it down the shaft. It fell only ten feet to the bottom.

Spur had to investigate. He went down the ladder with one hand, holding the torch with the other. At the bottom he found footprints, including some that could only belong to Libby.

He listened. Far off he thought he heard voices. But they faded out. There was only one direction to go. He had to duck now as the new tunnel was barely five feet tall. It had no rail tracks down it as many mines did. They worked simply here with wheeled carts men pushed.

A minute of walking down the tunnel revealed only two short drifts and no more shafts. Then the tunnel forked, moving out at forty-five degree angles. He checked both for footprints, but the soil was hard and packed and showed nothing. He picked the right hand tunnel and moved faster now.

Fifty feet down it he paused to listen, but could hear nothing. Ten minutes later he came to the end of the tunnel. Picks and pry bars and drive drills lay at the head of the tunnel as if they had been dropped at the end of a working day, but never picked up again.

Spur jogged back the way he had come to the fork in the tunnel, took the other one and moved cautiously. Here and there he saw footprints. Twice he stopped to listen, and the second time he heard a woman's voice, high and irritated.

Libby!

He moved quicker. His torch burned lower. It would go out in another few minutes.

He smelled smoke. It drifted toward him now as an air shaft somewhere sucked it from the tunnel. Wood smoke. They had built a fire ahead. Spur rounded a gradual curve in the tunnel and saw the glow of a fire. He put out his torch at once and moved slowly forward, careful not to make a sound.

The voices came clearer then. The man arguing, the woman firm and positive. He worked closer until he could hear what they were saying.

"Absolutely no way anybody is going to find us in here," a heavy man's voice said. "For sure not one man, that Spur McCoy you talk about. He's no miner. He'd get lost after the first shaft. Probably down on the sixth level now blundering down one tunnel after another."

"You can't keep me here forever," Libby said her voice strong and assured. "All the food is back in the cabin. What do you have for breakfast?"

"Worry about that in the morning. Got my Waterbury, know exactly what time it is." He paused.

Spur worked silently forward. The firelight was in their eyes. Neither one of them could see beyond its glow. He had the advantage.

"I could just rip your clothes off and force you, you know," the man said.

"You might. I'm stronger than I look, and Alexander showed me ten ways to stop a man from raping me. Want to learn all ten of them?"

"Come on, you've had a man or two since Alex died. I've heard stories."

"Stories are what they are. In any event, I'd choose my lover, not the other way around."

Spur was in range. He lifted the Remington pistol. The man moved closer to Libby. She pushed him away. He laughed. Spur aimed again and just as he fired, the man lunged forward. The round aimed at his chest, caught him high in the right arm as he moved.

He screeched in pain.

The sound of the pistol shot in the tunnel was like an echo chamber slamming the sound waves around and around, bouncing them forward and back and forward again so it felt like the sound would never fade out.

The man had been flung to the side by the shot and Libby scrambled toward the sound of the gun. Spur snapped another shot at the man, forcing him backward out of the firelight.

"Come this way away from the fire so he can't see you, Libby," Spur called. She darted in his direction at once. The other man did not fire. Then Spur saw his revolver on the ground near the fire. He had been cleaning it.

"Give it up," Spur called. "Come out now and you'll only face kidnapping charges. This is a lousy place to die."

"Die? There's a dozen ways out of this tunnel," the man shouted.

"I'm betting you're wrong. The other tunnel ended. Figure this one does too. You don't know every turn in this mine."

"Know enough. I'm gone. Next time I see you I'll be topside with my rifle waiting for you to come out the entrance to the mine. Then you'll be quick dead." The man laughed and the sound trailed off fainter as he ran down the tunnel.

He had no light. Spur moved up where Libby was and she rushed into his arms.

"Oh, Spur! I'm so glad you came! It was just terrible. Can we get out of here? I hate the mines."

A scream echoed through the tunnel before Spur

could reply. He took her hand and walked to the fire, picked up two torches and lit them, then they moved down the tunnel toward another scream.

"Easy, he must be in trouble. We don't want to fall into the same trap."

They worked forward slowly. Soon they saw the edge of a new shaft that had been started. Spur pushed the torch over the edge and looked down.

A man stood on his tip toes at the bottom of the ten foot deep shaft. Shovels and buckets and picks had been stacked neatly to one side. The man was trying to reach the buckets to stand on them. The whole bottom of the pit seemed to be moving. Spur dropped one of the torches into the hole. The moving floor was a sea of rattlesnakes, shaken out of their hibernation by the human thing dropping in on them.

"For Christ's sakes, get me out of here!" the man wailed. Then he screamed as a snake blinded by the bright light struck out but missed his leg.

"No rope," Spur said. "Stand on the buckets, maybe I can reach you."

The man grabbed the torch from the floor and cleared a path through the writhing snakes to the buckets, and tried to stand on them. They caved in, rusted through. He fell and only the torch kept him from being attacked by the furious rattlers. He burned two of them and they slithered back.

Spur pulled off the light leather jacket he wore and took a firm grip on one sleeve. The other sleeve he lowered into the pit and then stretched out flat on his stomach at the edge of the hole.

"Grab it and use me as an anchor and climb out," Spur said.

The man tried to catch the leather sleeve, but missed it. Spur stretched lower and the kidnapper caught the sleeve.

"Drop the torch and grab the sleeve with both hands," Spur ordered. "Libby, sit on my back, give me some support." She lowered on him to anchor him in place.

The man in the pit grabbed the leather and put his feet on the wall. An underground seepage made the wall slippery. He tried to step up but slid down.

The torch sputtered on the floor, frying a rattler, the light coming weaker and weaker. His foot slipped again and as it dropped down, a coiled rattler struck two feet through the air and fastened its fangs on the unprotected calf. The man screamed and dropped the jacket sleeve, falling to the bottom of the pit.

Spur held the second torch low, rattlers swarmed over the man. He screamed again and again, then looked up and one large rattler struck and fastened his fangs into the kidnapper's throat. As the poison gushed directly into the human bloodstream, Spur could see death come. It was a terrible way to die. He pushed Libby off his back and stood.

Slowly he slid into the jacket and led her back toward the fire.

"He's gone?" Libby asked.

"Yes. Nobody deserves to die that way. He paid for all of his sins in full that last five minutes."

"You gave him a choice."

At the fire they paused.

"Libby, are you strong enough to climb back out of here?" he asked.

"Yes, but is it a good idea?"

"Only one left up there who can be waiting for us, no two I guess. I tied up one of them." Spur watched her. "Might be better to wait for daylight. Then the other two will probably high tail it for town and then into Idaho somewhere."

"Let's stay right here," Libby said. "He found a blanket. It's not clean, but better than the tunnel floor."

Spur watched her, a small grin grew on her pretty face.

"We may have to sit close together to stay warm," Spur said.

"I'm counting on that. I've never stayed over-night in a gold mine before."

"Deal," he said. He found some of the square set timbers that had been broken apart in some ore car crash, and brought them back for wood. After building up the fire, he spread out the blanket and pointed their toes at the fire. He had stacked the twelve by twelve timbers on the opposite side of the fire so the heat would reflect off the timbers and toward them.

"You've made a campfire or two in your time, I'd guess," Libby said.

"A few." She sat down beside him, pushed in so their hips touched and then turned. She smiled but through it he saw the fear that was still ebbing from her features.

"They had you scared, didn't they?"

"Yes. I've never felt so alone, or so vulnerable in my life. He . . . the man back there, would have had his way with me eventually. I had figured on that. I could live through it without any worry. But I was really afraid he would never let me leave the mine."

"Your worries are over."

"All over. I'm glad you came." She reached over and kissed him, and he felt her begin to relax.

"We could just stay warm," he said.

"We could. But right now I'm so glad to be alive that I want to see how it feels to be a woman again. I don't fuck around very often."

She grinned at his surprise that she used the word. "And I don't talk dirty unless I'm really starting to feel horny. Would you please hurry up and give me a little bit of encouragement?"

12

Spur watched Libby and slowly grinned. "Seems like I could at least offer more than encouragement." He bent and kissed her lips and she smiled at him.

"You can do better than that," she said.

Libby's mouth was open when he kissed her the next time and he let his tongue dart into her hot, eager opening. She caught his tongue with her teeth and growled at him, then let go and tried to get her tongue into his mouth.

For a moment they battled, then he let her enter and as she did his hand slid between them and closed around one of her covered breasts.

"Oh, god yes!" she said, then pushed back inside his mouth and pressed against his hand. Her mouth came away from his and nibbled at his ear, then she nestled against him.

"Tell me how you like to make love the best," Spur said, his hand working on the buttons of the dress top.

"With a man," she said impishly. "Although it's

interesting with a woman. I've never had a more tender loving than with another female. Another woman seems to know exactly what pleases a female.''

She kissed him and rubbed his crotch where she felt the growing erection.

"Of course a woman's fingers are no real substitute for the real thing!'' She worked at unbuttoning his pants. Spur spread the top of her dress open and lifted the soft silk chemise. Her big breasts swung out full and bouncing as they glowed in the soft firelight.

"God but breasts are beautiful, do you realize that? Most animals use the rear end to attract the male. But with women the breasts have been developed down through the ages to attract the male of the species and also to suckle her child. So first great tits are essentially for beauty but practical, too.''

"Now you're getting poetic. I've never heard of a man who didn't go wild over bare tits.''

He kissed her and slowly pushed her down on the blanket. She finished the kiss, then sat up.

"I want to undress you first. Every stitch. Right now.'' She patted his bulge. "Darling, you'll have to wait your turn, I like all parts of a man.''

She took off his jacket, then his leather vest and his shirt.

"Oh, a hairy chest! I do love to play with man tits through his chest hair.'' She bent and kissed them both, then moved her kisses down his hard belly to his big heavy brass belt buckle.

"Oops . . . some more undressing to do here.'' She opened his belt and the last of the fly buttons and pushed his pants down. Spur wore cut off drawers and she jerked at them, eager to get to the important parts as she had said.

"My stars! Look at him! Such a big one. She laughed. "He's a big boy, but I bet he can do a man's job."

She pulled his boots off, then his pants and drawers and warmed her hands over the fire. Then she turned and began a strip tease for him, slipping out of her chemise first, letting her dress top fall to her waist.

For a few moments she did a sexy little dance, waving her breasts at him, humping her hips toward him and then going to her knees in front of Spur and letting one breast dangle so he could kiss it and chew on it.

"I didn't realize I was so hungry," Spur said munching away.

"Just leave some room for dessert," she said. She pulled away and lifted the dress off over her head. Instead of the usual knee length drawers common for women of the day, she wore silk panty underwear that fit loose and inviting.

"Like my short panties?" she asked. "All the women in Paris are wearing them I hear."

She knelt in front of him, her big breasts bouncing, the soft pink areolas large and glowing with hot blood. Her nipples stood up tall, enlarged by her desire.

"I'd rather see you not wearing them," Spur growled, his hands reaching for her.

"Tear them off me with your teeth! Bite your way right through to the soft, wet, and wonderful place!"

Spur bent forward, pushed her back on the blanket, her legs spread and he lowered his face into her crotch. She moaned in delight. He caught the silk fabric in his teeth and jerked upward. The fabric tore. He held the side of the panties with his hand and bit and ripped upward, exposing a slice of white thigh. Again and again he bit and tore at the silk with his teeth until it hung in shreds over her crotch. Then he parted the strands and moved toward her black muff. He parted the rich midnight hairs and exposed her pulsating quim.

The outer lips were swollen already speading outward. He bent and kissed her pussy softly, then again and she trembled.

"Do that once more and I'll squirt all over you!" she yelped. He kissed her again and she screeched in pleasure, her body jolting and pounding upward, her hips doing a little dance as he watched. Again and again tremors pulsated through her body, shaking her, rattling her until she growled in animal delight. She pulled his naked body on top of hers and her hips pounded upward a dozen times as the spasms kept rocketing through her slender body.

"My god! Nobody has ever done that for me before!" She kissed him and then licked her lips. "I can at least do the same for you." She gathered their clothes to make a pillow for her head lifting it forward so she could accept him, then motioned to him. Spur straddled her shoulders with his knees and bent forward.

Her hand caught his penis and pulled it down into her mouth. She took a deep breath and nodded and he began to slide in and out of her.

Spur had been so worked up it didn't take long. She held off on it as long as he could, then she moaned in anticipation and he couldn't stop it, and the life substance of the universe jolted through him and gagged her momentarily until she swallowed. Then she sucked him dry and at last he rolled away and panted on the blanket, as she lay on him like a warm cover.

When Spur could talk he bobbed his head. "Marvelous, wonderful. Who taught you that?"

"Alex, he taught me everything I know. God bless you Alex, even though you have ceased to exist."

He looked at her. "Alex is not in heaven?"

She laughed. "Long ago Alexander convinced me of the total folly of all religion. He said religion is for fools, the lazy, or those who need some crutch because they are too weak to stand on their own two feet and face life. They want somebody to blame and commiserate with."

"But religions have been around since man crawled out of the slime of the prehistoric oceans millions of years ago."

"So has strong drink, evil men and prostitutes, but nobody says you have to think they are good or worship them."

Spur laughed softly. "I've never had a theological argument before with a naked woman."

"Alex used to say never ague with a naked woman, the man will always lose."

"Alex must have been some man. Religions, don't they do some good? What about the moral principals, the standards, the ethics?"

"Those are man manufactured. They have no basis in religion, they are man made. Some of them are commendable. "But don't think that only religion produces ethics and morality. That's a narrow viewpoint of man. Remember the Crusades where hundreds of thousands of innocents were slaughtered all in the name of church? Look at the days of the Inquisition. Those were religious leaders of the Christian Church, notably the Holy Roman Catholic Church, who were tearing those 'heretics' limb from limb for the glory of god. Some god."

Spur smiled. "What about the missionaries, the Catholic priests who went across the Southern U.S. establishing churches?"

"The main purpose of the Catholic Church was to spread the control of the church. Which allowed them to collect more money. To promise the peasants glory in heaven even if they were destitute in this life and gave all their money to the church."

"You are tough on them," Spur said. "No church, no resurrection, no life after death?"

"Of course not! Life after death is a logical contradiction. Does a tree live after you cut it down? Does a horse live after it is shot in a gunfight? Using the same logic neither does a man or woman or child live after they take their last breath. As Alex used to say, they simply cease to exist."

"Like I said, you are tough on religion." He kissed her soft lips and they kissed back. "Since I'm arguing with a naked lady, I can't win. It doesn't matter, I have little use for religion myself. Now what say we get warm by the fire, and figure out what other games we can play?"

They made love three more times that night, then dozed and woke and slept again. Spur kept the fire going to discourage any wandering rattlers, and by morning they were dressed again, but chilled and sore from sleeping on the ground.

"No breakfast," Spur said.

Libby rubbed the sleep out of one eye and sat up. One of her breasts poked out from where she had not buttoned up the front of her dress. Spur bent and kissed it, chewed on the nipple until she pushed him away. "I have a meeting to get to by nine o'clock, can we make it?"

"The Relocation Committee?"

"Yes."

"We'll get there as quickly as we can."

Spur lit two torches, checked his watch and they started to retrace their steps. The time was eight fifteen A.M. They came to the ladder that led up to the next level tunnel and checking closer, Spur saw that the rungs were not in as good a shape as he had thought on the way down.

Two of the cross bars were gone completely, and another weakened. He helped Libby get past the broken one, and soon she was in the tunnel above and off the ladder. He swung up to the next rung but when he put his weight on it, it broke in half and his foot slipped from the rung below. He crashed six feet to the bottom of the shaft and dropped the torch.

"Spur, are you all right?" Libby called. She held the torch down low until she could see him.

"Damn ladder broke," Spur said. I'll try again and spead out my weight more." He left the torch blazing away on the bottom of the shaft and tried the ladder again. This time he stepped on the rungs close to where they were nailed to the uprights, and grabbed them with his hands against the uprights as well.

It worked. He got past the broken ones and crawled over the edge. Libby kissed him.

He took the torch and they worked back the tunnel watching for snakes and shafts. They came to the next shaft and went around it and soon were at the metal stakes between the two mines.

Spur loosened the six-gun in his holster. She looked at him.

"You expect them in this far?"

"This is where I'd be if I was waiting for someone. Catch them before they were ready." They moved cautiously. Spur kept the torch well away from his body and made sure Libby stood on the other side as they walked. A shot at the torch would probably miss his hand and warn them.

They stopped twice to listen, but heard nothing. At last they saw the light from the tunnel opening ahead. Spur put out the torch and they crept ahead cautiously.

At the entrance he edged around at twelve by twelve beam and looked out. Nothing. He saw no movement, heard nothing. No smoke came from the chimney of either building.

He moved back where he had left Libby. "Stay here. I'm going to make a run for the buildings and see if they are waiting for us. There are two of them still alive."

Spur paused at the entrance, then with his six-gun out, he raced out of the tunnel and the twenty yards to the first building.

Nobody fired at him. He looked around. The buggy was still there with its horse still in the traces. Two saddle horses were ground tied near by.

He edged around the building and darted ten yards to the back door of the second structure.

Again nobody fired at him. Inside there was no one except the two dead men. Spur checked the three rooms, then outside and at last holstered his gun and walked back to the mine.

"They've left, Libby. Come on out."

When she left the mine she gave a big sigh of relief and hugged Spur in thanks, then frowned.

"What time is it? We have that nine o'clock meeting in town."

"It's a little after nine now. Sorry it took so long. Better to be a little late than a little dead."

Spur brought around the buggy, checked where he had left the yahoo tied up under the building but found him gone. He figured the lookout had heard the shooting, got there too late to help, found the bound man and they both lit out like their tails were on fire. He tied the spare horses to the back of the buggy and headed for town. One more stop at the end of the lane where he had left his rented horse, and with her fastened on the buggy as well, they hurried into town.

It took them a little over an hour to travel the four miles over the rough mining roads.

Libby thought for a moment about her appearance. She never went out in public without her company dress and her hair perfect. Today would be an exception.

The pale blue dress was mud and dirt splotched. One sleeve was torn nearly off where one of the kidnappers had grabbed her. She did not even pause to wash her face but knew it must be smudged and dirty. Her hair was a mess. It fell around her shoulders but in straggles and ropes, and she was sure it looked as if it hadn't been combed for a week.

But she would testify.

They rode into town and somebody shouted in recognition and hurried to tell the sheriff that the most important woman in town had been rescued from her kidnappers.

Spur drove straight to the town hall where the meeting was being held. He tied the horse to the hitching rack and asked someone to take the other horses to the livery, then hurried inside with Libby.

He was sure they made a grand appearance marching into the hushed Territorial Senate Relocation Committee hearing. They looked as if they had slept in their clothes deep in a coal mine.

Someone was testifying.

"That's Rufus Laidlaw," Libby whispered to

Spur.

Spur helped her sit down in the front row, heard the surprised whispers of the senators on the panel, and then walked up to Laidlaw.

"Mr. Chairman, pardon this interruption, but my name is Spur McCoy, I'm with the United States Secret Service. I'm here on official business."

"If it could wait, Mr. McCoy, Mr. Laidlaw is testifying on an important matter."

"You'll have to get a deputation later, sir." He turned to Rufus. "Is your name Rufus Laidlaw?"

"See here, we're in the middle of an important matter, Laidlaw said."

"Are you Rufus Laidlaw?" Spur asked again, his voice a parade grounds bellow.

"Yes," Laidlaw whispered.

"Then by the authority granted to me by the United States government, I'm arresting you for conspiracy to commit murder, for kidnapping, for attempted murder, and for involvement in the deaths of four men hired by you to commit felonies."

Spur took Laidlaw by the arm, lifted him from the chair and marched him down the aisle and toward the door.

Just before they got there, Laidlaw drew a hideout .38 derringer from under his left arm and fired point blank at Spur. The round slanted off Spur's big brass belt buckle and pentrated the side of the room. Spur staggered back by the force of the blow on his belt and tumbled to the floor.

Laidlaw surged past him, out the door and down the street. He still had one shot left in the double barreled derringer.

Helpful hands lifted Spur. Libby ran up, her face a mask of fear.

"I'm all right," he shouted. "Which way did

Laidlaw go?'' Several men pointed the way and Spur
raced into the street. He saw the fat man lumbering
into a store across the street and he rushed that
way.

The store was a Chinese laundry. Spur pushed in
the door and heard singing from behind a curtain.
An elderly Chinese with a skull cap and a long braid
looked up expectantly.

"Did a man come through here? Where did he
go?''

The old Chinese bobbed his head, bowed and
pointed behind the curtain. Spur rushed past the
curtain and the singing promptly stopped.

There were a half dozen Chinese women and girls
doing laundry in round tubs, others hanging the
laundry to dry in the empty building, and other
folding sheets and clothing items at a flat table.

"The fat man, which way did he go?'' Spur asked.

One of the Chinese ladies smiled.

"No English,'' she said in a sing song voice.

Spur looked in every possible place, but there was
no spot where Laidlaw could hide. Spur ran to the
back door and looked down the alley.

Half way down he saw Laidlaw puffing along. He
stopped to check a rear door to a business but it was
locked. He tried the next and ran inside. Spur was
half a block behind him.

The place where Laidlaw vanished was Manny
Logan's, a small but classy bordello where some of
the best men in town could be found. Spur charged
in, saw a staircase for confidential visits. He ran up
the steps, knew at once what the place was and
began opening doors.

Screams and strings of swear words followed each
opening. The fourth room was empty, the fifth had
only a girl in a housecoat lounging on a narrow bed.

She smiled at him but he shook his head.

"No tits," he said. She threw a book at him.

Two doors down he found where Laidlaw had been. He had ripped off a window screen and went out the opening to a one story roof below. A couple on the bed humped in the final moments of a mutual climax and they never even noticed Spur.

He slid out the window and down the roof. Laidlaw had dropped off the roof into a wagon and then scrambled to the street and dashed into the general store.

Spur was twenty seconds behind him but as soon as he opened the general store door, a shot exploded inside the store and a slug slammed into the casing beside him.

"One more step and I'll blow this lady's head off!" Laidlaw shrilled. "I mean it. I got nothing to lose and you know it, McCoy. Just one more step and you kill this woman."

"Hold it, Laidlaw. You kill her and you'll hang for sure. Best you get now is ten years. You can do that time while you're planning your next scheme."

"Not prison. My dad used to lock me up in a closet where it was dark and cold. I couldn't live five days in prison where they locked me up."

Spur saw him now, crouched behind the small counter near the money drawer. The woman was standing in front of him, Laidlaw's arm around her throat, the derringer against the side of her head.

"I'll kill her, so help me god! Got nothing to lose. You stand back. Get outside!"

"Can't do that, Laidlaw. I'm a federal law officer. It's my job to take you in. I don't even know that woman. Why should I care if you kill her? Lots of women out here in the west now. Ain't like it used to be twenty years ago."

"You're bluffing, McCoy."

"You shoot her and I shoot you at the same time. You that eager to die? Is there life after death, Laidlaw? I can guarantee that you'll find out if you pull the trigger. You just have one shot left. Ain't like you had a six-gun."

"Damn you, McCoy!"

"You tried to kill me three times, didn't you, Laidlaw?"

"Yes, damn you, one of them should have worked."

"Don't hire boys to do a man's job, Laidlaw. Now put down the gun and live until tomorrow. You interested in the sunrise? You'll never see it you keep that derringer up there much longer. I'm not a patient man."

"Why didn't you just stay out of this town?"

"Lady needed some help. I see why. Give it up Laidlaw."

"I can stand here as long as you can, McCoy."

"But the logic is working on you. You're not stupid. You know how bad your situation is. Why make it worse? And besides, you're not sure about life after death, are you? Want to test it out and see if you're right? Why not give it a try, Laidlaw? You'll either be flying around as a happy ghost laughing at us all down here on earth, or you'll be in a long dreamless sleep from which you'll never wake up. Which is it going to be?"

"Christ! Give me the old time lawman who shot first. All this talk is confusing."

"Just put the little gun on the counter and it all will make sense, Laidlaw. The sheriff just came in the back door. Didn't you hear it close? He'll have his gun on you in about half a minute. He's the kind to shoot first. Make up your mind, now!"

"All right! All right, I'm putting down the derringer. My hands are in the air."

The woman fell against him and slid to the floor in a dead faint.

Sheriff Palmer stepped out of the supply room and eased his six-gun against Laidlaw's neck. His voice surprised the man. His appearance also surprised Spur who had bluffed the idea.

"Easy, Laidlaw," Sheriff Palmer said. "I got a nice cell waiting for you."

Spur walked up and tried to revive the woman.

"McCoy, sometimes I think you're taking all the fun out of being sheriff. We could have had a dandy of a shootout here."

"Right and two maybe three of us would be dead by now."

"Guess you're right," the sheriff said.

"The lady clerk here is damn sure that I'm right," Spur said. "She's one of the ones who would have been dead."

13

Lawrence Taylor watched the disruptive exit of the two men and gaveled sharply on the special board.

"Gentlemen, ladies, we will have order. Close the doors, and come to order. This is a Territorial Committee meeting. The officer was within his rights to arrest the gentleman, now we must continue with our business.

"Mrs. Adams, you were the first witness, and since you were not present when we began, we moved Mr. Laidlaw into your place. If you're ready, we will proceed."

Libby walked to the front of the chamber and sat in the witness chair. For the first time she seemed concerned about her appearance.

"Mr. Taylor, I thank you for allowing me to testify. As you may know I was kidnapped last night by five armed men. They were hired by Rufus Laidlaw specifically to keep me from speaking before this committee. Only now have I returned after spending all night in an abandoned gold mine trying to find my way out.

"I assure you my state of dress and even my dirty face, are no reflection on this committee. I was determined to get here, even looking the way I do.

"What I have to say is important, because it is vital that we move the territorial seat of government closer to the life lines of communication and transportation, and closer to the center of the territory so all sections of Montana can be served. You gentlemen know the geography of our territory. Helena is near the center from north to south, and in the middle of the area which we project will have the greatest population growth.

"One of the largest growth potential elements is the railroad. The Northern Pacific is even now drawing up final plans for its line through Montana, and the best information we have at this stage is that the general route will follow down the Yellowstone River valley to Livingston, then swing west and northwest to Helena.

"I don't need to remind any of you how the presence of a railroad line is a tremendous boon to any community and area, opening it up for trade and for development and as an artery for quick transportation of goods and services to points both east and west. That will make Helena the ideal place for our territorial and we hope soon our Montana state capital.

"I'm sure the mayor and the county board of Commissioners will have a lot to tell you about Lewis and Clark County. Gentlemen of the committee, do you have any questions for me?"

There was one.

"Are you positive about the route of the Northern Pacific through Helena," one of the men on the committee asked.

"I am. I hope the railroad is. If I were a gambling

person, I would put all of my money out right now that the rails will be coming through Helena."

There were no more questions. Libby smiled at the men on the committee. "Thank you, and if you don't mind, I'll go and get cleaned up a little before our dinner at twelve-thirty sharp at my house as planned."

She stepped off the witness stand and walked quickly out of the room.

Irv Nelson, owner, editor-publisher of Helena *Graphic*, called to her as she entered the hallway.

"Mrs. Adams. Do you have time to tell me about what happened on your kidnapping? I want to write a story about it for the paper."

"I really don't have time. The committee is coming for dinner this noon . . ." She paused. "If you'll drive me to my house we can talk. I'll tell you what I know. Then you see Spur McCoy and the sheriff for the rest of it. All right?"

Nelson grinned, helped her down the steps then handed her into the carriage and drove it to her house and into the stables in back just off the alley.

She talked constantly as they drove, and he made notes as fast as he could. At the house he thanked her and she hurried inside to find Charity staring at a box of food that had come from the general store.

"Dinner!" Libby said and hurried Charity and the cook into making a fantastic feast for dinner for the committee as she heated water for a long bath.

If everything worked out right dinner would be on time and she would be clean and combed and dressed before the four men arrived at twelve-thirty.

Spur McCoy had found the sheriff in and pushed all three hundred pounds of Rufus Laidlaw at him. The man was quickly led to a cell and Spur told the sheriff what had happened during the kidnapping, including where he could find the three bodies out at the old Laidlaw mine.

"I'll take your word for the third one. The other two need to be brought in and identified for the record. You say there are still two of the kidnappers free?"

"Somewhere out there. We got Libby back for her talk to the committee. Is it that important?"

"Damned important. I'm going to tell them how the sheriff's department will be enlarged as needed to take care of normal policing activities for the territorial capital, and that we will cooperate in any way with all territorial policing agencies now in place and any that might be created. If we can nail down this relocation, Helena will boom."

"Hope it works out for you." Spur relaxed in a chair in the sheriff's office. "You going to need me for the trials?"

"Damn right. We'll get them set up early, be a week, maybe a week and a half at the most. Without you to testify we have no case."

"Done. Figure I can spend a week or so going after a Grizzly bear. You know a good guide who could get me into Grizz country?"

"Reckon I could scare up one or two. You do any fishing?"

"Some. Guess I'll have enough things to do for a week."

"Make it my business to see that you do," the sheriff said.

Spur stood and stretched. "Guess it's high time I have a bath, and then a nice big dinner, couple of steaks sounds good. Then about a full day of sleep to catch up. You ever tried to sleep in a cold gold mine tunnel with just a little fire and one blanket to keep you warm?"

The sheriff shook his head. "But then you forgot something. You had Libby Adams along as well to keep you warm."

"Yeah, true," Spur said noncommittally and walked out into the sunshine.

He strode with purpose toward the hotel where he figured would be the best spot to take a bath at one of his rooms. As he crossed the street a .44 blasted somewhere ahead of him and a slug slammed over his head and out of town. Spur reached for his gun but saw a man standing thirty yards down the street, the smoking gun still in his hand and aimed at Spur.

"Wet met last night, McCoy. You didn't give me a fair chance. Figure I owe a damn lot to three of my friends so I'm gonna put you out of your misery."

Spur tried to recognize the man, but it had been dark. This would have been the one at the mine that he tied up and pushed under the building.

"You're lucky to be alive. Why don't we leave it that way?" Spur called.

"Not the point. You made me look bad. I was outside. I cost the lives of three of my friends. I won't sleep until I even the score with you."

"You try and there's the chance that you might never sleep again." Spur checked the street, and scanned the buildings on both sides.

"Don't worry, I'm alone. The lookout in the tree you went around lit out for Denver last night. I don't scare nowhere near that easy."

"Do you bleed?"

"You got no choice, smart mouth. I'm putting my iron back in leather. You better get ready. You're packing. Next time I draw, one of us is gonna die. I'm bettin' it's you."

"Mighty big bet. It's your life on the line."

"Done it before, won before. You ready?"

"No way to talk you out of it?"

"Shut up and draw."

The man went for his iron and Spur beat him to the draw, he thumbed the hammer back with his left palm and fired when the six-gun was waist high and still moving upward. The round took the man in the right shoulder and shattered it. The gun spinning out of his hand.

The man roared in pain and hatred. The jolt of the lead bullet had slammed him four feet backward and dumped him on the ground. He crawled to his gun using only his left hand. The man fisted the weapon and turned, but Sheriff Palmer's right boot smashed into his wrist, breaking it and separating the left hand from the gun.

"Don't, son. You'd just be dead, and we need a star witness against Rufus Laidlaw," Palmer said. He looked down the street at Spur. "Didn't tell me you was a gunsharp as well. Thanks for hitting him in the shoulder. He'll talk his head off to stay off a scaffold."

"Just the way we planned it, Sheriff," Spur said and continued on his way toward the hotel, pushing out the spent round and shoving a new one in to complete the five live ones. Never could tell when a body might need five shots.

At the hotel desk he asked for his key and the desk clerk gave him a message in his box. Before he read it he ordered five buckets of hot water and a bath tub brought to his room, then went that direction.

The note was short: "Spur . . . please come to dinner at my house at twelve-thirty. I'm entertaining the Relocation Committee and need your moral support." It was signed, Libby.

Spur shrugged. Why not? The only other problem on his list was the Will Walton ranch, and the killers he was sure were there. They would not be going any place. That changed his plans about a long nap. But he had to eat. Suddenly he realized he was as hungry as a starved caribou.

The bath lasted until the water turned cold. He soaked out the grime and the aches from the night in the mine, then toweled himself dry and dressed in a set of clean clothes he had left in the room so it would look lived in.

He brushed off his low peaked, brown hat, the one with the ring of Mexican silver pesos strung around the crown, and decided after he shaved he would be fit company, even for a Montana Territorial Committee.

He was early. Spur stopped by at the Lewis and Clark county courthouse and talked to the county registrar.

"Yep, found it," the tall, balding man with half glasses said. "Recorded all right here in the book. Owner is listed as Mrs. William (Martha) Walton. Grant deed is free of any incumbrances, no co-owners."

"When was it recorded?"

"Let's see. Date is May twelve of eighteen and sixty-seven. Little over three years ago, seems."

Spur thanked him and strolled to the mansion on the corner with five minutes to spare. The other guests were already there. Charity welcomed him, stepping close to him and rubbing his crotch, then grinning and led him into the parlor where the other four men waited for Libby.

Spur introduced himself again to the men, who welcomed him.

"You get that Laidlaw feller?" one of the men

asked.

"Yes, undamaged and ready to stand trial as soon as the judge can get here."

"Good. He's been a thorn down at the capital. Friend of some sort of the governor, 'though I don't know why."

Libby came into the room and the men all stood automatically.

"Beautiful!" the chairman of the group said. "Now that is what I call a transformation!"

"Is this the same bedraggled woman who testified before us this morning?" another man said.

"Thank you, gentlemen. I warned you this morning I was not in my best state of repair. I'm glad you like the new model."

She had turned with one hip toward them emphasizing her narrow waist and the dress did the rest, plunging between her breasts showing just a hint of each on the sides. Spur was sure she wore nothing under the top of the dress. When she walked forward her breasts bounced and jiggled enticingly and he knew that she had this committee eating out of her carefully manicured hand.

"Dinner is served," Charity said from the door.

"Good, right on time. Gentlemen, this way, and I hope that you're feeling hungry. My poor cook has been up all night getting things ready."

Not true, Spur thought as he brought up the end of the line. She seated him at the far end of the table with the committee chairman on her right.

For a mid-day snack it was something of a banquet.

It began with asparagus soup, moved on to a green salad and then two exquisitely roasted pheasants, each with the showy tail plumes extending from the cooked birds. They had been basted with wine sauce of some sort. Spur was impressed.

Libby charged into her mission. "Gentlemen, is there anything else I can tell you about Helena, the ideal spot for the new territorial capital!"

"Mrs. Adams, I don't think so," the chairman said. "From what you've said, and the prospects prepared by your city council, we were strongly leaning your way anyhow. Then this morning a railroad man said he would give us a hundred to one odds if we wanted to bet that the Northern Pacific rails did not come through Helena."

"That's good enough for me," another member said. "I think the territorial legislature will go along with our recommendation when we get back."

Libby lifted her wine glass. "I propose a toast to Helena, the future capital of the territory of Montana!

They all stood and cheered then drank.

"Now, I have something really serious to talk about. Most of you know that Senator Marlowe introduced my bill in the legislature to give women the right to vote. They have it in Wyoming, used to have it in New Jersey. How come women are second class citizens here in Montana?"

"Mrs. Adams," the smallest of the men on the committee said. "I've read your bill, frankly I'm against it. Most women I've talked to just aren't interested in politics or in the lawmaking process. Women are interested in their homes, their husbands, having babies, and raising them. That's their job."

"Most men are not interested in politics either," Libby countered. "I suppose you know that less than twenty percent of those men eligible to vote do so. That means less than one out of five men are interested. Why not give one out of five women the same chance to send our lawmakers to the legislature?"

"Wouldn't work."

"It does in Wyoming. I went down there during their last election. It worked extremely well. They even have four women elected to the legislature. Are you really saying women are too stupid to be lawmakers?"

"Now, Libby. . . ."

"Am I too stupid? I am currently operating twenty-three business firms here in Helena. True, I inherited them from my late husband. But in the past six years, the net worth of these companies has increased by twenty-seven percent. I have bought six new firms, and have plans for three more. I have more than four hundred employees in this area, most of them men. Am I too stupid to be a legislator?"

"Of course not, Libby," the chairman said. "Granted you have a point, but you also have a majority of the men who don't want women to vote. That's just the way it is. Might take fifty years to change it." He grinned. "But, by god, you keep trying!"

The next course arrived, delicate mountain trout fillets that had been baked and covered with a thick cheese sauce. The men forgot politics and ate.

Spur went around the table and whispered to Libby.

"I have to go. One more little job for me to take care of while I'm here."

"Right in the middle of dinner?"

"Sorry. You push your problem. I'll be back." He said goodbye to the other diners and slipped out the front door.

It took him fifteen minutes to get his horse outfitted, find his Henry repeating rifle, and tie on a blanket roll and a minimum supply of dried rations for an emergency. Never could tell when a afternoon's ride would turn into something longer.

He stopped by the undertaker and left ten dollars for a casket and funeral for Will Walton, then rode for the ranch. It was only a little after one o'clock.

Less than half a mile out of town, Spur checked his back trail and saw a rider there. Lots of people moving around. He went another half mile toward the Walton ranch and kept checking. The rider had turned off the trail when he had and followed him into a heavy wooded section on a small ridge. There was no reason anyone should be going exactly this way unless the man was trailing him.

Spur tied his horse to a tree and backtracked a quarter of a mile at a trot, put the Henry against a ponderosa pine and settled down to wait. Ten minutes later the rider came up fast, monitoring the easy trail Spur had left in the leafmold under the trees.

Spur sent a rifle round over the rider's head.

"Hold it right there!" Spur bellowed.

The rider pulled up.

"McCoy? Is that you? Tried to find you in town, but by the time I caught up with you, you had moved out this way. My name is Kennedy, U.S. Marshal here in Western Montana."

Spur relaxed a minute, kept his rifle ready and stood.

"You afraid of something, or can I lite and talk a spell?" the marshal asked. He had a silver pinned to his leather vest.

Spur nodded. "Lite, but go easy. Far as I know there aren't any U.S. Marshals assigned to Montana

Territory right now. Budget problems they tell us. What was your name again?"

"Kennedy, Marshal Bob Kennedy. I work out of Denver usually. Sent me up here to check on some rustled cattle. But mostly I'm finding gold mines and some Indian trouble."

"Sounds about right."

The man had eased to the ground. He had a hogsleg on his left hip and Spur watched him.

"Who's the chief marshall in Denver?" Spur asked.

"What is this a test of some sort? His name is Chief Marshal Bill Barber, less he's been replaced in the last two weeks."

Spur grunted. Let the rifle muzzle drop. Barber was the man, but half the west knew about Bill.

"What did you need to talk to me for?" Spur asked.

"The Laidlaw thing. Just heard. Sounds like you got him wrapped up and tied with a noose."

"Not quite, but I'll be around to make sure."

"That's fine. I can get on with my work. Thought I'd offer my services if I could help."

Spur stood ready, still not convinced. "Thanks, but it's all done. Say, I hear all you marshals got issued new service revolvers, that brand new one from Remington. Like to take a look at it if you don't mind."

"New . . . Hell not me. I'm the last one to hear about everything. They keep me on the run."

"Strange. I talked to Bill in Denver three weeks ago, and he said no man would go on assignment without the new weapon. Jody said he had plenty to go around."

The man shook his head and turned. "Damned if I know what went wrong." Then his eyes widened and his head made a tiny involuntary movement as his right hand darted to his gunbelt and scratched at iron.

He was fast. Spur came up at the same time with his weapon and dove for the protection of the ponderosa. Both guns exploded black powder, driving .44 slugs out six-inch barrels. Spur took a glancing hit on the heel of his boot as he gained the safety of the three foot tree.

The other man screeched with a round in his left shoulder. He dodged behind at tree. Spur put a rifle round close past the tree hiding the imposter.

"No way out, whoever you are. You try to run, I nail you."

"I won't run. I owe you. Four of my friends you slaughtered."

"Two matter of fact. One jumped into a pit of rattlesnakes in the mine. Another one is in jail in town talking his head off. He said you took off for Idaho."

"That was the plan. Only I was supposed to bushwhack you just out of town. You moved too fast and there warn't no cover."

"The man in the tree out at the mine, that's you."

"Yeah. Made me look bad."

"Try it."

Spur darted to another tree ten feet away and crouched behind it. The kidnapper heard Spur but couldn't know where. He edged around the tree and Spur saw his legs. Spur's rifle round bored through the outlaw's left thigh and he screamed.

A minute later the man came around the tree limping, both hands holding six-guns as he stormed at Spur's tree. He fired as he came, keeping Spur behind the safe tree. After six shots Spur leaned out at ground level and fired one round that caught the kidnapper in the throat and ripped the side of his head off, dumping him to the ground where he twitched a few times, then lay still.

Spur sat up, moved to the dead man and rolled him over. He had done his last kidnapping. Kid looked no more than twenty-five or six. That was seeming younger to Spur all the time. He took the two pistols the man carried, and a rifle from his saddle boot and put them with his gear. He untied the horse and whacked it on the rump. It would wander back to the road and someone would find it. Then he turned and continued on his way toward the Walton ranch.

One more little task to take care of . . . a murderer.

14

Spur lay in a scrabble of brush a quarter of a mile from the Martha Walton ranch. It was truly hers now with the real Will Walton dead. He had been watching for fifteen minutes and the only movement he saw was Hans running quickly from the barn to the side door of the house.

Spur had no real chance to shoot him, and he wanted to talk to the man first anyway. A short time later the boy left the side door and walked to the privy. When he came back he looked all around as if trying to see if someone were riding up. The screen door banged as he went back inside.

Smoke came from the kitchen chimney.

Spur searched for cover closer to the house. The outhouse was too close, the well house too far away in the small gully. Thirty yards on this side of the house lay three boulders big enough to cover a man. Spur mounted up and rode hard out of the brush to the boulders, making turns and changes in speed to throw off any rifle aim.

He had just bailed off his horse when the rifle

174

spoke. A round went high and by the time the sound had echoed away into the hills, Spur was belly down in the dirt behind the big rocks. Now he was plenty close enough to call.

"Martha Walton inside the house. This is Spur McCoy, U.S. lawman. Your husband is dead, the real Will Walton died in the doctor's office in town."

A shotgun blasted from a crack in the front door but few of the pellets got the thirty yards to the rocks.

"I'm here to take in Hans for questioning. You send him out and we won't have any trouble."

The rifle barked again three times in quick order, which told Spur the man had some kind of a repeater. He ducked lower.

"Before Walton died he told the sheriff that both Hans and Martha were in on the killing."

"No!" a thin boy's voice shouted.

"Ain't so! My mom wouldn't kill nobody!" A defiant Will Walton Junior stood in the open doorway for a moment before a big arm came out and swept him aside and slammed the door.

"Might as well come get us, McCoy," Hans called. "We're not coming out." Another rifle round spanged off the rocks.

"A matter of time, Hans. I got all day. You have a ranch to run. Cow going to need to be milked about five."

The side door swung open and the seven year old rushed out. He ran twenty yards away from the house and hid behind the privy.

"My Ma didn't try to kill my Pa!" the boy shouted. "I know she didn't. She was in the house."

The shotgun roared and the outhouse took the full load of buckshot. The boy was unhurt. Twice the rifle drove rounds into the wooden structure.

"Lay down behind the privy, Will!" Spur called. He sent two shots from his pistol through the window of the house and then motioned to Will, waving him to run for the barn. As soon as Will took off for the barn, Spur pumped his last three pistol rounds at the rear door, then two rifle shots. Two pistol shots came from the house but Will reached the barn safely.

"Send the woman out, Hans. I don't want to hurt her. You're the only one on my arrest order."

Two more rifle rounds answered him.

In the quietness that followed, Spur could hear the couple in the house shouting at each other. The door came open once and was slammed shut.

Again the door swung open and Martha rushed out, looked at the barn, then ran toward the outhouse.

Spur had reloaded his pistol and he sent three shots through the side door. He thought she would make it. Then the rifle in the house spoke sharply and Martha stumbled and fell six feet from the small structure.

Spur used the rifle now, sent the rest of his magazine of rounds through the open door and the window on that side. Quickly he reloaded his pistol and pushed the loaded magazine he had taped to the stock of the rifle, into the Henry with twelve more rounds.

"Give it up, Hans. You'll never get away. Come out and take your chances with a jury. Locals didn't know Will, they might let you off easy."

Spur watched the house. Out of the corner of his eye he saw Martha move slightly, then she lifted and tried to crawl the six feet to protection behind the outhouse.

McCoy fired three times through the back door,

then once more. The rifle inside the house fired twice and Spur saw one of the slugs hit Martha. She screamed, then did not move.

Spur watched the house but saw no movement.

Will Jr. showed himself at the barn door for a moment, saw his mother near the privy and screamed in fury as he ran forward. Spur tried to cover him by shooting at the house, but this time there was no response from inside the ranch house.

Will reached the safe haven and pulled the still form of his mother behind the small building.

The house was too quiet. Spur noticed now that he was masked by the bulk of the house. Someone could go out a back window and get to the corral and then go unseen to the back of the barn.

Spur looked up at the edge of the barn and saw movement. He lifted up and raced to the small outdoor convenience. He dropped to the dirt where Will Jr. held his mother's head in his lap. Tears streaked his dirty face.

Blood showed on the front of her dress. One arm was bleeding.

"Is Ma dead?" Will asked.

"No, she's bleeding." He touched her throat and felt a weak and rapid pulse.

"Mrs. Walton." Spur said. He bent and pinched her face a moment in his hands. "Mrs. Walton!"

Her eyelids fluttered open, closed then opened again.

"It's all right. You're safe now. Will is here."

He bent and kissed his mother. She smiled.

"Will, this is your ranch. You pay heed to what McCoy here says. He's like your Pa. Understand?"

Will nodded through his tears.

"Ma, you got to get well!"

"No, Will. Hurt bad. You take the ranch, and run

it. Make . . . make me proud.'' She looked at him.
"Inheritance, in the bank in town. Yours, now. Ten
thousand dollars. More coming. From your real Pa's
family. You be a good boy.''

He bent and kissed her and when he lifted away
the last earthly breath of Mrs. Martha Walton
whispered into eternity.

"Will, you stay here with your Ma. I'll be back.''
He raced for the barn, expected to find Hans gone,
and he was. He looked out the back door and saw a
rider galloping hard for the hills.

Spur ran back to where his mount had been
grazing after he jumped off her, and stepped into the
saddle. He pushed the Henry in the boot and waved
at Will, then rode at a canter toward where he had
last seen Hans.

Hans had proved before that he was no expert
man in the woods, yet he angled toward the first
timber he found. Spur watched the tracks of the
horse and slowed his own. Most horses used west of
the Mississippi could run a quarter of a mile at a flat
out gallop and faster than any racehorse. But then
they had to slow and rest. Spur grimly studied the
tracks, then pushed on.

They went over the bridge, down the other side,
through a small valley and into the timber again.
This ridge had only Douglas fir on it, with hundreds
of small trees sprouting, and making the passage
that much harder. The trail was easy to follow. Spur
knew the man had a rifle, a Sharps maybe, but more
likely a Henry from the sound of it back at the ranch
house.

Spur estimated he had traveled a little over a mile
from the house when he stopped and listened.

The sound came from ahead, a high piercing
scream. The sound of a horse in pain.

Spur picked up the pace, watching carefully now. When he topped the rise he saw the horse below, it had foundered and gone down. The man had simply ridden it to death. It still pawed the ground on the grassy slope. Hans sat six feet away, one of his legs bent at an unnatural angle.

The horse screamed again. Spur dismounted, took out the Henry and steadied the barrel against a fir tree and refined his sight. The rifle spoke sharply in the cool, clear mountain air. The .44 rim fire slug smashed through the air and hit the horse in the head, putting it out of its misery.

Hans screamed when the sound of the shot died.

"McCoy, you bastard! Come and get me. You'll pay if you want to take me in. Ain't one to be in prison. Yanks let me out of a Tennessee prison during the war. Ain't going back to another one."

"Won't be all that hard, Hans," Spur called. Two rifle slugs sang through the air near him. Spur slid behind the fir and peered around. Hans had crawled to cover.

It took Spur fifteen minutes to work his way around the killer near the dead horse. There wasn't much protection there, but he had found a depression and two trees to hide behind. Now Spur had passed the trees and he had the high ground.

The Secret Service Agent put a rifle round into the dirt beside Hans' good leg. The German turned and fired four rounds from his pistol, then began frantically to reload.

"Give up, Hans. Being dead is no fun. Think about it."

Three more rounds powered into the brush over Spur's head, then Hans lay waiting.

Spur made a series of safe moves from tree to tree working the thirty yards down the slope toward

Hans. Spur could have killed Hans a dozen times, but he wanted Hans to hang for Will's death and for Martha's murder.

Spur stepped out from behind a covering Douglas fir ten feet from Hans, his pistol muzzle centered on Hans' chest.

"Drop the iron," Spur demanded.

"No," Hans said. He lifted the gun, swung it past Spur and put the barrel in his mouth.

"I think you're out of rounds," Spur said. "Anyway, that's a coward's way out."

Hans pulled the muzzle out of his mouth and snorted. "Why do you suppose I was in a Rebel prison, I was afraid to fight!" He put the gun barrel back in his mouth, shrugged and pulled the trigger.

Hans died at once. The round tore off the top of his skull spewing blood and bone across the virgin forest. Spur's eyes squinted for a moment, then he moved forward and pulled the pistol from the dead fingers and checked it.

Hans had saved the last round for himself.

A half hour later Spur had taken Hans' wallet for identification and both his weapons, and climbed up the hill to his horse. That was when he checked the Henry repeating rifle Hans had used. It was out of rounds as well.

As an afterthought, Spur rode back to the dead horse and pulled the saddle and bridle off. They belonged to the WW ranch, might as well take them back.

Will Jr. was hard at work digging a grave when Spur rode into the ranch yard. He put the tack in the barn, tied up his horse and took up a second shovel that was beside the just begun grave. It was on a little rise near a cherry tree that had been half frozen off during some hard winter.

Spur hadn't said a word. Will Jr. sniffled now and then, once wiped his nose on his shirt sleeve. Neither of them looked at the body sprawled behind the outhouse.

When they had the grave down three feet, Spur caught Will's shovel.

"Will, be best for you to go in and get some clothes and things together so you can live in town for a while. We'll need to get things sorted out, find somebody to run the ranch, and you'll need to go to school in the fall."

"No more school," Will said quickly. "I got a ranch to run."

Spur dug a few spades full of the rich black soil.

"You want to run the ranch right, do a good job?"

"Sure."

"A smart man will do it much better than one with no book learning. I have a lady in town I want you to meet. She never could have a family. She might like you, keep you at her house and help you with your homework. Way things are these days with the tough competition, a man's got to be as smart as he can to run a big ranch like this."

Will Jr. stared at him.

"What would your Ma want you to do?"

"She always said I had to get a high school diploma. Held real strong to that."

"So there you are, Will."

The lad watched Spur a moment, his big blue eyes steady and the scruff of light hair moving in the breeze. He looked over where his mother lay, closed his eyes a minute and nodded, then turned and walked to the house.

When Spur had the grave dug down five feet he climbed out and found Will dressed in his Sunday best holding his mother's head in his lap. Tears glistened on his cheeks.

"Why did she have to die, Mr. McCoy?"

"I don't know, Will. Things just happen and not always the way we want them to. That's why we have to learn as much as we can so we'll be ready to make the good things happen to us. The more we know, the better we can be sure that we make those good things come."

"Ma never had but the third grade. She said I had to go to school. Only been a little bit so far, we moved around a lot."

Together they placed Martha Walton's body in the grave. Spur said a few words targeted at the boy, not at anything else. Then together they filled in the gaping hole until it was humped up.

Will sat on the porch with hammer and nails pounding together a cross of two by fours.

"I want it to last a long time until I can get a proper marble marker," he said.

They found an ink pen and Spur wrote her name on the cross in strong block letters.

Will insisted on driving the pointed stake of the cross into the mound. Then he dropped the hammer and cried again.

Two hours later, Spur McCoy and Will Jr. rode up to the fence outside of the mansion and tied their horses. Spur untied the suitcase from Will's saddle horn and carried it as they walked up the steps to the big door.

Charity opened it before he knocked.

"We wondered when you were coming back," she said. "Mrs. Adams has been having a stroke." She looked down. "Well, and who is this handsome stranger?"

Spur introduced them and then Libby ran into the entranceway hall.

"Spur McCoy! I've been waiting all..." She stopped quickly, her frown turning into a smile as she stared at Will Jr. "I'm sorry, I didn't mean to shout. I didn't know we had real company. And who might this be?"

Will stood stiff and erect. He held out hand as Libby walked up. "How do you do, Mrs. Adams. My name is Will Walton, Jr. and I own the WW ranch outside of town."

Libby dropped to her knees and shook his hand. If Spur thought he had seen her beautiful smile before, he was wrong. Now she had the most marvelous smile he had ever seen and she showered it all on Will. He could see her holding back. She wanted to grab the boy and hug him to pieces.

"Well, young man, how do you do? I'm pleased to meet you. You have your suitcase, I hope you can stay for a while." She stopped. "Say, Charity has been making ice cream in the kitchen, would you like to go with her and see if it's ready to eat yet? She said it should be soon."

"Ice cream?" he said. Then brightened. "Oh, yes! Ma calls it cream. We had some once in Kansas City I think it was. I like it!"

Charity held out her hand. "Let's sample it. We'll be first. We might need to turn the crank a few more times."

Will took her hand and several steps then he hung back and looked at Spur. "Mr. McCoy, is it all right?"

"Sure, Will. Anything Mrs. Adams says is just fine."

Will grinned and they hurried out.

"Will Walton, Jr.?" Libby asked when he was gone.

Quickly Spur told her the story of the disturbed

soldier and how he tracked his missing family here.

"So, Will is all alone. I figured he might be able to stay here for a few weeks until a judge can get it all sorted out and legal. There's also an inheritance of ten thousand dollars in your bank under his mother's name."

"McCoy, you figured get the kid in the house and let her take care of him for a few weeks, and she'd adopt him and never let him go."

Spur shrugged. She caught his arm. "Yes, Libby, something like that. Will has had the raw end of life so far. I figured he deserved a break." He smiled. "And so do you. A kid like that could do wonders for that tough business woman shell you're starting to build up around yourself."

"Why you . . ." She stopped and laughed softly. "I think you're right. First we'll have to find a family who needs work who can run a ranch. Then the ranch will need some more grazing land, probably some good breeding stock from Billings, or maybe from Kansas. Will can live on the ranch during the summers and come in here in the fall to go to school.

"I've been thinking of looking over the school to be sure it has the best possible teachers and materials. There was some talk about needing a new school house as well. I could make a sizeable donation to get it started."

Spur grinned. "Sounds like you're still undecided about Will." He laughed gently. "I've got to go see the sheriff. You save me some of that cream or I'll make another batch myself." Spur hurried toward the front door.

Libby stopped him. "McCoy, you're a schemer."

Spur shook his head. "Not a chance. I'm a dreamer. I figured Will Jr. has had enough hard knocks. Today he watched his mother die and then helped bury her. Not many people have to go through a double emotion blast like that. He's made of good stuff. I know, I saw his father, a hero of the Civil War."

Spur went out the door, set his low crowned hat on his head firmly and hurried to report the deaths to the sheriff.

In the kitchen Will stared around in surprise.

"This whole room is just the kitchen?" he said. "It's as big as our whole ranch house!"

"Yes, Will," Charity said. "And this is the ice cream freezer. Turn the handle and see if it's hard enough." Will tried. He looked up in surprise.

"I can hardly turn it!"'

"Good, let's take the top off and taste it," Charity said.

Will watched in wonder as she unlatched the top of the hand crank freezer, took the ratchet off and then lifted the slender metal can out of the ice cold salty water. Carefully she turned the lid and pulled it off.

Soft, pink ice cream showed on the lid and in the can.

"Looks about right," Charity said. She scooped some off the lid with her finger and tasted it. When she nodded and held the lid out to Will he did the same.

"Wow! that is good!"

Libby Adams stood at the kitchen door watching. Things were going to change around her house now. Big changes. Somehow she felt they would be the best days of her life. Here was a brand new human being she could help train and mold and bring up to become a fine man. Somehow she would find a way to lessen his pain and make him remember only the good parts about his mother.

She would treasure these years of watching Will Jr. grow up, and she could pour into him all the love and care she could never give a child of her own. It was like a gift from heaven, even a heaven that she didn't believe in. Libby blinked back the start of a tear and went to sample the ice cream before it was all gone.

15

Spur stepped into Sheriff Palmer's office and spun his hat on his finger. The lawman looked up.

"What this time? You through disrupting this county?"

"Through, Sheriff. You can close the books on the Will Walton shooting. I went out to talk to Mrs. Walton. She and the boy ran out of the house and her hired man, Hans, gunned her down. Little boy saw the whole damned thing.

"By the time I caught up with Hans he had galloped his horse to death in his panic to get away. Hans broke a leg when he went down and couldn't run. Soon as I moved in on him he saved his last round and put it through his mouth."

"God! Least it saves the county the cost of a trial."

"I'll go out with a deputy to bring in the body if you want me to. I put the horse out of its misery."

"Better go out there. Have enough light?"

"We can make it. Oh, I brought the seven year old boy Will Walton Jr. into town. He's staying at

Libby Adams' place. Think she might want to keep him there if it's all right with the county."

"Hell, county don't have much say in such matters around here. If it's fine with you and with her and the boy, we'll say good work."

"Done."

Spur and the deputy brought back Hans' body just after dark and turned it over to the undertaker. Whoever his people were would simply never find out what happened to him. He had no papers, nothing to indicate any relatives or a home address. Spur shrugged. It was his choice. He'd never thought much about it, but he decided that a man had a right to end his life if he wanted to. He had no idea why anyone would want to.

Spur rode to Libby's stable and put his horse in a stall, then went in the back door. Libby was still in the living room having a second cup of coffee.

Will Jr. worked on his third dish of ice cream. He had been washed and combed and still wore his best shirt and pants.

"Will and I have been making plans!" Libby said, the eagerness and joy gushing out of her words. "Tomorrow we'll go down town and get some new clothes, and then try and find a bicycle that he can ride. We'll need a pony for him too, and just so many interesting things."

Will kept eating the ice cream. He looked up at Will and grinned once, then finished the dessert.

"I'm going to have to stay around town for a week or two for the Laidlaw trial," Spur said. "Is my welcome still good here, or should I go back to the hotel?"

"You can't run out on me now," Libby said. "Will wants you to go along when we get his clothes."

Spur nodded. "Might work in a fishing trip to one

of the lakes, if you like fishing, Will.''

"Yes sir, I'd like that.'' He looked at Libby, then at Spur. "May I be excused now, please?''

"Of course, Will. You have the rest of the house to explore. We need to pick out which room you want for your very own. Then we'll decorate it and fix it up any way you want to.''

"Yes, ma'am.'' Will got off the chair, looked at both of them and then hurried out of the big dining room.

Spur moved closer to Libby and sat down.

"Don't go overboard on the boy,'' Spur said. "He's bound to be a little moody for a while. Just lost both his parents, two fathers in two days. Hard to take.''

"I'll try to be . . . conservative. But I just want to buy him everything in sight that he wants!''

"He's had almost nothing before this. Go slow and easy. Make do for a few weeks. Do things for him gradually. I talked to the sheriff. He says you can keep Will here if you want to. The county doesn't have any facilities or any money.''

"Good!'' Libby said.

"Remember, just go slow. Will is coming from a small ranch where they struggled just to get food on the table and to stay warm in the winter.''

"Yes, oh wise one,'' Libby said. "Are you coming to the rally tonight at the church?''

"Votes for women rally?'' Spur asked.

"Of course. Eight o'clock. I've invited all the women in the town. But you can come as our security force.'' She saw his great lack of enthusiasm. "Please, McCoy. I . . . I want you there.''

"There shouldn't be any more problems for you.''

"I know, that's not why I want you there. I just

want to be close to you when I can. If I let you go you'd just end up in some saloon pinching the dance hall girls and playing poker half the night."

"I'll go, I'll go." She went to him and kissed him quickly.

"We have to leave in fifteen minutes. Do you want to change?"

"For polite society, I guess I should. I'll come in after it gets started."

Spur went to the kitchen where Charity had a tray ready for him with three sandwiches, a pot of coffee and a big bowl of ice cream.

"Have to eat up the cream before it all melts," Charity said. She smiled at him. "You ever get lonesome, give me a call."

Spur ate in the kitchen, heard Libby leave and then went up to his room and washed up and changed into a dark suit, string tie and spanking new low crowned white cowboy hat, and walked down to the church.

When he stepped inside, Libby was going full steam ahead.

". . . so the only thing we can do is to flood the legislators with letters. I write ten letters every day to various legislators urging them to vote for our women's rights bill. That's what each of you should be doing. I've had twenty copies made of the names and addresses of eight important legislators you should write to.

"If more of you want the names, please share the lists. I know we can get the bill passed this session of the legislature if we push hard on it. I'm going to Billings and then to Bozeman and Butte and Great Falls to get women to write letters.

"It doesn't matter if you're no good at writing a letter. Just tell these men what you want them to do. Remind them that the hand that rocks the cradle also rocks this territory."

The fifty women in the church applauded politely. A few asked questions and when it was over, Libby thanked everyone and the meeting broke up.

On the way back to her house, Libby held Spur's arm and sighed. "I don't know if we'll ever win. It seems such a hard fight when the men have all the power, the voting power."

"A lot of times money is power, Libby. Did you ever think about that? You could support the men you wanted elected, run a man sympathetic to your cause against men in any district where the man was against you."

"Possible, but our next election is a year away."

"Take you that long to hire a good political consultant, pay him to study the men in the legislature and target the districts you need votes from. And of course get a hundred percent backing by all the districts around Helena."

"Who could I get to do the job?"

"Write some letters to St. Louis and Chicago."

"I'll think about it."

Back at the house, Charity met them at the door. She undid two locks and let them in.

"Will Junior stayed in your library for a while, then he went up to his room, Mrs. Adams," Charity said. "I think he was lonesome and bored."

"I'll go up and talk to him," Spur said. He climbed the open staircase and went down the hall to the smallest bedroom. That was the one Will had picked.

Spur knocked, then went in. Will lay still fully dressed on top of the bed.

"Hi, pardner," Spur said.

"Hello." Will sat up. "There's *nothing to do*

here," Will said. "At the ranch I could feed the chickens, or go for a ride, or just play with my rabbits."

"Give it time. This is your first few hours. Bound to be a little strange. Takes some time to get used to things. You're getting plenty to eat, and that bed looks lots softer than the one I usually sleep on out on the trail. Looks like you found yourself a mighty good place to live."

"But it ain't home, Mr. McCoy."

"That's for sure, Will. But then, I haven't been home to St. Louis even for a couple of years. Two things you need to remember here, seems to me. Book learning. Your Ma was strong about that, you said. And you got to give yourself some time to grow up so you can run the ranch."

"Did anybody milk old Bessie tonight?" Will asked.

"Not sure. I'll ask. Mrs. Adams was going to send someone out to take over running the WW. I'm sure Bessie got drained out right on schedule. Mrs. Adams is an efficient lady. She does things when they are supposed to be done."

Will nodded.

"Just worried about Bessie. I'll need to feed my rabbits tomorrow. Do we have to buy clothes?"

"No clothes tomorrow. You and I will ride back out and check on the ranch."

"Good. I'd like that."

"Now, time for you to get out of your clothes and into that night shirt and dive into bed. Bet you'll sleep good tonight."

"Hope so."

"Will," Spur said. "I'm sorry your real Pa died before you got to know him. He got wounded in the war, shot in the head, and he kept forgetting who he

was and even where he lived. He tried to come home,
for all those five years he was trying. His head just
made it impossible.

"Sorry about your Ma, too. But things are going
to be better tomorrow and all the tomorrows after
that."

"Hope so," Will said.

Spur waved at him and went out the door. Will
was going to make it. Spur had the feeling the young
man would do just fine.

Downstairs, Spur found Charity had gone to bed,
and Libby sitting in the living room waiting for him.

"How is Will?"

"Scared, still in shock about his Ma being killed
that way. Worried about what he's doing here. And
homesick. Outside of that I think he'll make it. He
and I are going clothes shopping tomorrow, we're
riding out to check on the milk cow and to bring
back his pet rabbit. We'll make room for the hutch
out by the stable."

"Should I look in on him?"

"Not tonight. Let him settle down a little."

"All right. Tomorrow will be much better for him.
Glad that is all settled. Now, I'm glad you're
staying for a while, McCoy," she said.

"Why?"

"Because you owe me."

"What do I owe you?"

"You owe me a soft, gentle loving in a clean bed
with our shoes off and a nip of brandy on the
bedstand.

"I try always to pay my debts. Do I bring my own
bottle?"

"I can find one and a small snack. In fact, they're
already in my bedroom." She kissed him softly on
the lips. He kissed her back, only their lips touching.

Her hands fluttered around his shoulders, landed slightly and she leaned against him.

"You'll never know how good that feels, to have a man I like with his hands on me. Could you carry me up to my bedroom?"

Spur scooped her up and headed for the stairs. She nuzzled against his neck, bit him gently and looked up.

"I can be an animal, did you know that?"

"A soft, cuddly animal I hope. Keep your claws retracted." He kissed her nose.

"Alex used to . . ." she stopped. "Never talk about one lover when you're with another one. I forgot the rule."

"He sounds like a smart man, all the way around. He knew you were bright enough to handle his fortune, to run his businesses. He was right. If he could see you right now, I'm sure he would be proud of you."

"He was before he died. I had been managing four firms for about a year. We were in competition with two of his other stores. Usually my stores won. I paid higher salaries, got a key man away from him and we showed more profit."

"Sneaky," he said pushing open her bedroom door. Inside it was a woman's room, nearly twenty feet square, with a canopied bed, a square specially made bathtub built into the corner with a curtain that could be pulled around it.

The scent of sashay drifted to him and the delight of fresh cut flowers in three different vases. The room was decorated with a pink theme, from the soft rug on the floor to the spread on the bed and the canopy over it.

He lowered her onto the softness of a silk bedspread and she sank into the goose down mattress.

"Lay on top of me," she said. "I want to be dominated. Alex was ahead of his time when it came to sex. He said nothing was an unnatural act if both parties wanted to do it. Anything was fine, as long as it didn't hurt and was accepted. He was so smart about everything. He said women didn't always have to submit if they didn't want to. He said most women think it's a duty to fuck their husbands. But it shouldn't be that way.

"Alex said the woman should be having as many thrills as the man in sexual intercourse. I agree. I enjoy sex, don't you?"

Spur grinned, bent down and blew hot breath through her dress onto her right breast. She giggled.

"Yes, I enjoy sex. It's the most intimate, satisfying and delightful experience that two people can have together. Does that kind of talk excite you?"

"Yes."

"I want your body. I want to see it all bare and pink and trembling and I want you panting, just eager as hell for me to ravish you."

"Ravish! what a wonderfully exciting word. Are you starting to ravish me yet?"

"It's a slow ravish. First I open your dress, like this.' He undid buttons down the front. "Then my hands *violate* your breasts."

"Call them tits, tits is a good word."

"Then my hands grab your big tits."

"Now it seems like you're starting to violate me." Libby giggled like a stranger. "Damn, I wish I were a virgin again. I wish it had been someone like you."

He spread back her dress top and pushed aside the silk chemise. Her breasts, even when she lay on her back, were full and heavy. The pink areolas tinged a darker shade now, as her heart raced.

"We were both sixteen and on a church picnic and got lost in the woods and we started exploring each other's bodies. He was a virgin too, he told me later. We both were just curious as hell. We just fumbled around and tore off clothes and got more and more excited until I wouldn't let him stop. It hurt for just a minute, then bliss!"

"Take off your dress," Spur commanded, rolling away from her. "Get it off now!"

She blinked, then sat up and pulled the dress off over her head and three petticoats. She had on the silk and lace panties again, all loose and enticing.

Slowly she undressed him, and soon they were both naked and lying side by side on the bed.

"The first time?" he asked.

"Dominate me. On top and hard and fast. Don't wait for me, make me catch up."

He plunged into her a moment later and she gasped at the burning of the dry flesh against dry, then it eased and he slammed into her again and again. She scowled for a minute, then laughed and ground her hips against him in a furious race to catch up and did at last and then sped past him, exploding before he could.

She yelped and squealed and bounced and made him lose his rhythm, then she faded into a series of long, sharp spasms that left her drained.

Just as she finished he went over the top and powered his seed deep into her and then fell exhausted beside her on the soft bed.

"You won," he said when he could talk. They lay there in each other's arms for ten minutes. Softly she cried, but he didn't ask her why. Another three or four minutes and the tears ceased and she brushed away the last of the wetness and rolled over on top of him.

"Sometimes when it's tremendously wonderful, I just have to cry. I wonder if you can understand?"

"No, not being a woman, I could never understand that one. But I can agree that it has validity and meaning for you. Does that come close enough?"

"Close enough." She kissed him. "I'm going to do everything I can to keep Will here, and make him happy. Makes up for some of the joys I've missed."

"There will be some tears as well, goes with the territory. Just no way to have one without the other."

"I realize that and accept it. I'm going to do everything possible to make Will's life here more joy than tears."

"Good, where's the brandy."

She motioned to the bedstand. He rolled out of the bed and brought it back with two glasses. Spur poured two fingers in each glass and handed her one.

"Medicine for the strong hearted."

"My kind of medicine," she said then leaned forward and nuzzled her ear. "You ever think of settling down somewhere? Letting someone else chase the bad guys?

"Thought of it."

"Always a chance you could find some young widow lady with more money than she could rightly know what to do with. Might even get into bed with her." Libby took one of his hands and put it on her breasts.

"You could probably ravish her if you tried, and the lady could work out a joint venture of some sort, like general manager, or chief executive officer. She would have an adopted son to mother and to tutor and to raise."

He bent and kissed both her breasts and she made small noises in her throat.

"That kind of a set up would be damn hard to find. Might not be more than one in the whole wild west."

"Just what I was thinking," she purred. "We seem to think a lot alike. We could always talk about it."

He sucked half of one of her breasts into his mouth and worried it for a minute, then let it go.

"I don't feel much like talking right now. Any other ideas?"

"One but you might not like it."

"What's that?"

"On the floor with my ankles on your shoulders. If you're ready."

"Hell, woman, it's been ten minutes, I'm ready!" They both laughed and left the bed for the soft pink rug.

"You will think about it, about that sexy widow with the money and a real need in her life that needs to be filled."

"Yes, I'll think about it." He spread her legs and drove forward hard. "I wonder if this will help fill her need?"

Libby giggled and then lifted her feet and put her legs on his shoulders as Spur adjusted forward and watched her get ready to shatter herself to pieces.

He stopped moving.

"What are you doing?" she asked.

"You said I should think about it. I'm thinking."

"Damn you, not now! I've got a much more urgent problem for you to solve than that other. This is a problem that has to be penetrated completely to be evaluated."

He stared at her unsmiling.

"McCoy, if you don't keep on fucking me deep I'm going to crown you good!"

Spur laughed and continued. "Just checking to see if you had dropped off to sleep yet."

She hadn't. Neither of them did until almost three in the morning.

16

Spur woke at five-thirty as usual the next morning and completed a fast needed half mile walk around town. When he returned he found Libby in a dressing gown pacing the living room, her hair uncombed, tears showing on her face.

"He's gone! Will Junior left sometime last night. Nobody heard a thing. He's just gone."

Spur took her into the kitchen, poured a cup of coffee for her and added a shot of whiskey and watched as she drank it.

"He's alone and scared and doesn't really know who his friends are yet," Spur said gently. "He's probably gone back to the ranch. Have you checked the horse he rode in on yesterday?"

She shook her head. Charity found his door open that morning when she got up to help the cook with breakfast.

Spur went to the stables behind the big house and found one stall empty. All had been filled last night. Will was too small to saddle a horse. One bridal was missing. He could probably ride bareback as well as with a saddle.

Back in the house, Spur told the women. "Give me a cup of coffee and about six of those cinnamon rolls and I'll go take a look. Chances are, he's back at the ranch by now, depending when he left.

"Explain to him . . ." Libby began, then stopped.

"Yes, Libby. I'll try to explain. Will had a lot of things pushed on him all at once. Remember, we talked about going easy, slow with him? That is more important than ever now. If I find him we'll be back only if he wants to come. We can't make him stay in town if he doesn't want to."

"I sent a family out late yesterday afternoon to run the ranch. He's a former rancher who lost his spread in an Indian raid. He's a good man. Name of Kingman, Frank Kingman. Couple and two kids . . ."

"But you'd rather Will stayed with you than with the Kingmans. I know. I'll see what I can do. Stay busy." Spur took the wrapped rolls and saddled his horse and rode away toward the ranch. He wasn't sure what he was going to say when he got there.

Chances were good that Will would be there. Will might try to set it up to stay with the foreman's family. Such things were fairly common.

Spur rode for half an hour toward the ranch. He had just turned into the long valley from which the finger valley extended where the Walton ranch lay, when he saw the Indians.

There were six, obviously a hunting party on their horses with hackamores and barebacked. Each brave carried a lance and two had rifles. The six sat motionless on the brow of a small hill, outlining themselves plainly.

They wanted him to see them. They were probably Crow in this part of Montana. He rode toward them at a canter to let them know he was not afraid and was eager to talk with them.

The six remained in position and an older brave came from behind them on a large white horse that pranced and skittered as if it was not used to being ridden. The old Indian put the animal under control with soft words and by rubbing its neck. Spur stopped and the Indian stopped. They were ten feet apart.

Spur used the universal Indian sign for welcome or hello and waited. At last the old Indian gave the same sign, his hand raised, fingers straight palm outward.

The Indian looked pointedly at Spur's Henry rifle in his boot, then lifted both his hands to his forehead and made buffalo horns. It was the sign for buffalo.

Spur shook his head no, then held his first two fingers of his right hand outward in a "V" against his left eye. He had not seen any buffalo.

The old Indian sighed, nodded. Then he touched his thumb to his chest indicating himself and with his palm upward, he moved his hand back and forth in front of him.

It was the sign for "go" Spur knew. He nodded and turned his horse and rode away at a slow walk, to prove his bravery by exposing his back to six potential enemy.

The Crow were comparatively at peace with the white settlers. The Indians kept to the higher hills and valleys and left most of the whites alone. Now and then there would be a raid for horses and to capture rifles and ammunition. But it was a time of peace with the Crow in that corner of Montana.

Spur rode a quarter of a mile then looked back. The six hunters had vanished, only the old Crow sat on his horse watching the white man.

Spur thought little more about it as he moved on down the trail toward the Walton WW ranch. He had seen fresh tracks in the dust. These were of an unshod horse and the insects and worms of the night had made no tracks through the hoof prints. The prints had been made in late night or early morning.

He came to the ranch as before, saw smoke over the chimney in the virtually windless morning, and rode on down.

Will met him before he could dismount.

"Had to come back and check on Bessie," Will said.

"Figures," Spur said. "How are your rabbits?"

"Hungry. I fed them." Will watched Spur. "You come to haul me back to town?"

"Nope. Came to see if you were all right. Libby was worried about you. Just like your Ma would have been if you ran off."

"She's rich, she doesn't have to worry."

Spur chuckled. "Will, the rich people worry about more things than we do. They have more reasons to worry. She likes you, Will."

"She's a nice lady . . . but I'm a rancher. I have this spread to run."

"She sent out a man and his family to do that for you, Will."

"I met them. But I can do it myself." Will glanced up at Spur who said nothing. "Well, I can." He dug one toe into the dirt. "With a little help, I can. This man, Mr. Kingman, doesn't know where the stock is, or anything."

"You going to help him?"

"Soon as I milk Bessie. Come on."

Will led him to the barn and took an upside down milk pail off a wooden rack. He put a three legged stool beside a red and beige milk cow and sat down and cleaned off her udders. Then he began milking her with sure, steady pulls. The milk splashed on the side of the bucket, then into the bottom, churning into a froth of bubbles.

An old yellow Tom cat strolled up and sat down. He meowed once and Will looked at him and grinned.

"You ready, Yaller?"

The cat meowed again. Will turned one teat toward the cat and sent a long stream of warm milk squirting his way. The cat adjusted easily, caught the stream of milk in his mouth and when it stopped coming, he swallowed, licked off the drips on his fur and walked out the other side of the stall making sure everyone knew that he owned the whole spread.

"That old cat's got you trained mighty good, Will. I bet you could bring him back to town with you, if you're thinking of going back. I keep thinking what your Ma said about you getting a diploma and all."

"Yeah, I think about that, too."

He finished the milking, and carried the two gallons of milk back to the house. Inside he introduced Spur to Molly Kingman and their two boys, who were six and seven.

"You had your breakfast, Mr. McCoy?" Molly asked. She was in her late twenties, already starting to show the strain and wear of a ranch wife's hard life. Her smile was open, honest.

Spur said he had eaten, thanked her and said he'd be glad to take a list of supplies she needed when he went back to town and have them sent out on a wagon. She smiled and began deciding what to ask for and writing things down with a stub of a lead pencil.

Will tugged Spur outside to see his rabbits. He had a pair and hoped he would have young ones soon.

"I better clean out the cage," he said. He brought fresh straw and moved the pair of large white rabbits to a second cage.

Will reached into the hutch with a rake to pull out the used straw when he yelped.

"Mr. McCoy, come quick!"

Spur looked where Will indicated and saw eight small, wiggling, nearly hairless newborn rabbits.

"Well now, you're a grandfather!" Spur said. "Best get the mother back in there and keep the buck in another cage. Sometimes the male will kill the youn'ens."

Will's face held a brilliant smile as he tended to the newborns, moved the females back and put out feed. He found some leaf lettuce in the garden and fed them both by hand.

A man left the barn and moved toward them. He was medium height, solidly built and wore a straw hat. He had a friendly face that was weathered. He held out his hand.

"Howdy, you must be Spur McCoy who Will has been talking about. Glad to have you here. I'm Frank Kingman. Will says he's going to show me where the stock is, and where the property boundary lines are. Good thing to know."

"Morning, Frank. Will just got himself a litter of rabbits."

"Fresh rabbit fryers in two months!" Will said.

Frank laughed. "Now there is a real rancher. Knows we produce critters on a ranch to feed bellies."

Will grinned.

"Will, this be a good time to go for our ride around the spread?" Frank asked.

"Sure. Mr. McCoy, can you come, too?"

It took them three hours to ride the ranch, poke into the spots where the cattle congregated, and to roust a few out of some brambles. When they got back, the hundred and sixty acres looked to Spur to be a beautiful little spread. Plenty of water from the stream, lots of good basic sod grass and meadows of wild grass that could be cut for hay.

At the house, the noon meal was ready and Spur sat down with the family.

Molly had a long list of basics she needed. Will finished eating as the adults talked, and went outside with the boys. Spur and Frank smoked black, thin cheroots in the living room, then Spur went out to find Will.

He was kneeling down, sitting on his feet at his mother's grave. Spur came up and sat on the grass beside him.

"Seems a long time since yesterday morning," Will said. Tears splotched his cheeks.

"Long time," Spur said. "I know you loved your mother, but now that part of your life is over. Time to move ahead, to take on new things, to go to school and prepare yourself to run your ranch, the WW."

"I know. I wanted one last look. Mrs. Adams said she would get me a tutor to help me catch up with my grade. I don't want to start in first grade, I'm seven."

Spur nodded. "Figures. Now, we better see about taking the rabbits back to town."

Will shook his head. "Nope. The boys want to take care of them. I gave the rabbits to the boys. They need something of their own here. But . . . could we take Yaller back? He might like it in town."

Spur grinned and they went to find a cardboard

box they could carry the scrappy old tom cat in.

An hour later they had just topped a small rise when twelve Indians formed a line across the trail. All had rifles or bows and arrows in hand.

For a moment Spur sensed danger. Then the line of braves continued down the ridge without a second look at them. One of the Indians was the old hunting chief Spur had talked to that morning. In the valley on the far side of the rise, Spur saw a herd of about twenty buffalo grazing. They were the first he had seen in this area. Evidently the Indians had been tracking them and lost them in the night.

Now they moved slowly down the hill through the pine trees getting in position to attack the herd. The braves were upwind from the buffalo so the beasts could not smell the man scent.

Spur stopped and moved with Will forward where they could see the attack.

"One day soon the buffalo will be gone off the plains and out of the mountains, too," Spur said. "Watch this, you can tell your grandchildren about it."

Nothing happened for a half hour. Yaller yowled and Will talked to him and petted him through a slit in the top of the box.

Below the buffalo wandered closer to the edge of the timber. Then without warning the old bull leading the pack snorted and bellowed a call of danger.

Within two or three seconds, three rifles blasted. Two of the shaggy beasts near the center of the group went down. The others charged away toward the opening of the valley. The Indians streamed after them, six ahead of them trying to cut off their escape, firing at the lead bull who charged directly over one Indian pony without stopping. The brave dove off the horse at the last second and rolled out of the path of the sharp hooves.

The thunder of the hoofs continued for several seconds, as a dozen more shots stabbed through the still mountain air, then all was quiet. The braves who had ridden after the herd came back. Three of the shaggy animals lay still on the grassy valley. At once two of the braves rode off to the north to direct the squaws and ponies with their hunting camp equipment back to the site.

Before darkness, the small band of Crow would have set up a hunting camp, and have butchered out the first animal.

"These Indians get almost everything they need to live on from the buffalo," Spur said. "Robes to keep warm, skins to cover their tipis, food, dried jerky for winter. They use every part of the animal."

The pair rode on, and arrived at Libby's house in Helena just before dark.

Will dashed into the house and found Libby in the living room. It took him a half hour to tell her about the birth of his new bunnies and then how he and Spur had watched the Indians hunting buffalo.

When he was done they had supper and he was still talking.

At last she touched his hand.

"Will, have you decided to stay here in town?" Libby asked.

"Yes. I . . . I guess so. Ma told me to get book learning. This is the only place. If you can put up with me and Yaller."

Libby had been surprised by the cat, but they had put it in the basement along with food and water so he would get used to the area and know where home was.

"Will, I think I'll be able to get along with both of

you. Try not to be too hard on me. Mr. McCoy has to stay in town for a while to go to the trial. I remember he promised you a fishing trip."

"Yes," Will said looking at Spur. "We're going tomorrow. Then the next day we're going to ride into the mountains and try to shoot a grizzly bear!"

Spur laughed. "The fishing sounds fine, but the more I think about the old grizzly, the more I've decided to let him stay up there in the hills. I don't have a fight with any of them."

Spur and Will played dominoes that night. He thought about St. Louis and the office there. He'd have a week here for the trial, which he figured would last about two hours once the judge came to town and it got started. That was the way most trials went out west. No long harangues, no fancy lawyers, just meataxe law that was usually fair but always quick.

Then he'd be back at work. He wondered just where he would go next? First he'd have to get to a telegraph and report in.

His biggest regret on this job had been Will Walton senior. He had been a true victim of the horror of the Civil War. He was killed by the war just as surely as if he had fallen at the Wilderness. May he rest in peace.

Spur remembered Will Junior. He was going to do fine in town with Libby. He'd spend summers at the ranch, and winters in town. If he was as sharp as his Pa, Will would do just fine.

Spur grinned and relaxed. Between Will during the day, and Libby and Charity at night, he was going to have an interesting week!

**Get more adventure for your money with Special Giant
Editions of the wildest Adult Western Series around!**

*More gunslinging gangs, more wild women, more non-stop
Western action in every low-cost volume!*

**SPUR GIANT EDITION: TALL TIMBER TROLLOP
by Dirk Fletcher.**

When a ruthless gang started sabotaging the biggest
logging operation in Oregon, the Secret Service called
in Spur McCoy. Spur had to figure out how to stop the
gang, how to protect the flirtatious daughter of the mill
owner, and how to cool the fire of a flame-haired torch
singer — or he would end up a pile of kindling.

__2788-7 $3.95

*The Adult Western series with more punch
than a barroom brawl . . .*

#27: FRISCO FOXES by Dirk Fletcher.
____2664-3 $2.95 US / $3.95 CAN

#26: BODIE BEAUTIES by Dirk Fletcher.
____2635-X $2.95 US / $3.95 CAN

#25: LARAMIE LOVERS by Dirk Fletcher.
____2597-3 $2.95 US / $3.95 CAN

#24: DODGE CITY DOLL by Dirk Fletcher.
____2575-2 $2.95 US / $3.95 CAN

#23: SAN DIEGO SIRENS by Dirk Fletcher.
____2519-1 $2.95 US / $3.95 CAN

#21: TEXAS TEASE by Dirk Fletcher.
____2475-6 $2.50 US / $3.25 CAN